Potent Magic,

Carried on the Hot Winds of the Night

Hugh could not prevent himself from reaching for her as he had once before in the sultry gardens of the rajah's palace. Eden turned toward him, and her eyes met his. Suddenly, she was in his arms. Her body was enchantingly soft and slender beneath the rough kaftan, and the scent of rose petals clung to her skin.

Touching his mouth to hers, Hugh found her lips sweet beyond belief. Drawing her closer, he lowered his head and kissed her insistently, parting her lips with the pressure of his own. It was a long kiss filled with a drugging wonder, and Eden felt as if there were nothing in all creation for her to cling to but the mouth that moved slowly, sensuously upon hers . . .

ELLEN TANNER MARSH

TAME THE WILD HEART

AVON
PUBLISHERS OF BARD, CAMELOT, DISCUS AND FLARE BOOKS

TAME THE WILD HEART is an original publication of Avon Books.
This work has never before appeared in book form. This work is a novel.
Any similarity to actual persons or events is purely coincidental.

AVON BOOKS
A division of
The Hearst Corporation
105 Madison Avenue
New York, New York 10016

Copyright © 1988 by Ellen Tanner Marsh
Published by arrangement with the author
Library of Congress Catalog Card Number: 87-91617
ISBN: 0-380-75219-0

First Avon Books Printing: January 1988

AVON TRADEMARK REG. U.S. PAT. OFF. AND IN OTHER COUNTRIES, MARCA
REGISTRADA, HECHO EN U.S.A.

Printed in the U.S.A.

K-R 10 9 8 7 6 5 4 3 2 1

Prelude

Meerut, India
May 1857

A dawn sun, shrugging free of the foothills, chased away
the long-reaching shadows and lifted the hovering veil of
early morning mist. The faint breeze blowing on its heels
rustled through the elephant grass and churned the dust
beneath the hooves of a lone horse galloping headlong across
the plains. Its rider leaned low in the saddle, features obscured by the loose end of a muslin turban unraveled and
pulled across the face in the manner of a native from the
Khyber hills. A sense of urgency was evident in the slim
lines of the rider's body, a tension that seemed to com-
municate itself to the horse, causing it to increase its stride
until the lion-colored ground passed in a blur.

Eden Hamilton, tightening her hold upon the reins,
could feel her heart beating in furious rhythm with her
mount's drumming hooves. Lifting her eyes to the horizon, she saw that the purple shadows stretching across the
canyons were fast disappearing and that the burning rays
of the sun had already reached the rugged peaks of the
distant hills and painted them with fire.

You fool! she thought, aware that she had been gone
far too long and that she'd never be able to return to the
Meerut cantonment without being caught. Already she
could hear the scolding of Mrs. Percival, with whom she
and her cousin Isabel were staying, and envision the look
of horror on that normally patient woman's face at the
discovery that Eden had once again ridden out without

escort dressed in little more than a vest and loose-fitting muslin salwars.

"I cannot imagine that your father permits you to leave his house dressed no better than a native," Mrs. Percival would doubtless say, shaking her head in utter disbelief. "And it is out of the question to let you go riding at four o'clock in the morning, Eden! Perhaps you're accustomed to such odd behavior in Lucknow, but while you're staying in Meerut you'll do neither, is that understood?"

"Yes, ma'am," Eden would invariably reply, standing outside the bungalow where the first of many such confrontations had already taken place.

Regrettably it was Mrs. Percival who did not understand, for it was simply far too hot to ride at any other time of day, and one couldn't possibly sit astride a man's saddle wearing pinafores and petticoats, the proper attire for any fourteen-year-old girl who, like Eden, was growing up amid the restrictive tenets of the Victorian age. The turban, too, was an unavoidable necessity, for how else was one to keep the rising dust from blowing into one's nose and mouth during a gallop?

While Eden had never intended to openly defy her well-meaning guardian, she had been quick to discover that the *chowkidar*, the night watchman, could easily be bribed into leaving the back gate unlocked, and that it was a simple enough matter to steal away for a gallop before anyone in the bungalow awakened. Even Isabel, who shared a room with Eden, was unaware of these nocturnal excursions, and to Eden's way of thinking they were thoroughly harmless—provided she wasn't caught.

Today, however, she had strayed too far, entranced by the sight of the stars dimming in the heavens and the pale gold and apricot of the coming dawn washing the ancient faces of the cliffs. Her fleet-footed mare, Mumtaz, seemed to have shared her feelings, for she had spent the morning chasing the wind across the sweeping plains, and Eden had not reined her in until they had reached the distant banks of the shimmering river. Here they had startled a herd of black-buck into flight, and Eden had watched them bound toward the shadowy hills until nothing remained of their passage but a streak of silver dust. Of course Mrs. Percival would see that she paid for such dalliance, and Eden's dark blue eyes were suddenly bright with anger.

"If only I were older!" she whispered, knowing no one would dream of denying a grown woman the chance to ride wherever she chose. Furthermore, she intended to be an army commander as soon as she grew up, and by then she would be in charge of a regiment of sepoys as proud and well trained as her father's. And no one would dare banish an officer of the Honorable East India Company's Bengal Army to the house of a well-meaning but dreary widow who hadn't the vaguest recollection of ever having been young!

Catching sight of the sprawling buildings of the Meerut cantonment over the rise ahead, Eden urged Mumtaz to a faster pace. The cantonment, surrounded by trees and a high, whitewashed wall, lay on the outskirts of the crowded bazaars of the city, and it was in a pleasant little bungalow standing directly across from the parade grounds that Eden and her cousin currently lived. Both the bungalow and the services of the fussy Mrs. Percival had been provided by Colonel Carmichael-Smyth, commander of the Third Light Cavalry and a former classmate of Eden's father from their years of training at the East India Company's military college in Addiscombe. Though Eden thought Colonel Carmichael-Smyth pompous and dull beyond words, she was grateful that he had arranged for Mumtaz to accompany her mistress from Lucknow and provided her with a stall in the cavalry stables.

Colonel Carmichael-Smyth, Eden felt sure, would not approve of her early morning rides any more than his housekeeper did, and he certainly possessed the authority to put the stop to them, which Mrs. Percival did not. Yet even that did not really matter to Eden, who had no intention of discontinuing her unseemly ways until the colonel was apprised of them and actually forbade her to leave the cantonment grounds.

"That may happen sooner than you think," Eden decided with a scowl, convinced that this time the long-suffering Mrs. Percival could not be prevented from carrying through with her threat to inform the colonel on the score of the Hamilton girl's continued disobedience. It was her own fault, really, Eden decided glumly. She shouldn't have strayed so far this morning.

Lifting her head, she saw that the long row of domed bungalows was bathed in rosy light, and the wild thumping of her heartbeat slowed as a sudden surge of hope rose within her that perhaps it was still early enough after all to steal back into the house undetected. She began to hum softly at the prospect and reached up to unwind the strip of muslin cloth that obscured her features. In the next moment, however, she was nearly thrown from the saddle as Mumtaz, galloping ever closer to the cantonment gates, threw up her head and shied violently.

"What is it, *piari?*" Eden asked, bending forward to stroke the mare's neck.

The unexpected crackling of gunshots brought her head whipping about, and she gasped as she caught sight of the dark columns of smoke rising from the treetops above her. For the first time she realized that the red glow illuminating the buildings of the British lines was not in fact the reflected light of the coming dawn, but the ugly glare of leaping flames.

Kicking Mumtaz into a gallop, Eden turned her toward the wide-standing gates, but for the first time in her life the valiant little mare refused her mistress's commands. Blowing loudly, she balked and swerved, and when Eden tried to guide her with her heels, she reared and fought the bit. Dismounting, Eden took her by the reins, but Mumtaz tossed her head and backed away, and it was then that Eden saw what was causing her to panic.

It was the body of a British soldier sprawled facedown in the dust, his cavalry uniform slashed and his blond hair clotted with blood. Eden's breath caught on a gasp, recognizing him as young Colin Jeffries, one of Colonel Carmichael-Smyth's orderlies. Lifting her horrified eyes to the gates, she saw another body lying a short distance away . . . and another . . . and another.

"No!" she whispered. *"No!"*

A smattering of gunfire from the barracks sent her fleeing for the compound walls, keeping under cover of the thick stands of scrub and pulling the trembling Mumtaz behind her. Leaving the mare tethered in a tangle of undergrowth, she scaled the wall and huddled behind the concealing branches of a *neem* tree. The smoke was thick here, stinging her eyes and obscuring her vision, and the crackling flames added to the torturous heat of the morning.

There were more bodies sprawled on the roadway across from the mall and on the hot stretch of grass between the parade grounds and the magazine. Eden looked upon them with disbelief, for these were not soldiers but innocent civilians: a white woman and two children and a number of Indian servants. She thought she recognized the woman as Lieutenant Wickham's wife, but it was difficult to tell since the body had been badly mutilated.

Hearing a fresh crackling of shots, Eden cowered back amid the branches and her breath caught on a gasp as half a dozen sowars, native cavalry soldiers armed with rifles, galloped past on horses that had obviously been appropriated from the garrison stables. *"Maro! Maro!"* she could hear them shouting. "Kill the *feringhis!* Let none escape!"

A fusillade of gunfire met them from the powder magazine, where a handful of British soldiers must have dug in to take a stand against them. These were quickly and effectively silenced by several well-aimed shots from the sowars, who raised their fists triumphantly as the last of their unchallenged reports faded into silence.

"Let us go, brothers!" one of them shouted. "There are other *Angrezis* waiting to be slain! Let us ride for Delhi!"

"No!" Eden whispered as she watched them gallop away amid a cloud of dust. "No, it isn't true! It cannot be happening!"

Yet she knew that it was. Wasn't this exactly what her father had foreseen and what he had tried so hard to warn his superiors against? They had refused to listen, scoffing at his fears and pointing out that there had always been rumblings of mutiny from the sepoys, the native infantry soldiers who served in the armies of the Honorable East India Company, the powerful British firm that governed all of India. Why should the company fear such talk when it always amounted to naught?

Eden's father had refused to be placated by such blustery assurances, aware that the dissatisfaction was spreading from the sepoys and the sowars into the hearts and minds of the Indian people themselves. At the bottom of their growing unrest lay the East India Company's enforced policy of annexation: the taking over of even friendly Indian states and replacing their rulers with the company's own commissioners. When one thought about it, Colonel Hamilton had bitterly maintained, the entire system amounted to little better than barefaced stealing of the land, which the people of India could not be expected to tolerate overlong.

Unbelievably, the company made no attempt to conceal the fact that it was well aware of what it was doing. Yet its directors were far too greedy to leave even the poorest Indian state untouched and too insufferably arrogant in their certainty that they were leading a backward nation down the lighted path of progress and modernization to attempt to trade honestly and fairly with them. And what did it matter that they deposed long-ruling and quite popular rajahs and queens of the territories they seized? These were naught but inferior beings, puppet figureheads who ruled a race of "coloreds" and "blackies" and were therefore quite unfit to rule anything at all. What, they had argued scornfully, was there to fear from such ignorant savages?

Fourteen-year-old Eden Hamilton, panting and close to tears, shrank farther into the protective branches as a pair of grinning sowars appeared on the verandah of a bungalow directly below her. Their uniforms were stiffened with blood that was not their own, and they carried between them a sack bulging with stolen loot. The sight of them was a shock to Eden since they wore the uniforms of *resaidars*, junior Indian officers promoted from the ranks—men who should have been expected to remain loyal to their British regiments. If the *resaidars* had not been true to their salt, as all Hindus who took the military oath swore to be, then what had become of the sepoys, who, as her father had predicted months ago, were seething for mutiny?

Eden heard one of them curse as the heavy musket he carried slipped from his grasp and clattered down the verandah steps. "Wait, brother, I cannot carry both!"

"Leave the weapon," the other advised. "There will be more for the taking and I value our booty far more than thy rusty jezail!"

Both of them laughed, and with the sack between them they hurried across the withered grass to vanish amid a rustling bamboo brake on the far side of the bungalow.

Holding her breath, Eden waited only long enough to make certain no one had followed them, then leaped from the wall and raced across the hot stretch of lawn to scoop up the discarded musket. It was a cumbersome weapon and far too heavy for her, but it was loaded, and she knew how to shoot it. Gathering it against her breast, she began to run, keeping to the protective shadows of the thorn scrubs.

Tears of relief welled in her eyes as she reached the flowerbeds bordering Colonel Carmichael-Smyth's tidy bungalow and saw that it had not been set afire. Yet there seemed to be an odd, empty look about it, and what on earth, Eden wondered, was that thing there on the verandah lying partially obscured by the opened doorway? Her eyes widened with horror as she recognized the body of the colonel's fat Mohammedan cook, Mumfaisal. A trail of discarded belongings lay scattered across the steps and on the lawn to tell its own terrible story.

"Mrs. Percival! Isabel!" Eden screamed, starting up the steps at a run.

"Eden! Eden-baba!"

Eden whirled, lifting the heavy jezail in anticipation of firing only to lower it with a dry sob as a small Hindu woman in a torn sari hurried toward her through the glaring sunlight.

"Sitka!" she breathed on a note of pure relief.

"I thank the gods thou art still alive!" the woman wept, clutching Eden in a fierce embrace. "I have been waiting for thy return from the plains! For the first time in my life I do not curse thy wayward habits!"

"Oh, Sitka, what has happened?" Eden cried, reverting to the vernacular of the woman's native Hindustani. "Is it the sepoys? Have they risen against us? Where are Mrs. Percival and Isabel?"

"Hush, *piari*, do not speak! We must hide! Listen, canst thou not hear the shooting? The sowars are searching the grounds for any *Angrezis*, any English, who may still survive!"

Pulling Eden behind the sprawling plumbago bushes planted on the shaded side of the bungalow, the Hindu woman whispered fearfully: "Thy father, the colonel-sahib, was wrong in thinking it would be safer here in Meerut where so many *Angrezi* regiments are stationed. It is here that the tinder has been struck. The mobs in the bazaars are howling for the end of company rule, and the bloodshed has begun!"

Eden shivered as she stared into the terrified face of the woman who had been her *ayah*, her nurse, from the first hours of her birth. "Have the sepoys mutinied, then?" she whispered.

"The sepoys and the sowars, the cavalry and the infantry" Sitka answered tearfully. "And they have risen not o ly against their *Angrezi* officers, but against the memsahibs and the babas. No *feringhi*, no foreigner in all Hind is safe this day!"

"Why have they done this?" Eden demanded. "My father felt certain there was still time to make concessions!"

"Thou hast not yet heard the news," Sitka explained. "Eighty-five sowars of the Meerut Brigade were court-martialed yesterday and sentenced to life at hard labor."

"Court-martialed!" Eden's breath caught on a gasp.

"Colonel Smyth-sahib himself handed down the sentence. Perhaps thy father, Hamilton-sahib, remembers him as a man of honor and sense, but it must be that the years have robbed him of his reason, for never have the people spoken of a sentence so unjust!"

"What in God's name have the sowars done?" Eden demanded.

Sitka twisted her gnarled brown hands together. "It is said they refused to use the company-issued cartridges in their new rifles, and for this reason the colonel-sahib and General Hewitt-sahib chose to make examples of them.''

Eden's thoughts whirled. She had heard her father speak of the cartridges before, calling them the devil's poison and predicting that their distribution among the ranks would ignite a burning torch that would engulf all India in flames. The cartridges, greased with the fat of hogs and cows, had to be bitten open in order to be used, and it was to this that the sowars and the sepoys objected. The tasting of beef fat was considered defilement by a Hindu, as was the eating of pork by a Mussulman.

"The sepoys spoke of the cartridges as a company plot handed down to destroy their caste," Sitka added, and she shivered, for to destroy a Hindu's caste was to destroy the most sacred of all his institutions. "When the men of the Meerut Brigade refused to touch the cartridges, Carmichael-Smyth-sahib charged them with insubordination, and the general-sahib ordered them publicly stripped of their uniforms and led away in shackles."

The fools! Eden thought, and the constriction that had clogged her throat ever since she had seen Colin Jeffries lying murdered outside the cantonment gates grew tighter still. It was incredible to think that while she had been riding oblivious across the plains, a seething mob from the city had stormed the prison to free the martyred sowars and turned upon the British who had so shamed them. Their simmering resentment had erupted at last, and it was far too late for knowledgeable men the likes of Colonel Dougal Hamilton to stem the raging tide.

Crouching in the hot shadows of Colonel Carmichael-Smyth's looted bungalow, Eden Hamilton could feel the sweat trickling between her shoulder blades and hear the dull hammering of the blood in her ears. Lifting her face to the hot blue sky, she wet her lips and tried to make some order out of the confusion of her thoughts. She couldn't exactly remember when the dawn had come, or when she had first grown aware of the heat or her raging thirst, but it seemed to her as if an eternity had passed since she had left Mumtaz tethered beyond the compound gates.

"What of the other regiments?" she inquired hoarsely. "Why haven't they come? Surely they must have heard the shooting by now!"

Even as she spoke she was remembering how empty the Grand Trunk Road had seemed to her when Mumtaz had galloped across the length of it on the way back to the stables; empty of even the ordinary morning traffic from the outlying villages: the *ekkas* of the memsahibs from the British town, the donkeys and drays of the vendors, the lumbering elephants, even the ubiquitous bullock carts. . . .

"The sowars have been boasting that all the Europeans in Meerut have been slain," Sitka told her. "We must flee before they find thee! I have been hiding here in the shadows for hours, child. Mumfaisal was not as fortunate as I. She did not think the sowars would harm us, that it was just the sahib-log they wanted. But I saw them break down the door—" She broke off without warning and began to weep, softly and despairingly, her face buried in her hands.

"What of Mrs. Percival and my cousin?"

Sitka shook her head. "I do not know what has become of the memsahiba, but thy cousin fled the house when the soldiers first came. I hid here in the shrubs and as yet have not found the courage to go back inside." Her voice dropped to a whisper. "It is in my mind that everyone is dead. All of them have been slain, Eden-baba, all of the memsahibs and the children of the cantonment. We must leave while we can, for though the sowars have gone on to Delhi to seek new sport, the *budmarshes*, the riffraff from the city, will follow on their heels to see if there is anything left to loot. They, too, will be crazed with greed and the desire to kill."

Lifting her head, she wiped away her tears with the embroidered edge of her sari. Some of her panic fled as she looked down into the pale, beautiful face of the British child she loved as her own and whose dark blue eyes were clouded with shock. "There is still hope for us, *piari*. Dressed as thou art, thou mayest yet pass for a *chokra*, a native boy, but we must go now if we are to escape at all."

"No," Eden said unexpectedly, and when she lifted her head to look at the Hindu woman there was suddenly a stubbornness on her heart-shaped face that told Sitka it would be futile to argue. "We cannot leave, not until we find Isabel and see for ourselves if there are others here in need of our help. Let us take what we can in the way of supplies and search the grounds before we go."

"Very well," Sitka said reluctantly, "but if there is any sign that the sowars remain or that the *budmarshes* have come, we will flee at once. Thy word on this, child!"

Eden nodded solemnly.

"I have a cousin who lives in Dargunj," Sitka added on a brighter note. "If talk is to be believed and it is truly unsafe to show thy face in Meerut, we will go to him there. He can be counted on to hide us."

"Then let us hurry," Eden urged. Peering down the dusty length of the mall and seeing nothing more than the heat haze shimmering across the sand, she scrambled through the thickets and up the steps, turning her gaze deliberately from the bloated body of Mumfaisal.

When she saw what the looters had done to the pleasant rooms of the bungalow, she grew sickened with disbelief. Every stick of furniture had been smashed to pieces, and all of the *chik* blinds had been ripped from the windows. Paintings and bric-a-brac lay slashed and broken amid the scattered contents of the colonel's antique armoire, and an overturned brandy decanter spread an ugly stain on the beautiful Persian rug.

"This cannot have happened!" Eden gasped uncomprehendingly. "It cannot!"

"Hurry, child!" Sitka hissed, rummaging frantically through the kitchen cupboards in an effort to fill her canvas haversack.

Eden hurried across the hall and into Colonel Carmichael-Smyth's study, finding to her great relief that his gun case had not been tampered with. Starting toward it, she froze suddenly and her heart seemed to leap into her throat as her eyes fell on the body sprawled before her.

Mrs. Percival was lying on her back, her wide crinolines spread about her and her small red mouth opened in a soundless scream. Her sightless eyes stared into nothingness, and Eden, looking down at her with her hand pressed to her throat, could see no mark on her that might have indicated how she died. For a long, dragging moment she did not move, then she swallowed hard and forced herself to step over the stiffening body.

Her hands shook as she unlocked the door and took out powder and shot. Sitka might consider food and water of paramount importance, but Eden was not about to leave the bungalow inadequately armed.

Stuffing the bags of powder into the pockets of her loose-fitting trousers, she swung the glass door shut and froze abruptly, hearing the sound of heavy footsteps pounding up the verandah steps. Swiftly she ducked behind the lacquered screen that served in summer months to conceal Colonel Carmichael-Smyth's *punkah-wallah*, who operated the ropes that moved the reed blades of the ceiling fan back and forth.

. The floorboards in the front hall creaked, and Eden, peeping through a slit in the screen, inhaled sharply as a shadow fell across the threshold. She could see a pair of polished black boots and blue-piped trousers and then, incredibly, the deep scarlet of an infantry officer's uniform. The features above the tight black collar were indistinct, but it was an unmistakably British face, and Eden could feel the terror ebb from her.

Oh, thank God, she thought, and was about to step from behind the screen when the roar of an explosion somewhere on the cantonment grounds halted her in her tracks. It was answered immediately by a fury of rifle shots, and the British officer, who had paused near the doorway to listen, cursed savagely under his breath.

Eden's eyes widened in disbelief as she saw him kick Mrs. Percival's body aside and begin to rummage through Colonel Carmichael-Smyth's desk. Prying at one of the drawers with a letter opener, he gave a satisfied grunt as a thin strip of wood came loose in his hands. Reaching beneath it, he withdrew a small tin box of the sort commonly used to hold loose tea or tobacco and which Eden recognized immediately as the one her father had entrusted to Sitka upon their departure from Lucknow. She hadn't thought much about it at the time, believing it to be a gift for Colonel Carmichael-Smyth, but now she stared openmouthed as its contents spilled onto the desktop. Blood-red rubies, some of them larger than robins' eggs, lay winking on the blotter amid shimmering ropes of iridescent moonstones and sapphires. Carved emeralds sparked and flared, their facets reflecting the muted sunlight in haunting, brilliant green.

"I'll warrant you were after these yourself, weren't you?" the officer inquired of Mrs. Percival's slackmouthed corpse.

"Huzoor, I beg you, do not take the jewels!"

The officer stiffened, and for a dreadful moment Eden, too, imagined it was the dead woman who had spoken.

"Huzoor, please, the memsahiba promised me she would take them with her, and— Oh! Oh, she cannot be dead!"

"Sitka!" Eden whispered, recognizing that voice.

The Hindu woman's eyes were filled with panic as she hurried across the room. Stumbling over Mrs. Percival's body, she tried to claw the box from the officer's grasp. "Please, Huzoor! I swore to Hamilton-sahib that no harm would befall them!"

"Get back from me, woman! Are you mad?"

Backhanding her brutally, the officer sent Sitka reeling against a nearby chair. Turning to scoop up the mound of glittering jewels, he failed to see her stagger to her feet and snatch up the letter opener lying on the desk beside him.

While Sitka may have had the advantage of surprise, she was old and not strong, and though she brought the sharp blade down with every intention of plunging it through his heart, she succeeded in doing little more than tearing his neat scarlet uniform. It was enough, however, to bring the blood welling, and with a yelp of pained astonishment the British officer hit her again, this time with a force that sent her crumpling to the floor.

In the next moment he found himself leaped upon by a furious little creature that bit and clawed him savagely, and only with an effort was he able to free his hands and catch it by the throat. Shaking the hair from his eyes, he looked down and found himself staring into a heart-shaped face whose dark blue eyes blazed with murderous fury from beneath a muslin turban. A look of utter surprise crept over his features.

"It's only a child," he murmured aloud. "An Indian boy—"

A volley of shots coming from the cantonment road seemed to tear through the hot shadows of the room and drown out the sound of Eden's labored breathing. Abruptly the grip about her throat eased, and she heard someone pounding on the door.

"Lieutenant! Lieutenant, are you there?"

Thrusting Eden from him, the officer scooped up the tin box. "I'm coming, Caulfield!"

"Hurry, sir! We haven't much time!"

Holding her bruised throat, Eden scrambled after him only to draw up short on the verandah at the sight of a yelling mob that was pouring through the cantonment gates wielding rusty jezails, scythes, axes, and sticks. Seeing the pair of uniformed men racing from Colonel Carmichael-Smyth's bungalow, they surged forward, clamoring for the deaths of these surviving sahibs.

Shading her eyes against the blinding sunlight, Eden saw the young lieutenant who had so carelessly murdered Sitka mount a waiting horse and whip it into flight. With a wounded cry she leaped from the porch to give chase, unmindful of the furnace heat and the howling of the mob at her heels. A lone bullet whined past her head, and Eden flung herself to the side, sobbing with fright and hopeless frustration. The next moment she screamed with terror as she was lifted up by the seat of her trousers and thrown onto the front of a wildly plunging horse.

"Sit still, thou centipede!" a Hindu voice roared in her ear as she struggled. "Sit still or thou wilt endanger us both! I almost did not recognize thee, and these *bander-log* are mad enough to slay their own kind!"

Even as he spoke a bullet smacked into the sand in front of him and another tore through his sleeve. He cursed and pushed Eden down in the saddle, urging his horse with voice and heels to a faster pace. Eden's face was pressed against stifling folds of cloth, and her head spun from the heat and the dizzying gait. She tried to fight her way free of the arms that imprisoned her, only to feel the world tip and tilt about her; and then the terrible events of that horrible, unreal day seemed to fade away, and quite unexpectedly everything around her went black.

Chapter One

A pearl-gray dawn stole softly over the foothills, and the first breath of morning wind blew across the plains, stirring the dry sand and whispering through the half circle of tents pitched beneath the ancient *sal* trees near the riverbed. Though the sun was little more than a faint glow on the cliffs, the heat was rising rapidly, and the man who thrust aside the tent flaps paused for a moment in their shadow to draw a disheartened breath.

"By God," he grumbled aloud, "I'm bloody sick of India! Another day's travel in this infernal heat, and I vow I'll put a bullet through my brain!"

"No need for that, old chap." His companion, a weathered Yorkshireman by the name of Harry Deas, gestured toward the shadowed canyons shimmering in the distance. "The rajah's palace should be somewhere beyond those foothills. No more than twelve miles at most."

"It's not just the heat," Captain Arthur Molson growled, flicking his half-smoked cheroot into the fire and watching moodily as the smoke spiraled into the paling sky. "It's Lamberton's bleating zeal in getting that cursed treaty signed. I vow his incessant whining is eating at my nerves! The rajah of Mayar has been dead all of four months. What harm could there have been in waiting until cooler weather before seeking out his mewling heir?"

"The new rajah is said to be a difficult young man," observed Mr. Deas, the local district officer and a twelve-year veteran of Indian civil service. "Though the old rajah remained loyal during the mutiny, one cannot know what lies in Prince Malraj's mind. Small though the kingdom may be, it boasts formidable soldiery, and one cannot trust him not to use it.''

"Quite right, Mr. Deas," agreed a sallow-featured gentleman who had emerged from an adjacent tent in time to overhear the district officer's words. "Crown Prince Malraj, or I should say His Highness, the new rajah of Mayar, is a thoroughly unpredictable fellow, the sort who vacillates continuously on the score of his loyalties. All the more reason to get a treaty of peaceful coexistence in hand and a British residency established within the borders of the state.''

"Pompous ass," Captain Molson muttered as the speaker wandered off behind a cluster of thorn scrub to relieve himself. "Lost his seat in the House of Commons last election, but no sooner is he appointed British resident of Mayar then he's acting like he's been elevated to the bloody peerage.'' The captain's lips thinned beneath his drooping blond mustache. "I'd like to know why the Political Department decided to mollycoddle this Malraj fellow in the first place, especially since most of his peers lost their territories when the rebellion was snuffed out. This'll only serve to worsen his overblown sense of importance, and Lamberton doesn't know nearly enough about handling blackies to convince him otherwise." His eyes grew flinty. "Mark m' words, Harry, there's bound to be trouble. India's no place for a man like him!''

"Or you, apparently," observed the district officer tartly, watching the captain's hands shake as he rolled another cheroot. Molson's spasms and ghastly color, as Mr. Deas well knew, were the lingering effects of dysentery, which had dogged the poor fellow relentlessly since their departure from Rawalpindi.

"Demmed right," Captain Molson agreed without heat. "I'd never have accepted this brevet if I'd known it would entail leaving 'Pindi for a haul across sweltering desert in the company of loutish civilians!'' Uncrossing his legs, he added quickly: "Present company excepted, of course. You've been more than helpful, Harry. Can't imagine how we'd have made it this far without you as guide. Rajputana hills all look the same to me, I'm afraid, the way they fold in on each other like bloody strips of carpet. I'd have been hopelessly lost even with the maps I've got.''

"Quite all right," the district officer assured him. Coming to his feet, he slapped the dust from his khaki slacks. "Might as well tell the bearers to strike camp. Can't say I'm looking forward to a daytime march, but Lamberton was adamant on the score of reaching Pitore before evening.''

Captain Molson muttered something unintelligible beneath his breath, though the insult it conveyed was obvious. "Now there's another bloody enigma for you," he added, changing the subject unexpectedly as his narrowed gaze fell on a tent pitched some distance from the others.

"What's that?" The district officer turned to see a darkheaded man in worn breeches step from the tent to exchange words with one of the bearers. His face and bare chest were deeply sunburned, and the profile that was turned toward them seemed strangely intimidating in the pale morning light.

"Oh, you mean Roxbury. What's with him?"

Captain Molson hesitated, aware that the district officer held an incomprehensibly high opinion of the man despite the fact that he himself considered Roxbury the most unpleasant individual he had ever met. "It's an odd thing, that," he said lamely. "Can't for the life of me understand why the undersecretary asked the duke of Roxbury to accompany the British resident to Mayar. He's impatient, high-handed, and bloody arrogant—not exactly qualities you'd care to find in a diplomat, eh?"

If he had hoped the district officer would shed some light on this particular mystery, he was to be disappointed, for the district officer merely laughed. "You're certainly right on that score, old chap."

Scowling, Captain Molson chose to let the matter drop, though he would have been surprised to discover that the duke of Roxbury tended to view the prospect of paying his respects to the troublesome ruler of a tiny, defeated Indian state as being more than a little tedious. Furthermore, the prospect of enduring the protracted ceremonies that would invariably mark their reception in Mayar bored His Grace no end, and he was heartily sick of having to spend additional time in the company of both Captain Molson, commander of Lamberton's military escort, and Edgar Lamberton, the new British resident himself.

Pack of fools, the duke of Roxbury was at this very moment thinking as he made his way down to the eddying shallows of the river. God alone knew why he had chosen to remain with them this long. If the heat didn't end up driving him mad, then boredom invariably would, and he'd had quite enough of Edgar Lamberton's zealous posturings and the incessant complaints of Captain Molson's cavalry escort. He hadn't come to Rajputana to take part in any royal sideshow. It was his own fault, really, for having agreed to join the British deputation in the first place, something he never would have done had it not been for the insistence of the undersecretary, a man he owed several favors.

"Wouldst thou care for a swim, Hazrat-sahib?" inquired the wiry servant who had trotted down to the river behind him, carrying a shaving kit and towels.

"Not this morning, Baga Lal." A faint smile touched the duke of Roxbury's lips and widened momentarily over his thin, sunburned features. It amused him that Baga Lal insisted on calling him "Highness" despite the fact that the royal blood within him was by now too many generations removed to count. But as it annoyed both Molson and Lamberton as well, and since both men were accorded considerably less respect by the natives, Roxbury hadn't troubled to forbid his bearer to use it.

"A shave, Baga Lal," he ordered in fluent Hindustani, though he rarely addressed his servants in anything other than English whenever he was in camp. "And see that thy blade is quick."

"The Hazrat-sahib is impatient today," the young Hindu observed, squatting to open the tooled leather kit, a smile lighting his normally solemn features. "He is thinking no doubt of the beauties who inhabit the rajah's zenana, though it is unlikely we will be permitted to see them. *Afsos!* How very sad! Perhaps in honor of the arrival of such august visitors, the rajah will see fit to parade them before us?"

"Not a chance in hell," the duke responded. Grinning he settled back on his heels and watched as Baga Lal began to strop the razor. Around them the pearl-gray dawn was giving way to a hot, breathless morning, and as the sun shrugged free of the foothills and washed the river with shivering gold, he laughed unexpectedly.

"No, thou art an ambitious dreamer, Baga Lal. I seriously doubt the rajah will permit his womenfolk to receive us even if they were not living in *purdah*. Not if there is the slightest chance they will appear wilted in the heat."

"A harem of fresh young beauties is certainly an asset of which any ruler can be proud," the Hindu agreed affably, and his dark eyes gleamed. "Perhaps it might be possible to convince the rajah that— *Dekho!*" he interrupted himself suddenly, lifting his head as he spied a thin cloud of dust on the distant horizon. "What is that? Has the rajah perhaps sent us an escort?"

"It is but a single horse," said the duke, whose eyesight was keener. Rising to his feet, he followed Baga Lal's pointing finger across the flat expanse of plain. He was silent for a moment, watching the animal's whirlwind approach, and then he frowned. "It appears to be out of control."

"*Hai mai*, a runaway!" Baga Lal exclaimed, shading his eyes against the glare. "There is someone clinging to his back, a boy from the look of it! Dost thou see him?"

"Aye," said the duke. "And he's going to break his leg if he falls."

"Or his neck if that maddened creature should put its foot in a badger hole."

The duke's eyes narrowed. "I suppose someone will have to make certain it doesn't."

Baga Lal frowned. "I do not understand, Hazratsahib."

But Roxbury did not answer, and when Baga Lal turned it was to see his master already halfway across camp, throwing his leg over the back of a horse just unhobbled in anticipation of grooming. The big animal snorted and whirled beneath the insistent voice and heels, then took off at a flat gallop, his long tail streaming like a banner behind him.

"*Shabash!*" Baga Lal exclaimed proudly. "Truly the sahib is a prince among princes! If the gods decree the wretched animal can be stopped, he is the one to do so!"

"I would not wager a single *anna* on that," snorted an elderly Mussulman who had trotted down to the river to watch. "The boy has a considerable lead."

Baga Lal's eyes gleamed. "Thou art talking through thy beard, Kulum Azar. An *anna* to prove as much."

The Mussulman smiled benignly. "Done."

As they watched, the runaway horse veered to avoid a rock-strewn *nullah,* losing ground as it did so. Baga Lal grinned broadly in response. "The wager will be easily won, my father! The sahib need only ride a hard right path to intercept it. Child's play, I tell thee!"

At the moment it did not appear that way at all to the duke, who had lost considerable time fording the sandy shallows of the river while the trail of dust behind the runaway grew visibly smaller. Yet his horse was fresh and the ground on the other side hard-packed and ideal for galloping, and the two of them settled down quickly to close the yawning gap.

A herd of black-buck exploded from a stand of thorn scrub as they passed, while a hyena foraging nearby panicked and slunk away toward the river. Roxbury paid no attention, yet when the drumming of another set of hooves came from somewhere behind him, he risked a quick glance over his shoulder. He was startled to see not Baga Lal or another of the bearers of his own camp giving chase, but a roan gelding he had never seen before carrying an Indian youth who leaned low in the saddle.

Turning away, Roxbury urged his mount to draw ahead and, using his whip, managed to come level with the tiring animal at last. Rising in the stirrups, he leaned across and snatched up the reins, jerking the panicked horse to a stop just as its rider uttered a helpless cry and tumbled to the ground.

Dismounting, the duke knelt beside him and turned him over gently. It was a boy of some nine or ten years who stared up at him with a dazed expression. "Art thou harmed?" the duke demanded in the vernacular.

Before the boy could answer, the roan gelding skidded to a halt beside him amid a stinging spray of dust. "Jaji! came the shrill cry from the youth who leaped from the saddle.

"I—I am unharmed, Choto Bai," the boy said breathlessly, struggling to sit up. "The sahib—the sahib stopped me in time. He saved my life!"

Roxbury waved this aside. "Thy mount would have spent itself eventually."

"But not before I would have fallen. I couldn't hold on any longer." Jaji coughed and attempted to straighten his turban, though his hands were shaking visibly. "Tukki is young and foolish," he added tremulously. "I suppose it was wrong of me to let him have his head."

"He is no more young and foolish than his rider," chided the youth called Choto Bai, and knelt to offer him a water flask. A scarlet turban was pulled low over his brow, and one end of it had been unraveled and tucked over his nose and mouth to protect him from the choking dust. Despite the oppressive heat, he wore a knee-length *achkan* of green quilted cotton buttoned tightly at the collar and wrists.

Regarding him curiously, Roxbury was startled to notice that his eyes were fringed with thick black lashes much like a girl's and that they were of an uncommon blue, as dark and hauntingly blue as the rarest of lapis. Men of the hills, particularly Pathans, the duke knew, had blue or gray eyes, but he remembered clearly the undersecretary having told him there were no Pathans living within the borders of Mayar. Perhaps the boy was of mixed blood? Unlikely, for the little fellow here would not have addressed a half-caste as "Choto Bai," meaning Little Brother, and his riding skills were far too impressive to dismiss the likelihood that he was not of Rajput blood.

Lifting his head at that moment and meeting the duke's speculative gaze, the youth stiffened unexpectedly and lowered the goatskin flask. "Come, Jaji," he said gruffly, "we must go back. Awal Bannu will be searching for us."

Attempting to rise, Jaji uttered a pained cry and fell back into the sand. "I can't! My leg—it hurts!"

"It doesn't seem to be broken," observed the duke, stripping away the boy's trouser leg and probing his ankle gently. "Though I daresay the sprain is a painful one." His harsh features softened as he noticed Jaji's pallid cheeks. "Doubtless it would be better if thou didst not ride Tukki home."

"Of course he will not," the youth said tersely. "Jaji will ride with me." His expression grew hostile as the duke's questioning eyes met his. "If thou wouldst be kind enough to lift him into the saddle, sahib?"

A frown pulled at the duke's mouth, serving to give his face a sinister cast, but Choto Bai merely gazed at him steadily, his eyes challenging above the folds of scarlet muslin.

"Cocky little bastard, aren't you?" Roxbury said at last, speaking in English.

The dark blue eyes did not waver. "Sahib?"

"Fetch thy mount," the duke ordered curtly, and a moment later Jaji was safely installed upon the gelding's back.

"Our thanks, sahib," Choto Bai said, and his manner was suddenly courteous once again. "It is unlikely Jaji would have escaped serious injury without thy intervention."

The harshness of the duke's features eased a fraction, realizing the boy's earlier antagonism had stemmed from concern for his young companion. "I am not at all certain of that, but I am glad to have been of assistance." He stood holding the bridle while the youth mounted and took up the reins.

"*Dekho*, Choto Bai!" Jaji exclaimed at that moment, pointing eagerly to a trio of riders galloping along the banks of the river toward them. "Is that not Awal Bannu?"

Choto Bai turned in the saddle and uttered a low curse of annoyance. "No, Jaji, I think not. Those must be other sahib-log. Come, let us leave before they arrive."

"Are they friends of thine, sahib?" Jaji inquired interestedly.

A faint smile pulled at the corners of the duke's mouth. "Not exactly, my son."

"Do not scowl so, Choto Bai," Jaji admonished in the next breath. "It does little for thy looks. Let us stay and meet them. The one in the lead seems angry, does he not? Look how red his face is! What is the matter with him, sahib?"

"Jaji, please!" Choto Bai warned, and it was clear that he would have wheeled the roan and fled but for the fact that the duke had not yet relinquished his hold on the bridle.

"Damn you, Roxbury!" the duke could hear Captain Molson shout as the half-dozen horsemen galloped into earshot. "What in hell do you mean expending Bolivar like that when you know I planned to ride him into Pitore this evening? How dare you risk him in this heat just to save some bloody little nigger boy a fall?"

There was an audible gasp from the older Indian youth, but because it was muffled in the folds of muslin covering his face, Roxbury did not hear it. His own smile faded, however, and there was a tightness about his mouth that deepened as Captain Molson reined in savagely before him.

"No harm done, Molson," he drawled softly. "But if I were you, I'd think twice before addressing the natives with such objectionable terms. In India appearances are not always as they seem."

"Oh, for God's sake, whatever are you talking about?" Captain Molson demanded irritably.

The duke's shoulders lifted. "Only that we're less than a dozen miles from Pitore, and these lads here might very well come from the royal palace. I sincerely doubt the rajah would care to have members of his family referred to as coloreds."

"Not bloody likely!" Captain Molson snorted, his eyes flicking contemptuously over both the boys. His scowl faded, however, as he took in the richness of their attire and the lavish trappings of the blooded animal upon which they sat. "Well, it's perfectly obvious that neither of them understands English," he blustered. "And furthermore, there's nothing to prove they're from the rajah's palace."

"His Grace may be right, sir," one of the junior officers spoke up hesitantly, pointing at Jaji. "The *sarpej* on that one's turban could well mean he holds some position of prestige."

"Yes, I suppose you've got something there," Captain Molson conceded, studying the glittering ruby pinned to the folds of Jaji's turban. "Perkins," he added tersely, "your Hindustani is better than mine. Tell the boy I'm relieved he's unharmed, and then come along. We've no more time to waste, and it's already too bloody hot for marching as it is." Wheeling his horse, he cantered off in the direction of camp.

"What the devil?" young Perkins exclaimed as a scuffle of hooves and a frantic neigh broke the uncomfortable silence that settled in his wake. Turning his head, he was astonished to see the duke of Roxbury jerk aside just as the older Indian youth lashed out unexpectedly with his whip. The leather tip whistled through the air, missing the lean cheek by inches. Outraged, the duke's hand shot out to clasp the boy's wrist.

"Whatever are you doing, you young spawn of Satan?"

"Damn you!" Choto Bai was leaning over him, addressing him, unbelievably, in English. His blue eyes flashed with hot anger, and he seemed oblivious to the painful fingers gripping his arm. "Nothing has changed, has it? Your kind still insists on calling them *coloreds*, *blackies*, the inferior native race! In God's name, didn't the mutiny teach you *anything?*"

The coat sleeve ripped as Choto Bai jerked his arm free of Roxbury's grasp. Wheeling the roan, he sent it thundering away with Jaji perched precariously on the crupper.

"I imagine we'd better return to camp, Your Grace," young Perkins said, speaking hesitantly into the ominous silence that settled in their wake. "The captain will be wanting to start for Pitore."

"Yes, perhaps we should," the duke agreed slowly. Swinging himself onto Bolivar's back, he stared thoughtfully at the trail of dust marking the roan gelding's passage, and his dark expression was tinged with something that was not at all pleasant.

"Why did you attempt to strike the tall one with your whip?" Jaji asked curiously as the roan pounded across the length of a rock-strewn ravine and, slowing to a trot, began picking its way down a deeply scored hillside. Below them the Pitore road unwound across the flat, lion-colored plain, and in the distance the buttresses of the ancient capital of Mayar shimmered in the heat haze.

"To repay insult with insult," Choto Bai answered curtly.

"Ah, then the one with the ludicrous beard did say something unkind! I thought as much! What was it?"

"It does not bear repeating."

Jaji's lower lip protruded. "That isn't fair, Choto Bai! Just because your English is better than mine—"

"Which it wouldn't be if you applied yourself more diligently to your studies."

"I wonder what these sahib-log want in Mayar?" Jaji mused, changing the subject for fear of a familiar lecture. "Do you suppose they've come to sign that treaty of alliance with Malraj?"

The older youth's hands stilled suddenly on the reins. "This is the first I've heard of such a treaty, Jaji."

The boy looked smug. "There! That proves you do not know everything that goes on in the palace!"

"Only because I do not make it a habit of listening at doors like some people I know."

"Well, how else could I have found out that Malraj is expecting *Angrezi* visitors?" Jaji demanded defensively, then added with considerable disappointment: "I had hoped there would be more of them, or at least a big military escort. Malraj will not be greatly impressed. Except perhaps with the tall sahib, the one who stopped Tukki from running away. He was not the least like the others, was he?"

"No," Choto Bai responded, and frowned, recalling how the sahib's pale blue eyes had seemed to peer right through him.

"You did not like him, did you?" Jaji asked shrewdly.

"No," Choto Bai said again, and fingered his whip, his eyes suddenly bright and hard.

"You are being unfair," chided Jaji. "Remember, it was the one with the yellow beard who behaved like a hysterical old woman."

"I promise you they are all the same," Choto Bai said impatiently. "Even the sahib who spoke such admirable Hindustani."

"Hai mai," said Jaji, wagging his head from side to side. "I would certainly like to know what the yellow beard said to have offended you so!"

"I've told you before that it does not bear repeating."

"So you have, and you needn't be so cross about it." Jaji's face brightened unexpectedly. "Will Malraj hold a durbar in their honor, do you think?"

Choto Bai could not help but laugh. "Oh, Jaji, really, you mustn't ask me so many questions! I've no idea what your brother has in mind!" Lifting his head, he rose suddenly in the stirrups and pointed. "Look there! Did I not tell you Awal Bannu would be searching for us?"

Jaji shaded his eyes and frowned as he saw a small band of riders crossing the rock-strewn *nullah* directly below them. The scored ravine was dry now, though during the monsoon months it was transformed into a shimmering river that turned the valley green and lured the wild pigs and *chinkara* down from the hills. "You won't tell him Tukki ran away with me, will you?" he inquired anxiously.

"How else are we to explain his absence?"

"Yes, I suppose you're right," Jaji said, sighing.

A hot wind stirred the elephant grass and rustled through the thorn scrubs as they trotted onto the road where Awal Bannu and his companions awaited them. To Jaji's relief there appeared to be nothing save concern in the lined face of the elderly Hindu who had been the boy's personal bodyguard from the moment of his birth.

"This is bad news indeed," was all Awal Bannu had to say, listening gravely to Choto Bai's account of how Jaji's black gelding had come to be left behind. "The rajah will be greatly displeased, my prince. You know you are forbidden to ride out alone. Perhaps when you are older—"

"I shall still have an army of servants, bodyguards, and wet nurses dogging my heels!" Jaji flared unexpectedly, and suddenly the resemblance between the angry boy and his lean, hawk-featured brother, Malraj, was striking. "I am never permitted to go anywhere alone! Always there is someone in attendance to make certain I behave! If I hadn't crept out while that fat, silly eunuch Nadhoo was nodding at the door, he would have summoned the guards to stop me. My sisters, the *rajkumaris,* can do as they please, and so can Choto Bai! Why can't I?"

"Because you are heir presumptive to the throne of Mayar," Awal Bannu said soothingly, "and until the rajah has chosen another wife who will bear him many strong sons—"

"I'm to be coddled and protected because I am incapable of looking after myself." Jaji's eyes filled with tears, and suddenly he was no longer the spoiled, demanding Rajput prince of a moment ago, but merely an unhappy little child. "Oh, yes, I have heard them say it, Awal Bannu: the Begum Fariza and the *rajkumaris,* all of the women in the zenana! They think I am a baby still!"

"As well they should," the white-bearded Hindu said gently. "Consider what happened when you disappeared on your own. You've lost the fine horse your brother presented you, and if that sahib had not stopped its maddened flight in time—"

"Perhaps we should go now, *cha-cha,*" Choto Bai broke in quickly, addressing the elderly man as "uncle." "Prince Jaji's ankle should be examined by his hakim, and I profess a great hunger for tiffin."

Awal Bannu frowned at him, yet after a moment his betel-stained beard twitched. "As always you are right, child. No one should be called upon to account for his behavior while his stomach is empty." His expression softened likewise as he peered into Jaji's unhappy face. "I will send a syce to fetch Tukki, my son, and unless the sahib-log think to mention the affair to the rajah, no one will be the wiser."

"You are kind, Awal Bannu," Jaji said quickly, cheered by the prospect of evading punishment. In fact, by the time the horses had reached the carved gates leading into the city, he was enthusiastically describing his encounter with the sahib-log and embellishing the tale with such grandiose lies that Choto Bai was hard-pressed to keep his expression composed.

The royal palace of the rajahs of Mayar sat atop a windswept plateau overlooking the crowded city of Pitore. Its lower stories resembled a fortified castle wall that was flanked on all sides by carved elephant gates. Fortresslike buttresses and battlements embellished them, reflecting a time when Mayar had been besieged by invading Mughal emperors. High above, however, the imposing structure gave way to a maze of breathtaking kiosks, ornamental towers, and crenellations that lent a pleasing beauty to the numerous courtyards, gardens, capacious durbar halls, and private audience chambers of the palace itself. Shrines and temples dotted the extensive grounds, and just inside the heavily guarded *Hathi Pol,* the elephant gate, stood sizable storage facilities for grain and water that had been used in times of siege and a stable large enough to house the war elephants and horses of the rajah's army.

The life of a Rajput ruler, however, was not always given over to feuding with rival clans or waging wars against Muslim emperors, so the inner courtyards of the palace were designed to please the eye and remind its inhabitants of the more sybaritic aspects of existence. To that end the glittering audience chambers of the *mardana* were lined with hammered gold and delicately carved marble and lapis, and the walls and lamp niches of the durbar hall were lavishly displayed with Rajput mirrorwork, murals, and friezes of hand-painted miniatures. Lotus flowers and other decorative symbols, most noticeably peacocks and elephants, were carved into the delicate *jali* screens fronting the balconies, and behind the royal treasuries stood extensive workshops staffed by custodians, draftsmen, and artisans charged with the sole task of refurbishing such priceless handiwork.

Prince Jaji, accustomed from birth to such breathtaking beauty, paid not the least bit of attention to the magnificence of the pink marble arches with their painted peacock motifs that rose from the courtyard where the lathering horses were finally brought to a halt. His only thought at present was breakfast, and his stomach had begun to rumble alarmingly in response.

"Will you please let me know the moment Tukki has been returned?" he inquired with uncharacteristic humility of Awal Bannu.

"Of course, my prince." Awal Bannu's hard black eyes softened with affection as he peered down at the youngest of the late rajah's sons, plump little Jaji, who had always lived in the shadow of his handsome, talented older brother. But for the friendship of Choto Bai, Jaji's life would have been empty indeed, for he had been pitiably neglected since his mother's death and even more so since his father's. The old Hindu's gaze was no less kind as it moved to the older youth who was also swinging himself out of the saddle.

"It is fortunate indeed that you saw the *rajkumar* leaving from your window and had the sense to give chase, my child. Your loyalty should not go unrewarded."

"This is payment enough for me, *cha-cha*," Choto Bai responded with a grin, untucking the end of his turban and drinking deeply from the flask handed him by a *bheesti*, one of the hovering water-bearers.

"I will see that the court hakim examines the prince's ankle," Awal Bannu added, motioning one of the syces to lift Jaji from the saddle. "And you yourself should rest, child. You seem weary."

It was a dismissal Choto Bai was only too happy to obey. Promising to look in on Jaji as soon as the hakim had gone, he ran lightly up the wide, flat steps of the terrace and through the maze of glittering corridors and antechambers of the palace. Once inside his own rooms, he dismissed the hovering servants and drew together the silk hangings across the arching doorway. Halting before a tall, gilded mirror carved with a border of cranes and lotuses, he unraveled the hot turban. Tossing it aside, he deftly unpinned the chignon that had been plaited to accommodate the heavy headgear. The uncoiled curls sprang free beneath his hands and fell in a honey-colored wave to his hips.

Choto Bai sighed and loosened the string at the waist of his trousers, stripping off the dusty garment. The heavy coat and the sequined *choli* beneath it quickly followed, so that he soon stood naked before the glass, stretching slim, sun-browned arms in an effort to relieve the stiffness of riding.

Where a moment before a handsome youth had been peering into the age-tarnished mirror, the reflection now revealed a breathtakingly beautiful woman, delicately boned and small-breasted, her long legs lean and muscled from hours in the saddle. The dark blue eyes that had so interested the duke of Roxbury took on a disturbing beauty when viewed with the finely molded features of her heart-shaped face. Her nose was slim and straight above a mouth that was generous without being overly wide and which curved beguilingly as she secured the heavy tangle of her hair with a tortoise-shell comb and slid into the waiting bath.

Rose petal–scented water lapped against Eden Hamilton's naked body, and she sighed as she felt the grit of the morning's ride soak away from her skin. Save for the rustling of the silk hangings and the flap and cooing of pigeons on the roof, the room was tranquilly silent. The subdued voices of the women in the zenana, the wailing of a fretful baby, and the clatter of pots and pans from the distant kitchens came only dimly through the opened windows. They were soothing sounds, and long-familiar ones, and Eden allowed them to lull her as the warmth of the water drew the last bit of stiffness from her limbs. Awal Bannu had told her that she looked tired and in need of rest, but as Eden's thoughts drifted lazily back to what the elderly Hindu had said to her, her eyes suddenly widened. Rising quickly from the bath, she reached for a towel, the water running in rivulets between her breasts and down her calves.

Rest while *Angrezis* were to be found within the borders of Mayar? Not bloody likely!

Kneeling, Eden rummaged through the inlaid chest in which saris of every imaginable color lay folded amid sheets of scented tissue. Though several servants waited without to help her dress, she did not summon them. Wrapping herself in a sari of cream-colored silk, she stepped through the archway of blue-and-silver mirror-work that separated her room from its private garden. Here the air was redolent with flowers and noisy with the desultory droning of bees. A light breeze ruffled the fronds of the palms and shook the fragrant petals from the orange trees. For once, however, Eden was oblivious to the beauty that surrounded her, and when she paused in the shade there was a fretful frown upon her lovely face.

She had known all along that the British government would send an official representative to Mayar someday, yet she hadn't expected it to be quite this soon. The old rajah had remained staunchly loyal throughout the mutiny, after all, and there had been other, more troubled Indian states the British raj had been forced to deal with once the rebellion had been put down. Perhaps the tiny kingdom of Mayar might have escaped their notice indefinitely had Crown Prince Malraj not begun to openly criticize British supervision the moment he ascended the throne. Eden suspected that his complaints had come to the attention of the Political Department in Calcutta and alerted the secretary of state for India to the fact that no treaty of alliance had ever been drawn up between them. Immediate steps had apparently been taken to rectify that particular oversight.

Immediate indeed, Eden thought with a scowl, for it was obvious to her that little forethought had gone into the selection of the men who made up the British deputation. She was convinced that Malraj would never agree to sign a treaty with anyone as narrow-minded and offensive as the British officer she and Jaji had encountered today. And as for the arrogant, dark-headed sahib she had attempted to strike with her whip—

A rueful smile touched the corners of Eden's mouth. She hadn't exactly meant to do that, not after he had single-handedly stopped Jaji's runaway horse and berated the one called Molson for using such an unspeakable word. But he had been standing closest to her, and there had been something in his manner that had aroused her resentment from the first. Furthermore, she felt certain that despite his kindness toward Jaji, he was no different from the callous *Angrezi* fortune-seekers whose kind had descended like a conquering horde upon India the moment the company's raj had fallen.

"Not *Angrezis*," Eden berated herself, speaking aloud in her mother tongue, a language that had become thoroughly unfamiliar to her in the last three years. "English. They are English, Eden, and they are here in Mayar. What do you intend to do about it?"

Not a bloody thing, she decided, her chin tilting. She had no desire to make her identity known to the odious Officer Molson or the tall sahib. She was safe here in the rajah's palace, and should either of them think to ask indiscreet questions concerning the youth who had addressed them so fluently in their own tongue, Eden was confident that neither Malraj nor his ministers would choose to enlighten them.

The faint smile lingered on Eden Hamilton's lips as she stepped back into her room and caught sight of her reflection in the floor-length mirror. Except for her blue eyes, which could easily belong to a woman of the hills or an Indian of mixed blood, and the widow's peak of honey-colored hair visible where the embroidered veil of the sari fell away from her brow, she could easily have passed for a native. The strong Eastern sun had browned her skin, and the Begum Fariza's endless lessons in speech and deportment had transformed her completely from a coltish British child to a seemingly graceful young Hindu.

Abruptly the smile faded. No, Eden thought with a sigh, she was not a Hindu and claimed no blood relation to the late rajah of Mayar or to the royal princes and princesses and the numerous wives, uncles, aunts, cousins, servants, slaves, *nautch*-girls, and courtesans who made up the colorful population of his extended family. Yet she had lived for the past three years as one of them, indulged by the late rajah, tolerated by his wives, and treated like a brother by Jaji, who had christened her Choto Bai when she had first arrived in Pitore looking every inch a native boy in her turban and baggy salwars.

It was doubtful that any of them ever paused to remember that Eden Hamilton had been nothing more than a frightened *feringhi* child when the rajah's soldiers had brought her to Mayar three long years ago. In truth it was difficult for Eden herself to remember as much, for she had spent the time since then speaking, thinking, and dreaming only in Hindustani and taking an active part in the bustling world of the palace zenana. She had learned the art of making perfumes and scented oils, how to cook the delicate curried dishes that were the staples of the Indian diet, and to sew the beautiful stitches that adorned the embroidered saris she wore. She had been scolded and petted and praised in turn by the junior Rani and the Begum Fariza who had taken her under their wing and treated much the same as the other young women of the palace.

Indeed, she had been treated exactly as though she had been born of their caste, Eden thought with a profound sense of gratitude. Even the *rajkumaris,* the royal princesses, had not received a more extensive education, and no one in the palace had ever made her feel either with a spoken word or gesture that she was different—except in the question of *purdah.* All of the women of the zenana, including the powerful Begum and the junior Rani, lived in strict seclusion as was Hindu custom, guarded night and day by immense eunuchs armed with scimitars and jezails. They were never to consort with or even speak to strange men or allow a strange man to gaze upon their uncovered features. To do so would forever defile them.

Eden, too, had been taught to follow the tenets of *purdah* unerringly, yet unlike the other women of the palace, she had never been prevented from seeking out the company of the late rajah and his sons or to sit companionably with Awal Bannu in the *mardana,* the men's courtyard, listening to the bubble of his hookah fill the murmurous darkness. Wearing a turban and loose-fitting trousers to protect her modesty, Eden had even hunted

alone with Malraj and his syces and gone regularly to Jaji's rooms to play *shatranj* in the cool of the evenings if
she so desired.

Indeed, as Choto Bai, she had enjoyed freedom and
privileges the likes of which she had never dreamed. She
had grown happy here, and it was not difficult to understand why the arrival of a deputation of British should
arouse within her such suspicion and animosity. Their
presence made her think of the distant rumble of thunder
before the onset of the monsoons; but where the coming
of the rains had always been welcomed, Eden could not
help but feel that the charge she could suddenly feel in
the air portended ominous change.

"Be-wakufi!" she said aloud. "Utter nonsense!" And
laughed at herself because she sounded exactly like old
Dunna Gin, the court astrologer and master of the books,
who was forever predicting wildly improbable catastro-
phes. Of course it was unsettling to discover that the sahib-log had finally arrived in Mayar, but that didn't mean
her own way of life was in any way threatened!

Slipping her feet into the embroidered slippers standing
by the door, Eden went outside to join the women gathered in the painted courtyard to partake of the morning
meal. As she listened to their careless chatter and the
sound of their tinkling laughter, she was drawn once again
into their world—a world that had long since become her
own. Putting the unpleasant encounter with the sahib-log
from her mind, she promptly forgot it.

Chapter Two

With the exception of the junior Rani and the Begum Fariza, none of the women of the zenana had ever seen an *Angrezi* before. It was therefore not surprising that the announcement of the pending state visit of over a dozen sahibs should cause a considerable stir in the palace, and there followed endless speculation on the subject of their speech, their looks, their behavior, even their merit as men. As the newly appointed authority on foreigners, Eden was called upon to answer countless questions, and she was grateful that her misadventures with Jaji had not as yet come to light among the women of the zenana. She knew she would not have been granted a moment's peace if it had been otherwise.

Eden was herself admittedly curious about the *feringhis* and frustrated because she had been forbidden to take part in the numerous celebrations marking their arrival. Only the junior Rani, the last surviving wife of the late rajah, as well as her two daughters, had been permitted to attend even one of those events: a brief reception staged that evening to officially welcome the *Angrezis* to Mayar. Heavily veiled and seated behind a concealing *purdah* screen, they had seen next to nothing of the visitors, and the vague descriptions offered afterward by the giggling *rajkumaris* had proven equally as unsatisfying as the rumors circulating throughout the palace.

"It is unlikely we will learn anything about them," sighed Ammita, a sloe-eyed *nautch*-girl who, by virtue of being the rajah's favorite dancer, mingled freely with the higher-born women of the zenana. At present she was seated on a tassled cushion in Eden's room, slim ankles crossed beneath her as she nibbled *jellabies* from a brass dish and lamented the fact that she had not been asked to dance for the rajah's guests. Ammita was sixteen and slimly beautiful, and while her vaulted position might otherwise have aroused jealousy in those less well favored, she possessed a sweetness of nature that endeared her to all, in particular to Eden, with whom she had closed a strong friendship.

"In two days' time they will be gone from the palace and we will not even have laid eyes on them," she added unhappily.

"Except for the one who will be staying behind," Eden reminded her. "He is to become a *kotwal*, a headman for our district. The *Angrezis* call him a 'resident.' "

"Bah," said Ammita, wrinkling her nose disdainfully. "I don't care if he plans to succeed Malraj to the *gaddi*. It is said he is dull and in poor health and that his Hindustani is atrocious. Why would anyone be the least bit interested in him?" Resting her chin on her cupped palm, she added dreamily: "I would have enjoyed seeing his cavalry escort, though. It is said they wore brilliant scarlet uniforms and clanking swords when they rode beneath the gates of the city."

Though none of the zenana women had seen it, Malraj had sent a procession of gaily caparisoned horses and elephants under the command of his prime minister, Pratap Rao, to escort his guests to the palace yesterday afternoon. The citizens of Pitore had flocked to the streets in great numbers to welcome them while Eden and Ammita had stolen up to the covered balcony atop the soaring Tower of the Winds to watch. Unfortunately there had been little to see, for the cluttered houses of the city stood too close together to permit a clear view, but they had heard the noisy procession pass below them and the accompanying roar of the crowd.

"Perhaps thou wilt be asked to dance at the *tamarsha*," Eden said to Ammita, referring to the festivities planned for the following evening. "Surely thou wilt see them then."

Ammita looked doubtful. "Malraj has been behaving vastly tiresome since their arrival. I am not certain he wishes me to appear at all." Her antimony-darkened eyes regarded Eden curiously. "And thou? Thou hast shown little interest in meeting them, and yet they are of thine own blood."

Eden bent her head quickly over the small bowl of henna she had been stirring. The fragrant essence of sandalwood enveloped the room, and the oil lamps had been lit to dispel the gathering darkness. Her head was uncovered, and the faint tinge of color that crept to her cheeks would have been obvious to Ammita but for the fact that her face was lost in shadow.

"I have no desire to look upon them," Eden said with a shrug. "They will either be fat and bad-mannered or young and impatient as all sahib-log tend to be."

"Perhaps thou art right," Ammita agreed with a laugh. Losing interest, she leaned back against the cushions and motioned one of the servants to begin the intricate task of painting her palms and the soles of her slim feet with henna.

It was a ritual that would take considerable time, and Eden found herself seized by a sudden restiveness. She had never completely adapted to the leisurely pace of life within the zenana, and at times she felt decidedly sorry for the ladies-in-waiting, the maidservants and concubines who, by virtue of their minor positions, were never permitted to leave the harem grounds. Even the spirited Ammita was content to spend her days strolling in the *purdah* gardens, eating sweets and gossiping endlessly about the royal ladies in the upper echelons of the harem, and anointing herself with henna and scented oils so that she might look beautiful for the rajah.

Such activities had never held any particular appeal for Eden, and she certainly had no patience for them now. Covering her head with a veil, she excused herself and quickly went outside. Though the sun had set several hours before, the grinding heat of the day still lingered, radiating from the stones and burning through the thin soles of her slippers. It was far too hot to sit and watch the other women playing *chaupar* in the courtyard, and at any rate Eden did not feel inclined to listen to their desultory talk. She much preferred the solitude of the *mardana* gardens, knowing they would be deserted this time of evening while the rajah and his court held durbar for their visitors.

The elderly eunuchs at the gate were familiar with her solitary wanderings and allowed her to pass unchallenged. And it was indeed cooler in the *mardana* courtyard, where a steady breeze, unimpeded by the concealing cloth *shamianahs* surrounding the *purdah* gardens, ruffled the lily-choked lotus ponds. Rather than the cloying fragrance of incense, the air was perfumed with the heady scent of blooming frangipani and tesu flowers, and the jasmine-hung walkways were pleasantly deserted.

Savoring the tranquil silence, Eden paused in the cool of a domed pavilion to watch the stars spark and glitter on the artificial lake. Far in the distance a conch brayed in some ancient village temple and a peacock called to its mate while the hum of the zenana and the throbbing night beat of the Indian city was lost amid the murmur of the fountains. Fireflies flitted through the groves of tamarinds and cherry trees, spangling the darkness with pinpoints of light. Eden watched them for a moment, recalling young Jaji's delighted screams when she had helped him catch them in a crystal perfume bottle during her first summer here, and experienced a twinge of sadness knowing he considered himself far too old to indulge in such pastimes now.

Was it possible, Eden wondered idly, that Malraj had honored his little brother by permitting him to appear in durbar this evening? Eden's lips curved at the thought, picturing Jaji sitting proudly at the rajah's side in his jeweled collar and knee-length *choga* of stiff, quilted gold. It pleased her, too, to envision the expression on the odious Captain Molson's face when he found himself confronted by this youthful prince—who happened to be the same native boy he had so callously denounced two days ago.

A faint tug on the *dupatta* covering her head made Eden turn, and she gave an exclamation of annoyance seeing that the breeze had lifted the trailing end and caught it on a thorn. Bending, she unraveled it carefully so as not to prick her fingers or tear the delicate silk. As she straightened she froze abruptly, the smile going rigid on her face as she saw two men entering the pavilion from the steps on the far side.

Eden recognized one of them immediately, for the glittering pendant pinned to his courtly turban identified him as Lala Dayal, one of Malraj's numerous uncles. The other was a stranger, and for a dreadful moment Eden was convinced he had seen her, for she saw his stride check as he lifted his head in her direction and moved quickly to lay a restraining hand on Lala Dayal's sleeve.

Gasping, Eden retreated behind one of the pillars, her hand at her throat. It was obvious that their meeting was not intended for other ears and eyes, for nothing short of the clandestine would prompt Lala Dayal to leave the durbar hall in the company of a single sahib. Oh, yes, inexplicable as it may seem and despite the fact that she hadn't been able to see his face, Eden knew that the other man was British.

Fortunately he seemed not to have noticed her after all, for Eden saw him turn toward Lala Dayal at last and speak in low, fluent Hindustani that held no hint of urgency. And yet her breath caught painfully in her throat at the sound of his voice, for it was all at once painfully familiar. Dear God, it couldn't be the same sahib she had met out on the plains, could it? Surely she had to be mistaken!

Holding herself perfectly still, Eden strained to hear what was being said but could understand nothing of the softly uttered words. She knew better than to give herself away, however. Not if there was the slightest chance that she was listening in on a meeting of any importance. Furthermore, Lala Dayal would be furious with her if he found her here in the *mardana* gardens on the night of a durbar, for that in itself was strictly forbidden.

A tingling cramp began to steal through Eden's rigid limbs as she stood quietly in the shadows, and she was seized by the sinking despair that their conversation might very well drag on indefinitely. After a long moment, however, she was relieved to overhear the polite exchange of farewells, and the breath she had been holding was expelled in a soundless sigh of thanks.

Waiting another minute to make certain both of them had gone, she peeked cautiously around the pillar. To her dismay she saw that the sahib still lingered, leaning with his shoulder against the statue of a charging elephant in an attitude of seeming negligence—or was it watchfulness? Lifting her head, Eden looked up into his face, and her heart ground to a halt as she saw that he was staring directly into her eyes.

"You might as well come out," he said politely in Hindustani.

For a panicked moment Eden was tempted to run, though the memory of the hard fingers that had closed about her wrist once before checked the impulse. Instead she drew a deep breath and attempted to still the racing of her heart. Tilting her chin because, after all, she had nothing to hide, she stepped boldly from her hiding place.

Hugh Alexander Gordon, sixth duke of Roxbury, gazed with considerable annoyance into the veiled face that peered calmly into his. He had known all along that a woman was concealed in the shadows, for he had seen the blur of her sari when she had ducked behind the lavishly carved pillar. Thinking that she had stumbled upon them by accident, he had refrained from revealing her presence to Lala Dayal, not wishing to embarrass either of them by compromising her *purdah*. Yet it had since occurred to him that no woman in seclusion would dare venture onto the *mardana* grounds, not even on a night when all of the men of the rajah's court were sequestered in durbar, and had decided that her behavior warranted closer investigation.

Seeing the exquisite beauty of the embroidered veil she wore as she came toward him in the moonlight, he experienced a genuine shock, for this was obviously some high-born lady of the zenana and not a mere handmaiden. Hugh Gordon frowned, for he was familiar enough with the habits of royal Indian ladies to know that they spent a great deal of time, and much of their wealth, intriguing from their private palaces against the British. It was entirely possible that this one had deliberately broken the laws of *purdah* in order to spy.

"Thou art far from the zenana gates, sahiba," he observed sardonically as she halted before him. Studying her intently, he knew his earlier suspicions to be correct, for her attire was of the richness and ethereal loveliness one associated only with a high-born Indian lady. The *dupatta* covering her head was of pale coral tissue edged with silver, and the farhi pyjamas encasing her slim ankles were of shimmering salmon-and-blue-striped silk. She was tall, the top of her head coming level with his chin, and through the diaphanous veil her tilted eyes met his without fear.

Without fear . . . The duke's frown deepened, realizing that she was displaying none of the modesty expected of a woman nurtured in a closely guarded zenana. His narrowed gaze pierced her veil, saw there was no caste mark of powdered *sindoor* upon her brow, and that her eyes, though as large and magnificent as those of a Rajput princess, were of a deep, translucent blue.

A muscle in his jaw tightened, and his fingers closed without warning about her wrist, jerking her toward him so that her head snapped back and the veil parted to reveal the unmistakable, heart-shaped face he had seen once before.

"You!" he exclaimed.

The blue-eyed gaze did not waver, though the pressure of his fingers was unbearably painful. "Sahib?"

"Don't give me your wide-eyed innocence," the duke said impatiently, speaking in English. "I know who you are, Choto Bai."

Her eyes widened, and Hugh Gordon found himself thinking in an unguarded moment that she was incredibly beautiful, the color of her eyes in the starlight like nothing he had ever seen before. Her bone structure was delicate, her mouth wide and of a disturbing fullness, and where her face had seemed far too smooth-skinned and fair for the boy Choto Bai, it took on a compelling beauty when viewed as a woman's. There was nothing remotely fragile or sweet in its mulish expression, however, and the duke's hold tightened about her wrist.

"If you would please let me go, sir," Eden said with admirable calm, though she was rather nonplussed by his appearance. She was certain that he hadn't been quite this tall or of such a whipcord leanness the first time they met—or had he? While it was true that she had been greatly preoccupied with Jaji's welfare on the occasion of that meeting, surely she should have at least recalled him being so unnervingly . . . *large* and handsome—in the manner a hunting tiger was considered handsome, Eden decided uncharitably.

"I see no reason to let you go until you tell me who you are," the duke was saying unpleasantly.

"Yes, I am called Choto Bai," Eden admitted, deciding there was no sense in denying the truth. "But that gives you no right to—"

"By God," he interrupted, "so I was right. You're Scots, aren't you? I wasn't certain at first, not when you were speaking Hindustani. Would you mind telling me what in hell you're doing here?"

"I cannot see how it is any business of yours," Eden responded coldly.

"Can't you? It would seem to me that anyone caught eavesdropping on a private conversation between a British dignitary and the uncle of the rajah of Mayar would have a great deal of explaining to do."

The lovely chin tilted in what the duke suspected was a not uncommon manner. "You know perfectly well that I couldn't hear a word you were saying, nor was it my fault that you chose to meet in a pavilion already occupied."

Hugh knew a flash of admiration for her, aware that anyone else thus accused would have resorted to a lengthy outburst of affronted dignity. Her dark blue eyes continued to regard him coolly, and he found his gaze inadvertently drawn from their stormy depths to her lips, which were slightly parted and of a warm, rich redness. By God, she really was a beauty, and there was a sweetness in the unawakened passion of her curving mouth that made him forget of a sudden what she had been saying.

The heavy fragrance of blooming flowers was potent in the hot night, and Eden, staring up into the sahib's face, found herself suddenly and inexplicably frightened by the look upon it. Her pulse raced beneath the hard fingers clamped about her wrist, and she was seized with a panic-stricken urge to flee.

Calming herself, she lifted her head and looked past his shoulder, and suddenly she gave a sigh of relief. "Oh, but I am glad thou hast come, Dinna Chand!"

The duke turned questioningly, but even before his searching gaze confirmed to him that there was no one else in the pavilion, he felt her twist free of his grasp. A moment later he heard the sound of her light, running feet and then, outrageously, the whispered echo of her laughter.

Malraj Pratap Gaswarad, rajah of Mayar, sat in a private audience chamber adjoining the durbar hall upon a fabulous *masnad* draped with silk brocade curtains. The throne cushions upon which he reclined were of blue velvet studded with semiprecious stones, and the four corners of the carpet beneath them were weighted down by pieces of ivory carved in the shape of lotus buds. No less resplendent was the Rajput ruler himself, whose ankle-length coat was of deep-pink-and-gold silk brocade woven with orange and blue. A *patka* studded with pearls was tied about his waist, and his slippers and headdress were elaborately strewn with emeralds.

Other members of the royal court were seated on cushions throughout the *chitra shala,* the painted hall, and as a mark of courtesy the British delegation had been provided with chairs. Lavish refreshments had been carried out on silver trays, but the rajah and his courtiers did not touch them, for it would have polluted them to eat in the presence of casteless men.

Dark eyes watchful in his proud, hawkish face, the young rajah studied his guests in pensive silence. He did not care at all for Lamberton-sahib, the new British resident, and it annoyed him that the word of this insignificant little man could weigh more with the British raj than his own. Was he not a Rajput prince whose kind had ruled Rajasthan, the land of princes, for two thousand years? And did not all Rajputs of royal blood claim direct descent from the sun itself while Lamberton-sahib could boast only the feeble ancestry of common mortals?

Yet the fact remained that should Lamberton-sahib find fault with him, he need only whisper into the ears of the political-sahibs in Calcutta and Malraj Pratap Gaswarad, rajah of Mayar, would find himself swiftly dispatched into exile. *Hai mai!* A noble end indeed for a Rajput prince! Perhaps he should listen to the entreaties of his prime minister after all and abandon his fight against the British and their encroachment upon Hind. Malraj scowled and stroked his beard and wondered if he could do so. His dislike for *Angrezis* was equally as strong as his father's affection for them had been, and his pride forbade him to openly seek their approval as other ruling princes were doing. *Hai mai!* he thought again. If only the great mutiny had succeeded in driving the sahib-log from Hind for all time!

Despite the rajah's dour thoughts, the mood in the *chitra shala* was festive, for the issues raised in durbar had been effectively settled, and all were looking forward with anticipation to the *nautch*-girl Ammita's performance of the hypnotic kathak dance. The British delegation, seated on chairs of silver repoussé, exchanged polite remarks with their neighbors while they waited, and so it came to be that Pratap Rao, the diwan of Mayar and eldest uncle of the rajah, fell into conversation with the duke of Roxbury.

The duke had returned to the durbar hall in something of a temper. Annoyed that the woman called Choto Bai had once again managed to elude him, he had spent the remainder of the courtly session imagining the pleasure of twisting her slender neck between his hands. He had not forgotten the insult she had dealt him by attempting to strike him with her whip, and the fact that she had seen him meeting privately with Lala Dayal disturbed him. He must find out more about her, for the evidence presented him in their past encounter suggested that she was high-spirited and of a lively intelligence, and therefore endlessly troublesome. Furthermore, he found it decidedly odd that a Scotswoman was permitted to roam about the rajah's palace of her own free will—dressed as a boy, no less. A disturbing mystery indeed, and the duke frowned and wondered to whom he might best address his pressing questions.

"Your command of our tongue is most admirable, sahib," Pratap Rao was saying politely. "Am I to understand that you have spent considerable time in Hind?"

The duke's pale blue eyes warmed visibly. "Twelve years of my life, Rao-sahib, though not all of them at once. I've traveled back and forth at length between Hind and *Belait,* and have only just returned for the first time since the mutiny."

"Ah." The elderly Hindu's expression did not change at the mention of that bitter conflict, for he, like his brother the late rajah, had pledged his loyalty to the British. "You live now in *Belait,* no doubt?"

A faint smile curved the duke's lips. "For the last five years I have, yes. I came into an inheritance from my mother's side, and as it required considerable management I had no choice but to settle in England."

"I am curious if your years in Hind were spent in the service of the company." The carefully modulated voice remained polite, yet it was apparent from the sudden spark of anger in the old man's eyes that Pratap Rao, while an ally of the British, had never condoned the manipulative behavior of the East India Company.

"As a matter of fact I sat on the board of a rival company," the duke informed him obligingly. "Perhaps you've heard of it? Before its charter was broken it was known as Gordon and Blair of Calcutta and Delhi."

The diwan's manner changed instantly. "Yes, of course I have heard of it," he said warmly. "And with your mention of its name I recall my brother Lala Dayal having told me that one of the sahibs traveling with the new resident was not unknown to him. Obviously he was referring to you. I understand he made your acquaintance many years ago in the palace of Badahur Shah?"

A murmur of voices from the shadowed doorway caught his attention and he added with a smile: "It would seem the *nautch*-girl is prepared to make her entrance. You will be charmed, sahib."

"Assuredly," agreed the duke. Politely declining the proffered *pan,* he settled back in his chair and watched as

Pratap Rao helped himself to the betel leaves and opiates stored in the jewel-encrusted box. The tinkling of ankle bracelets heralded the *nautch*-girl Ammita's arrival, but the duke's attention was elsewhere of a sudden, caught by the flash and glitter of gold from somewhere above him. Lifting his head, he saw that three shadowy figures had entered the long gallery running along the upper length of the vaulted hall and were seating themselves unobtrusively behind a carved *purdah* screen. One of the women wore a sari of black silk cross-barred with gold, and it was the rich gilt embroidery reflecting the lamplight that had caught the duke's eye. His lips twitched as he studied the proud tilt of her head before she vanished with the others behind the pierced marble screen, for he suddenly knew unequivocally who she was.

"It is curious that *purdah* is not as strictly observed by the ladies of Mayar as it is elsewhere in Hind," he remarked in a conversational tone.

Pratap Rao's keen eyes followed his to the carved *jali* behind which the women had vanished, and he grunted and shook his head. "It should not surprise you at all, sahib. The custom of *purdah* was not brought to Rajasthan until the Mughal invasions, and thereafter it was adopted only very slowly. Mayar itself did not come under the thumb of Emperor Akbar until the late sixteenth century, and perhaps that is why Muslim influence was never felt very strongly here. You can see the truth of this not only in the seclusion of our women, but in our architecture, our daily customs, and our language."

"I see. Then the royal ladies of the palace are permitted to move about as they please?" the duke inquired interestedly.

Pratap Rao smiled. "Not as much as they would wish, I am certain. The junior Rani, of course, is permitted to leave the zenana as she desires, and my nieces, the *raj-kumaris*, make appearances at all religious processions. On the other hand, the Begum Fariza, who is the late rajah's foster mother and the only Mohammedan lady residing in the palace at present, keeps *purdah* devoutly. I myself have only looked upon her face three times, and yet I have known her these forty years past."

"I have heard talk of a woman known as Choto Bai," said the duke, feigning great interest in the entrance of the *nautch*-girl Ammita, lavishly attired in gossamer silks and preceded by veiled handmaidens sprinkling the floor beneath her feet with rose petals.

"Ah, yes, Choto Bai," said Pratap Rao with a complacency that clearly revealed his fondness for the girl. "She has been a delight to all of our hearts, my late brother's in particular. It is good that you speak of her, sahib, for if you wish, I see no reason why she cannot be presented to you at the conclusion of the dance. She is an *Angrezi* like yourself, and I am certain she would be most pleased to make your acquaintance."

"I would be honored," the duke murmured, his face expressionless.

Pratap Rao was true to his word, for at the conclusion of the *tamarsha* a servant was dispatched to inform the serving women guarding the entrance to the gallery that their mistresses' presence was requested below. There followed a lengthy wait while the painted hall emptied of all save the rajah and his personal servants and the handful of bored and yawning British detained by Pratap Rao.

The duke himself had not anticipated such a considerable delay. It was long past midnight, and the first of the rajah's summons had wakened him before dawn that morning. Not only was he tired, but he had been looking forward with anticipation to a few hours of solitude away from the noisy environs of the royal court.

The moment he saw the flash of annoyance in Choto Bai's veiled eyes as she followed the junior Rani and the giggling *Rajkumari* Krishna Dai into the circle of lamplight, however, he decided that the loss of his private time had been well worthwhile. Bowing politely to acknowledge Pratap Rao's introductions, he waited until the admiring attention of his companions had turned to the giggling princess before he moved unobtrusively to confront Choto Bai.

"I am honored to make your acquaintance at last, sahiba," he said in Hindustani, a mocking smile curving his lips. "It was high time we were formally introduced."

The peak of Eden's sari was pulled low over her brow, and only her eyes were visible through the gauzy veil. Dark blue and tilted at the corners, they regarded him with cool hauteur, though when she spoke her tone was equally polite. "Indeed, Huzoor. I am pleased that the Rao-sahib thought to do the honors."

"He was most formal, wasn't he?" the duke agreed affably. "Though not entirely truthful, for I know very well that Choto Bai is not your given name." He gazed down into her quickly averted face and switched to English, the mocking light in his eyes deepening. "I am Hugh Gordon, the duke of Roxbury, and you, sahiba, are a Scotswoman of considerable mystery. The Rao-sahib must be a formidable ally of yours, for he gave no indication to anyone but myself that you were not of the palace born."

Eden's head jerked about, and the gold thread of her veil glittered in the light of the lamps. "Surely there is no need for such intense curiosity, Your Grace," she said stiffly.

"Perhaps not," he agreed rudely, "but I am not often bested twice by a woman, especially a Scotswoman living the life of an Indian princess in the palace of a Rajput ruler."

Once again he saw the annoyed flash of those magnificent blue eyes behind her veil. "It was never my intention to fan sparks of intrigue, Your Grace. My story is actually a simple one and doubtless not unique." Her chin tilted. "If you must know," she said in a tone that clearly indicated he had no right to, "my given name is Eden Hamilton. My father was Colonel Dougal Hamilton, commander of the Fourteenth Bengal Infantry stationed in Lucknow, who fell in fifty-seven defending the residency there. I was brought to Pitore by the late rajah, who had promised my father he would see to my welfare in the event the sepoys mutinied, and who risked his own life and the safety of his family to see that promise kept. There, does that satisfy you?"

"How did your father manage to extract such a promise?" the duke inquired, ignoring the jibe.

"My father spent several years in Pitore upscaling the rajah's army before his marriage to my mother," Eden said impatiently. "At the time it consisted of little better than untrained men carrying rusty jezails, and a stable full of aging war elephants. The two of them became good friends." A trace of sorrow crept into her voice. "My father always said that the rajah was a very enlightened man."

"And why did you not return to your own kind when the rebellion was put down, Miss Hamilton?"

She seemed startled by the sound of her name falling from his lips. A slim, restive hand reached up to secure the edge of the sari more closely about her face, an obviously nervous gesture that caused the duke's eyes to narrow. "The time has come to bid you farewell, Huzoor," she said quickly in Hindustani, pressing her palms together and speaking as though they had been exchanging nothing more than simple pleasantries. "Good-bye."

As she made to turn away the duke put out a hand to detain her, but the shocked look on the hovering diwan's face told him clearly the folly of attempting anything so forward. Scowling, he let his hand drop and watched her walk gracefully to the seated rajah and make her devotions there before exiting with her companions through an archway that led by means of hidden passages back to the zenana.

Eden Hamilton. The name danced tauntingly through his mind, every bit as lovely and uncommon as the woman it belonged to. The duke stared thoughtfully toward the painted arch through which she had vanished. A pair of guards in scarlet turbans and glorious gold tunics had taken their places before it, armed with tulwars and menacing expressions. *Eden Hamilton.* He had found out her name, but what good had it done him? She was every bit as mysterious to him now as she had been before.

Chapter Three

"Shabash, butchas! Khabodar! Khabodar!"

Though the sun had barely cleared the soaring temples flanking the durbar hall, the polished stones of the court-yard seemed to radiate the fierce heat, and the shouts of the mahouts driving their elephants into line only added to the growing confusion. Fully five hundred retainers in crisp scarlet turbans were assembled in the shadows of the pavilions, among them *punkah* bearers, peacock-plume bearers, mace-bearers, and those of higher rank who were to carry the hallowed images of Sita Rama at the head of the royal procession.

The half-dozen elephants were caparisoned in gay colors and draped with silken finery, and the *howdah* that was to carry the rajah was carved of pegged ivory richly upholstered with crimson velvet. Ropes of wild flowers bound the straggling animals together, their heady scent mingling with the rosewater being sprinkled on the hot stones by a pair of chanting priests.

The rajah of Mayar and his guests were preparing to embark upon a tiger hunt. While the British resident and his chief secretary had been accorded the dubious honor of riding in the royal *howdah*, the rest were to follow on horseback. Hugh Gordon, standing slightly apart from the noisy assembly of men, was pleased at the prospect of finding a horse between his knees once again, for the lengthy receptions, the lavish meals, and protracted cer-emonies of the past few days had left him restless and chafing for exercise.

The fiery barb stallion presented him seemed of a sim-ilar mind, and the duke looked him over approvingly as he was led snorting and prancing from the royal stables. Once in the saddle he held the animal on a tight rein and spoke to it soothingly before taking his place amid the restive crowd.

"Quite a handful you've got there, Your Grace," observed Harry Deas, the district officer from Bharatpore. Since the elderly mare upon which he sat looked every bit her age and seemed incapable of causing similar trouble, he could afford to express his amusement as the nervous stallion turned its head and attempted to sink its teeth into the duke's booted calf.

"I'd wager money he's the son of a *puka* devil," Hugh agreed with a laugh, clearly enjoying the challenge of subduing him. "I only hope I can keep him from charging before this bloody procession gets under way."

"I believe it has," said the district officer, hearing the sound of singing drifting back from the head of the line. "The minstrels will be offering a hymn of praise to the rajah as his elephant passes beneath the *Hathi Pol,* so I imagine he's given the command to march. I only wonder if you can keep that devil calm until our end starts to move," he added, echoing the duke's earlier thoughts as he guided his mare out of reach of the stallion, who had lashed out with his hind legs at a group of brightly attired bearers pressing too closely.

"It's every man for himself, Harry," said the duke, and a grin widened over his aquiline features. "*Shabash, shikari*-sahib!" he called to a young Hindu in the uniform of a royal spear-bearer who demonstrated remarkable agility in leaping out of reach of the stallion's plunging hooves. "Well done!"

The Hindu grinned in return, his even white teeth flashing in his dark face, and made an obeisance of respect before vanishing into the crowd.

A feeling of excitement pervaded the air, and good-natured jostling and insult calling spread among the gathered men. The stallion tossed its head in response to their mood, and the duke reached down soothingly to pat his neck. As he did so he saw a familiar face materialize out of the crowd: a wiry Hindu who pushed his way toward him and took hold of the stirrup leather. It was Baga Lal, disheveled and out of breath, and the duke's eyes narrowed beneath the brim of his pith helmet.

"What have you discovered, my friend?"

Baga Lal responded in Pushtu, the language of the Pathans, which he, born on the northwest frontier within sight of the mighty Hindu Kush, had spoken since birth and which the duke understood tolerably well. "I have found the answer to your question, lord. The late rajah did indeed offer the *feringhi* girl sanctuary in Pitore on the strength of his friendship for Hamilton-sahib. There was nothing more to the arrangement."

Hugh frowned. "Then why did she not return to Lucknow? Surely someone would have taken her in."

"It is said she feared reprisals against the rajah and his family."

"That I can understand," the duke conceded after a thoughtful pause, recalling that the British troops who had beaten back the mutineers had been appallingly brutal in their methods. "Remember Cawnpore!" had been their rallying cry, and they had carried out their terrible vengeance in memory of the innocent white women and children who had been hacked to pieces in the Cawnpore residency and thrown down a dry well by the murderous sepoys. Poisoned by hate, the conquering army had shown no mercy even to those who had not raised arms against them, and throughout the vast continent of India innocent men had been hanged merely because of the color of their skin.

"It is possible that the British could have marched on Mayar believing that the girl had been held there against her wishes," Baga Lal agreed, "for it was a time of great madness. Yet if her word is the truth, and I think that it must be, then she cannot be the one who has been whispering into the rajah's ear."

"I believe you may be right, Baga Lal." The duke's eyes narrowed thoughtfully as he watched the unruly line of men, elephants, and horses pass beneath the cusped arches of the gate ahead. The sea of faces around him showed dark and inscrutable, and for a moment he knew the futility of finding the answers he had come in search of. How was he to discover which man among these multitudes was responsible for inciting the excitable young rajah to intrigue against the British?

"There is one more thing, sahib." Baga Lal was trotting beside him now, clutching the stirrup leather as the stallion set off at a brisk walk. He had reverted to his native tongue, for he no longer considered it necessary to mask his words. "I do not think it has any bearing on what thou wouldst wish to know, but I thought it of sufficient interest to warrant mention. It concerns a contract drawn up by the late rajah and the rana of Bharadpur arranging a marriage between the Yuveraj Malraj and one of the rana's younger daughters. I was told that negotiations had been under way for the better part of a year before the old rajah's death, yet it is now rumored that the new rajah has decided not to honor it."

Hugh frowned. "I thought Malraj was already married."

Baga Lal made a contemptuous sound. "He was betrothed at nine to the sickly little daughter of the rana of Udaibas, who died two years ago delivering her first child. It was stillborn, and both their deaths are not surprising considering the unfortunate little rani was all of fourteen years old at the time."

When the duke spoke again he seemed preoccupied and in a temper. "What does the rajah's decision to cancel his marriage have to do with any of this?"

"Only that a *daffadar* whose brother is a *khansamah* in the palace has told me that the rajah wishes to make a far more advantageous marriage than one with the second daughter of some minor princeling. He has referred often of late to unions of mixed race and has spoken at length of the prestigious position enjoyed by Lady Wheeler, the wife of the general-sahib who once commanded the troops at Cawnpore."

"She was an Indian lady," the duke recalled. "But what—"

"There are many who believe that a marriage of mixed blood may be of great advantage in gaining the approval of the British raj," Baga Lal pointed out. "Perhaps the rajah, who is already conveniently acquainted with a certain *Angrezi* lady, feels the same?"

There was a short pause, then: "Good God!" said the duke with appalled apprehension. "You can't mean to say that Malraj is thinking of marrying the daughter of Colonel Dougal Hamilton?"

"I make no presumptions," Baga Lal stated cautiously. "I only repeat what I have been told, and it is said that the *daffadar* is a man to be trusted."

Taking advantage of the confusion that arose as the last of the procession passed beneath the gate, he quickly touched his turban and slipped away, leaving the duke to ponder this startling disclosure alone.

"Good God," the duke said again after a lengthy silence. He couldn't even begin to imagine a woman as spirited and innocently lovely as Eden Hamilton married to the insufferably pompous rajah of Mayar. They were of a similar age, it was true, yet their backgrounds and customs and beliefs were so utterly, glaringly dissimilar. Furthermore, there was no end to the talk Hugh had heard in Delhi concerning Malraj's arrogance and his intense dislike of foreigners. And what he himself had seen of the rajah in the past few days had left him notably unimpressed, for one didn't have to look overlong to recognize the cruelty in those proud black eyes or the lines of dissipation already visible on the ruler's hawkish face.

"Oh, bloody hell, what does it matter?" the duke murmured aloud, annoyed by his preoccupation with Baga Lal's claim. Why couldn't Malraj simply take an *Angrezi* wife if he so desired and if his priests permitted? And why could it not be a young woman who had lived in the same palace with him for nearly four years and of whom, according to Jaji, the rajah was genuinely fond? Eden Hamilton must be at least eighteen, a grown woman even by Western standards, and as such certainly old enough to marry whomever she wished.

Perhaps you are the clever one after all, Malraj Pratap Gaswarad, the duke of Roxbury thought, gazing down the length of the road to the swaying *howdah* containing the rajah and his guests. Clever because the British Political Department would be more than pleased if an Indian ruler took a British wife, and because the rajah would be gaining a lovely and endlessly interesting woman in the bargain.

The land lying beyond the walled boundaries of Pitore was sparsely wooded and filled with torturous folds of dry hills and canyons. Ancient *nullahs* crisscrossed the dusty plains while the flooding of seasonal monsoons had long since scored the roads built in Emperor Ackbar's time with impassable ruts. The royal procession could move only slowly, and the afternoon sun hung hot in a pewter-colored sky before a halt was called at last along the blinding white banks of the river.

Here a veritable city of richly appointed tents had been erected in which the rajah and his guests were to refresh themselves. Since cooking fires would only add to the grinding heat, foodstuffs had been prepared in advance and transported via carts from the palace, and the camp settled down contentedly to a light meal of chupattis, lychees, fried mangoes, and custard apples served with cardamom tea.

Afterward they stretched themselves out on charpoys to rest while the molten heat within the tents was held at bay by *punkah*-bearers and the flies and crawling insects whisked away by turbaned servants armed with peacock feathers. Those of the camp who were forced to make do without such amenities sought refuge in the shade of the *neem* trees growing near the breeze-cooled riverbanks while the mahouts stretched themselves out between the legs of their elephants to sleep.

No one seemed at all unwilling to idle away the hottest hours of the afternoon by napping. Yet as a murmurous silence settled over the camp, the plaintive voice of a child could be heard exhorting an unseen companion who was dozing in the crook of a tree root some distance downriver of the tents:

"It isn't fair, I tell you! How can this be called a tiger hunt when all one does is eat and sleep? I'm going to find Malraj and tell him exactly what I think of such sport!"

Awal Bannu, arms propped beneath his head, opened one eye lazily to regard the irate little boy standing over him. "You would truly interrupt his rest, my prince? He will have you sent back to Pitore at once."

"Then let him!" Jaji declared, crossing his arms before his chest. "I'd rather spend the afternoon listening to Dinna Chand recite mythology than hunt tigers in this laughable fashion!"

Awal Bannu grunted, his eyes once again closed.

"I mean what I say," the boy threatened.

The elderly Hindu sighed and raised himself up on one elbow. "The tiger cannot be lured out into the open until dusk," he explained patiently, "for that is when he will appear at the *jheel* to drink. By that time your brother and his gun-bearers will already have taken their places in the *machans*. Since the structures are made of wood and far from comfortable, is it not better for them to take their ease elsewhere until then?"

"Yes, but—"

"Is it not?" Awal Bannu persisted.

"Oh, I suppose it is!" Jaji burst out, stamping his slipper. "But I am not the least bit tired, Awal Bannu, and I don't want to lie around pretending to sleep! What shall I do in the meantime?"

"You can come with me," Eden suggested, coming up behind them in time to hear his plaintive words. "Khaji Bad has given me a sack of sugarcane for the elephants."

Jaji brightened visibly, for he was normally forbidden to go near the enormous animals when they were housed in the palace stables. "Could we really feed them, Choto Bai?"

"Of course. Come along now so that our poor ancient friend here can get his rest. May your dreams be auspicious, *cha-cha.*"

"Off with you both," Awal Bannu grunted good-naturedly, closing his eyes on Eden's smiling young face without waiting to make certain that she obscured it with the folds of her turban before joining the company of mahouts and horse syces. She would be safe with them, he knew, for all were fond of her, and it would do Jaji good to spend some time for once away from his overprotective attendants. Drifting off into the light sleep of old age, he smiled, thinking he could already hear the boy's eager laughter.

"*Dekho*, Choto Bai!" Jaji was indeed shouting jubilantly at that very moment. "He likes me, does he not?"

"Hold the cane steady or you will drop it," Eden warned, watching as Jaji gingerly extended his hand toward the enormous bull elephant.

"Thou hast spoiled him, Choto Bai," complained the mahout who reclined nearby. "Look how he searches thy pockets for treats."

"He is clever enough to know when he will be rewarded," Eden responded with a smile, and spoke affectionately as the velvety tip of the elephant's trunk nuzzled the peak of her turban. "Thou art a prince among princes, Bulkulli."

"May I feed him again, Khaji Bad?" Jaji pleaded. "Please?"

"There is more sugar cane in the sack there, my prince."

In the shade of a nearby tree two men sat in silence watching the antics of the excited little boy. Presently one of them observed: "The rajkumar grows bold. Look how he runs between the creature's legs unmindful of being trampled."

"It is the *feringhi* girl who shows more courage," the other said. "Bulkulli's temper is reported to be evil, yet he allows her liberties that few would dare to take. Khaji Bad, who is my cousin, says there are not many whom he likes."

"Bah," said the first curtly. "That is only because she spends all her time in the stables playing with him as though he were a pampered pet. Such behavior is more befitting the *nauker*-log than a woman of the zenana."

His companion made no reply, for he knew full well that Gar Ram, the rajah's head syce, bore considerable ill will toward the *feringhi* girl and that he had done so ever since she had brought down with a single shot the *sambhur* Gar Ram himself had attempted to kill last year and had unfortunately missed. Though he was one of the finest *shikari* in the kingdom, Gar Ram accorded himself considerably more respect than was his due, and it had seriously pricked his pride to be bested by a woman, an *Angrezi* sahiba at that. His grudges and sulking temper were well known throughout the palace, and even the Rajkumar Jaji had once likened him to a puffed-up peacock.

"I have always thought it unseemly for the *Angrezi* girl to adopt the customs of Hind," Gar Ram added, the expression on his thin face contemptuous as he studied the young woman in cotton trousers and tunic who seemed oblivious to his presence. "It is a mockery of our ways to keep only those customs she deems suitable and ignore those which are not."

"Choto Bai may not lead a conventional life," argued his companion, who genuinely liked the girl, "yet she has always kept *purdah* devoutly and never shamed or compromised the late rajah's affection for her. *Ohé*, I would not be surprised if the gods grant her special favor and see that she is reborn a Hindu when she dies."

"Bah," said Gar Ram again.

"Thou wouldst be wise to curb thy tongue," he was warned impatiently. "If talk is to be believed and the rajah does indeed join her life to his, she will be a power to be reckoned with."

The face of the head syce was suddenly still. "What nonsense is this?"

"It is only talk," the other said uneasily, realizing belatedly that his temper had prompted him to speak unwisely. "One always hears talk in the palace which never amounts to anything more than sand grains on an anthill."

"And yet such talk could not have been invented." Gar Ram stroked his beard and fell silent, and presently the other said soothingly:

"Have no fear, brother. The rajah would never take to wife a woman who is without caste. To do so would forever defile him."

"Perhaps it would be better if the *feringhi* girl were dead," Gar Ram said darkly. "Her presence in Mayar has been an insult and a pollution to our people. It is a pity the late rajah never realized as much."

"*Chup!* Thou wouldst be wise to hold thy tongue," his companion warned again. "There is a sahib coming up from the river on horseback. There! Dost thou see him?"

"He is but one of the *yeh*-log," Gar Ram responded contemptuously, "and doubtless understands nothing of our language. Besides, the distance is too great for him to have heard us. Silence thy womanly bleatings, Shoki Lal. Thou art a contemptible coward."

On both counts, however, Gar Ram had been mistaken. Not only was this particular sahib fluent in Hindustani, but the hot, still air had carried the sound of the syce's voice far enough for Hugh Gordon to have heard the words he had uttered. Taking care not to acknowledge their presence, the duke rode slowly past them and halted his mount some distance away.

A sleepy syce in a grass-stained dhoti hurried up to take the stallion away, and only then did the duke surreptitiously turn. He caught sight immediately of Eden Hamilton chatting with Jaji and several laughing mahouts near the hobbled elephants, dressed impudently as one of them in loose-fitting cotton salwars and a muslin turban. She seemed unaware of his presence or that of the two men sitting in the shade watching her, one of whom was wearing the uniform of a lance-bearer, the other that of a syce.

So Eden Hamilton did have enemies in the palace, Hugh thought with interest. Her fairy-tale existence was not without danger, and he wondered if she was aware of it. Of course it did not matter to him one way or the other. Intrigue and politics and the hatred and jealousy their practice aroused abounded like a plague in the seemingly peaceful environs of every Indian rajah's palace. It was clearly no concern of his that Mayar was not immune to them.

"Ah, there you are, Roxbury," came the voice of Captain Arthur Molson from behind him. "I was just about to send one of the syces after you. The rajah is awake and has requested our presence in the durbar tent. Seems we're to be prepped before the big hunt. By God, it's hot!" Sighing, he mopped his brow with a sodden handkerchief. "Have an interesting ride? Harry Deas said you'd taken the stallion out for a run, but I said he must be mad to believe that. Not in this heat, and not when you could've been lying prone for a glorious hour with a *punkah*-nigger making cooling breezes for you.''

An unpleasant light entered the duke's eyes, but Captain Molson was unaware of it. Had he been able to guess the nature of His Grace's musings he would have experienced considerable alarm, yet the duke merely shrugged and said pensively: "*Interesting* is apt indeed, Molson. Now, what is it the rajah wants?''

The camp was already stirring as the two men entered the durbar tent, yet by the time they emerged once again the sun had begun its downward spiral from the heavens, and the march to the *machans* was ordered to begin. The blinds that the hunters were to use had been built along the south side of a nearby waterhole from which, two days earlier, frightened villagers had brought *khabar*— news of a tiger sighting. Only the rajah and his gunbearers and several favored courtiers would be permitted into the *machans,* and as a mark of honor the members of the British delegation had been invited to join them.

As the considerably smaller but by no means less festive procession left camp, the duke caught sight of Eden Hamilton riding away through the elephant grass in the company of Prince Jaji and a bearded Hindu unknown to him. It did not surprise him to see that she sat a horse as though born to the saddle or that her attire gave her the appearance of a handsome Rajput youth. He was forced to grin. She was certainly an unusual girl, and the more he saw of her the more he became convinced that she was worthy to be the bride of any Rajput ruler. A pity, he thought, the smile abruptly fading, that it had to be Malraj.

"Will the Rajkumar not be joining his brother in the *machans?*" he inquired of the bearer who walked beside his prancing stallion.

"No, Sahib. He was heard to complain that he would not be able to see a thing above the *shikaris'* heads. The rajah therefore graciously granted him permission to view the kill from the far side of the *jheel.* Since the beaters will drive the tiger to the opposite bank, the Rajkumar should have an excellent view.''

This was clearly true, for Awal Bannu himself had selected the site, and it was no more than twenty paces from the banks of the shallow lake surrounded by a thick stand of thorny *kikars* that would prevent the tiger from seeing them when it appeared. Since the *machans* stood farther down the same bank, the prince and his companions would be well out of the line of fire, and Jaji, looking eagerly about him, pronounced it more than satisfactory.

"Now we must wait patiently, my prince," Awal Bannu warned. "It may take some time before the beaters come, for they will have to circle far north of the *jheel* in order to make certain the tiger does not elude them.''

To his credit Jaji displayed remarkable patience, for the ensuing wait did prove considerable. Afternoon waned, and a breeze rustled through the lion-colored grass, yet nothing stirred on the plains beyond. There was no sign of movement in the distant *machans*, either, and surprisingly enough it was Eden who found herself growing restless. Try as she might she could not stop dwelling on the thought that Edgar Lamberton's cavalry escort would be leaving Mayar in the morning and that the duke of Roxbury would be among them. Though she was not sorry to be seeing the last of that particular individual, she found herself oddly disturbed by the knowledge that, come morning, she would once again be the only *feringhi* left in Mayar.

No, that wasn't entirely true, for the new British resident and his aides would be remaining behind. Yet Eden could not help but view Edgar Lamberton in the same unfavorable light that Ammita had. He was not exactly the sort of person to foster feelings of friendship, yet for some inexplicable reason his presence and that of the other sahibs had inadvertently awakened within Eden a deep hunger to seek out her own kind. She had never imagined that she would enjoy speaking English again so much, or that standing face to face with a man who couldn't care less that she had compromised the laws of *purdah* could seem so deliciously adventurous, even forbidden. For the first time since the fortified gates of the royal palace had swung shut behind her, Eden Hamilton found herself wondering about her fellow countrymen and what they thought and did and how many of them still remained on the vast continent of India that lay beyond the borders of Mayar.

"Listen! Listen, they are coming!"

The stillness of the waning afternoon was broken by the creak of a stirrup leather and Jaji's excited whisper, and the low hills seemed to take up the echo so that at first Eden, who had straightened quickly in the saddle, could hear nothing at all. Then, faintly over the dry rustle of the elephant grass, she could make out the sound of drums as the small army of beaters circling the sparse woodland a mile or so north of the water hole pounded on their copper vessels in an effort to drive the tiger into the open.

Sensing her sudden tension, her mount sidled uneasily, and Eden tightened the reins to signal that he was to stand quietly. Her eyes flicked to the distant *machan*, where Malraj was undoubtedly already sighting down the barrel of his prized English-made rifle. The *machan* would be crowded with men, she thought, for the rajah never took a shot without his syces and gun-bearers and half a dozen other retainers in attendance. The sahibs would be with him, too, and she wondered fleetingly if the duke of Roxbury would have a taste for the coming kill.

The horse beneath her pricked its ears and snorted softly, and Eden looked up quickly to see that a black-buck was wading out into the shallows to drink, apparently unconcerned by the noisy approach of the beaters.

"If the tiger was somewhere nearby, would the buck not be afraid?" Jaji whispered with obvious disappointment. "Perhaps the beaters let him get away!"

"Do not be too quick to make assumptions, my prince," Awal Bannu said softly. "Look there."

Eden's head turned, and she caught her breath seeing that something had alarmed the black-buck and had sent it exploding for the treeline. Her hands tightened unconsciously about the reins, although the gesture was unnecessary, for the gelding had been well schooled and knew to hold itself still. A breathless silence seemed to fall over

the vast plain, for even the beaters had ceased their
drumming, and it was as if all eyes, all ears, strained toward the *jheel*.

"Be very still, my prince," Awal Bannu cautioned as
Jaji gave a crow of excitement. Using the pressure of his
knees, he moved his horse closer and pointed with a
gnarled forefinger. "Look there among the reeds. If the
tiger comes, he will appear there."

Even as he spoke the tall grass twitched and danced,
and suddenly the great barred beast had padded out into
the open, moving so swiftly and silently and remaining so
well hidden against the sun-dappled reeds that at first
Eden did not realize she was looking directly at it. Then
it lowered its massive head to drink, and she saw the rip-
ples of water fan out beneath its lapping tongue, and she
shivered and felt the hair at the nape of her neck rise in
a wholly primitive fear. Without being aware that she did
so, she reached slowly for the jezail that rested on the
saddle before her, and out of the corner of her eye she
saw Awal Bannu doing the same.

Abruptly the tiger lifted its head, and Eden saw clearly
the whiteness of its throat and the long, tensed line of its
body. Though they were standing downwind of it and the
horses had not moved so much as a muscle, some sixth
sense seemed to have warned it of their presence. Eden
held her breath, terrified and fascinated at the same time
by the sheer magnificence of such evil beauty, and it
seemed to her as if creation itself had ceased its infinite
motion and was centered in those hypnotically glowing
coal eyes, waiting . . . waiting . . .

In the distant *machan* Malraj Pratap Gaswarad smoothly
squeezed the trigger. The shot cracked in the stillness and
was followed closely by another—so close, in fact, that
the sound of it was lost amid the collective sigh of the
watching men as the tiger's body twitched convulsively
and collapsed.

"*Shabash, ma-baap!*" someone cried, and suddenly the
silence was broken by a chorus of eager shouts. Everyone, it seemed, wanted to be the first to congratulate the
beaming rajah, and all of them rushed forward to do so—
all of them save the duke of Roxbury, who stood holding

aloft the barrel of a rifle he had deflected at the very moment that the syce Gar Ram had pulled the trigger.

"What is the meaning of this, sahib?" Gar Ram demanded furiously.

"Thy weapon seems to have discharged itself by accident," said the duke in soft, polite Hindustani, yet the accompanying look on his face was one that checked the syce's angry words as effectively as a blow across the mouth. "It is fortunate I was able to deflect it, as it would have been fired into the very trees in which the rajkumar and his attendants were watching the hunt."

Gar Ram paled and swallowed noisily and made to wrest the rifle from the other man's grasp. The rigid arm that held it aloft was as if made of whipcord, however, and after a moment the Hindu's gaze faltered and slid away.

"I do not know how it happened, sahib," he mumbled. "I will take more care in the future."

"See that thou dost so," the duke responded grimly. "I would not care to hear news of further negligence from Lamberton-sahib after I am gone."

Gar Ram jerked his head, and his eyes flickered nervously. Satisfied that his meaning was clear, Hugh let the man go, yet his expression remained forbidding as he stared through the waning daylight toward the distant line of trees.

Chapter Four

"I won't believe a word of this! You're lying! You haven't the faintest idea what you're talking about!"

Eden Hamilton's eyes were bright with anger as she stared up into the duke of Roxbury's intractable face. The two of them were standing in the shadows of the ornamental tower that dominated the main courtyard of the palace. Moonlight filtered through the upper balcony and illuminated the embroidered silver border of Eden's sari, which sparked and glittered as she moved her head in angry denial of his words.

"Do you know the risks I've taken by agreeing to meet you here?" she demanded furiously. While she had not forgotten that she was compromising *purdah* by meeting clandestinely with a sahib, her voice had risen unnoticed in her anger and was borne away easily on the still night air. Seizing her roughly by the wrist, the duke pulled her deeper into the shadows.

"Keep your voice down," he said curtly, "unless you want the *chowkidars* to hear us. I saw one of them walking over by the gate there not too long ago."

"Jaji told me you had something of importance to discuss with me," Eden went on, ignoring him. "Had I known you were going to make such utterly preposterous accusations I would never—"

"For God's sake," Hugh interrupted irritably, "you cannot imagine the trouble I had sending word to you privately, especially during all those bloody rituals celebrating Malraj's bagged tiger. Do you think I'd make such an effort merely to tell you lies? Gar Ram would have shot you if he'd had the chance, and I'm convinced he did so because he considers you a threat."

Eden's dark blue eyes flashed scornfully. "A threat? Oh, come, Your Grace, surely—"

"A threat to his exalted position as master of the horses and head syce to the rajah," the duke continued brusquely. "If Malraj were to marry a casteless woman, he would be forever defiled. Perhaps the priests would even strip him of his own caste and force him to abdicate, which would put Prince Jaji on the throne in his stead. From what I've heard there is little love lost between the rajkumar and his brother's head syce, and it isn't surprising that Gar Ram was prompted to act out of the unreasonable fear that he would be banished from Mayar. Furthermore, it isn't the least surprising that he attempted to do away with you, for his dislike of *Angrezis* is obvious."

"Then what do you suggest I do?" Eden inquired haughtily. "I hope you don't expect me to bring your concerns before the rajah, for he will only dismiss them as utterly absurd." Her tone indicated that she felt the same, and the duke, looking down into the proud young face illuminated by the rising moon through the carved friezework of the balcony, found himself in danger of losing his temper.

"I don't give a bloody damn what you decide to do," he said unkindly and, at the moment, quite honestly. "I only thought it wise to inform you of the truth. You might wish to consider returning to your own kind. If you like, we could provide you with escort to Delhi tomorrow morning."

"You mean leave Mayar in the company of a man of your reputation?" Eden demanded disbelievingly.

"Just what do you know of my reputation, Miss Hamilton?" the duke asked quietly.

Eden was too angry to take heed of his tone. "Your actions speak loud enough, sahib. I had only to consider your curious meeting with Jaji's uncle, Lala Dayal, and the fact that your bearer has been asking a great number of questions of the servants in the palace. Oh, yes, you needn't look surprised. There is little that escapes the attention of those of us in the zenana, despite how discreet he may have been. While I haven't any idea what you've been up to, I cannot believe it is entirely scrupulous."

"I'm not at all surprised," the duke pronounced darkly, "that Gar Ram tried to do away with you. Be careful you don't one day go too far, Miss Hamilton."

"I'll try to remember," she said lightly, and then gasped as he caught her arm. "What are you doing? Let me go!"

"Be still!"

Something in his tone warned her to obey, and she ceased her struggles and quieted in his grasp. The courtyard in which they stood was mainly used as an assembly ground for the rajah's religious processions and was surrounded by public rooms and balconies that most often stood empty. For this reason Eden had suggested the duke meet her there after she had received his request for an audience through Jaji, who had been delighted to play abettor in such secretive work and had promised not to breathe a word of it to anyone.

Yet someone else was out there now, and it was the sound of a low, dry cough that had alerted the duke to his presence. Footsteps echoed faintly on the hot marble tiles, coming closer until they halted just beyond the tiny, domed pavilion where Hugh and Eden stood. The moonlight was sufficiently bright so that Eden, turning her head a fraction, could easily see the reflection of a man in the polished mirrorwork on the door opposite. The duke had seen it, too, and he pulled her deeper into the shadows of the pillars.

It had to be a *chowkidar*, Eden thought with dismay. If he should see them and raise the alarm . . .

"Art thou here, brother?"

The unexpected whisper came from somewhere close by, and Eden caught her breath as a second man stepped out of the shadows. There was something oddly furtive about his movements, and it occurred to her that he could not possibly be a night watchman. Was it possible that she and the duke had stumbled upon a meeting as secretive as their own? Her breath quickened, and she felt the duke's hand tighten in warning about her arm. Lifting her eyes, she saw that his hawkish profile was still and watchful against the long-reaching shadows.

"Why hast thou called me?" the first man demanded in a whisper, joining his companion near the low marble wall. "It is dangerous for me to be here. If I were to be seen—"

"*Chup!*" the other interrupted. "There is news."

"From Delhi?"

"No."

"What, then?"

The first man glanced quickly over his shoulder, but it was obvious that the enormous shadowed courtyard was deserted. Lowering his voice nonetheless, he spoke at length, and though Eden strained to listen, she could hear nothing but the measured rise and fall of his words. Beside her she could hear the duke curse softly, yet when she glanced up at him he put his finger to his lips and motioned her to silence.

They stood without moving for some considerable time before the two men concluded their business and began walking slowly back in their direction. As they came closer it was possible to hear what was being said between them, and the nature of their conversation caused the breath to catch in Eden's throat:

"It is spoken here in Pitore that Malraj is considering taking an *Angrezi* bride," one of them was saying darkly. "She is the daughter of the colonel-sahib of one of the *pultons* in Lucknow, an *Angrezi* colonel who died defending the residency against our noble sepoys."

"I do not understand why this should trouble thee, brother. It has nothing to do with us."

"*Hai mai!* The rajah of Mayar intends to wed a *feringhi!* Is it not enough that he entertains such a notion?"

The other gave a contemptuous laugh. "What care I if thy preening peacock wishes to seek the approval of the British raj in this manner? He may take a thousand memlog in marriage for all the difference it will make. Our quarrel is not with him. Leave him in peace, brother, and go about thine own affairs."

"But is it not—"

"Enough! I must go. And do not summon me again unless the cause is truly urgent!"

The speaker slipped away into the shadows, leaving the other to stand for a moment alone in the courtyard. Presently he, too, turned and strode away, muttering angrily beneath his breath. As he passed by the tower room the moon fell full on his features, and Eden's heart checked painfully in her breast as she recognized him. It was Gar Ram.

"Who was that other man?" the duke inquired after the syce had vanished, and the sound of his voice served to bring Eden out of the paralysis that gripped her.

"I don't know. I've never seen him before. But I'd swear he was one of the headmen from the nearby village. What on earth could he be plotting with Gar Ram?"

"I couldn't imagine," said the duke, yet Eden, peering up into his face, suspected that he knew exactly what the two of them had been talking about. Opening her mouth to say as much, she was prevented from speaking by a hand that moved swiftly to cover her lips.

"Be quiet," the duke said curtly. "None of this need concern you. It's merely a bit of trouble the Political Department has been investigating."

Eden's eyes widened. "What sort of trouble?"

"I'm sure you realize," he said obligingly, "that not all of Hindustan accepted British domination peacefully, and there have been isolated reports of *bairagis* and *sadhus* attempting to spread new seeds of discontent. The Punjab has been especially vocal, but Rajputana is not altogether immune."

"Do you mean to say that the man we saw talking with Gar Ram is trying to organize a new rebellion?" Eden demanded incredulously.

"I believe so."

Eden's eyes narrowed. "And you say you've been investigating the matter on behalf of the Political Department?"

"As a favor to the undersecretary, yes. Since Lala Dayal and I have known one another for a number of years, it seemed perfectly reasonable that I accompany

Edgar Lamberton to Mayar in order to question him about rumors of unrest in the territory.''

"So that was why you met him in the *mardana* gardens on the night of the durbar!"

"My dear Miss Hamilton, of course it was. Fortunately the fanatics who would instigate another mutiny are few in number, and Pratap Rao, as diwan of Mayar, has already taken steps to have them arrested. I should expect it to happen within the next several days."

A faint line creased Eden's brow. "Why are you telling me this?"

"Because you are a meddlesome creature in whose hands a few half-truths could cause a great deal of damage," Hugh said bluntly. "By satisfying your curiosity now, I can be assured that you won't go about asking foolish questions later."

"Prying, you mean!" Eden flared.

He inclined his head politely. "If you wish."

"And if I choose to tell Malraj what you've been up to? I take it he knows nothing of this because you first suspected him of being responsible for the unrest in Mayar?"

"We did, but he obviously has very little idea of what goes on in his subjects' minds, or cares, for that matter. By all means, tell him if you wish, Miss Hamilton, but I find it curious that you would want to deliberately further an anti-British cause. Surely your sympathies lie with your own country?"

He had expected her to speak up in her defense, yet Eden said nothing. She merely looked up at him, her eyes filled with hostility. Though she had been heavily veiled when she had first met him on the steps of the tower, she was disheveled now, thanks to his rough handling, and her face was bared. An indignant flush had crept to her cheeks, giving her skin a warm ivory cast, and once again it occurred to Hugh that she was far lovelier than any woman had a right to be.

The scent of rose petals clung to the fabric of her sari, and when a faint breeze sprang up unexpectedly it lifted the end of her veil and blew it softly against his cheek in what could almost have been a lover's caress. Hugh's eyes were drawn powerlessly to her lips, and his loins tightened seeing that they were parted and moist in the moonlight.

Without giving the matter any thought, he reached for her, yet before he could touch her she stepped away as if some primitive instinct had warned her of his intent.

"I see no reason why I should return to my own kind, Your Grace," Eden said somewhat breathlessly. "Nothing seems to have changed since the company's raj ruled Hindustan. I only wonder why we British continue to delude ourselves into thinking it is the *natives* who are the barbarians?"

"By God, perhaps you ought to stay," Hugh agreed with considerable annoyance, though it was mainly aimed at himself for having entertained even for a moment the notion that he wished to kiss her. "I'll see to it that the Rao-sahib has Gar Ram arrested, and afterward you'll be quite safe to accept Malraj's offer—provided, of course, that you want to marry him. It's obvious to me that he is not at all involved in any seditious plots against the British, despite his verbalizing to the contrary. 'A hot-headed young cockerel with plenty of wind to complain and little backbone to back it up.' That's how Sir Hilary Tremain described him to me, and I'm inclined to agree with him. But by all means, Miss Hamilton, marry him if you wish."

"Perhaps I will," Eden said tightly.

His expression did not change. "Good for you. What woman wouldn't consider herself fortunate spending the rest of her life engaged in nothing more strenuous than daily rounds of devotions and playing dice with her handmaidens while awaiting summons to the rajah's bed? It's an ambitious goal and doubtless will suit you admirably. Good-bye, Miss Hamilton."

He turned heel and left her standing there trembling with anger and wishing she had something to throw at him. How dare he speak to her like that! Just because he had the authority of the British raj behind him didn't mean he could pass judgment on how she chose to live her life!

"He makes it sound as though I'd be living in a gilded cage!" Eden said indignantly, and the sound of her voice sent a hovering fruit bat whirring away in alarm. "Well, I'm not! And I wouldn't waste my time doing all those silly things he said! I wouldn't!"

Gathering up the trailing end of her sari, she ran lightly across the courtyard. In the quiet of her rooms she tossed aside her slippers and threw herself facedown on the cushions. Though the dawn was little more than an hour away, Eden found she could not sleep. Indignation simmered within her, and she could not thrust away the image of that lean, mocking face. Time and again it returned to taunt her, and it was not until she felt the warm trickle of tears on the back of her hand that Eden realized she was crying.

The fact appalled her, and she drew breath to loudly denounce the absent duke in a language equally as foul as any native's from Bagar, yet little more stirred the silence of the room than a choked whisper: "It isn't like that here in the zenana! It isn't like that at all!"

"Baga Lal, you worthless creature! Where the devil is my mess kit? I told you to pack it this morning, and I'll be damned if I can find it!"

The bearer's expression remained deliberately bland. "I will search for it, Hazrat-sahib," he murmured, and made a deep obeisance before hurrying away.

"*Wah!*" exclaimed another bearer dispatched on his heels in a similar manner. "The sahib's temper is foul indeed! What cause is there for such anger?"

"Hold thy tongue," Baga Lal answered curtly. "I have served the sahib for many years and warn you to make haste when he speaks in such a fashion. Ah, here is the kit! Place it in his saddlebag, Mahan Dal, and be quick in thy task."

Though the fierce heat of the day had long since waned, the stones of the courtyard in which the British delegation was making preparations to depart simmered like flatirons, and the plains beyond the opened gates wavered in the heat haze. Few onlookers had gathered to watch them go, for the novelty of having *feringhis* in Mayar had since worn off, and no one cared to stand about in the grinding heat merely to watch a handful of horses and pack carts rumble away in the dust.

The rajah of Mayar had bid his guests a formal farewell earlier, presenting them with gifts while his priests sprinkled them with rosewater to bless their journey. Edgar Lamberton, who would himself be remaining behind, had made a lengthy and predictably dull speech, and afterward Hugh had taken a few moments to speak privately with Lala Dayal in the cool green shadows of the throne room.

"Baga Lal," he said now as his bearer hastened to secure the cinches on the saddle of his mount, "hast thou received word from the zenana?"

He had reverted to Hindustani, and Baga Lal answered in kind: "No, lord. I let it be known that the way was open for the miss-sahib through us, but there has been no reply."

"I cannot say I'm disappointed," the duke observed dryly.

"Are you ready, Your Grace? I'd like to give the order to start. By God, I'm bloody glad to be leaving this place!" Captain Molson's jovial mood was heightened by the knowledge that he had discharged his duties in an honorable fashion and that his beloved Rawalpindi lay little more than a two-week march beyond the distant hills. "All set, then? Good!"

"That one is an idiot," Baga Lal observed as the captain hurried away humming "God Save the Queen" beneath his breath. "I will not be sorry to see the last of him."

"Or of this bloody place." Hugh smiled cynically. "Mount up, my friend. There is no reason to delay our departure."

With a shout from Captain Molson and the accompanying creak and rattle of wagon wheels, the small group of mounted men and the carts that carried their belongings started slowly toward the *Hathi Pol*. Ahead of them lay a nine-day march through torturous terrain in relentless, simmering heat, yet the men of Captain Molson's escort seemed undaunted. Indeed, they were laughing and trading insults as they clattered across the bridge spanning the rocky *nullah* that encircled the citadel's foundations. Hugh Gordon was the only man among them who thought to turn his head and look one last time at the soaring walls of Malraj's palace. His narrowed eyes pierced the carved *jalis* surrounding the numerous balconies, but apparently he did not find what he was looking for. After a moment he shrugged and turned away, and the procession continued onward in leisurely fashion to Pitore.

While the residents of the royal palace may not have been interested in watching the departure of the sahib-log, the citizens of Pitore were of a different mind, and the short stretch of road leading through the outskirts of the city was lined with curious onlookers. The general mood was a festive one, and the crowd cheered and waved small paper flags as the horses and heavily laden carts rumbled past. Captain Molson inclined his head with appropriate dignity to acknowledge the honor, and they were almost past the thickest part of the throng when the off-side wheel of one of the carts lurched into a rut and sent its contents spilling onto the ground.

Immediately the roadway filled with swarming, shouting children who crawled between their elders' legs to gleefully make off with whatever they could find. The captain, who had at first presumed they were assisting in the recovery of the scattered bundles, lost his affable smile and sent his horse bowling into the midst of them.

"You bloody little devils! Put those down! Perkins, Holiday, fetch them back this instant!"

The duke had drawn rein to watch, his expression amused as the red-faced captain and his corporals charged to and fro, unable to recover so much as a single canvas-wrapped bundle. Meanwhile the rest of the captain's men sweated and grunted to right the sagging cart.

"Personally I don't begrudge the little beggars a thing," confided the district officer in an undertone, halting his mount beside Hugh's. "They're poor enough, and God knows we're certainly loaded down with more equipment than we'll ever need."

"My feelings exactly," Hugh agreed with a smile, "but I think we'd better see to Molson before the poor fellow has an apoplexy."

"This is an outrage!" the captain shouted as they pushed their horses through the collection of onlookers who were noisily lamenting the behavior of their children while making little effort to bring them to heel. "We'll have to return to the palace at once to report this!"

"You'd have the rajah arrest a handful of children?" Hugh inquired blandly.

Captain Molson's face darkened from a dull red to mottled purple. "This is a blatant insult to the British Cavalry and cannot be overlooked! I have every intention of— Ah, Perkins, you've got one, have you? Good lad!"

Hugh turned to see the officer engaged in a struggle with a thin-featured native boy who was loudly proclaiming his innocence. The matter of dispute seemed to be a bulging haversack that the two of them were tugging back and forth between them.

"Caught him red-handed, sir," panted young Perkins, for the boy was putting up a considerable struggle. "Says he was bringing it back to us, but I wouldn't believe that for a moment. He's probably never told a truth in his life."

"Thou art the liar, and a fool," countered the boy angrily. "A thousand curses upon thy mother's house!" He was tall and very thin, and only his eyes were visible above the folds of a thick puggari turban. "Sahib, wilt thou not tell him the pack was not stolen?" he appealed to the duke, and for a brief moment their gazes met and held. Hugh was hard-pressed to conceal his start of surprise in recognizing that dark, unmistakable color of blue.

"Let him go, Perkins," he said quietly.

The young man looked up at him in astonishment. "Your Grace?"

"I said let him go."

"Are you mad?" Captain Molson demanded, pushing his way between them. "You've no authority in this matter! I'll be damned if you—"

"I have every authority in this matter," the duke contradicted, and though he spoke very softly there was something in his face that put an immediate end to the captain's indignant protests. "The boy is a distant cousin of my bearer's who asked to accompany us back to Delhi.

As he was recently orphaned and no longer happy in Mayar, I saw no reason to refuse him. We can always use another *bheesti* or a syce.''

"Good lord, I've never heard such a preposterous tale! It's obvious the two of them—your bearer and that dirty beggar—concocted it in order to rob us blind the first night we make camp!''

"No, it is true, Huzoor,'' Baga Lal insisted, appearing fortuitously at his master's side. "My mother's people come from nearby Jaipur, where the boy, too, was born. By the gods' good fortune he recognized me when we arrived in Pitore and begged me to show him kindness. He has been unable to find employment in the rajah's elephant lines and so lives from day to day in the streets and alleys of the city. I appealed to the Hazrat-sahib in the matter, and through his blessed generosity—''

"Oh, good Lord, that's enough!'' Captain Molson's eyes narrowed as he saw the amusement on the duke's face. What kind of man was this to forever entangle himself in his natives' affairs and actually seem to enjoy treating them as equals?''

"I'm afraid you can't prevent me from hiring an extra syce,'' Hugh said blandly.

"No, I cannot,'' the captain agreed, tight-lipped. "But I intend to take the matter up with my superiors as soon as I return to 'Pindi. You have no right to—''

"Up into the wagon, boy,'' the duke interrupted brusquely. "And I want to hear no complaints should the ride grow uncomfortable. Is that understood?''

"The sahib has made himself clear,'' the boy muttered, though he scrambled dutifully enough amid the sacks of grain.

At a curt order from Captain Molson the procession got under way once again, and though the townsfolk had discreetly withdrawn—no doubt, as the captain dourly observed, to take stock of their booty—the duke of Roxbury and his bearer remained unusually alert. Citing the probable presence of cobras, Baga Lal withdrew a loaded jezail from his pack and tucked it beneath the crook of one arm, while the duke inspected the firing mechanism of his pistol before slipping it carefully into the saddlebag before him.

His narrowed eyes fell briefly on the boy jouncing amid the grain sacks in the trailing cart, and his mood was not pleasant. It wouldn't do, of course, to tell Molson who the boy really was, for he would only fear the rajah's wrath and insist on returning him immediately to Pitore. Nor would it help Eden Hamilton's reputation any were it to become known that she was about to spend the next nine days trekking across the plains in the company of a dozen unmarried men, half of them natives of questionable morals. Better to continue the charade until they reached Delhi, since Miss Hamilton's seeming return from the dead would cause enough of a sensation as it was. Hugh sighed, not entirely pleased with the prospect of shouldering such a troublesome responsibility and suspecting, rightly so, that the journey back to Delhi was going to be trying indeed.

They camped that night near the banks of the river where four days earlier the duke had intercepted the black gelding Tukki and encountered for the first time the haughty Indian youth known as Choto Bai. There was no need to pitch tents this time, for all of the men of the expedition were accustomed to sleeping under the stars, and it was only Edgar Lamberton and his secretaries who had insisted upon using them.

As he dismounted Hugh saw Eden descend stiffly from the grain cart. Though she was doubtless bruised and sore from the jolting trip, she set about immediately unsaddling the horses and giving them water. Hugh knew better than to speak to her, for her tight-lipped expression told him that she was far from happy. His presence would be no comfort to her, Hugh decided, and he made no effort to seek her out even after the cooking fires had been extinguished and the others had retreated with their bedrolls to sleep upon the cool sand.

Once, late in the night when the stars were already paling in the sky and the jackals were slinking back to their lairs, he awoke briefly and without apparent reason. Lying with his arms propped beneath his head, he listened to all of the night sounds peculiar to the Indian hills and tried to pick out the one that had disturbed him. It seemed unlikely that the rajah had sent a deputation to fetch Eden Hamilton back to Pitore since an envoy would have caught up with them long before this, yet Hugh was not about to dismiss that possibility.

Being by now fully awake, he was able to listen more closely when the sound came again. Yet it still took a moment for him to realize that what he was hearing was the sound of someone weeping, the muffled sobs coming from underneath one of the carts standing nearby.

Bloody hell, Hugh thought with a stab of helpless anger. It was bad enough that he had saddled himself with the responsibility of seeing Eden Hamilton safely to Delhi. He didn't need to start feeling sorry for her as well.

Chapter Five

"*Dekho, chokra!* Dost thou see them? There among the *kikars!*" Mahan Dal spoke in a whisper, his pointed finger indicating a flock of sand grouse emerging cautiously from a stand of thorn scrub near a wide turn in the river. Dawn was breaking over the foothills, painting the shallows and the sand banks with a wash of pearl. Narrowing her eyes against the faint light, Eden nodded and reached slowly for the ancient fowling piece lying across her saddle.

"They are too far," grunted an elderly Hindu who had ridden onto the plains with them. "Do not waste thy shot, child!"

"Thou hast forgotten, my father," Eden responded with a grin, "that I was taught the art of hunting by a Rajput warrior, to whom hunting means all things. I do not intend to miss."

As she spoke she lifted the heavy weapon to her shoulder. Sighting carefully down the pitted barrel, she pulled the trigger. The grouse scattered amid a whirring explosion of wings while Eden, quickly accepting a second weapon from the waiting gun-bearer, squeezed off another shot.

"*Shabash!*" Mahan Dal exulted, despite the fact that he himself had missed. "That is two more for thy pouch! We will dine like kings this night!"

"Come, brothers, let us go," said the elderly Hindu who was a *chuprassi* in the services of Harry Deas, the district officer from Bharatpore. "The dawn grows long, and the sahibs will be impatient to march."

They returned to camp at a hand gallop, and Eden knew a measure of contentment listening to the idle gossip of the men around her. The fact that they had so readily accepted her as one of them had helped ease the gnawing misery she had felt at leaving Mayar in so secretive a fashion, without even taking time to bid farewell to Jaji. She especially liked old Sudhoo, the bearded bearer who served Harry Deas, for he reminded her in a way of kindly Awal Bannu. For six days now she had marched and eaten and slept in their midst, and it was Sudhoo who had asked Molson-sahib for a spare horse so that she might accompany them on the hunt.

I have well repaid Sudhoo's faith in me, Eden thought contentedly, for the leather pouch slung over her shoulder was filled with fresh game.

They emerged from the distant folds of the canyons amid a cloud of dust, and Baga Lal, who had been watching for them, grunted and slipped away to inform the Hazrat-sahib.

"I wonder what would happen if they were to discover that the boy they have befriended is in truth a Scotswoman who might have been the rani of Mayar," Hugh mused aloud.

"Assuredly they will not take kindly to the fact that they have compromised their caste in the presence of a memsahib," Baga Lal said softly.

"I should never have permitted that to happen," Hugh agreed. "The truth was to have been hidden mainly from Molson-sahib, who is a fool and a coward and would have insisted on sending her back to Mayar. Nor did I wish to encourage untoward talk in Delhi." His lips thinned. "Yet I did not realize that the sahiba would fool the rest of them so completely. Thou art right, Baga Lal: the others must never learn the truth."

"*Beshak,* it is hard to believe they will ever do so, for she could pass as any one of my brothers. And they are wild ones, I promise you." Baga Lal shook his head as he watched the horses canter into camp and the slim young woman swing herself effortlessly from the saddle. "Perhaps," he added thoughtfully, "it is wrong of us to assume that the Hamilton-sahiba will find happiness in the world of the mem-log.''

Though Hugh would normally have scoffed at his bearer's doubts, he himself was growing daily more unsure. Watching Eden sling the shotgun over her arm in the manner of someone who felt completely at ease handling heavy weapons, it occurred to him that few self-respecting Victorian ladies were schooled in the art of stalking and killing wild game. Likewise the strict and admittedly stuffy tenets governing the lives of British women both at home and abroad would never suit anyone with Eden Hamilton's upbringing. Indeed, Hugh already strongly suspected that she would chafe against their restrictions as surely as her fellow creatures would label her a pariah— unfit for proper company—the moment they laid eyes upon her.

''Bloody hell,'' the duke said aloud, thinking once again of the enormity of his burden. He was, after all, responsible for her reintroduction into polite society, and the fact that she seemed far more at ease in the company of gray-bearded Hindus did nothing to reassure him on the score of her success. All he could hope for was that Miss Hamilton would adapt quickly to her old way of life, yet that, he decided in a dark moment of doubt, did not seem bloody likely.

''Baga Lal,'' he said curtly, making up his mind, ''tell thy cousin I wish to speak with him this night. It is time for him to confront his future.''

A flicker of surprise showed briefly in the bearer's eyes. ''I will tell him, Huzoor.''

Though the terrain across which they traveled that day was so torturous as to preclude a total of more than a dozen miles, the prospect of dining on freshly roasted partridges compelled Captain Molson to call an early halt. At his order camp was made while the burning sun still hovered like a disk of molten metal over the distant hills and twilight with its cooling breezes lay several hours away. Yet the captain's decision was met with enthusiasm, for the ascent of the last, steep hill had brought the party to a level plateau across which a shallow river cut a silver swath, and there were shade trees to cool them and grass for the horses.

"I'm going for a swim, Baga Lal," Hugh announced immediately upon dismounting. Leaving his horse in the care of a syce, he strode down to the riverbank and stripped off his boots and sweat-soaked shirt. The water was tepid, yet after riding all day through the broiling sun Hugh found it refreshing. He swam for a half mile against the sluggish current before turning over on his back and floating back to the spot where he had left his clothes. Coming to his feet in the waist-deep water, he pushed the hair out of his eyes and flexed his arms, glad to have the opportunity at last to work off some of his restless energy.

"Aren't you afraid of muggers?"

Hugh shielded his eyes against the blinding sun to see Eden Hamilton squatting on her heels in the sand, her features swathed in a length of muslin unraveled from her turban.

"If you mean crocodiles, no. They know better than to bother me." Hugh grinned, wondering if she was aware of the fact that he was standing before her naked. He was inclined to doubt it, for though she seemed rather disconcerted by the sight of his bare chest, she was displaying none of the fierce embarrassment he was certain would consume her were he to take another step or two out of the water.

"What are you doing here?" he asked, propping his hands on his hips.

"Baga Lal said you wished to speak to me. He said you were beginning to grow impatient."

"Did he? Perhaps I am. But I've no intention of talking to you while you wilt before my eyes." There was no shade anywhere along the riverbank, and the blinding white sand seemed to shimmer in the heat. Hugh could see damp patches of sweat on the brow of Eden's puggari. "Why don't you join me?"

He saw hot color flare across her cheeks in response and was hard put to hide his amusement. So there was a good deal of the chaste Victorian maiden in Eden Hamilton after all!

"I don't know how to swim," Eden lied, wishing belatedly that she had waited until nightfall before seeking him out. She was confused by the behavior of this impudently grinning man, not at all certain if he was teasing her or trying deliberately to make her feel uncomfortable. Well, he wasn't going to make fun of her if she could help it. Eden's chin tilted, and she stared boldly into his eyes.

"I imagine you are angry with me for having avoided you since we left Pitore." Her voice was cool and measured, as if she found nothing in the least bit odd about addressing him from a sandy riverbank while he stood in the shallows before her, water running down the tanned expanse of his chest. "I suppose I should have at least explained to you why I—what happened that night."

"I imagine it isn't easy to talk about, Miss Hamilton." She shrugged offhandedly. "I'd be lying if I said I didn't miss them, especially Jaji. No one ever paid much attention to him after his mother's death, you see, until I came to Mayar. I hope he doesn't think—" She broke off with a catch in her breath and looked quickly away.

"I'm sure he'll understand," Hugh said brusquely. Bloody hell, all he needed was for her to start crying again!

Fortunately Eden seemed determined to shed no tears before him, and after a moment she squared her shoulders and said resolutely, "I had to leave after what you said to me that night. You made me realize that should I become the rani of Mayar I would no longer be allowed to comport myself as I'd become accustomed. While I could do just about anything I pleased as Choto Bai, it would have been unseemly for the wife of a rajah to compromise *purdah* in any way. I would never have been permitted to leave the zenana on my own again, or to hunt with Malraj or fly falcons with Jaji. The thought was intolerable, so I chose to run away."

"You chose to return to your own kind, Miss Hamilton, which is by far the more courageous decision."

"Is it?" she inquired doubtfully.

"Did you tell anyone you were leaving?"

"Only the Begum Fariza. She understood my reasons for wanting to go, and arranged for me to be among the crowd of onlookers in Pitore. The overturning of your cart was not an accident, by the way. Neither of us could be certain how Malraj would react if he knew I was planning to leave, so we decided that my departure must be carried out in utmost secrecy."

"Surely he would have sent a patrol after you by now if he suspected you had gone with us."

"The Begum said she would let it be known throughout the palace that I was indisposed with an illness. I doubt my absence will be noticed for several more days."

"And the Begum? How will she protect herself from the rajah's wrath when he discovers she has been your abettor?"

He heard her soft laughter. "You do not know the Begum Fariza, sahib."

"You mustn't call me that anymore," he said harshly. "You are a Scotswoman, Miss Hamilton, and the Rajput Choto Bai no longer exists."

He saw the laughter die from her eyes, and for some inexplicable reason it exacerbated his temper. "And I trust you will make every effort to comport yourself as a proper English lady once we arrive in Delhi."

"Oh, you needn't worry on that score, Your Grace," Eden retorted, stung. "I wouldn't dream of embarrassing you by behaving like a hoyden."

"That isn't what concerns me," he said shortly.

"No?" she countered. "Then perhaps you are afraid that I will tell everyone how easily you were fooled by a woman—one disguised as an Indian, no less?"

She saw a muscle in his cheek twitch as though he could still feel the blow she had attempted days ago with her whip. "By God, someone should have drummed that arrogance out of you a long time ago."

"Do you think you're man enough to do it?" she mocked, unable to resist taunting him.

"Why, you bloody little bitch—"

Eden's eyes widened, and she sprang to her feet in alarm as he waded menacingly out of the water. Dear God—until that moment she hadn't had an inkling that he

was standing before her stark naked! She took one look
at his hard male body, at the muscles that tapered across
his flat belly to the dark patch of hair between his lean,
muscled legs, and a burning wave of color flared across
her face. Turning, she bolted like a frightened deer, and
behind her, maddeningly, humiliatingly, she could hear
the sound of his deep, throaty laughter.

Eden spent the remainder of the day in helpless misery, terrified of running into the duke inadvertently and
being forced to meet his eyes, knowing she would die of
embarrassment at what she would see there. How *could*
he have stood there speaking to her so calmly when all
the while he hadn't been wearing a scrap of clothing?
Eden's cheeks burned as an unwanted vision of his hard,
muscled body rose before her. She was glad that the swift
Indian twilight had settled over the hills and that her face
was hidden in shadow so that old Sudhoo, who sat smok-
ing his hookah nearby, was unable to see her expression.

It was because she had spent the last three years of her
life in a zenana, of course. Hugh Gordon was not ignorant, and he would know that many of the women who
lived within its glittering walls were kept exclusively for
the rajah's pleasure. It was a natural-enough mistake for
him to assume that Eden, too, had been similarly schooled
in the art of erotic love.

Well, I haven't been, and I'm not one of them! Eden
thought resentfully. While she was by no means ignorant
of the duties a concubine was expected to perform for her
lord and lover, her innocence had been zealously guarded
by the Begum Fariza, as befitting any high-born daughter
of a noble house. Despite what anyone might be tempted
to think, Hugh Gordon's naked body had been the first
Eden had ever seen, and her resentment grew as she remembered his amused laughter when she had fled from
him like some foolish, blushing maiden.

God above, how could anyone blame her for running
away from a sight like that? His naked body had been
shocking in the extreme, after all, and she would never
have dreamed that anyone could be so large and muscular
and hairy. And as for actually *lying* with someone who
looked like that—

"*Chut!* The stitches will hold without such sweating and cursing, my son."

Eden looked up quickly from the bridle she had been mending to find Sudhoo's heavy-lidded eyes regarding her curiously from across the fire. "I'm sorry," she said sheepishly. "My thoughts must be elsewhere."

"A thousand miles or more," the old man agreed affably, the slow bubble of his hookah filling the night. "I have never known thee to be troubled, child. Is it the decision of Molson-sahib to take thee to Rawalpindi that distresses thee?"

The methodical movement of Eden's heavy stitching needle abruptly stilled. "This is the first I have heard of it, my father."

"Ah. This I did not know."

"What is it Molson-sahib said?"

"Only that he wishes thee to travel with him when the road divides and his men turn north to Rawalpindi. It is said there is much work for a young syce of thy talents in the *rissala* of the *Angrezi* army."

"Has this already been decided by Molson-sahib?" Eden inquired quickly.

"I think not. It was only a question he was heard to place before the Hazrat-sahib."

"And what did he say?"

Sudhoo's dark eyes gleamed with amusement. "He is never one to give a simple answer, the Hazrat-sahib! *Ohé*, sometimes I believe he thinks too much like a man of Hind!"

"I see," Eden said slowly, though it was obvious from Sudhoo's words that Hugh Gordon did not care one way or the other what her decision would be. Turning her head, she stared off into the night, wondering what she ought to do and unable to explain to herself why his indifference should depress her so immeasurably.

Long after the campfires had burned low that night and a pale sickle moon had ascended above the ragged peaks of the hills, a low whisper awakened Hugh Gordon from sleep.

"Who's there?" he demanded, instantly alert.

"Sahib?" The low voice came again above the murmurous rustle of the elephant grass in the wind.

Hugh lifted his head from the mess pack that served as a pillow to find someone crouching in the nearby shadows, and he knew at once that it was Eden.

"What is it?" he asked curtly.

She glanced cautiously over her shoulder before squatting down beside him. Her face was bared, and her eyes were dark and troubled in the moonlight. "Captain Molson's company is heading north for Rawalpindi tomorrow," she said in a whisper. "I wanted to ask if you'd made arrangements for me to go with him or not."

Hugh sighed and came up on one elbow. "Your timing is remarkable, Miss Hamilton. Couldn't this have waited until morning?"

"You know it could not," she said coldly. "If I'm to go with him, he'll have to be told who I am, and I'm not entirely certain that's wise. Since I haven't the faintest idea what you plan to do with me in Delhi, I thought it better to ask first."

"My dear Miss Hamilton," Hugh said dourly, "I haven't the faintest idea what to do with you, either."

Eden started visibly. "But I thought—"

"Good God," interrupted Hugh ill-temperedly, "what do you expect? I know next to nothing about you or your family, and since you haven't been particularly helpful in enlightening me, how can I possibly decide what's to be done with you?"

"I suppose I should have told you something about myself earlier," she admitted reluctantly.

"That would have been helpful," he agreed.

Eden longed to slap his face, but the sudden gleam that appeared in his eyes told her he was perfectly aware of her thoughts and was not above reciprocating in kind. "I cannot say that I like you very much, Your Grace," she couldn't prevent herself from saying.

To her annoyance he merely threw back his dark head and laughed. "No, Miss Hamilton, I don't imagine you do. But since fate has seemed inclined to throw us together, perhaps you might be cooperative enough to tell me a bit about yourself?"

Eden's lower lip protruded, and she suddenly looked more like a recalcitrant child of seven than the beautiful, self-assured young woman to whom Hugh had been officially introduced in the glittering *chitra shala* of the rajah's palace. "What is it you wish to know?"

"You have no family residing here in India?"

"No," she said flatly. "They were murdered by sepoys."

Hugh's brows rose. "All of them?"

As it turned out Eden's mother alone had escaped such a fate, for she had died of childbirth fever two days after Eden had been born. She had been nearly forty at the time, far too old by the standards of the day to bear children, and the unsanitary conditions of the field hospital in the district where her husband had been stationed on maneuvers had ultimately sped her untimely demise.

"They'd been married for ten years before I was born," Eden said quietly, "and I suppose they'd given up hope of ever having children. I must have been a considerable surprise to them. After my mother's death my father arranged for an *ayah* to care for me."

"Is she still alive?" Hugh inquired.

Eden's expression turned to stone. "No."

"And your uncle?"

"Uncle Donan never had the military inclinations my father did. He was a planter who made his home in Ceylon. When the threat of mutiny became apparent he sent his daughter Isabel to stay with us in Lucknow, and Papa eventually moved the two of us to Meerut." Eden turned her head and looked off into the darkness. For a long moment she was silent, watching the heat lightning flicker across the distant hills. "He said we would be safer there. Odd, isn't it, when the sowars in Meerut were the first to rebel?" She gave a bitter laugh, and Hugh found the defensive profile presented him in the moonlight oddly touching.

"Do you know for a fact that both your uncle and cousin were killed?"

Eden shrugged. "After the rebellion was put down, the rajah—Malraj's father, I mean—tried his best to find out what had happened to them, but without success. It was

assumed they were dead, and since I had no one else to
turn to there seemed little reason for me to leave Mayar.''

"You have no relations left in Scotland?''

"None that I know of. My father lost touch with
everyone on Bute when he and Uncle Donan emigrated
to India. As for my mother—'' Eden frowned. "She cannot have gotten on well with her family because my father
never spoke of them to me. I think she must have run
away from home when she was very young, or done
something terrible enough to make my grandparents dis-
own her. Why else would she have left Scotland to become a governess for some wealthy nabob in Lucknow
who had a sickly wife and a half-dozen children? I understand he overworked her dreadfully, and it was a
blessing when Papa took her away to be married.''

"Then that's a dead end, too, isn't it? You've no idea
where her people might have come from?''

Eden shook her head.

"Well, Miss Hamilton, I'm afraid that doesn't give us
much to go on,'' Hugh said at last. He was annoyed with
himself for the pity that stirred him as he looked at her
averted face. "In any event I would suggest that all inquiries concerning your family be directed to Scotland. It
shouldn't prove too difficult to find your relations, provided they are still living on Bute.'' He paused thoughtfully. "In the meantime I've decided to send you to a
friend of mine in Delhi. Colonel Frederick Porter has two
daughters who should be around your age by now. They'll
be happy to take you in.''

"That's very kind of you,'' Eden said awkwardly.

A lengthy silence fell between them, broken only by
the scratching and foraging of some unseen creature in the
nearby thorn scrub.

"I suppose I ought to thank you for all you've done
on my behalf,'' Eden resumed at last. "After all, you're
not to blame for the fact that I had to leave Mayar.''

"With a British resident living in Pitore, your story
would have come out sooner or later,'' Hugh observed.

"Yes, I suppose so. Still, I'm very grateful, and I
wonder—'' She lifted her head, which had been resting

on her knees, and regarded him solemnly. "Do you suppose we might be friends?"

"Friends? Of course, Miss Hamilton," Hugh said gravely, though the very idea of a man of his character and reputation being friends with a woman amused him greatly. Turning his head to look at her, it occurred to Hugh with no small measure of surprise that there was something oddly compelling about the intimacy of sitting here in the darkness beside her. Above them the wide sky was spangled with countless stars, and nothing broke the stillness save the distant murmur of the river.

There was a potent magic in the hot night, and Hugh could not prevent himself from reaching for her as he had once before in the sultry gardens of the rajah's palace. Eden turned toward him as he did so, and her dark, solemn eyes met his. Both of them grew still, and suddenly, without either of them knowing how it happened, she was in his arms. Her body was enchantingly soft and slender beneath the rough fabric of her kaftan, and the scent of rose petals clung to her skin.

Touching his mouth to hers, Hugh found her lips sweet beyond belief. Drawing her closer, he lowered his head and kissed her insistently, parting her mouth with the pressure of his own. It was a long kiss, slow and filled with a drugging wonder, and to Eden it seemed as if the very firmament itself were being swept away beneath her feet. It was as if there were nothing in all creation left for her to cling to but the hard mouth that moved slowly, sensuously, upon hers.

Something stirred deep within her as Hugh's lips continued their gentle assault, a strange, insistent heat that crept through her blood and centered at last in that secret womanly place between her legs. Perhaps Hugh sensed as much, for he loosened one of his arms from about her waist and pushed aside the stiff material to cup her naked breast. His fingers were strong and very sure, and as the nipple hardened beneath his touch, the fire fanned hotter within her until it fairly sang through her blood. She insinuated herself closer, her body melting against his.

"My God," Hugh whispered, and in that drawn, ragged breath there was wonder as well as passion.

At that moment the unexpected whinnying of a tethered horse tore through the stillness. Perhaps a foraging mongoose or the scent of a jackal pack borne on the breeze had startled it from sleep, yet though it quieted immediately and roused no one else in the sleeping camp, its call had served to act upon Eden like a dash of cold water in the face.

She had been lying in Hugh Gordon's arms, her head resting against his shoulder as he kissed her, and in a moment of pure panic it was no great feat to jerk her elbow backward and deliver a crashing blow to his gentlemanly parts. Instantly his arms loosened about her, and he gave a low grunt of pain. Scrambling to her feet, Eden stood staring down at him, the knuckles showing white as she pressed her trembling hand to her lips.

"Now I know why you were so willing to help me escape!" she breathed, and her eyes were suddenly hot and bright with wounded anger. "Doubtless I'm nothing more to you than another of Malraj's concubines, aren't I? Well, you're sorely mistaken on that score, I'll have you know, and should you ever attempt anything like it again, you're really going to regret it!"

"Believe me, Miss Hamilton, I already do," Hugh assured her painfully.

Lifting up the trailing ends of her kaftan, Eden turned heel and vanished into the darkness. Groping her way to her bedroll, she threw herself upon it. For a long time she lay without moving, her heart pounding and her breasts rising and falling with every agitated breath she took. At first she was certain that he would come after her, yet as the agonizing minutes ticked by and nothing stirred from the far side of camp, Eden drew a long, shuddering breath of relief. Thank God he had decided to leave her alone. She didn't know what she'd do if he tried to kiss her again!

Rolling onto her back, she stared up at the vast canopy of twinkling stars, and after a moment she traced her bruised lips with a hesitant finger.

Dear God, she had never known, had never suspected, that a kiss could feel like that! She had heard endless talk of the ways of love from the women of the zenana, yet never, never would she have suspected that the simple touch of a man's hard mouth could rob the breath from her body so completely.

''I cannot stay here another moment,'' Eden whispered into the empty darkness. ''Not with him! I must go to 'Pindi with Captain Molson!''

She suspected that the captain would not be particularly sympathetic upon discovering who she was, yet that possibility and the fact that he might insist upon returning her to Mayar was not in the least bit as daunting as the confusion Hugh Gordon had instilled within her with a single kiss.

I mustn't think of him, not ever again, and I must get away at once, Eden thought. I cannot face him, not after this!

Rolling over onto her side, she closed her eyes, yet not until the first pale streaks of dawn were creeping across the distant foothills was she permitted the dubious luxury of a fitful sleep.

Chapter Six

Above the rose-tinted walls of Delhi soared the minarets and turnip-shaped domes of Shah Jehan's Grand Mosque, its carved stone columns and silverwork gleaming in the sun. Against the sprawling ridge rising beyond the city, the battlements of the Red Fort shimmered in brilliant red, and dust devils danced beneath the ancient, arching gates. Other domes filled the crowded skyline, their curved moon symbols of Islam giving evidence to the influence of the Moslem invaders who had laid the first cornerstones of this ancient city of the plains. The trade roads they had carved into the desert sands existed still, and despite the heat of the afternoon they were crowded with pilgrims and beggars, bullock carts and camels, and the elegant carriages of the memsahibs.

Eden Hamilton, drawing on the off-side rein so that her mount might avoid a sacred Brahmini cow grazing in the center of the road, gazed about her with open wonder. She had forgotten what it meant to be in an Indian city populated extensively by British. Everywhere she looked, frock coats and hooped skirts with stiff, foaming petticoats were as much in evidence as dhotis and saris and the dark-colored bourkas of the Moslem women. Young English couples strolled leisurely, and a noisy group of soldiers ate a picnic luncheon beneath one of the ancient gates, their boisterous conversation interspersed with snatches of song. It seemed difficult to believe that only four years earlier the last, brave defenders of the Delhi residency had been brutally hacked to pieces on that very spot by a howling Indian mob.

"They've forgotten, haven't they?" Eden inquired softly of the elderly gentleman who rode beside her.

"Forgotten? No, I don't think so," replied Colonel Frederick Porter, understanding her instantly. "We British have never been a vindictive lot, and sometimes I confess it's easier to act as if the unspeakable never happened."

"It's easy for the victors to say that, isn't it?" Eden said with a trace of bitterness. "I don't think any of y— any of us," she amended quickly, "have ever paused to consider how the Indian people must feel having risked their lives to escape the oppressive boot of John Company only to find themselves newly forced beneath the thumb of the British Crown."

Colonel Porter looked down at her as she trotted beside him, her face solemn beneath the brim of a small black derby. He did not envy Eden Hamilton the task of picking up the threads of her former life while in her mind and heart she had become very much a Hindu. And yet she had made remarkable progress in the past six days, and in her riding habit of powder blue trimmed with black braid she was thoroughly unrecognizable as the turbaned youth who had been ushered into his house late one night by the duke of Roxbury.

Colonel Porter's lips twitched beneath his graying drundeary whiskers as he recalled the scene. She had been clearly out of sorts with Roxbury, her irritated escort. Never had the colonel seen two young people going at each other quite like that: Miss Hamilton with her slim nose in the air and those astonishing blue eyes glittering with dislike, while Roxbury, never the most patient of men to begin with, had all but shoved the girl at him and fled out the door. Thank goodness his bearer, Baga Lal, had ridden ahead to warn the colonel of their arrival, and that Mrs. Porter and the girls had been away at Hobson House to celebrate Celia Hobson's pending marriage; otherwise there would have been the devil to pay. Mrs. Porter, being hellishly proper, would never have tolerated having her home invaded by half a dozen dusty men freshly returned from the plains, among them Indian natives in the service of the duke of Roxbury, and a young woman shockingly disguised as a syce—the daughter of a colonel of British infantry, no less.

The colonel had instructed the staring serving girls to provide Miss Hamilton with proper clothes and hot water for washing, and had sent the duke's bearers round to the verandah, where they had been served refreshments. He had then managed to persuade His Grace to withdraw to the study, where he had listened in his solemn and uncensorious manner to Roxbury's telling of the Hamilton girl's astonishing story.

"Of course she can stay here, m'boy," he had said at once, considerably intrigued by the prospect. "Wouldn't turn her out into the street, b'gad!"

Hugh Gordon had made no effort to hide his relief. While he had known Colonel Porter for many years and had suffered no qualms on the question of his support, he was more than ready to terminate his responsibility for his troublesome charge. By God, if he'd known what a virago Eden Hamilton could turn out to be, he would never have attempted to kiss her that night on the plains! He'd had more than enough of her icy stares and haughtily turned shoulders since then, and he was heartily annoyed with himself for letting her behavior affect him as it did. Not a day had gone by during the long trek that followed when he hadn't found himself wishing that he'd let her go on to Rawalpindi with Captain Molson instead of losing his temper and insisting she travel with him to Delhi.

"She won't be easy to tame, Fred," he had warned the older man, sitting in the darkened study listening to the creaking of the *punkah* fan and idly watching a gecko lizard hunt insects on the ceiling. "Are you certain you won't think it over?"

"Nonsense," the colonel had assured him. "Can't say I've ever shied away from a bit of a challenge, and it wouldn't be right to turn one's back on a daughter of Bengal Infantry, eh? Besides, just between you and me—" His voice dropped to a conspiratorial whisper, though no one could hear him save the yawning *punkah-wallah*. "It's been crashingly dull here of late, what with everyone gone to the hills and the regiments sitting idle. It's the heat, I tell you, and Mrs. Porter, I'll confess, hasn't been the most pleasant because of it. Ought to do her a great deal of good to get her mind off the weather and play Lady Bountiful to a poor orphaned girl. Benevolent works, that's the thing for my Clarissa.''

Privately, Hugh decided that looking after someone as willful and temperamental as Eden Hamilton could not exactly be considered in the same light as doing ''good works,'' but then again he knew Clarissa Porter fairly well and suspected that she was quite up to the task. She was gregarious and authoritative, generous without being overly sentimental, and her position as a ruling matron of Delhi society should guarantee that she knew how much restraint to use where Eden Hamilton's introduction into the city's upper circles was concerned.

''I'll stop by the chief magistrate's first thing in the morning,'' Colonel Porter had added, ''and see if we can't track down her relations. After all, there must be someone here on the continent who'd be willing to take her in, don't you think? As for Clarissa—I think it best if we don't tell her exactly how Miss Hamilton spent the last few years of her life. Zenanas and maharajahs and the like all sound good and fine in a fairy tale, but it won't do here in Delhi where respectable young women simply don't mix with the natives, b'gad! I'll do my best to keep the gossip down to a bearable level.''

''That's very good of you,'' Hugh said with distracted relief, and declined an invitation to stay for another brandy. He had pressing business to conduct in Delhi, he explained, and was expected in Calcutta at the end of the month to appear before the governor-general and the council. Perhaps he might then return and see how Miss Hamilton was faring, but at the moment he wasn't entirely certain.

''I understand,'' replied the colonel with a hearty handshake, knowing better than to ask questions. The duke of Roxbury's cool blue gaze had always hidden a great deal, and he respected the younger man far too much to dare risk `offense by asking something as thoughtless as an explanation for his appearance before the council or his reasons for journeying to Mayar.

He had always suspected that it wasn't the lucrative Indian trade alone that had brought Hugh Gordon time and again to India, and that the man had the dangerous predilection of seeing the Indian side as readily as that of the white man. But that, too, had become an invaluable asset since the days of the great mutiny, and if the governor-general had seen fit to call upon the duke in some capacity—strictly unofficial, of course, since His Grace was neither an Indian civil servant nor of military rank—then Frederick Porter was not about to make meddlesome inquiries into the matter.

The two men were silent as they stepped onto the verandah, where Baga Lal and the duke's syces and *chuprassis* squatted patiently in wait for him. Once more the colonel offered Hugh his hand, and this time there was genuine warmth in the younger man's eyes as he gripped it.

"My thanks, Fred. There aren't many who'd take in an orphaned British girl with no questions asked."

"I'm only doing it because you're the one who asked," the colonel responded with a smile. "Don't you want to wait and bid her farewell?"

"Thank you, no," the duke responded dryly, and there was a tightness about his mouth that the colonel had seen before and recognized. Wandering back to his study, he was unable to stop the sudden doubt concerning the wisdom of his decision. How very difficult was it going to be having a strange young woman suddenly thrust into his care? Perhaps he should have taken up the matter with Mrs. Porter before giving such hasty consent. His wife was, in all honesty, very set in her ways, and one never knew how she would react to such a disruption of her well-ordered household.

To his infinite relief, Mrs. Porter had not only been delighted, she had declared herself in utter sympathy with Eden Hamilton's distressing plight. Of course the girl must remain here with them; she wouldn't hear of anything else! Furthermore, she would make immediate arrangements to provide Miss Hamilton with appropriate clothes, since the few saris the girl had brought with her in her dusty haversack would never do. Why, her eldest daughter, Allegra, had *dozens* of gowns that needed only a bit of alteration to fit Miss Hamilton's taller frame.

"And of course you must stay here no matter how long it takes to locate your relations," Clarissa Porter had concluded, feeling quite in charity with this poor, motherless creature.

"You are too kind," Eden had murmured with downcast eyes, and the listening colonel had found himself wondering why on earth the duke of Roxbury had ever thought to label this lovely young girl difficult.

The braying of a conch in a nearby temple and the babble of countless voices recalled Colonel Porter's thoughts to the present. Looking about him, he was startled to see that their horses had already reached the outskirts of the Chandi Chauk, the Avenue of Moonlight that served as the main thoroughfare of Delhi. The sun beat relentlessly upon the flat rooftops of the buildings surrounding it, and on the far side of the city walls the Jumna River shone like a molten riband of silver. The colonel blinked and glanced in bemusement at his pocketwatch, wondering where the time had gone.

"Dear me," he said with considerable disappointment to Eden, "I had wanted to show you the Kutab Minar and the Tombs of the Seven Cities, but I'm afraid we've run out of time. Cottington will be impatient if we're late. This way, my dear."

If Eden felt the least bit nervous about stepping into the imposing reception room of Government House and finding within it three strange men, all of them staring at her with undisguised interest, she gave no indication of it. Seating herself in the offered armchair, she smoothed down the skirts of Allegra Porter's borrowed habit and tilted her chin to regard each in turn with cool dignity from beneath the brim of her hat.

The air was oppressively hot, and the creaking of the punkahs only served to contribute to the closeness of the shuttered room. No breath of air stirred the drawn *chik* blinds, and a potted plant standing near the doorway drooped in the heat. After formal introductions had been made and the turbaned bearer with his refreshment tray had been dismissed, Colonel Porter and the three remaining gentlemen seated themselves amid a subdued scraping of chairs.

Cool and impenetrable as her gaze might be, Eden could not still a flutter of nervous anticipation as a heavy silence fell over the room. Her gaze came to rest on the man Colonel Porter had introduced to her as William Cottington, a political officer of the Intelligence Department of the Northwest Provinces who had traveled from Oudh expressly to see her. Feeling her solemn eyes upon him, Sir William cleared his throat and sorted through the sheafs of paper spread on the small secretary before him.

"I'm sure Colonel Porter has already told you that your father did not survive the siege of the residency in Lucknow, Miss Hamilton. I was, however, able to recover his personal affects, and these I wish to give you. They've been kept in storage in our Oudh bureau these three years past."

"That's very kind of you, sir," Eden murmured.

"At that time we also conducted an extensive search for any other surviving relations of Colonel Hamilton's," Sir William continued, "and I believe you have already been told that the investigatiion yielded naught." He squinted at a sheet of paper before him. "Your uncle, Donan Hamilton, was killed in Madras at the onset of the mutiny, and his daughter, Isabel, is believed to have been among the thirty-odd Europeans slain in the Meerut massacre. I understand an additional search is currently being conducted for relations who might still be living in Scotland."

"Quite right, quite right. I'm seeing to the matter myself," said Colonel Porter promptly, and gave Eden a reassuring smile. "We expect something to turn up before too long, b'gad."

"I'm glad to hear it," said Sir William politely. If the truth must be told, he was a harassed and quite overworked civil official who cared not at all where this young woman had suddenly come from or where she had spent the long years since the onset of the rebellion. His sole responsibility lay in transferring Colonel Dougal Hamilton's personal effects to his daughter, and once that duty had been satisfactorily discharged, Sir William had no further interest in what became of her. Signing to his secretary, he watched with a trace of impatience as the young man retrieved a small wooden box from the desk and placed it in Eden's hands.

"I'm afraid it isn't much, Miss Hamilton," the young man apologized.

Eden lifted her strained face to his. "Thank you," she said quietly.

An expectant silence fell over the hot room, yet she made no move to open the box in her lap. It felt absurdly light, and she resisted the impulse to shake it and prove to herself that, yes, there was actually something inside, something of her father's that did indeed prove he had once existed.

"Perhaps you'd like a few minutes to yourself, Miss Hamilton?"

Eden looked up into the kindly face of a blond Englishman whose name, she recalled, was Henry Pascal. He was, as Colonel Porter had mentioned during the introductions made earlier, some sort of adjutant to the administrative commissioner of the Punjab, and as such the only man in the room who was actually employed at Government House. He was forty-one, vigorous and good-humored, and, unbeknownst to Eden, an old friend of the duke of Roxbury.

"Yes, thank you. That would be kind."

Ushering Eden into a small office across the corridor, he started to close the door behind him, then paused. "Take as long as you like, Miss Hamilton. It's my office, and I'll see no one disturbs you. Oh, and I wouldn't let Cottington's manner throw you," he added with a grin. "He's a thoroughly distasteful toady with no more tact than a charging elephant."

Eden was forced to laugh at this, and her smile lingered as she turned to set the box on Pascal's desk. Taking a deep breath, she untied the jute and lifted the lid. Cottington's secretary had been right: little indeed remained of the man who had once been Colonel Dougal Hamilton, commander of the Fourteenth Bengal Infantry. There were several medals and an assortment of other decorations, tarnished now by heat and neglect. The gold

saber sash Eden had seen her father wear during dress parade was folded neatly in the bottom of the box underneath his military bandolier, which was itself stiff and
badly mildewed. Lifting them aside with fingers that
shook slightly, Eden found a small stack of yellowed letters tied together with a tattered ribbon, the ink faded and
barely legible.

Sudden tears sprang to her eyes. They were the first she
had shed for her father in many a year, and a feeling of
helpless despair clogged her throat. Dougal Hamilton had
given his life for India, the land he had loved as much
as, perhaps even more than, his wife and child. It seemed
inconceivable to his daughter that nothing should remain
of him but the tattered remnants of his uniform, a handful
of letters, and the few tales of bravery still being told by
the soldiers in Lucknow who remembered him.

"It isn't fair!" Eden whispered. "It isn't fair that this
should have happened to you, Papa!" And with sudden,
painful clarity she realized, too, that she could never leave
India now, not after her father had given his life to defend it and make it safe once again for his own kind; to
do so seemed tantamount to betraying him.

Fresh tears scalded Eden's eyes, and she rested her
cheek for a moment against the neatly folded sash, then
carefully returned it to the box. With a rustle of petticoats
she went to stand before the monsoon-tarnished mirror
hanging behind Henry Pascal's desk. There she scrubbed
her eyes with a crumpled handkerchief, tucked the few
stray hairs of her chignon back into place, and squared
her shoulders resolutely.

When Eden returned to the reception room several
minutes later, there was no trace of tears on her face, and
her chin was once again tilted in its usual, forthright
manner. In her blue eyes burned the determined look of
a woman who has made an irrevocable decision, as indeed she had, and her voice was cool and measured as
she offered her hand in farewell to William Cottington.

"Thank you for your help, sir. It was kind of you to
go to such trouble on my behalf."

"I'm sorry we couldn't do more, Miss Hamilton," Sir
William said, clearing his throat. Lovely little thing, he

was thinking to himself. A pity fate had chosen to treat her so unkindly.

Henry Pascal alone accompanied Eden and Colonel Porter to the front hall, where a smartly uniformed Gurkha of the Queen's Own Guard snapped to attention as he opened the door. "If there's anything else we at Government House can do for you, Miss Hamilton, please don't hesitate to ask."

Eden peered up into his face. "Thank you, sir. You are very kind."

Pascal bowed over the slim, gloved hand that was placed in his, and as he watched her sweep gracefully down the wide marble steps, her trim back straight in the powder-blue habit, he was moved to make a remark that caused a passing clerk to regard him with startled curiosity: "Blood and thunder! Roxbury must be utterly mad!"

"I hope that wasn't too painful for you, my dear," Colonel Porter remarked worriedly when they were once again trotting their horses across the hot trunk road leading toward the distant ridge where the British cantonments stood. "Being confronted by so many memories after this much time—it couldn't have been pleasant."

"On the contrary," Eden said softly. "I'm grateful that I finally have something of Papa's to keep. What with our bungalow having been looted and burned, I'd thought all of it was gone."

"I'm glad to hear it," the colonel said with patent relief. Unbeknownst to Eden, he had been expecting a painful exhibition of female histrionics—exactly the sort that always made him feel so dashed helpless and inadequate whenever Mrs. Porter or one of his daughters chose to indulge in them, which they did with a frequency that quite dismayed and bemused the poor colonel. Yet gazing into the composed young face of the girl riding beside him, he came to the conclusion that Miss Hamilton possessed not only an admirable temperament for a woman, but an extraordinary amount of courage.

"We'll have you reunited with your family before too long," he told her heartily, wanting to offer her some sort of encouragement. "What with our new telegraph system

and the steam ships plying the seas between Bombay and
Aden, we ought to be hearing something from Edinburgh
quite soon.''

Eden smiled in response to this and wondered what the
colonel would say if she were to tell him that she had no
intention of leaving India no matter how eagerly her Scottish relations might be waiting to take her in. He would
think her mad, of course, and appeal to the duke of Roxbury to make her see reason, and that, Eden decided with
a toss of her head, was not about to happen. His Grace
was one man she certainly never intended to take orders
from again.

Of course, it was not going to be easy to persuade any
of them to allow her to remain in India. She was under
age, for one thing, and the inheritance her father had left
her was, according to Sir William Cottington, pitiably
small. That, and the meager compensatory pay she would
receive from the British army would never be enough to
support her, and what sort of work could a single woman
of modest means find in India?

Colonel Porter had already warned her that a new India
had emerged from the bloodshed and horror of the rebellion. No longer a backward nation exploited by the greedy
directors of the East India Company, British India had
become a fast-developing country governed by political
and military councils concerned with the building of
schools, mills, and factories and the laying of extensive
railroads. Yet Eden was intelligent enough to read between the lines and draw the conclusion that this vast,
restless land was nonetheless still governed by a plump
and notoriously humorless British monarch, a queen
whose own personal morality and unshakably stuffy beliefs had molded the thinking of an age—and forced the
countries of her ever-expanding empire to embrace every
bit of her stifling prudery. Clearly Victorian India was not
a land of opportunity—or even one of sympathy—for the
plight of a single woman.

If I were wealthy, Eden thought suddenly, none of
them, not even His Perishing Grace, the duke of Roxbury, could tell me what to do. Surely a woman of in-

dependent means may do whatever she pleases, despite what the disapproving populace may say!

A determined light deepened the blue of Eden's eyes, and her soft lips curved in a manner that would have alarmed anyone who knew her well. It was suddenly and completely obvious to her that what she needed was a fortune of her own, and if she plotted carefully and luck was on her side, she knew exactly where to go about finding one. . . .

On a worn Persian rug below the massive doors of Shah Jehan's Grand Mosque sat the bearded brass hawker known to all Delhi as Mohammed Hadji. Though the hour was late and the sky above the soaring minarets was awash with stars, the steps of the mosque above him were still crowded with beggars and pilgrims engaged in prayers.

Mohammed Hadji's hookah glowed as it chuckled softly in the darkness. Once he had been a proud Afridi warrior who had fought at the side of Akbar Khan against Lord Elphinstone and the British troops who had attempted the entrenchment of Afghanistan. But that had been many years ago, and since then he had grown old and fat and tamed to the bazaars of Delhi. Yet there were many who remembered him still as a man of cunning and courage, a spy who was said to have eyes and ears in every province north to the Great Frontier. His name was known to all who resided in the ancient city, and it had not taken many inquiries on Eden Hamilton's part to find him.

Tonight, as on every night for the past week, Eden left the horse she had appropriated from Colonel Porter's stable tethered at the foot of the marble steps and seated herself cross-legged on Mohammed Hadji's rug. She was dressed once again as an Indian youth, and the long tail of her puggari had been unraveled and wrapped about her head so that it completely concealed the womanly features of her face.

Because Mohammed Hadji himself had summoned her this night, Eden waited patiently while the glow of the water pipe faded, knowing that he would speak in his own good time. Setting the pipe away at last, Mohammed Hadji pulled significantly at his beard and began to talk at length, his voice low so that no man passing by could overhear a word of it.

A frown drew Eden's brows together as he spoke and remained that way for some time after he had lapsed into silence. "I thought as much," she said at last, striving to hide her disappointment. She pushed a handful of rupees across the rug, and Mohammed Hadji scooped them up with a plump hand.

"I will ask again," he promised, feeling unaccountably sorry for the slim youth seated across from him. "My cousin did his best to make inquiries, but as you know, the answers you seek are known only to the *sirdar* in Meerut, and there are few who have his ear."

"Perhaps I should ride to Meerut myself," Eden mused aloud, though she knew that it would be impossible to cover the distance there and back in the course of a single evening.

"There is no need for that," Mohammed Hadji assured her. "I will speak again to my cousin. Perhaps there is yet another way."

Eden thanked him politely, yet without much hope. Because she had no idea when the Porters were expected to return home from their soirée, she bade Mohammed Hadji farewell and untethered her horse. For five nights now her luck had held, but she couldn't be certain that the Porters might not, on some occasion in the near future, return home early from a social engagement and find that she had not retired to bed with a headache, as she had told Hila Deem, Colonel Porter's bearer, but that, in fact, her room was empty and one of the horses in the stable was gone. . . .

Lost in thought, Eden trotted across the darkened bazaar in the direction of the Kashmir gate. Here her mount nearly ran down a beggar who, having stepped behind the shadows of a pillar to relieve himself, had imprudently failed to look left or right when returning to the roadway.

"A curse on ye, spawn of shaitan!" the beggar cried furiously, leaping out of the way in the nick of time. He was blind in one eye and covered with sores, and though the fault had not been hers, Eden drew rein long enough to toss him a handful of coins.

"Take care the loose-wallahs do not rob thee, old man," she called after him, and urged her mount through the gate and out into the black tangle of the Kudsia Bagh.

Scooping up the coins, the beggar looked nervously over his shoulder and took to his heels as he saw that someone, indeed, was lurking in the shadows behind him. It was a tall Hindu who could easily have overpowered his less fortunate brother had he chosen to do so. Much to the beggar's relief, however, he seemed to have no interest at all in the coins that had been flung onto the street. He seemed not to have been aware of them at all, in fact, for he was staring after the vanished horseman with a disbelieving expression on his face.

Turning heel himself, the Hindu hurried back in the direction of the Grand Mosque and, asking questions of the beggars seated in the narrow doorways and along the marble steps, was eventually directed to the rug of the brass hawker Mohammed Hadji. Though the fat Afridi was not particularly willing to reveal his confidences to a Hindu, a liberal greasing of his palm removed whatever reservations he might have felt, and he spoke freely to his visitor of what the boy Choto Bai had requested of him.

"He has been most anxious to discover the names of all the *pultons*, the regiments, that took part in the siege of Meerut on the first night of the glorious rebellion. I referred at once to my cousin, who lives in Meerut City, and was told that there were two *Angrezi* pultons under command of Colonel Carmik-al-Ismeet (Carmichael-Smyth) lodged in the garrison and native *rissalas* of the Third Light Cavalry and the Twentieth and Eleventh Native infantries. But this, it would seem, the boy already knew."

"Then why did he come to you?"

Mohammed Hadji shrugged. "He claims there was another *pulton*, or at least an *Angrezi* officer of unknown origin, present in Meerut that night, and he would wish to know his name. My cousin," Mohammed Hadji explained importantly, "is a *daffadar* of unquestionable standing in the Meerut garrison. Regrettably he has been unable to learn the answer, as it is difficult to make inquiries about the *gora*-log without appearing indiscreet."

"But why would the boy wish to know these things?" the Hindu persisted.

"I am not at liberty to say," Mohammed Hadji remarked guardedly.

Another coin was extended, and he pocketed it readily. "It is a sad story indeed," he pronounced promptly, shaking his head. "The boy tells me his mother was killed in the massacre by this particular *Angrezi*, and that he wishes for a reckoning. I have not the heart to tell him that it will do him little good even if the man is found. There has been no justice in Hind since the sahib-log have been making the laws."

"That is indeed the truth," the Hindu agreed. For a moment he remained seated in thoughtful silence, then came to his feet and gave the Afridi another coin for good measure, although he knew full well there was little sense in attempting to buy the Muslim's silence. Mohammed Hadji would waste no time in informing Eden Hamilton of his encounter with this decidedly inquisitive Hindu the very next time they met.

Without another word he hurried away into the darkness, aware that he must act quickly in order to avert what he sensed would be disastrous trouble.

The gods protect me! he thought, knowing it was probably too late, and then groaned aloud as a new thought struck him. *Hai mai!* The Burra-sahib will be furious when he hears of this!

Chapter Seven

The duke of Roxbury, travel weary and covered with the grime of two hundred miles of hot, dusty road, reined in his mount in the darkened garden of a white-roofed house not far from the Kashmir gate. A wine-colored moon hung in the sky and poured its pale light onto the lawn and the flower beds that flanked the soaring stucco walls of the house. Fruit bats whirred overhead, and the night beat of the ancient city of Delhi throbbed through the still, hot air: the beating of drums, the barking of pi dogs, and the incessant whining of insects. From the opened windows of the house opposite came the sound of high, feminine laughter, and in the garden the *chowkidar* muttered unintelligibly to himself and scratched distractedly at his private parts.

Hugh's boots echoed hollowly on the verandah boards, and the wide front door opened to admit him.

"Good evening, Huzoor," said the *khidmatgar*, bowing deeply.

"Good evening, Hira Singh. Is thy master at home?"

"*Nahin*, Huzoor. He has gone to the house of Meade-sahib to dine. Would the Huzoor care for refreshment?"

"I'll help myself to a brandy in the study, thank you. Tell Baga Lal I'm here, and have a bath drawn up, if you would."

Apparently Baga Lal had already been apprised of the duke's arrival, for he was waiting in the study, bowing deferentially and inquiring if the Hazrat-sahib had had a pleasant journey.

"You know damned well I didn't," Hugh growled, pouring himself a brandy from Henry Pascal's elegant sideboard. "Nahdeem met me in Allahabad with your message, and since then I've been riding like the devil possessed to get here." He grimaced and tipped down a healthy swallow of the fiery liquid. "Doubtless I've set a new record for the distance from Calcutta to Delhi! Now, what is it that prompted you to send me such urgent summons?" Seating himself in the chair behind the desk, he crossed his dusty boots before him and regarded his bearer with a cynical eye.

"It is the miss-sahib," Baga Lal began at once, and the words tumbled out of him as the duke's expression darkened in response. "Fortunately Porter-sahib knows nothing of her undertakings," he concluded, "and she has not been back to the bazaar but once since then. Still, I have heard from the servants that she has indeed left the house several times while the colonel-sahib and his women were away, and Hila Deem vows he saw her returning to the cantonment one night dressed as the boy Choto Bai."

There was a moment of silence while Hugh absently swirled the contents of his glass. "Why the devil did Porter leave her home alone to begin with?" he demanded at last.

"It would seem the memsahib did not wish her to visit other mem-log without proper *Angrezi* clothes. The unworn dresses of the eldest daughter were to have been prepared for her, and perhaps they are finished at last, for she has accompanied them tonight to Meade-sahib's to dine."

"Has she now?" Hugh inquired unpleasantly. "I suppose I'll have to make an appearance there myself to see what she's been up to—" He broke off and stared irritably into his glass. "What the devil can she have meant, telling that fat Mohammedan in the bazaar that her Indian mother was killed by British?"

"It is a puzzlement to me, Huzoor."

"No matter, I'll find out soon enough." Setting aside his glass, Hugh rose to his feet with a sigh. "I suppose I'd better have a bath and a shave first, otherwise I'll give poor Lady Meade a fit of the vapors." He grinned abruptly and slapped his bearer on the back. "Thou art a worthless dog, Baga Lal! I could flay thee for making the situation seem so dire when it is only the miss-sahib causing her usual trouble."

"Then thou art not angry with her?" Baga Lal inquired with considerable surprise. "I had thought she gave her word not to cause the colonel-sahib undue sorrow."

"To her way of thinking, she probably hasn't. The colonel knows nothing of her nightly exploits, after all, does he?" And without another word Hugh started up the stairs, whistling tunelessly to himself and unbuttoning his sweat-stained shirt as he went.

The two-storied stucco house inhabited by Henry Pascal and his Portuguese wife, who was currently away visiting friends in Simla, had withstood the siege of Delhi remarkably intact. Unlike Hugh's bungalow, it had not been looted and later leveled to the ground by a badly aimed artillery volley from the beleaguered Delhi magazine. Hugh, who had left for England fully a year before the uprising, had not been able to return until well after Campbell's vengeful Highlanders had recaptured the city from the last, desperate sepoys and marched in a terrible path of death and destruction onward through Lucknow.

What he had seen upon his return, however, had shaken Hugh to the soul. Gordon & Blair, his highly successful import firm, was gone, the building razed by mutinous sowars, and the Indian factory workers who had remained faithful to him (and there had been many) had been brutally murdered at their work stations. All of his servants were dead, his fortune dwindled to nothing, and the only comfort Hugh could derive from his loss was the fact that Baga Lal, shunning the teachings of the religion that forbade him to travel across the vast expanse of "black water," had accompanied him on that particular trip to England and thus been spared a similar fate. Baga Lal had served him faithfully these great many years, and Hugh did not know what he would have done had he lost him.

Freshly bathed and shaved, he shrugged into a coat of unrelieved black worsted that Baga Lal held out for him. It occurred to him in thinking of the past that he would eventually have to make the decision whether or not to build himself a new house here in Delhi. He couldn't go

on accepting Pascal's generosity indefinitely, despite the
fact that the stucco house was sufficiently large to prevent
him from disturbing Pascal and his wife whenever he was
in residence. Still, he hadn't entirely made up his mind
whether or not he cared to rebuild what the rebellion had
destroyed or go on living this divided life between two
continents. Furthermore, his holdings in England were re-
quiring more of his attention with every passing year, and
he wasn't certain how much longer he could neglect them
this way.

"The hell with it," Hugh muttered, scandalizing his
bearer by brushing past him without accepting the proffered gloves and hat. At the moment he had other dilem-
mas to occupy him, the most pressing of which was what
to do with the ever-difficult Miss Hamilton.

"Will the Hazrat-sahib require a carriage?" the *khidmatgar* inquired politely as he met the duke at the foot
of the stairs.

"Thank you, no, Hira Singh. I believe I'll walk."

His destination, after all, was not far: an impressive
Indian structure of countless towers and twisting turrets
known as the *Moti Mahal*, the Pearl Palace, which was
situated amid a cluster of towering royal palms not far
from St. James's Church. Here, before the days of the
mutiny, a Delhi nobleman claiming blood relation to Wa-
jid Ali Shah, the last king of Oudh, had kept a colorful
and intrigue-ridden court, all of it sadly gone since the
British had effectively crushed the rebellion. It was owned
now by a wealthy nabob who resided in England and who
had appointed a distant cousin to occupy the house and
discharge his daily affairs.

Sir Percy Meade was an overweight and vigorously
ambitious mercantile trader, a *box-wallah*, as the natives
called him, who found immense pleasure in entertaining
the notables of his day. On any given occasion one might
find at least a dozen wealthy Delhi merchants mingling
with Indian guests of noble blood—all of them male—beneath the glittering Belgian crystal chandeliers in the ballroom of his palace. Their numbers were always matched
by an equal compliment of British army officers bristling
with medals and decorations, and the high members of

the councils and political departments of Delhi government.

Despite the fact that Hugh possessed no invitation, he was readily admitted by the bowing head *chuprassi* and intercepted in the glittering foyer by Sir Percy himself.

"Back from Calcutta already, Your Grace? Splendid, splendid! Missed supper, I'm afraid, but there's plenty of libation and ladies eager for dancin', b'gad!"

Hugh's lips twitched mockingly as he noticed the mottled splotches of color on Sir Percy's fleshy face. Meade was a man who liked to drink and did so to excess. Even the forceful Lady Meade, who by now had spotted their guest and was bearing down on him with an eager smile, had been unable over the years to convince her husband of the imprudence of his habits.

"It's so good of you to come, Your Grace," she twittered gaily, unable to believe her good fortune. "Sophia and Rose will be simply *delighted!* We weren't even aware that you were back in India until Henry Pascal told us. Dear me," she added fretfully, scanning the crowded ballroom for a sign of her daughters, "I don't know *where* the girls might be."

"I'll be certain to pay my respects the moment I see them," Hugh assured her, and extricated himself as politely as possible from the gloved hand clutching his sleeve. The last thing he desired at the moment was to be cornered by Lady Meade's ever-so-eligible daughters.

"Hugh!" Another hand had reached out to grip his arm. "You're back, are you? How was Calcutta?"

"Dull as ever," Hugh responded, his smile deepening as Lady Meade's disapproving face was lost behind the broad, satin-encased shoulders of Henry Pascal. "The past six weeks have seemed like an eternity, I can assure you."

"Come on, then, and tell me about it. They're playing whist in the billiard room, but Meade won't mind if we use his study. Eh, excuse me, Lady Meade."

"You've no finesse at all," Hugh observed mildly, accompanying the other man up the short flight of steps from the entrance hall, but the laugh lines about his eyes and mouth remained.

"It's obvious your presence here has sent her into wild ecstasies, old boy," Pascal responded. "I'll wager she's willing to forgive me any faux pas simply because my being here has lured you into her house."

"You overestimate my popularity, Henry."

"Do you think so? I assure you that even my dubious esteem has been unquestionably raised in the eyes of every mama present this evening simply because you're here." Pascal gave a mock grimace of distaste. "You won't believe how much they mourned your departure for England the last time you left."

"I'm not certain I'd care to hear about it," Hugh said sardonically.

"Oh, by the way," Pascal added as an afterthought, shouldering his way through the crush of dowagers, sub-alterns, and young girls in rustling crinolines who were clustered about the periphery of the dance floor, "you'll be interested to know that your little butterfly is here to-night."

Hugh's brows rose. "My what?"

"The unmanageable little barbarian you brought back from Mayar, as you yourself chose to describe her." Pascal's whiskers twitched. "Though I've since come to the conclusion that you were either addled to say as much or that she has undergone a remarkable metamorphosis during your absence. Ah, there she is." He gestured in an offhand manner toward a glittering wall of mirrors where a number of chairs had been set up for the pleasure of those guests who did not care to dance.

Hugh could see nothing save a cluster of young men surrounding what appeared to be a slim, lovely girl in a white ballgown. She was smiling up at one of them with apparent amusement, and as she tilted back her head to laugh, the glow of the candles caught the richness of her carefully netted hair and set it ablaze.

"Good God!" said the duke, halting in his tracks. It had never occurred to him that Eden Hamilton might be blond—though the word was woefully inadequate to de-scribe the mass of shining hair confined in its proper chignon. He was reminded absurdly of wheat ripening on endless, sun-drenched acres, and Henry Pascal, hearing him mutter something to that effect, turned toward him with a look of surprise.

"You mean to say that you spent nearly a fortnight in her company and never even discovered the color of her hair?"

"Miss Hamilton was forever availed of a heavy pug-gari or hiding modestly beneath a *dupatta* and sari," Hugh replied, frowning. He had always admitted openly that Eden Hamilton was graced with unusual beauty, yet he never would have suspected that she could look so damned—*disturbing* in an unadorned white ball gown edged with absurd ruffles that billowed over maidenly crinolines. Her throat and shoulders were bare, the skin a golden brown, and from what he could see of her nipped-in waist through the circle of her admirers, it was small enough to be spanned with the breadth of his hands. Which, he suddenly remembered with uncharacteristic annoyance, was exactly what had happened when he had taken her into his arms and kissed her that long-ago night on the plains of Rajputana, finding himself caught up in an emotion he did not care to experience again.

A bright note of music spiraled through the high-ceilinged room, and the duke watched with narrowed eyes as Eden Hamilton was whirled away in the arms of a beaming young officer.

"Aye, she's a fetching piece," he remarked in a bored drawl, "and I'm not surprised the lot of 'em are panting after her."

Pascal's brows drew together. "You do her a grave injustice, I think."

"What's this, Henry? You've not developed an interest in the girl yourself?"

"Of course not! I've had the opportunity to speak to her a time or two, however, and I don't think she's quite the shameless baggage you've described."

Hugh might have agreed with him had the things Baga Lal told him earlier not sprung unexpectedly to mind. "Believe what you will, Henry," he said dryly. "I, for one, know better."

"Suit yourself," Pascal countered with a shrug, and followed him into Sir Percy's study.

* * *

When the dance ended several minutes later, Eden excused herself from her partner and sought out an empty chair at Mrs. Porter's side. Flounces spilled from the slim waist of her white brocade ball dress, and her wide skirts rustled as she leaned forward to accept a drink from a passing bearer.

"Are you enjoying yourself, dear?" Clarissa Porter inquired anxiously, aware of the girl's breathlessness and faintly flushed cheeks. This was Eden's first official appearance in Delhi society, and she had been fretting all evening over the possibility that something could go dreadfully wrong. To her relief, dear Eden had comported herself from the beginning as though accustomed to these functions, and it had further pleased Clarissa to notice that the child had not been lacking for partners since the dancing began. Naturally she would have liked to see just as many eligible young men clustering about Allegra and Alva, but then again Miss Hamilton was something of a novelty tonight, and wasn't it kind of all these young gentlemen to strive to put her at ease?

"I'm enjoying myself very much, thank you," Eden responded, and was rather surprised to realize that she was speaking the truth. She had not been looking forward particularly to attending this soirée, but until now none of the doubts that had been troubling her had proven in the least bit justified. No one, not even the most curious of gossiping matrons, had addressed her with a single question about her past, and all of the gentlemen who had danced with her thus far had declared with utmost sincerity that it had been quite unfair of the Porters to have hidden her away for so long. And if any of them suspected that she was wearing one of Allegra Porter's discarded ball gowns, not one of them had been ungallant enough to mention it.

"I cannot believe how well you've taken to dancing," Mrs. Porter added approvingly, "especially when one considers that you've never received formal instruction."

"It was far easier than I expected," Eden said with a laugh, remembering the tedious hours she and Isabel had spent in the music room of Colonel Carmichael-Smyth's bungalow under the strict eyes of their tutor, Mrs. Percival.

"Why, I do believe they're starting a waltz," Mrs. Porter observed, hearing the musicians strike up another tune. "I certainly hope Allegra hasn't accepted that Lieutenant Lawrence again! She's already danced with him three times, and convention won't allow— Why, isn't this delightful?" Mrs. Porter sighed dreamily, spotting her eldest daughter on the floor with a very eligible officer of Bengal Infantry. "Isn't that Major Robert Metcalfe? I understand he's extremely well heeled and currently unspoken for. I wonder if he's danced with Allegra before? Did you happen to notice, dear?"

But Eden was unable to reply, for she suddenly found herself surrounded by a group of hopeful young men begging for the honor of the dance. Unable to choose between them, she could only laugh and shake her head, saying that she was far too hot and tired, and would they think ill of her if she chose instead to escape to the cool of the terrace? There followed a moment's confusion as they vied for the honor of escorting her, yet Eden confounded them all by gathering up the train of her skirts and slipping away unnoticed in the midst of their arguing.

A sigh of relief fell from her lips as the noise and heat of the crowded ballroom gave way to the stillness of the warm, close night. Through a break in the shrubbery Eden could see the wide, white sandbanks of the Jumna River and hear the murmur of the current dragging at the bottom of the sloping lawn. In the distance the howling of a hunting jackal pack blended with the beating of tom-toms and lent their voices to the night sounds of India that Eden had known and loved since birth. Breathing deeply of the slight breeze with its myriad smells of the city, the inevitable sewage and the river, she wandered away from the squares of light falling from the windows behind her.

Unaccustomed as yet to the wide hoops that supported her crinolines, Eden bumped hard against the balustrade a full four feet before she reached it, and she gave a small gasp of annoyance as the whalebone stays dug sharply into her rib cage.

"I take that to mean you are not particularly happy to
see me, Miss Hamilton.''

Eden whirled and gaped in dismay at the tall man who
moved out of the shadows toward her. So he was back,
was he! She had never seen the duke of Roxbury attired
totally in black, and for some reason it served to heighten
the somewhat satanic cast of his sharply chiseled features.
There was nothing unfamiliar about the mocking arrogance in his pale blue eyes, however, and Eden bristled
with sudden annoyance.

"I wasn't even aware that you were back in Delhi,
Your Grace.''

"Apparently not," he agreed, having seen the look that
had crossed her unguarded face at the sight of him. Unaccountably annoyed himself, he said rather harshly: "I
thought it advisable to return as quickly as possible after
learning from Baga Lal the extent of your unacceptable
behavior.''

Eden retreated a step so that her petticoats were crushed
against the railing behind her. Though her first instinct
was to feign utter ignorance, she knew better than that,
and knew, too, that somehow he was fully apprised of
her nightly forays to see Mohammed Hadji. Lifting her
chin, she inquired haughtily: "Since when have I become
answerable to you, sir?''

Hugh regarded her for a moment in thoughtful silence,
his mouth not quite under control. It was in his mind to
rebuke her harshly or at the very least point out that he
was in fact completely responsible for her good behavior
as long as she remained in Frederick Porter's care. Instead he found himself saying, and in a tone that was far
more charitable than he would have liked: "Will you not
tell me what it is you seek in Meerut? Perhaps I can
help.''

Eden's eyes widened, and a pulse began to beat rapidly
in her throat as an inexplicable longing to seek his confidence shook her to the soul. In the next moment, however, bright anger blazed defensively in her eyes.

"No," she said coldly. "My business in Meerut need
not concern you—or anyone.''

It seemed to Hugh that she had withdrawn behind some invisible wall, as impenetrable as the *purdah* screens that had hidden her from view in the *chitra shala* of Malraj's palace.

"If you'll excuse me, Your Grace?"

Hugh watched wordlessly as she walked away from him, the heavy chignon adding a touching dignity to her youthful features. He expected her to return to the ballroom, but instead she sought out a shadowed bench on the far side of the terrace, the stiff carriage of her back indicating to him more loudly than words that she wished to be left alone. And he would have gone and left her there had Eden not forgotten that great care must be taken in sitting down properly when wearing a hooped skirt and crinolines. There was a muffled gasp, and Hugh's eyes widened incredulously as he saw Miss Hamilton disappear amid a frothing mountain of lace while the offending hoop whipped up to smack her ignobly in the forehead.

Hurrying forward to offer his assistance, he halted instead in his tracks and burst into laughter. Eden, struggling to subdue the foaming petticoats that billowed about her ears, was at first too indignant to even speak. After a moment, however, she, too, began to laugh, the sound mingling pleasantly with his.

"I confess I've not quite mastered these ridiculous things," Eden said at last. "I wasn't out of pinafores and pantalettes when I arrived in Mayar, you see, and of course it was far more appropriate to wear Eastern attire there."

By now she had managed to tuck the wide skirts about her in a ladylike fashion. Hugh seated himself beside her, and Eden cast him a swift glance from beneath her lashes. She saw that his body was relaxed and that nothing seemed to be troubling his conscience save the contemplation of Lady Meade's pleasantly overgrown garden. It astonished her that she felt not the least bit embarrassed to be sitting here beside him, her bare shoulder just brushing his arm, when by rights his nearness had always aroused some sort of resentment within her. Honestly considered, he had never really given her just cause to dislike him—unless one counted that unforgivable episode when he had kissed her on the plains and later refused to permit her to ride to Rawalpindi with Captain Molson and his men.

Eden stiffened at the thought. It was unfortunate that she had chosen to remember that particular episode now, what with the duke sitting beside her and the pale moon illuminating the sensual mouth that had drawn such a drugging response from hers. Something shivered through her as she remembered the touch of those hard, warm lips. It was almost as if her body seemed to betray her at the memory, and Eden strove frantically to still the rapid rise and fall of her breasts as her breathing quickened. She could feel her nipples hardening against her tight, scooped bodice, and suddenly she gave an angry exclamation and leaped to her feet.

"I believe I'll go back inside," she said coldly, hating herself for sounding so breathless. "The Porters will be wondering what's happened to me."

"It certainly isn't wise for you to be seen on the terrace with a man of my reputation," Hugh agreed, voicing her own condemning thoughts.

Eden saw the flash of his white teeth against the darkness of the night, and with a jerk of her elegantly coiffed head she turned away. Without warning a hand clamped down on her wrist to detain her, and though the fingers bit painfully into her flesh, she whirled to face him with open defiance. The expression on his face, however, was such that she could feel her breath catch in her throat, and a primitive tingle of fear fled down her spine.

"I warn you, Miss Hamilton," Hugh said softly, and he was no longer smiling, "that I intend to find out what you've been plotting here in Delhi during my absence. I'm certainly not about to permit you to run wild through the streets of a civilized city as though it were some feudal kingdom like Mayar. Different rules apply here, and I intend to see you abide by them."

"As I am not in the least bit answerable to you, I cannot see how you can possibly make me," Eden said frigidly, and detached herself calmly from his grasp. "If you'll excuse me, Your Grace?"

Hugh sat there for some time without moving after the rustling of her flounces had faded, and there was an untoward gleam in his pale eyes. Damn her! he thought, but not with annoyance at her haughty words. He was remembering instead the undercurrent of passion that had flowed tangibly between them as they sat together on the darkened bench. Lifting his eyes to the vast, star-hung sky, he cursed irritably and asked himself what in hell he had ever done to deserve Eden Hamilton in his life.

In the ballroom, meanwhile, a very agitated Mrs. Porter was pacing to and fro between the potted palms, her taffeta skirts rustling in time with her quick, fretful breathing. Whatever had become of Eden? How *could* the girl run off like this just moments before the duke of Roxbury made an unexpected appearance? Supposing she had gone out onto the terrace in the company of one of those dissolute young men who had dogged her heels all evening? Mrs. Porter shuddered to think what His Grace would say to such gross negligence on her part!

"Oh, my dear, thank goodness you've come back!" she exclaimed as Eden appeared before her, thankfully quite alone. Her fan fluttered in agitation. "You'll never guess who has just arrived!"

"If you mean His Grace, the duke of Roxbury, I've already seen him," Eden informed her. And thinking of him, she was unable to prevent herself uttering a terse invective in Rajasthani, one that fortunately was not understood by Mrs. Porter, though it caused a passing bearer of unquestionable Rajput origin to draw up sharply, nearly upsetting the contents of his tray.

"I'm certain he'll be anxious to hear how you've been getting on," Mrs. Porter added brightly. "Oh, Frederick, there you are! I understand His Grace has·returned! Isn't it marvelous?"

"I've already heard, m'dear," said the colonel as he joined them. "The whole drawing room's abuzz with it, though I'll be hanged if I know what brought him back from Calcutta so soon!"

"I do hope he asks Allegra to dance," Mrs. Porter confided with a nervous flutter, for her delight in the duke's unexpected return was fueled in part by pure maternal interest. "She was barely more than a child when he left India the last time, you'll recall, but now . . ." Her dreamy expression gave way to one of startled vexation as her eyes found her daughter engaged in private conversation with Lieutenant William Lawrence beneath a long, gilded mirror.

"Oh!" she gasped. "Frederick! Do put a stop to that at once!"

"Egad, woman!" the colonel protested, following her gaze. "I'll not make a scene simply because you've set your sights on another husband for the girl! Damned unacceptable choice, too, I might add," he stated baldly while Mrs. Porter gasped and declared herself on the verge of swooning. "Well, it's true, b'gad! Roxbury's not the right man for any daughter of mine!"

"I thought you held His Grace in the highest esteem," Mrs. Porter quavered indignantly.

The colonel's face reddened. "Of course I do! But Allegra needs a calm and quite devoted fellow for a husband, like young Lawrence there. She'd never withstand the rigors of marriage to Roxbury. No woman could, b'gad!"

Mrs. Porter stared at her husband as though he had sprouted horns. "Well, I never!" she gasped at last. "I thought you'd be delighted if Allegra were to become the duchess of Roxbury!"

Colonel Porter looked decidedly uncomfortable. "Perhaps we'd better discuss this privately, m'dear."

"Yes, indeed," his wife agreed stiffly, "though I promise you, Frederick, that *should* His Grace ask for Allegra's hand, I'll not think twice about accepting!"

To Mrs. Porter's bitter disappointment, the duke, with his usual propensity toward rudeness, chose to spend the remainder of the evening in conversation with several Indian guests and did not deign to dance once with Allegra. She was quick to mollify herself, however, with the knowledge that His Grace didn't dance with anyone else.

Eden, who had herself declined to dance with anyone after her return to the ballroom, was markedly silent on the drive back to the bungalow. Professing a headache, she begged to be excused as soon as the carriage drew to a halt before the door, and such was the extent of Mrs. Porter's own preoccupation that she let the girl go with only the briefest of good-nights.

Siva, the serving girl who acted as Eden's personal maid, was waiting for her in the lamplit bedroom. Though normally the two of them laughed together as Siva readied her mistress for bed, Eden spoke very little and dismissed the girl as soon as the magnificent ball gown had been unhooked and hung away. Lifting the *chik* blinds, she stood for a moment before the window, staring out into the hot, humid night. Though other girls would doubtless have been dreaming about the dashing officers with whom they had danced that night, Eden gave no further thought to the evening's glittering entertainment save for one glaring exception: the duke of Roxbury and his infuriating arrogance.

A surge of resentment swept through her as she thought of him. How dare he take it upon himself to tell her what she could or could not do? Her affairs were her own, after all, and her business in Meerut a private matter that need not concern him in the least. She was not, as she had tartly informed him earlier, in the least answerable to him, and to prove her point she ought to ride to Meerut herself to seek the information the bazaar monger Mohammed Hadji had as yet been unable to find.

A determined light began to burn in Eden's eyes. Yes, she would ride to Meerut tomorrow, and if Hugh Gordon happened to hear of it and dared to object, she would simply tell him exactly what she thought of his overbearing, meddlesome manner.

Eden unplaited her hair and wondered how best to obtain a horse from Colonel Porter's stable without encountering too many questions. Perhaps she would simply wait until he had ridden out to the lines and Mrs. Porter and her daughters had left to visit the Hobsons, as they did every Thursday morning. It seemed likely that none of them would object to her wishes to spend the day alone, and with that thought in mind Eden slipped into bed and fell at once into an untroubled sleep.

Chapter Eight

"Here you go, miss. Mind the step. The boards are somewhat uneven."

Once out on the verandah of the orderly room, where the barracks of the British infantry lines shimmered on the far side of the sun-baked parade grounds, the young officer who had escorted Eden outside paused to mop his brow and comment apologetically on the ferocious heat.

"I'm sorry you didn't find what you came for," he added, motioning a waiting subaltern to lead her horse around to the steps. "There aren't many left here in Meerut who remember the massacre. Most of them were assigned to other regiments years ago or sent home to England."

"I understand," Eden said politely, "and I'm grateful for your assistance. Please give my thanks once again to Major Morriston."

"Of course, Miss Hamilton, I'd be delighted." The orderly frowned of a sudden, looking down at the solitary horse that stood waiting below. "Why, what's happened to your syce?"

Eden smiled up at him. "I came alone."

"All the way from Delhi? But surely you must realize— What about the natives? Weren't you afraid they might—eh—"

"My dear sir," Eden said crisply, "I have never been in the least afraid of natives, and as for _dacoits_ or any other unscrupulous characters who might have crossed my path—" She broke off and gestured meaningfully to her saddle pack, where a rifled Enfield musket was thrust with military readiness into a well-oiled scabbard. Lifting aside

124

her skirts, she mounted without assistance, and the expression on her face was such that there was no need to make clear the fact that she would not have hesitated to use the weapon had the need arisen.

"My God," remarked the orderly as he watched her trot away through the glaring sunshine. "I do believe there's something entirely uncanny about Celtic women. They may be as beautiful as the houris of Paradise, but they've the hearts and minds of preying tigers."

"And the tempers to match," agreed the subaltern, whose Irish mother had always worn a similar expression of haughty defiance and had never, in his memory, ridden anywhere with proper escort.

Oddly enough, Eden would probably have agreed with them on the score of her misbehavior had she been able to discern their thoughts. At present she was feeling keenly the disappointment of her fruitless search for the British officer who had murdered Sitka and made off with her family's jewels and wishing that she had indeed brought along someone to act as her escort. She could not remember when she had ever felt quite this discouraged and alone, and it would have been soothing to have someone to confide in, even gruff old Colonel Porter.

How could I have been so naive as to believe a visit to Meerut would solve all my problems? Eden wondered with despair. After all, Major Morriston had made it clear that none but resident troops had been engaged in the actual fighting in Meerut and that, to the best of his knowledge, no other regiments stationed anywhere within the vicinity had been dispatched to lend aid.

Naturally this was exactly the news Eden had been dreading, for it merely confirmed her suspicions that the man she sought had arrived in Meerut alone with the express intent of stealing her uncle's jewels. How he had managed to discover their existence was a further distressing mystery. Perhaps Isabel had inadvertently revealed their whereabouts when she had brought them to Lucknow for safekeeping, and the unscrupulous officer who had stolen them had needed only the confusion generated by the uprising to commit his crime. Equally nagging was the question of how he had known exactly where in Colonel Carmichael-Smyth's study to look for them.

I suppose I'll never discover the answer to that, Eden thought, and even if I do, how on earth shall I recover them?

She was not so foolish as to imagine that he had kept the gems in his possession after all this time, and even if he had and she did manage to find him, how could she possibly prove that they had once been Hamilton possessions?

It's a fool's dream, that, Eden told herself angrily, and was annoyed at the tears that unexpectedly prickled her eyes. Better to forget she had ever seen those seductively glittering jewels, and better, too, to ride quickly for Delhi before anyone there learned of the utter foolishness of her quest. She would simply have to forget about the vast fortune that would have been—so she felt convinced—hers and Isabel's inheritance, and find another way of stopping Colonel Porter and the duke of Roxbury from sending her away from India.

Setting her horse trotting across the *maidan,* Eden glanced inadvertently in the direction of the mall, and her heart seemed to contract as she caught sight of the neat, familiar roofs of the British bungalows visible beyond a dense grove of trees. Though she had promised herself that she would not drag up old, painful memories by riding past them, she found she could not prevent herself from tugging at the off-side rein and sending her mount clattering across the bridge. A moment later she was riding past the tidy flower beds and hedgerows that separated the bungalows from the infantry lines.

The rambling dwelling that had been Colonel Carmichael-Smyth's had been entirely rebuilt, and a newly painted fence ran along the length of the neatly tended lawn. A wooden swing hung from the verandah on the same spot where fat, loyal Mumfaisal had died, and a pair of giggling children were being pushed back and forth by a patient, smiling *ayah.*

Hot tears rose unexpectedly to Eden's eyes, blinding her so that at first she did not recognize, or even notice, the tall man on horseback who halted suddenly beside her and demanded to know what the devil she was doing there. Startled, Eden turned to him, scrubbing furiously at her eyes, never realizing the effect that unconscious, childish gesture had upon him.

"Your Grace!" she breathed in disbelief as his dark, familiar face swam into focus, and all at once it seemed as if the vast, hazy sky and the dun-colored ground began to dance and blur before her eyes.

"Dammit," she heard him say from a great distance, "that's what you get for riding out in such heat."

Dismounting swiftly, he lifted Eden from the saddle, and though she protested, she could not prevent herself from leaning against his arm as he set her down upon the still swaying ground.

"Serves you right, you bloody little idiot," he said unkindly, and the unjustified insult sufficiently infuriated her to bring about a swift recovery of her bearings. Shaking herself free of his hold, she stepped away from him, dashing away the last of her tears with the sleeve of her habit. She was too proud, and perhaps a bit too embarrassed, to explain that it was not the heat but the onrush of painful memories that had precipitated that momentary dizziness.

Carefully shaking out her dusty skirts, Eden turned at last to face the duke, and though her chin had risen to its customary angle, her gaze inadvertently faltered as it met his. There was no mistaking the anger that smoldered within him. Steeling herself for the blistering dressing-down she sensed was forthcoming, Eden was startled when Hugh merely stared at her for a pensive moment before turning back to his horse. Taking down his water flask, he stood watching in silence as Eden lifted it to her lips.

"Now, then," he resumed when she had drunk her fill, "why don't you tell me what the devil you're doing here in Meerut?"

"I could ask the same of you."

Hugh's lips twitched, though there was nothing the least amused in the expression on his face. "I see you've recovered your wits remarkably fast."

"That's because I'm certain you're already well apprised of my reasons for being here," Eden said coolly. "Doubtless Major Morriston was more than happy to enlighten you as to the nature of our conversation."

Hugh's lips tightened. "My dear Miss Hamilton, it's far too hot for verbal sparring. May I suggest that I accompany you back to Delhi and that we continue our discussion at a more opportune time?"

Eden glanced up at him suspiciously but was unable to peer beyond the bland mask of his deeply tanned face. Though she was convinced that he had come to Meerut because of her, she was far too hot and disappointed to harbor any resentment toward him. Nodding her head to show her agreement, she allowed him to help her mount, and neither of them spoke as their horses trotted down the dusty lane that brought them eventually to the Grand Trunk Road and the burning plains that separated Meerut from Delhi.

"This is where I was riding that first morning when I saw the fires," Eden said unexpectedly, turning in the saddle to look at the domed rooftops and whitewashed walls of the cantonment behind her. "I thought it was the sun coming up. It never occurred to me that the bungalows might be burning." Her voice had dropped to a whisper at the memory, and Hugh, glancing down at her, was aware of an unexpected stab of pity.

"Mumtaz knew, of course," Eden continued softly. "Animals are always so much more perceptive than humans, aren't they?"

"Mumtaz?"

A wistful smile curved Eden's mouth. "My mare. I left her tethered in the scrubs that morning. Awal Bannu came to look for her afterward, but she was gone. We were never able to discover what happened to her."

"I'm certain whoever took her treated her kindly. Even mutineering sowars appreciate the value of good horseflesh."

Eden looked up, startled, and though there was nothing in his impassive expression to suggest that the duke had intended to be kind, his words inadvertently served to break the tension between them and send it ebbing away.

In oddly companionable silence they turned down the long trunk road leading toward Delhi.

It was a journey of less than thirty miles, yet as the sun climbed inexorably toward its zenith, the heat of the afternoon settled relentlessly upon them. Birds sat listless in the thorn scrubs with their beaks agape. Indian peasants and farmers traveling the Grand Trunk Road drew their bullock carts one by one off the roadway and crawled beneath them to sleep. Cattle that had been turned out from nearby farms to forage had long since ceased their grazing and lay motionless beneath the inadequate shade of sparsely scattered trees. Even the stones and the ruts of the roadway seemed to give off the terrible heat, and the pair of horses carrying Eden and the duke soon slowed to a plodding walk, their heads hanging.

Though he was wearing a thin shirt with the sleeves turned up at the elbows, Hugh could feel the sweat trickling uncomfortably between his shoulder blades. He was bareheaded, having ridden away from Delhi in sufficient haste to forget that simplest yet most vital of precautions against the scorching Asian sun—his pith helmet.

Glancing briefly at Eden, Hugh saw the weary droop of her head and the dampness of the upswept curls at her brow. She was wearing a pale blue habit that, though its color suited her and displayed the slender figure of its wearer most admirably, was far more appropriate for a brisk gallop through the Northwest Frontier than a sweltering trek to Delhi.

"I'm afraid, Miss Hamilton," he remarked abruptly, drawing rein, "that we will have to seek refuge in the shade until the heat abates." Anticipating a tiresome argument, he added curtly, "Unless you wish to court heatstroke by riding all the way to Delhi now?"

Eden glanced ahead to the shimmering length of uneven plain and the distant ridge behind which lay the minarets of Delhi, hidden in the haze. "No," she said at once, and without the protests and demurring another woman might have made. She was hot and unbelievably tired, and though she had had every intention of returning to the Porters' bungalow in time for tea, she no longer

cared if her absence caused them undue alarm. Surely His
Grace could explain the situation upon their return?

Hugh seemed to have the same thought in mind, for he
led them wordlessly into a grove of trees some twenty
paces off the roadway. Turning the horses loose, he offered Eden the flask, and she drank thirstily before sinking into the soft grass. Removing her derby, she leaned
her head against the trunk of a tree and gratefully closed
her eyes.

"I believe this is the first time I've ever felt quite in
charity with you, Your Grace," she murmured.

Hugh chuckled as he seated himself a short distance
from her. "I can, on occasion, make myself most agreeable, Miss Hamilton."

Eden smiled in response, and the drowsy droning of a
horde of locusts in the tall grass filled the hot stillness.
Then she asked unexpectedly: "Did you manage to accomplish all you'd set out to do in Calcutta?"

"As a matter of fact, I did," Hugh surprised her by
saying. Eden had already discovered that he rarely answered a question unless it suited him to do so; perhaps
the intimacy of sitting companionably beneath the spreading branches of a lone tree had provided the impetus that
prompted him to speak. "I assured both the governor-
general and the council that Malraj, though hotheaded and
inclined toward rash behavior, was not responsible for the
unrest in his kingdom. And since the new British resident
had already taken steps to arrest those men who are, they
were quite content to leave Mayar in peace."

"Oh, I'm so glad!" Eden exclaimed, for she had
thought often of Jaji and the Begum Fariza and all the
others in the palace, hoping that the duke's report to the
Political Department in Calcutta would not precipitate
some sort of harsh action against them. "Then there's
nothing left to keep you here in India, is there? I mean,"
she added hastily, "Colonel Porter told me you own
property in England that requires considerable supervision. Will you be returning there anytime soon?"

Though she had tried to keep the hopeful tone from her
voice, she had apparently not succeeded, and she had the

good grace to blush when Hugh observed blandly that the prospect seemed to please her.

"Actually, I'm considering an offer to join the political service and remain permanently in India," he explained before Eden could speak up in her defense.

Eden's eyes widened. "But—but I thought only officers of the British Crown or the East India Company army were admitted to the service!"

"My dear Miss Hamilton," Hugh informed her with considerable amusement, "I've received so many brevets in the past ten years that I'd probably qualify for any post they cared to offer me. I cannot even remember my present rank, though I wouldn't be surprised if someone chose to address me as 'Colonel' Gordon."

Eden regarded him with open astonishment. "Then why did they put Captain Molson in charge of the escort to Mayar when you clearly outranked him?"

"Because I've never officially accepted any of those commissions. As Baga Lal is fond of complaining, I already possess enough titles to drown a simple man."

He yawned as he spoke, and Eden, glancing wonderingly into his face, could not help but think that this exhibition of amused modesty was not at all in keeping with her previous, uncharitable opinion of him. She ruminated on his words for a time in silence, but after a while the heat and the shrilling of the insects served to make her drowsy. Her eyelids grew heavy, and her chin fell to her breast, and from the quiet, even rhythm of her breathing, Hugh knew that she had fallen asleep.

Turning his head to look at her, he wondered at the conflicting nature of his feelings for this woman. Though she was a tiresome and impossibly stubborn creature, he could not help but like her—a startling revelation since he had never had cause to actually *like* a woman before. Her presence in Mayar had certainly served to ease the boredom of his visit there, and despite the annoyance of dancing attendance upon her as she roamed the city of Delhi disguised as Choto Bai, he had to admit that the diversion she had offered him was lively indeed.

Yet was that all? Studying her youthful profile, Hugh could not deny that there was something infinitely dis-

turbing in the curving mouth that was softened now with
sleep and in the slim, lovely lines of her body that be-
spoke a woman of beauty and passion, albeit a passion as
yet unawakened. Staring at her, Hugh had a sudden and
entirely vivid vision of Eden Hamilton standing before
him with her severe chignon unpinned, the golden curls
spilling to her hips in a silken curtain to caress her bare,
ivory skin.

With an exclamation of annoyance he turned his head
away and deliberately closed his eyes. It would be infinitely wiser, he decided, given the unsettling heat and the
absurd nature of his thoughts, to sleep.

When he awoke, curiously refreshed and impatient to
be off, the shadows of the tree were long on the brittle
grass before him and the sun was descending in a shivering wash of scarlet toward the distant ridge of Delhi.
The creaking of cart wheels, the sound of lively voices,
and an occasional braying of a donkey told him that the
late afternoon traffic was brisk on the Grand Trunk Road,
though he could see little of the roadway through the
cluster of thorn scrubs.

He stirred and spoke briefly to Eden, but there was no
reply. Turning his head, he saw that she was gone, and
for a moment his heart cramped with a dreadful, irrational anger. By God, if she had left him and ridden alone
to Delhi in the appalling heat of the afternoon—if she had
met up with any of the *dacoits* who roved in number upon
the trunk roads looking for likely victims to rob . . .

"I'll break her neck," Hugh vowed through clenched
teeth, yet in the next moment he heard the familiar whinnying of his horse and the answering neigh of the mount
Eden had appropriated from Colonel Porter's stable.
Turning his head, he saw them grazing in the elephant
grass a short distance away. Then, through the thorny *kikars,* he caught sight of a flash of blue muslin: Eden was
bending to wash her face and hands in a nearby spring.
He watched as she lifted her face to the welcoming breeze
shivering across the water, and the slim line of her throat
and breast were revealed against the green and gold of

the swaying reeds. Hugh was conscious of an odd constriction above his heart, and he came slowly to his feet.

Hearing him approach, Eden straightened and turned, and her hands dropped to her sides. They stood looking at one another without speaking, separated by nothing more than a short stretch of grass, and an oddly expectant silence settled over them. Eden was aware of a tightness in her throat and a breathless urgency that seemed to fire the noisy beat of her heart. Unconsciously she began to move toward him, yet in the next moment she froze and gave a cry of alarm, her hands flying to her lips. Following her stare, Hugh went rigid seeing the cold gray coils moving slowly through the grass beneath her feet.

"It's a cobra, Eden. Don't move."

It took him only a moment to retrieve the rifle from his saddle pack, yet during that time the cobra had slowly unwound its deadly length, and Hugh's heart jerked to a halt when he returned to find it hissing and swaying a mere yard from Eden's frozen form.

"Don't move," he murmured hoarsely, flicking off the safety. Fear clogged his throat as he hastened down the sandy banks of the small *jheel* some distance from her, seeking an adequate vantage point for firing. Fortunately his approach through the reeds had distracted the cobra, and when Hugh squatted down in the grass several paces to Eden's right, he saw that it had turned its head and its obscene, flicking tongue toward him—and away from her.

The shot would be easier this way, with the spreading hood squarely before him, yet Eden stood less than a yard away, and Hugh knew well the consequences should he miss. Once again he was aware of a dryness in his throat and an uncharacteristic unsteadiness to his hands. He took aim nonetheless, reminding himself that he had repeatedly brought down moving targets at far greater distances, and yet—and yet—

The report sent a flock of brilliant green parrots screeching from the nearby trees and a spurt of dust exploding in the distance as the bullet slammed home. Tossing the rifle aside, Hugh did not even bother to watch the shattered remains of the cobra sink slowly back into its coils. Stumbling forward, he caught Eden in his arms as she put out a blind, groping hand to him. Her head fell against his chest, and Hugh drew her close, an unfamiliar ache closing his throat. Resting his cheek against her hair, he breathed deeply of its scent and willed the mad thundering of his heart to still.

"I didn't see it," Eden gasped. "I thought—"

"Hush, *chabeli*," Hugh whispered, and his lips moved in a comforting caress against the silken curls at her brow.

Eden sighed, and Hugh's arms tightened about her, his strong fingers moving slowly against the nape of her neck. Though her slim body still trembled with fear, the numbing terror that had coursed through his own veins was slowly giving way to another, equally elemental emotion.

Slowly and deliberately he bent his head, and his lips were no longer caressing her brow but were traveling warm and sure along the curve of her cheek. The touch of his hands, too, had subtly changed, for they were no longer gentle but caressed her with the firm, insistent need of a lover.

Eden grew still in response. A warm, drugging delight seemed to seep through her, blotting out her fear and loathing so that she was no longer rigid but soft and pliant in Hugh's arms. Lifting her head so that his seeking mouth might find hers, she was suddenly filled with stunned dismay as he wrenched himself without warning from her. She stumbled and nearly fell as he pushed her aside, and the short train of her habit tangled amid a clump of reeds.

Turning to look at him with eyes wide and uncomprehending in her white face, she saw that his mouth was tight with suppressed fury and that he seemed to be having difficulty maintaining a grip on his temper.

"Goddamn it," he ground out, "don't look at me like that! I'll be damned if I—if we—not after I swore—" He bit off his words and swung around savagely to retrieve his rifle. "Get your horse," he commanded. "If we're lucky, we'll make Delhi before dark."

But they did not, and the number of lights blazing in the Porter bungalow and the servants hovering anxiously near the doorway gave evidence to the alarm generated by Eden's lengthy absence. Alerted to her return by the watchful *chowkidar,* the entire family hastened outdoors to meet her. Colonel Porter, taking one look at Eden's drawn, weary face in the light of the flickering lamps, lifted her down from the saddle and brusquely ordered his wife to cease at once with her ridiculous lamentations.

"There'll be time for that later, madam!" he snapped in a tone he had never used with her before. "Can't you see the poor child is exhausted?" And Mrs. Porter, genuinely shocked, was cowed into silence.

While Eden was whisked away to her bedroom with considerable concern and solicitude by the Porter daughters and their weeping mother, the duke of Roxbury was left behind to face the waxing wrath of Colonel Porter. Eden's absence had given all of them an unpleasant scare since British girls did not simply disappear from their homes here in India—not unless, as Mrs. Porter had tearfully pointed out, they had met with some dreadful accident or unspeakably foul play.

Summoned from the lines that morning by his wife's hysterical posturings, poor Colonel Porter had endured a most tiring day as the victim of numerous unjustified recriminations and outright accusations concerning "dear Eden's" disappearance. It was no wonder, then, that his nerves were badly frayed by the time she returned, and his temper by no means mollified to discover that she had spent the day in the company of the duke of Roxbury, a man the colonel trusted implicity and who, b'gad, should have known better!

"Really, Hugh, this is too bad of you!" the colonel remonstrated, confronting the younger man alone in his study several minutes later. "I've spent the entire day scouring Delhi in search of the girl and enduring the most ghastly scenes here at home. Mrs. Porter was quite convinced she'd been kidnapped by some dissolute rajah or murdered by a roving band of *dacoits*. The least you could have done was send a message with your bearer that she was to spend the day with you! Damned impertinence," he added with a growl. "Anyone else and I'd have collared him properly for this, b'gad!"

Hugh took no offense at the old man's brusqueness, well aware that his bluster hid feelings of genuine concern for Eden. Yet there was little he could say in his own defense, for he was not about to mention Meerut or Eden's reasons for going there. That was between Eden and himself, unless she chose to say something to the colonel of her own volition. His tone was nonetheless curt as he made a brief and entirely inadequate apology and took his leave without another word.

Riding back to the city, he found his mood incomparably foul, and there was a grim tightness about his mouth. His responsibility toward Eden Hamilton should have ended the moment he had placed her in Frederick Porter's care. Why in hell, then, did he insist on continually involving himself in her madcap escapades? Let her make a public appearance at the next grand ball at Government House dressed as Choto Bai for all he cared!

I've been behaving like an unmitigated fool, Hugh thought angrily, and it's only because, if the truth must be told, I want to make love to her!

But such an admission did nothing to ease his anger or self-contempt one bit, and in a thoroughly vile temper he drew rein at last in the moonlit stableyard of Henry Pascal's stucco house.

"Baga Lal!" he roared, stepping into the dimly lit hall and sending the terrified servants scattering like a flock of panicked fowl.

"Huzoor?" the bearer inquired politely, descending quickly from the staircase above him.

"Pack my belongings and see your own are in order! We leave for Gujranwala in the morning!"

Baga Lal's expression remained bland. "Is there a specific purpose for this trip, Huzoor?"

"We're going after black-buck," growled the duke with tight-lipped impatience. "See that my guns are cleaned and oiled. I don't wish to find so much as a speck of dust on any of them, is that understood?"

"The Huzoor has always made himself quite clear," murmured Baga Lal, and hastened away to carry out his master's orders. The prospect of leaving Delhi for the wilds of the border country pleased him, for a few days camping alone on the frontier never failed to improve the

Hazrat-sahib's bad temper, especially if the hunting was good.

Hai mai, but I do not think a mere few days will serve this time, Baga Lal decided, suspecting quite accurately the reasons behind this particular outburst. I will have to see that we stay away at least a week!

He would have been greatly pleased if nothing more had been heard or said about the Hamilton-sahiba before their departure, yet the morning sun was still well below the horizon when a dusty, travel-worn courier arrived at the doorstep of the big white house demanding an audience with Gordon-sahib.

He was a *havildar*, a sergeant of Bengal Infantry and as such an officer not normally given to playing the role of messenger. Yet his duty, he explained after giving Hugh a smart salute when the two of them met in Pascal's study, was being carried out in honor of the memory of Colonel Hamilton-sahib, a man of rare courage and compassion whom the *havildar* had served faithfully before his death in the Lucknow siege.

"It is known in my regiment that the daughter of Hamilton-sahib seeks her father's people, for the political sahibs in Oudh and those of Government House here in Delhi have asked many questions of late. Regrettably there is little known to us about the colonel-sahib's family. That is why, when this packet arrived in Lucknow yesterday addressed to the memsahib, it was decided to bring it at once to Delhi. I was accorded the honor, and I bring it to you, Huzoor, for it was mentioned by Cottington-sahib that you have made yourself responsible for the girl."

As he spoke, he drew forth a leather satchel and removed from it a thick packet tied with jute, which he handed deferentially to Hugh. Thanking him gravely, Hugh turned it over and studied with interest the canceled seal of the Royal Post of Edinburgh. Clearly this was the reply all of them had been waiting for, and he was not about to turn it over to Government House, where it would probably lie undelivered for days upon the desk of some overworked clerk.

Seeing the *havildar* on his way, Hugh sent a disapproving Baga Lal round to the stable for his horse. Several minutes later he was galloping through the graying dawn toward the distant Delhi Ridge, the packet strapped tightly to his saddle.

The plains and the trees and the high white walls of the British compound were bathed in soft, pearlescent light as Hugh turned at last down the long, deserted drive leading to the domed bungalow belonging to the Porters. His horse lifted its head and whinnied softly, and Hugh's gaze narrowed as another rider materialized unexpectedly through the dim light, a slim woman dressed in a blue habit who drew sharply erect at the sight of him. Since the avenue was far too narrow to prevent her turning back without an encounter, she drew rein and calmly awaited his approach.

Hugh's expression was not pleasant as he halted beside her, his own mount so close that his stirrup leather brushed against her skirts. "You're out early this morning, Miss Hamilton."

"As are you, Your Grace."

Hugh leaned forward in the saddle. "It's most commendable of you to exercise your mount before the heat grows too fierce," he remarked conversationally, "especially after the long hours you spent in the saddle yesterday. Few young women of my acquaintance would be willing to venture abroad so early merely for the well-being of their horses." Seeing the wave of color that flared to her cheeks, he lifted a brow in mock astonishment. "My dear Miss Hamilton, surely you aren't riding abroad for something other than exercise? Wasn't yesterday's mishap enough to daunt you?"

He saw her lips thin and the gloved hands tighten about the reins. She said nothing in response, however, merely tipped her chin to stare coolly into his eyes.

"Come, Miss Hamilton," he said curtly, reaching over to take the reins from her. "It would be better if you went back home."

"I fail to see," Eden said tartly, snatching the reins from him, "why you insist on involving yourself continually in my affairs, sir! I can look after myself perfectly well without your constant interference."

"Can you?" Hugh inquired, and there was suddenly something in his face that unnerved her. Eden could not know that he was thinking of the cobra he had killed the day before and remembering the fear for her that had lashed at him.

"Why can't you just leave me alone?" she whispered, stung by what she took to be an indication of his contempt for her.

"Because it isn't decent, damn it! It isn't decent for you to be roving alone throughout the countryside, exposing yourself to all sorts of dangers in pursuit of God only knows what kind of foolishness!"

Eden's face was suddenly very white, and she flinched from his angry countenance as though he had struck her.

"Why do you do it?" Hugh demanded, the unconscious gesture unwittingly firing his temper. "Why do you insist upon taking matters into your own hands like this? You're barely eighteen, for God's sake!"

"Because I've no one else to help me," Eden whispered stiffly, and the full measure of her loneliness was suddenly and unwittingly revealed in her eyes.

Hugh's anger instantly left him. The look on that young and vulnerable face had suddenly made clear to him that he had been mistaken all along in thinking she was nothing more than a spoiled, willful chit governed by mad impulses rather than courage, and he was filled with a rare and unsettling remorse.

"I'm sorry," he said gruffly. "I had no right to speak to you like that, but didn't I tell you once before that I'd help you if I could? You had only to ask, you know."

Eden stared up at him, her lips parting on a gasp. "I didn't think—did you really mean it?"

"And why shouldn't I?" Hugh demanded, annoyed.

"Then—then you weren't merely being inquisitive?"

"My dear young woman, I am never 'inquisitive,' nor do I make it a habit of offering assistance without intending to stand by my word."

The color rushed once again to Eden's cheeks, and she gazed wonderingly into his face. "Why, you are very kind," she whispered.

Looking at her, Hugh became aware of an odd, insistent tugging at his heart. The feeling took him entirely by surprise, and for a moment he was overwhelmed by a queer, stunned amazement. No, it wasn't possible! It couldn't be happening—not like this! The horse sidled uneasily at the unexpected pressure of the hands on his reins.

"I don't believe you'll need to ride abroad any longer," Hugh said abruptly, speaking in a tone that was so inexplicably harsh that the color drained from Eden's face. "Not after you've read this." He extended the package to her as he spoke. "It was delivered to me earlier this morning by a *havildar* from the Lucknow residency."

Eden's fingers were stiff as she took it from him. "Thank you," she whispered, carefully avoiding his eyes because she could not understand why he should be so angry with her. "I'll see Colonel Porter gets it as soon as he—"

"Oh, for Christ's sake, woman, it isn't for the colonel!"

Looking blankly at the packet, Eden was startled to see that it bore her own name rather than Colonel Porter's, and a number of addresses, all but the one in Lucknow struck through with dark ink. Apparently it had traveled a great distance and across numerous desks to reach her.

"What—what is it?" she stammered, although she already knew.

"I would guess that it's a reply from your Scottish relations."

"Yes," Eden said almost inaudibly. "I suppose it is." She glanced up at him, looking so terribly young and vulnerable that Hugh was seized with the irrational impulse to tear the packet from her grasp. He was convinced suddenly that it would contain nothing more than the querulous missive of an elderly and cold-hearted relative commanding Eden to pack her trunks at once for the gray chill of Edinburgh, and for the first time since their return from Mayar he was moved to wonder if it had been fair of him to press so diligently for her departure from India. Acknowledging the possibility of having committed an error of judgment, however, was equally as unacceptable to him as this strange, unwelcome feeling of protectiveness for her that had suddenly sprung full blown within him.

"I imagine you'll wish to read it in privacy," he said unkindly, and took up the reins in obvious dismissal. "I hope the news is good and your voyage to Scotland a pleasant one. Good-bye, Miss Hamilton. It's doubtful that we'll meet again."

"Oh," said Eden on a gasp, and her voice was suddenly unsteady. "Are you—you sound as if you plan to leave Delhi!"

"My bearer and I intend to spend a few days hunting on the border. You'll probably be gone by the time we return."

Wheeling his mount more harshly than was his usual habit, he took off at a hard gallop down the long, deserted avenue. Behind him Eden sat as if turned to stone, the packet clutched to her breast and the dust raised by his departure stinging her eyes. After a moment she, too, wheeled her mount and brought her whip down sharply on its flanks. Startled, the big animal leaped away, and Eden made no attempt to slow his maddened flight.

Chapter Nine

"Eden Hamilton? Such a kind, dear girl, and the most agreeable traveling companion one could wish for! I'll admit she's somewhat unconventional, but, to be fair, one must take her Hindu background into consideration," stated Mrs. Harriet Trowbridge, her knitting needles clicking industriously. "Furthermore, I find it most refreshing to speak intelligently for a change with someone who isn't the least bit critical or overly maudlin about India."

"Birds of a feather, didn't I tell you?" said Mrs. Amelia Lawton in an undertone to her companion. "Hattie's spent the last eighteen years of her life in India, and you can see she's become quite obsessed with it."

"I fear I shall never grow accustomed to it," the other woman confessed with a shudder. "Not to the heat or to the cholera or those frightful natives. Thank goodness Colin has agreed to take me home for the summer."

"Yes! Just think," said Mrs. Lawton complacently. "In a few short weeks we'll be back in England!"

The steam packet *Isle of Wight* was churning through the surging waters of the Red Sea two days south of Suez while Mrs. Trowbridge and her acquaintances were seated as usual in the shade of a colorful awning spread across the weatherdeck. The topic of conversation had centered immediately upon Miss Eden Hamilton, who had quite shocked her fellow passengers the previous evening with an impassioned defense of Indian coloreds, her outburst being prompted by the drunken remarks of a colonel of native infantry retiring from India after thirty-two years of active duty.

Though Colonel Faircloth's prejudiced posturings had admittedly bordered on the offensive, they had not shocked those assembled in the saloon quite as much as Miss Hamilton's coolly disrespectful replies. Until that point none of them had suspected the girl of being a libertine! The women had looked on with stunned disapproval, the older men with thunderous miens, and the younger officers, who had little cause to like the pompous colonel, with pursed lips that had concealed secretive smiles.

The indignant colonel had, of course, demanded an immediate apology, and Miss Hamilton had further damaged her reputation by wordlessly removing from the saloon. Though her chaperone, Mrs. Trowbridge, had remained singularly aloof from the stir that followed, she had tired eventually of the twittering gossip and had, perhaps unwisely, risen at last to her young charge's defense. Her disclosure that Miss Hamilton had spent her childhood in the harem of an Indian rajah and thus should not be blamed for her views had been greeted with a renewed outcry of shocked exclamations.

"Why, it simply isn't decent, Harriet!" Amelia Lawson had gasped. "You should insist the captain give you a new cabinmate at once!"

"Nonsense," Mrs. Trowbridge had answered energetically, already regretting her impulsive words. "I quite like Miss Hamilton and find her company most refreshing. And I do hope," she added, looking about her meaningfully, "that all of you will be magnanimous enough to treat her with tolerance."

Naturally there were those who had no intention of doing so, and no sooner had Mrs. Trowbridge appeared on deck the following morning than she found herself quite overwhelmed by a collection of curious matrons avidly hungering for additional information.

"I know very little about Miss Hamilton's background other than what Frederick Porter told me," she said now, her fading but still lively brown eyes taking in with impatience the assembly before her. "If there's anything more you wish to know, I suggest that you ask Miss Hamilton herself."

But none of them would dream of being so forward, and they merely whispered and speculated among themselves until the events of Eden's past took on entirely exaggerated and unfounded proportions. Eden herself was well aware of the curious glances turned her way when she appeared on deck a short time later, yet she dismissed this attention with characteristic indifference.

After we reach Suez I shall never see any of them again, she reasoned coolly, and I don't give a bloody damn what they think of me!

"I do so hope you don't mind all this fuss, dear," Mrs. Trowbridge said to her later that day. "Shipboard scandal is usually the most popular form of easing the boredom of a long voyage." Her eyes twinkled. "And I'm afraid you've given them more than their usual share."

Eden was inadvertently moved to laugh. She had already grown fond of the elderly Mrs. Trowbridge and was glad that the Porters had arranged for them to travel to England together. Twenty years in India seemed to have given the older woman a tolerance and fondness for the land and its people rarely displayed by her fellow countrymen, and Eden suspected that she had not entirely disapproved of her outburst the night before.

"You were quite right to stand up to Josh Faircloth that way," Mrs. Trowbridge continued as though echoing her very thoughts. "I've known him for thirteen years, and I vow his views are thoroughly objectionable."

"No one else seemed to think so," Eden observed wryly.

"Oh, I wouldn't let that bother you, dear," Mrs. Trowbridge advised. "In two days we'll be on our way north to Cairo, and the rest of them will have quite forgotten about you."

Cairo! Eden gave a shiver of excitement. Oh, to see the beauty of that ancient Egyptian city and know that, upon reaching it, she would be more than halfway along with her journey, a journey that would end up taking her all the way to Scotland—and to her cousin Isabel, who awaited her in the distant city of Edinburgh.

Eden still could not believe that Isabel was alive. Gazing beyond the surging rail to the deep blue green of the sea, she tried to visualize her cousin's face. Isabel had always been the shy one, appalled at times by the wild behavior of her older cousin, yet Eden could not remember a time when the younger girl hadn't agreed to participate in any of the boisterous games she had suggested. They had been as close as sisters, and the only real sorrow in Eden's young life had been the fact that Isabel and her father lived far away—in Ceylon, where Donan Hamilton grew rice and mined gemstones and only rarely managed to bring his motherless daughter to Lucknow for a visit with his brother and her cousin.

Eden's heart cramped painfully at the memory of those happy times when she and Isabel had haunted the teeming bazaars of the city or played together in the cool, palatial courtyards with native children their own age. Her vision misted over, and suddenly the roaring green depths of the ocean and the width of the hot blue sky blurred and ran together before her tear-filled eyes. It was the pull of those beloved memories that had prompted her to leave India, and for Isabel's sake alone she had willingly packed her bags and undertaken the sweltering journey to Calcutta with Harriet Trowbridge. So speedily had her departure progressed, in fact, that she could remember little more than standing dry-eyed and silent by the rail as the packet veered away from its Calcutta anchorage and cut a slow, wide swath through the mud-colored water. The sand heads of the Hooghly River had slipped past the stern, and the last, brief, glorious Indian twilight had faded swiftly into darkness around her.

"I'll come back," Eden promised herself suddenly, the whispered words acting as a soothing balm to her ravaged heart. "I'll come back with Isabel as soon as I can, and we'll live together in Lucknow and never leave India again."

Isabel could not possibly be happy in Edinburgh, Eden had already reasoned, though her cousin's letter had mentioned only that she was living with an elderly Hamilton aunt somewhere near the Royal Mile. Like Eden, Isabel had been born in Lucknow within sight of the soaring stucco walls of the king's palace, and she could not have forgotten her love for that fantastic, colorful city no matter how much she had suffered during the mutiny.

They would set up house in the shadow of the golden-domed palace and the temples that flanked the teeming bazaar, Eden decided. And since Isabel's Hindustani was nearly as fluent as her own, the two of them could earn their living teaching English to the sons and daughters of Indian nobles. The duke of Roxbury had told her once that capable tutors were very much in demand by princes and rajahs eager to advance their positions with the British.

The bright expectancy died suddenly from Eden's eyes. She hadn't wanted to think about the duke ever again, for to do so would inadvertently remind her of the queer, breathless hurt she had experienced at his abrupt departure from the Porter bungalow weeks ago. Yet it seemed entirely likely that the two of them would run into each other on occasion when she and Isabel returned to India, especially if he did accept a position with the political service and settled permanently in Delhi. Still, she could soothe herself with the knowledge that Lucknow and Delhi were far enough apart to prevent the likelihood of chance encounters, and besides, what did it matter if she *did* see him on occasion? He meant nothing to her, nor she to him.

And yet a single thought betrayed her suddenly, and Eden was appalled to find herself remembering how Hugh had taken her in his arms after killing the cobra and how he had held her hard against him and called her "sweetheart" in the Hindi tongue. A faint trace of color crept to her cheeks. Had he really called her that? She had been so light-headed with relief at the time that she couldn't be entirely sure.

Abruptly she turned away from the rail, her expression one of angry reproach. Apart from that moment, and the few instances in which she had, absurdly enough, found comfort in his presence, she had never felt anything more than utter exasperation and dislike for the duke of Roxbury. As for the times he had made her feel as if the very earth was being swept away beneath her feet—

Sudden fury overwhelmed her at the thought, and with an angry rustle of flounces she retreated to her cabin.

The fierce rays of the Egyptian sun burned upon the packet's blistered decks. Beneath the taut white awning the female passengers gasped and moaned and fanned themselves in a frantic effort to seek relief.

Eden alone had not sought refuge in the shade of the weatherdeck. Wearing a sensibly thin cotton frock of ivory trimmed with green, and long accustomed to the sweltering heat of Rajasthan summers, she had taken her place by the entry port and was scanning with interest the scene below her. There was little to see of Suez itself save hot, sandy streets and houses built of wooden frames and crushed stone, the windows latticed to reduce the sun's fierce glare. Gulls bobbed listlessly in the muddy water that hissed and swirled about the wooden pilings of the pier, and the scent of sewage was strong on the hot, dry wind.

A voice called loudly in Arabic, and Eden turned to see that the steamer had been made fast against the wharf. In no time at all the deck was swarming with Arab coolies, and the still air came alive with the thumping and bumping of cargo in the holds and the scraping of trunks across the worn planks.

Mrs. Trowbridge appeared through the crush, her features shadowed by an enormous straw hat tied beneath her chin with varicolored ribbons. "Oh, dear, I'd quite forgotten about the heat and dust!" she gasped. "And here it is barely June! Thank goodness it won't be long until we're in Cairo. Keep an eye on our luggage, will you, child? They'll be loading it onto those wagons shortly, and I've learned from sad experience *never* to trust them!"

Eden was eager to leave the ship and examine Suez at closer quarters, but Mrs. Trowbridge, upon hearing her request, flatly refused to grant her permission to go. Suez, she pronounced knowledgeably, teemed with disreputable thieves and disease-ridden beggars, and under no circumstances was Eden to come into contact with them. Furthermore, there was nothing of interest to be seen beyond the sun-baked docks. Reluctantly Eden abandoned her plans to go ashore and spent the long, hot afternoon reading in their sweltering cabin.

Not until the first stars were brightening the evening sky and the call of a muezzin echoed from the spire of a nearby mosque was the announcement made that the vans were prepared to depart. At first Eden was inclined to look upon the horse-drawn vehicles that were to convey them across the desert to Cairo with a feeling of anticipation. It would be pleasant, she reasoned, to leave behind the stifling confines of the ship and view firsthand the sweeping panorama of desert and sky. Yet after several hours of being tossed about in a dark, airless, bucking wagon filled with the dust churned up by the horses pulling the vehicle ahead of them, Eden began to long for the journey to end.

Mrs. Trowbridge, with enviable ease, had fallen asleep on the seat beside her, and since the couple seated across from them showed no inclination toward conversation, Eden was left to stare alone out of the window. She could see nothing save the tilting, swaying sky and an occasional glimpse of moon-washed sand, and she tired quickly of the never-changing scene.

Leaning her head against the hard back of the seat, she closed her eyes and thought with longing of India. She had dispatched a letter to Jaji shortly before her departure, and her throat ached as she thought of him. This was not the first time homesickness had dragged forcibly at her heart, yet tonight Mayar seemed farther away to her than the remotest corner of the earth—or the mountains of the moon. A feeling of weary despair crept over her, and she was suddenly inclined to view her arrival in Edinburgh not as a joyous reunion with Isabel, but as a cold, empty exile from which there was no turning back.

Once in Cairo, however, Eden's unhappiness was quickly forgotten. The lush green oasis of the city, the red desert sands stretching to the flat yellow sandbanks of the Nile, the chatter of monkeys, and the sight of storks roosting in the minarets of the mosques provided endless enchantment for her. It was cooler here than in Suez, the high white walls of the houses and the soaring groves of sycamores providing shade for the teeming streets below.

They slept that night in comfortable hotel beds draped with mosquito netting, and Eden was up with the dawn, well rested and eager to view the sights of Egypt's most exotic city. Mrs. Trowbridge, having journeyed often to Africa in her youth, knew Cairo well and declared herself sufficiently recovered from the bone-jarring trip to accompany Eden.

Dressed in sturdy boots, a wide-brimmed pith helmet, and comfortable, loose-fitting clothes, she led her young charge out into the brilliant white and green and gold of the city. Fighting their way through the throngs of donkeys and camels clogging the narrow, twisted streets, they viewed the grand mosque of Ahmed Ibn Tulun and shopped the open-fronted stores of the old quarter of the city. When the temperature climbed uncomfortably, precipitating the arrival of clouds of flies, they quit the noisy bazaars and dined in a dimly lit Turkish restaurant, where the turbaned cook prepared them a dizzying array of exotic dishes. Afterward, at Mrs. Trowbridge's suggestion, they returned to their hotel to rest, yet Eden found it impossible to sleep.

The window of their room looked out upon the Nile and the profusion of blinding white sails that scuttled across the sulfurous water. Beyond them rose the pyramids, breathtaking in their size and mystery, the brilliant blue of the sky above their soaring peaks filled with scudding clouds. Camels plodded the desert sands in their shadow, and Eden rested her elbows on the sill and wished that she might ride one of them to the base of the Grand Pyramid and view for herself the burial chamber of the Pharaoh Khufu and his long-dead queen.

"There really isn't much to see," Mrs. Trowbridge told her regretfully over dinner that evening. "My husband and I toured all three of the pyramids in forty-six, when he had several months' leave coming to him and the train to Alexandria was delayed. I must admit the balky behavior of our camels and the shocking rudeness of our guide quite took the enjoyment out of it. I cried like a ninny the entire way back to the city, and poor

Major Trowbridge had no choice but to give his solemn oath that he'd bring me back one day. I'm certain he would have kept his promise,'' she added pragmatically, ''if he hadn't been killed fighting the Sikhs at Chilian-walah.''

Though Eden began to hope that their own train might be delayed, morning brought a hotel clerk rapping politely on the door to inform them that they must make haste in order to reach the station on time. They ate a hurried breakfast of omelets and fruit and afterward were driven to the station amid a crush of tourists, camels, and bullock carts. Mrs. Trowbridge possessed both the influence and income to commandeer a first-class compartment on the train, but Eden was sufficiently disappointed with their pending departure from Cairo to view their accommodations with only a jaundiced eye. The floor was decidedly unclean, and the worn leather seats were ripped in places and yellowed stuffing protruded.

''How nice it will be to have a compartment all to ourselves,'' sighed Mrs. Trowbridge happily. Seating herself with a rustle of crinolines, she unfolded a gazette and began to read.

The windowpane was of an odd violet shade and so grimy with soot that it was difficult to see out. Intrigued by the noisy crowd and the shrilling of policemen's whistles on the platform below, Eden forced the window open and leaned outside to look. She immediately attracted a mob of gesticulating vendors selling everything from loaves of unleavened bread to unappetizing plates of dried meat and moldy cheese. Accustomed to the similar clamoring of Indian bazaar mongers, Eden bartered skillfully in sign language, and by the time the train jolted slowly out of the station she had purchased a basket of fragrant oranges and two bottles of drinking water.

Mrs. Trowbridge dozed quite comfortably throughout the long trip while Eden did her best to make herself comfortable upon the narrow, lumpy seat. Once, during the night, the train chuffed to a halt for no apparent reason, and Eden, peering curiously out of the window, could see nothing beyond the grimy pane save the vast, star-hung sky.

"We're probably passing through some pasha's territory," Mrs. Trowbridge informed her, having been awakened by the jerking halt of their train car. "We'll be on our way as soon as he grants his permission."

By morning the rooftops and minarets of Alexandria lay before them, the Mediterranean shimmering in brilliant hues of green beyond its crescent-shaped harbor. Palms and cactuses dotted the landscape and filled the gardens of the pleasant white houses lying beyond the tracks.

Though their steam packet was not due to weigh anchor until later that afternoon, it was already coaling off shore, and with the aid of a kindly Egyptian official their luggage was soon loaded onto one of the smaller transport boats and sent across the oily water.

"Now, then," said Mrs. Trowbridge amiably, "we've plenty of time for sight-seeing. Why don't we get something cool to drink and then tour the city?"

They took a hackney coach from the docks and returned in the same fashion several hours later, wearied by the intense heat and by the number of sights they had made a point to see. The docks were crowded, for another train had recently pulled in, and anxious passengers were scrambling about exhorting indifferent coolies to exercise care in transferring their luggage to the waiting boats. Hackneys and elegant carriages clogged the thoroughfares leading to the piers, and to add to the confusion an enormous, weathered merchantman was being made fast at a nearby berth and disgorging a mob of sweating, swearing crewmen.

"Oh, dear," said Mrs. Trowbridge, pushing her way through the throng, her parasol brandished before her like a weapon, "I've never seen anything quite like this. Do have a care, young man! You're trodding on my flounces!" Pulling her skirts free of the offending boot, she wavered without warning and sat down heavily on a nearby crate, her mouth open and her breath coming short.

"Are you all right?" Eden inquired, bending worriedly over her.

"It must be the heat," Mrs. Trowbridge responded breathlessly. "I feel so dreadfully dizzy of a sudden."

She fanned herself vigorously and gave Eden a tremulous smile. "Do be a dear and fetch me some water, will you?"

Eden hurried away, not entirely certain where she ought to begin looking for it. Fortunately her white, anxious face quickly attracted the attention of a passing quartermaster, who promptly sent one of his hands back aboard the merchantman for a pannikin of water. Eden took great care not to spill it amid the jostling crowds, yet she might have spared herself both the frustration and the effort, for Mrs. Trowbridge was lying in an apparent faint on the hot planking when she returned. Several passersby were clustered about attempting to revive her.

Alarmed, Eden tried to push her way through the knot of onlookers. "Please," she said urgently, "let me through!"

No one paid the least bit of attention to her until one of the men who was kneeling by the elderly woman's head turned at the sound of her voice. A disbelieving look crossed his lean brown face, and he pushed his way to her side, taking her arm in a rough grip.

"Eden! What in God's name are you doing here?"

"Oh, please, what's wrong with Mrs. Trowbridge?" Eden gasped, accepting without question Hugh Gordon's presence. "She asked me for some water—" She held out the near empty pannikin for his inspection, and the harsh lines of His Grace's face softened slightly.

"I'm sorry, Miss Hamilton. I'm afraid she won't be needing it."

Eden stared up at him, her face very young and frightened beneath the brim of her rice straw hat. There were dark stains on her neat white blouse and blue cotton skirt where the water had sloshed in her haste, and Hugh thought with a pang of pained annoyance that she looked as bedraggled and bewildered as a child of seven.

"I don't understand," Eden whispered.

"I believe it's her heart," he said gently. "It simply gave out. Perhaps the heat or her age—"

"No," Eden said faintly. "No! You don't mean—it couldn't be! I won't believe it! We just returned from a tour of the city, and she said she was feeling a little dizzy and would I fetch her some water and—and— Oh, she cannot be dead!''

The pannikin fell to the ground with a clatter. "I must go to her!'' Eden said urgently, but Hugh refused to relinquish his hold on her arm.

"The woman is dead, Miss Hamilton. There's nothing you or anyone else can do for her.''

"I won't believe it! I won't! Let me go this instant!''

Looking down into her drawn face, Hugh uttered a harsh exclamation and pulled her roughly to a stone bench that stood in the shade of an overhanging balcony.

"Wait here,'' he ordered, making her sit. "I'll see if there's anything I can do. And under no circumstances are you to leave until I return, is that understood?''

Eden nodded silently in response to the authority of his voice, but Hugh knew her far too well by now to view her seeming acquiescence without suspicion. Returning to the docks, he collared a young man he recognized as a clerk employed at one of the local banks in Delhi and charged him brusquely with keeping an unobtrusive watch upon her.

When he returned a half hour later he was genuinely surprised to find Eden still seated where he had left her, her head bowed and her hands clasped tightly in her lap. Looking up at that moment, she saw him approach, and an expression of genuine relief crossed her face.

"Where have you been?'' she asked tremulously, hurrying toward him.

"Making the necessary arrangements.''

"For the—the burial?''

"Of course not. The Egyptian authorities will take care of that,'' Hugh said impatiently. "I was referring to your welfare, Miss Hamilton, and the fact that you've been stranded in Alexandria without a chaperone.''

"I don't need—''

"Oh, yes, you do,'' he interrupted brusquely. "You cannot travel all the way to England alone. And let me tell you that I've had the devil of a time making adequate arrangements for you. Your fellow passengers seem to consider you something of a pariah, and none of them wish to be responsible for you. I can't say I'm the least bit surprised," he added unkindly.

"I don't care," Eden said stiffly. "And there really is no need for you to—"

"Oh, but I'm afraid there is," Hugh said, interrupting her again. "I, for one, refuse to board the *Perion* knowing I'll have to endure the endless remonstrations of the matrons you'll undoubtedly shock. Unmarried Englishwomen, Miss Hamilton, simply do not travel alone all the way from India."

Eden's expression had gone blank with shock. "You're sailing aboard the *Perion?*"

"A charming coincidence, isn't it?" Hugh inquired in a tone indicating that he was no more enamored of the situation than she. "I happen to be on my way to England, too."

"But how did you manage to catch up with us so fast?"

Hugh Gordon's lean face settled into hard lines as he looked into Eden's dismayed blue eyes. "I was hunting on the banks of the Sutlej when an urgent summons from England was forwarded to me. Since it was far easier to travel to Bombay and catch a steamer there than return to Calcutta, that's exactly what I did. My luggage will be following directly."

There was suddenly a look on Eden's face that Hugh had not seen in a great while: one of bright expectancy and eagerness and undeniable longing. Misconstruing that look, he softened suddenly, yet the words he was about to utter were arrested as she breathed: "Then you traveled through Rajasthan, didn't you? Oh, tell me, please, did you go anywhere near Mayar?"

"I traveled north of Bikaner, nowhere near Mayar," Hugh informed her, and his voice was flat and inexplicably bitter. "It would seem the *Perion* is prepared to depart," he added as a high-pitched whistle sounded from the vessel. "May I suggest that we go aboard?"

I shall never be rid of him, Eden thought, glancing resentfully at the hard face of the man seated opposite her in the tiny boat that ferried them across the water. Once again he had appeared unwanted in her life, taking command of it as though he had every right to, and going about it with his usual, maddening arrogance.

She was *not*, Eden decided firmly, the least bit happy to see him, unless she was honest enough to admit to herself that his presence did indeed provide a measure of comfort given the shock of Harriet Trowbridge's unexpected death. Eden's breath caught on a pained gasp as she thought of her chaperone, for she had been genuinely fond of the other woman.

"At least she did not suffer," said Hugh softly, and Eden turned to regard him blankly.

"Mrs. Trowbridge, of course."

Eden nodded slowly, wondering if she would ever come to terms with her feelings for this man. He could be so awfully hard, even frightening, at times, yet just when she had decided that she disliked him thoroughly, he would say or do something unexpectedly kind and leave her quite confused.

Perhaps I've misjudged him, Eden thought, wanting to be fair. And since they would be traveling to England together, she ought to at least make the effort of behaving civilly toward him.

Yet by the time the *Perion* had discharged its Egyptian pilot and swung a wide path north through the bright green sea, Eden had already abandoned that particular resolution. As far as she was concerned she would be quite content never to lay eyes on Hugh Gordon again. The cabin he had selected for her was unacceptably small and hot and airless, for one thing, and Eden was appalled by his choice of a chaperone.

Mrs. Camille Severance was a woman of Hugh's personal acquaintance, a former actress who had been traveling by coincidence aboard the same train with him from Allahabad to Bombay. She had agreed to look after the girl at the duke's request, and, not surprisingly, Eden had taken an instant dislike to her.

Hugh had described her as a widow of good social standing, and Eden had pictured a woman of a similar age and temperament as Harriet Trowbridge. Yet Camille Severance was barely forty, heavily rouged and gaudily attired in violet satin, and wore about her person the overbearing and rather disagreeable scent of rosewater. Despite her limited contact with Western women, Eden had immediately recognized in her the same slatternly characteristics of the less favored concubines in Malraj's palace, and Mrs. Severance had not helped to dispel that impression by flirting quite openly with the duke. Eden had felt both awkward and resentful in her presence and had withdrawn stiffly from the cabin after introductions had been made, telling herself that she had no intention of tolerating the long voyage in Mrs. Severance's company.

"She cannot be the sort of woman he prefers," she whispered to herself, and there was a hot, hard lump in her throat she attributed entirely to anger and disgust.

Standing by the deck rail, Eden shaded her eyes and stared unhappily across the deep green water. Instead of the vanishing coastline of Egypt, however, her vision was filled with the hard, cool mouth of the duke of Roxbury. She found herself wondering if he had ever kissed Camille Severance's rouged, pouting lips as he had once kissed her own.

It was an intolerable thought, and in a way it made her feel coarse and young and ridiculously foolish. How he must have laughed at her for having been so angry with him that night he had taken her into his arms in the desert of Mayar! Camille Severance, Eden felt sure, would not have struggled in his embrace or flung childish accusations at him.

I cannot bear it! Eden thought, and there was a sudden heaviness in her breast as she envisioned the two of them together in the days to come, Camille laughing and leaning against Hugh's arm to whisper intimate reminders of the memories they shared. . . .

"I hope you've found the accommodations to your liking, Miss Hamilton?" came a voice in her ear.

Eden turned to find the duke of Roxbury behind her, and all at once she was seized with the inexplicable certainty that he was mocking her. An overwhelming impulse to slap his handsome face overcame her, and she struggled against it, determined not to give him any more reasons to think of her as immature or gauche. With an effort she schooled her face into an expressionless mask and said with cool dignity:

"Yes, thank you, Your Grace. Mrs. Severance and I will doubtless get on splendidly."

Lifting the short train of her traveling skirt, she swept away with her chin tipped at an imperious angle, the abruptness of her departure somehow conveying considerable insult.

Now what in hell, Hugh wondered, staring after her, has gotten into her this time?

Chapter Ten

As the *Perion* entered cooler waters the weather grew more pleasant, and Eden spent most of her time walking briskly in the sunshine and enjoying the stiff, salt-tinged wind that whipped against her cheeks. She rarely wore a bonnet, and her face was soon as browned as a seaman's, and the shining hair that was always rolled tightly into a modest chignon was streaked the color of the sun. She had made many friends among the crew, and though Hugh had at first looked with disapproval upon her habit of conversing with them, he knew better than to take her to task. Eden Hamilton was not a conventional woman, and it shouldn't surprise him that she felt more at home talking with lowly lascars and sailors than with her own kind. And because she seemed far happier these days than when the *Perion* had first left Alexandria, he made no move to intervene.

He was himself largely preoccupied with his own personal affairs throughout the voyage and, much to the disappointment of the majority of the *Perion*'s female passengers, kept mostly to himself. Owing to the fact that it had become fashionable among the upper classes to take an extended Grand Tour of India, the steamer was packed with numerous peers returning home from lengthy jaunts abroad, yet the duke of Roxbury was by far the most notable among them—as well as the most eligible, according to the hopeful mamas and daughters who sailed with him.

Eden was well aware of the interest Hugh Gordon aroused in her fellow passengers and of the fact that his mere presence could set even the most jaundiced feminine pulses fluttering. She was far more intimately acquainted with many of the European ladies than Hugh might have supposed and conversed with them often enough to be aware of their gossip. Yet despite the fact that she admitted to a certain amount of admiration for the duke of Roxbury herself, she could not bring herself to share their boundless enthusiasm for him. Camille Severance had seen to that.

With all the guile and experience that ten years of walking the London boards had taught her, Camille Severance had promptly set about spinning tales for the benefit of her innocent young charge, fanciful narrations concerning the duke of Roxbury's numerous and highly publicized sexual exploits. Though Eden refused to believe half of what Mrs. Severance divulged to her in the dark of their cabin, she had to concede that Hugh Gordon seemed at least the type of man who was capable of such shocking behavior. It never occurred to Eden that Camille's vitriolic confessions were fueled largely by jealousy.

In one respect Eden had been right about her: Camille Severance possessed an overabundance of womanly instinct, and she had sensed at the moment of their meeting the disturbing effect that the girl's golden beauty could exercise on the opposite sex. And being well schooled in the workings of a man's heart and mind, she had immediately, and with uncanny accuracy, drawn the conclusion that if Hugh Gordon had as yet failed to take Eden Hamilton to bed, it was only because of the unsuspecting girl herself.

How could anyone possibly be so ignorant? Camille had asked herself with baffled resentment. Wasn't the girl in the least bit aware of the beguiling power of her looks?

If I were only half as lovely, Camille thought bitterly, yet she knew that she was not, and because she knew, she could not prevent herself from blackening the image of the man she loved, to the shock and disbelief of the naive Eden.

Wretchedly uncertain about the credibility of what she heard, Eden took to avoiding the duke altogether or speaking to him with the barest of civility whenever that proved impossible. It was a considerable relief to her that

he spent most of his time writing letters in his cabin or
conversing with men of his acquaintance whenever he
made an appearance on deck. She had expected him to be
annoyed by her rudeness, or at the very least to comment
upon it in his usual mocking manner, yet as time went
by it occurred to her that he seemed scarcely aware of
it—or of her.

The discovery filled her with an entirely illogical and
inexplicable fury. Did he think that he owed her nothing,
not even an occasional exchange of common civility, now
that he had discharged his duties toward her? Or was it
possible, she wondered while lying awake in her bunk one
hot, sleepless night, that he no longer noticed anyone save
the beguiling Mrs. Severance?

Eden had been tossing restlessly upon the hard mattress
for what seemed like hours, telling herself it was because
the moon was falling in bright silver bars across her pillow that it was impossible to sleep. Yet now she lay perfectly still, her breath catching on a sudden constriction
in her throat as the reason behind Mrs. Severance's numerous nightly absences from their cabin became
wretchedly clear.

''No!'' said Eden aloud. ''No, I won't believe it!''

Suddenly, she could no longer stand the close confines
of the cabin. Throwing a shawl over her head, she ran
lightly up the steps and out onto the moonlit deck. The
number of passengers still milling about surprised her, and
she passed by them quickly and fled to the leeward side
of the ship, where the cabin wall threw a shadow across
the deck and offered her the welcoming privacy of darkness.

She paused by the rail and sighed, and could not be
sure if what she was feeling at the moment was relief at
being in the cool, fresh air or sadness. Turning her head,
she looked aft, where the moonlight shivered on the water
and illuminated the wide swath of churning wake in a
path of silver. The stars glittered dimly in a sky that was
more blue than black, and Eden sighed again, the emotions roiling within her beginning to ease as the beauty of
the night crept over her.

She could not say how long she stood there by the rail before some inexplicable sixth sense warned her that she was no longer alone. Turning her head, Eden caught her breath at the sight of someone a short distance away from her: a tall man with dark, wind-ruffled hair. Though his face was lost in shadow, she knew at once who he was.

Camille Severance was not with him, and Eden stood perfectly still, shaken by the discovery. He did not speak, and Eden was not at all sure that he was even aware of her presence. Still, for some reason, the last vestiges of the pain encircling her heart were suddenly, inexplicably gone. She made no move to acknowledge herself, merely turned again toward the vast, moonlit sea, and for a long moment there was silence between them.

"Shouldn't you be in bed, Miss Hamilton? It's very late, you know."

Eden was not at all startled when Hugh spoke at last, nor did she think it odd that he should have known who she was even though she was standing in the same shadows that had concealed his identity from her.

"It's far too hot for sleeping," she said, "and the night too lovely for staying below."

"An unqualifiedly romantic statement," Hugh observed with a grin, "and I'm afraid few of your fellow passengers would agree with you. Most of the ladies seem to be of the opinion that the sound of engines and the smell of coal smoke make for very disagreeable nights."

"Well, that shouldn't go on much longer, should it? Captain Pringle told me we should have Lisbon off the bow by morning."

Hugh came to stand beside her, propping one shoulder comfortably against a nearby lifeboat tackle. "I assume you're on your way to Edinburgh," he said, her comment having served to remind him that the end of their journey was near. "Did it turn out that you had relatives there?"

Eden nodded, remembering belatedly that he had not been aware of the contents of the package he had delivered to the Porters' bungalow that long-ago morning in Delhi. She told him something of it now, explaining how her cousin Isabel had survived the massacre of Meerut and been smuggled from the country by sympathetic Indian friends, and how she had ended up in Edinburgh in the care of an elderly Hamilton aunt.

"All these years she assumed I was dead," Eden concluded, "and it must have been as great a shock for her to find out I wasn't as it was for me to receive a letter written by her own hand."

Hugh had been listening without comment, his face lost in the shadows. "Miss Isabel's rescue seems to have been as dramatic as your own," he remarked at last. "You seem pleased by the prospect of a reunion."

"I wouldn't have left India for any other reason," Eden said carelessly, then bit her lip and stared up into his face with no small measure of consternation. "How odd that you yourself left India so abruptly," she went on hastily.

She had meant only to draw the conversation away from herself so as not to reveal to him that she planned to return East as soon as possible with Isabel in tow. Certainly she hadn't intended to inquire into his private affairs, for she knew perfectly well that he rarely divulged anything personal about himself, and she was rather surprised when he chose to reveal to her that pressing legal problems involving his estates in Somerset had necessitated his prompt return to England.

"I wonder that you've managed to keep both your home in England and a residence in Delhi," Eden said, digesting this piece of news with a thoughtful frown. "It cannot be easy to administer an estate while living half a world away."

"Believe me, it isn't," Hugh answered wryly, "and I'm in the process of deciding what's to be done with it. The estate, the Roxbury title, and all that it entails have only recently come into my possession, you see. I inherited them upon the death of my uncle, the ninth duke of Roxbury."

"Then you weren't born in India?" Eden asked curiously.

"No. I was eighteen when I first set foot on Indian soil. My intention was to visit an uncle serving with the Hundred and Third in Lahore, but instead I soon found myself drawn into the business of consigning wool and other textiles fabricated in England over to the East India Company army.''

"Wool?" inquired Eden, genuinely puzzled.

"It gets damned cold on the Northwest Frontier," Hugh reminded her with a grin, "and the army had an insatiable demand for uniforms. It wasn't difficult getting the business established," he added, a trace of bitterness creeping into his voice, "for the company was mainly interested in taking what it could from the Indian people— silks, tea, timber, and the like—and overlooking the fact that imports were just as necessary to its greedy, growing empire."

"You had a firm in Calcutta," Eden remembered, "and one in Delhi, too, Mr. Pascal told me."

"And both of them were lost in the uprising," he said, the bitterness deepening. "Twelve years of honest labor destroyed while I was playing the landed heir in faraway England. I was called away to the old duke's bedside shortly before the onset of the mutiny, you see, and since then I've done nothing but travel back and forth between both countries while my incompetent solicitors continue to make a muddle out of everything."

"And yet you've remained active in the India political service," Eden said wonderingly, recalling his recent visit to Mayar.

"I care about India, Miss Hamilton," Hugh said curtly, pausing to light a cigarette. The sulfurous spurt of the match revealed the harsh planes of his handsome face as he raised it to his lips. "I care about her people—and ours—and I suppose the governor-general considers my fifteen years in Delhi sufficient experience to call on me from time to time for favors."

"I think—I think you are being modest, Your Grace," Eden said unexpectedly, and he lifted his head to look at her, his eyes filled with humor.

"Am I?"

She could not prevent herself smiling back at him, and beneath the dark veil her lovely young face glowed. Abruptly Hugh turned away from her, swearing softly beneath his breath.

"I cannot imagine what's prompted me to talk to you like this," he said roughly, more to himself than to her. "I think perhaps you should go back to your cabin, Miss Hamilton."

Eden's puzzled gaze took in the strong hands that were suddenly clamped about the rail and the unexpected grimness about his mouth. "Yes," she said, sounding somewhat unsteady herself. "Perhaps I should. Good night, Your Grace."

He heard the sound of her footsteps fade into silence, and only then did he turn from the rail. A faint smile curved his lips, a smile that held no warmth and did not reach his eyes, and when he withdrew at last to his cabin it was to lay awake for some considerable time with his arms propped beneath his head, contemplating the slow, rhythmic swaying of the lantern hanging from an overhead beam.

Eden, meanwhile, had returned to her own cabin only to halt abruptly in the doorway upon finding Camille Severance there. For a moment the two women stared at one another across the small room. Without speaking, the older woman began to brush her hair while Eden quickly unhooked her crinoline and slipped into bed.

"You were out late tonight," Mrs. Severance observed at last. "What were you doing?"

"Looking at the moon."

There was a brief pause. "I'm not certain I approve of that, child. Suppose you had run into one of those unscrupulous deckhands in the darkness?"

"I saw no one but His Grace," Eden assured her.

"Do you mean the duke of Roxbury?" inquired Mrs. Severance with sudden sharpness.

"Yes," said Eden. "We met by chance on the weatherdeck."

"I see."

Eden held her breath, for something in the older woman's voice alerted her to the fact that she had somehow blundered, yet Mrs. Severance did not seem inclined to pursue the subject. After a moment she got into bed and extinguished the lantern on the tiny dresser beside them. Secretly relieved that she had been spared further questions, Eden pulled the thin sheet up to her chin and closed her eyes. In no time at all, it seemed, the rolling motion of the ship had lulled her to sleep.

By morning the *Perion* had not rounded the southern tip of Spain as Captain Pringle had so optimistically predicted. Engine trouble had necessitated several shutdowns during the night, and much to the disappointment and even alarm of some of the female passengers, the announcement was given out that a short layover for repairs would be made in Cadiz.

Eden was delighted to learn that the passengers would be permitted to disembark during the steamer's brief stay in port. After having endured the long voyage from Alexandria, she was looking forward to escaping the cramped confines of the ship, and in the company of several like-minded ladies she was rowed across the oil-smooth water to the ancient Phoenician city.

The sunny, palm-lined squares and charming gardens proved enchanting, and they spent several hours strolling along the promenades and admiring the medieval ramparts girding the rocky sea walls of the harbor. As morning waned into an uncomfortably hot afternoon, however, most of the ladies professed a desire to return to the ship. Only Miss Cynthia Neville, a devout lover of the arts, could not be dissuaded from leaving until she had made an excursion to the chapel of San Felipe Neri to view Murillo's famed painting of the Virgin.

Miss Neville was something of an oddity to everyone and the subject of considerable speculation among the *Perion*'s female passengers. A spinster at forty-three, she taught English to disadvantaged Indian children in the missionaries of Calcutta, and it was not surprising that the only person who had not shown herself reluctant or embarrassed to seek out her company had been Eden Hamilton. It was Eden who volunteered to accompany her to the church since it would not do for Miss Neville to go alone.

"I'm not at all certain you have enough time, Eden, dear," protested Mrs. Lawton, glancing worriedly toward the harbor. "It would be simply dreadful if you were to be left behind!" This was the same Amelia Lawton who had traveled aboard the *Isle of Wight* from Aden and who had been so shocked by Harriet Trowbridge's disclosure concerning Eden's Indian connections—until she had discovered that Eden was traveling under the informally declared protection of the duke of Roxbury, a revelation that had instantly altered her opinion of the girl. "I believe Captain Pringle made the announcement that we're expected to sail at two o'clock," she added fretfully.

"No, it was four o'clock," said Eden decisively, for Mrs. Severance had been kind enough to make inquiries on her behalf before the water taxi took them ashore.

Mrs. Lawton, lingering only long enough to exhort the two women to be careful, led the rest of the party back to the ship. Eden and Miss Neville, meanwhile, wandered down the closely knit streets to the inner town.

They were both of them hot and rather weary when they emerged a half hour later from the dim, oval-shaped interior of the church, and since it was barely three o'clock they agreed to rest for a time at a shaded sidewalk cafe and sip a refreshing *fino*. Miss Neville, when removed from the influence of the other ladies to whom she felt vastly inferior, proved a lively conversationalist whose plain features were transformed as she talked to Eden of her work as a missionary. Eden was delighted to discover that they shared a passionate love for India and that Miss Neville, unlike other European ladies of Eden's recent acquaintance, did not view her years in an Indian palace as the least bit shocking or immoral.

"I envy you, in fact," Miss Neville said with a sigh, "and it seems likely that none of us will ever be so fortunate as—" Looking over Eden's shoulder, she broke off with an alarmed gasp.

"What is it?" inquired Eden curiously, only to whirl about as she felt a hand clamp down hard on her shoulder.

"You little fool!" came a familiar, angry voice from behind her. "What in hell do you think you're doing?"

Eden looked up to find Hugh Gordon towering above her, his lean face dark with fury.

"Your Grace!" she exclaimed, startled. "What—?"

"I vow you are the most exasperating woman I've ever met," he snapped. "The *Perion* has been ready to sail for the past hour and a half, and here you are sitting on the sidewalk drinking wine as though you had all the time in the world! Didn't Captain Pringle make it clear to you that all passengers should be back aboard the ship by two o'clock?"

"Two o'clock?" Eden echoed indignantly, yet was permitted to say nothing more.

"They were prepared to sail without you, even Captain Pringle," Hugh went on unkindly, "until I decided to intervene once again on your behalf. I hope you have a suitable explanation for this, Miss Hamilton?"

"I—" Eden began, then fell silent. "No," she said quietly. "I've nothing to say."

Above her bowed head Hugh's face hardened into intractable lines, sufficiently cowing the listening Miss Neville into swallowing the defensive words she had been about to utter.

In silence the three of them were rowed back to the ship; once there, Eden, her face burning with shame, went immediately below. Mrs. Severance was fortunately absent from the cabin, and Eden threw herself down on her bunk, struggling to repair her shredded pride by envisioning the number of vengeful Rajput practices she intended to inflict on the buxom actress. But of course there was nothing she could do save refuse to give the other woman the satisfaction of knowing how much she had been humiliated. She suspected quite rightly that Mrs. Severance would have been more than delighted had the *Perion* sailed from Cadiz without her, though she could not, upon lengthy introspection, come up with a single reason as to why the older woman should want to be rid of her.

"I hate them both," Eden declared, illogically choosing to blame Hugh Gordon as well for the embarrassment she had suffered. In the future she resolved to treat both of them with the greatest possible disdain.

Fortunately the unpleasant episode did yield one favorable result for her: a strong friendship that flourished between herself and the plain but likable Cynthia Neville.

Miss Neville spoke Hindustani tolerably well, and the two of them soon found themselves reminiscing about India in that lovely, liquid language understood by no one else on board ship save the lascars and a few of the British officers who had spent a lifetime in the East.

For Eden the last few days of the voyage proved to be the happiest she had known since leaving Mayar, the magnificent palace and its colorful inhabitants coming alive once again as she described her life in Rajasthan to the deeply interested Miss Neville. So swiftly did the remainder of the voyage pass that Eden was taken quite by surprise when she came on deck one morning to find the coastline of England visible. The weather was cold and raw, and an icy wind gusted across the Channel, whipping the sullen water into whitecaps. The same surging swell was running in the Thames estuary, and by the time the *Perion* made fast at the enormous pier belonging to the Orient & Peninsular Line, many of the ladies had withdrawn below, fearing the onset of seasickness.

Though Eden had nothing to protect her from the chilly air save a thin shawl, she clung stubbornly to the rail, determined not to miss anything of this, her first sight of the city of London. It proved to be as disappointing as Miss Neville had warned: overwhelmingly crowded and bleak and covered with a sooty layer of grime. Yet its very strangeness and its vast difference to Calcutta was fascinating in itself, and Eden was scarcely aware of the confusion on the decks around her as she stood by the rail and looked her fill at the profusion of warehouses, church spires, and tall, narrow buildings that stood so close together they almost seemed to touch.

Most of the passengers were met on the pier by acquaintances and loved ones, and Eden saw Miss Neville throw herself into the arms of a thin young man who, judging from their resemblance, must be the brother she had spoken of so often. Mrs. Lawton and her peers were similarly well received by waiting family and friends, and it was only after the crowds on the deck and pier had begun to thin that Eden was moved to wonder if the steamer's delay in Cadiz might not have been responsible for the fact that no one was here to meet her.

She turned away from the rail in order to seek out Captain Pringle and saw Hugh Gordon standing near the entry port with a soberly attired gentleman who had come aboard to meet him. Hugh was shaking his head in response to something the man was saying, and the harassed look on his face was one that Eden easily recognized since she herself had been responsible for its presence on numerous occasions. Reluctant to disturb him, she started to slip away only to have Hugh lift his head and frown as his eyes met hers. Speaking curtly to his companion, he crossed the deck to where she stood. Scowling, he demanded to know why in hell she couldn't wait below until her escorts came to fetch her instead of standing about in the misting cold.

"Because there isn't anyone to meet me," Eden said with admirable dignity. "I was to have stayed the night with Mrs. Trowbridge's family, but I've a feeling they've forgotten all about me since the Egyptian authorities cabled them with the news of her death."

"I expect you're right," Hugh agreed, and did not look particularly pleased. "I suppose we ought to find out if you've missed your packet as well. Which one was it?"

Eden told him the name and watched with mingled resentment and relief as he vanished around the corner of the charthouse: resentment because she was once again forced to turn to him for assistance, and relief because she couldn't, in truth, help but feel a little lost and alone in this cold, foreign city.

As it turned out, the delay in Cadiz had indeed cost Eden her berth aboard the Dunfurmline-bound packet, and Hugh had not been able to obtain another booking until Thursday—three days hence. In the meantime, he told her, he had made arrangements for her to stay in Hampstead in the home of friends. He had imparted this information with such ill-concealed irritation that Eden, burning with helpless frustration, hadn't dared protest. *She* couldn't help it if her chaperone had met with an untimely death, could she? Whether she was at fault or not, Hugh Gordon was forever being called upon to extricate her from some unfortunate situation. She was grateful to

him for his continued help, of course, but he could be a
bit more civil about it, couldn't he?

Apparently not. Impatient himself to be off on the
lengthy journey to Somerset, Hugh did little more than
arrange for the transfer of Eden and her luggage to a hired
carriage that was to take her to Hampstead village and the
home of his friends, the Cannons. Brushing aside her
stammered thanks with a brusque farewell, he did not
even wait to watch her cab splash away through the rain
before he himself was being driven off in an elegant black
vehicle bearing an impressively wrought coat of arms.

The Cannons, as it turned out, lived in a dilapidated
yet pleasant cottage high on the heaths not far from the
outskirts of London. They were a large and noisy family
with children constantly underfoot, and Eden found that
she was to share a loft bedroom with three shy, giggling
girls of greatly differing ages. Mrs. Cannon had been head
housekeeper to the ninth duke of Roxbury and after
twenty years' faithful service had been handsomely pensioned off by his nephew Hugh. All of the Cannons, she
was quick to discover, spoke kindly, even worshipfully,
about the present duke, and Eden was inclined to view
their admiration with a good measure of well-concealed
skepticism.

There was no doubt, however, that Hugh Gordon had
sent her into an environment where she felt, curiously
enough, at home. Had he brought her to any number of
his wealthier, more aristocratic acquaintances in London's
fashionable West End, she would have felt compelled to
offer explanations about her past, answer endless inquiries
as to her admittedly curious relationship with the duke,
and apologize continuously for her abyssmal lack of an
adequate wardrobe.

The Cannons asked no questions and seemed quite
content to honor their visitor's distinctive customs. Since
Eden had learned to forswear meat while living among
Hindus, Mrs. Cannon cheerfully and without comment
obliged by producing a variety of cheeses, breads, and
tempting, meatless stews for their groaning table. Even
Eden's method of brushing her teeth or anointing her

freshly bathed skin with scents other than the lavender and violet water favored by English ladies were looked upon with deep interest by the female members of the Cannon household.

Unlike most of the British memsahibs Eden had met thus far, who were inclined to view with horror and ridicule her years in Mayar, the Cannons were fascinated and highly entertained by her past, asking again and again that she describe for them the palace in which she had lived. Accepted unquestionably as one of them, even in such a short time, Eden began to feel as if perhaps she had been mistaken in harboring the unspoken worry that her Hamilton relations—and even her cousin Isabel—would view her as odd, strange, even *foreign*.

On the morning Eden's packet was to sail, Mr. Cannon rose with the dawn to curry the big drafter that was to pull the wagon to the London docks. Though pressing work awaited him in the fields, Mr. Cannon would not hear of letting his houseguest drive into the city alone despite the fact that His Grace had provided ample fare for a cab.

Half a dozen piping voices clamored to accompany him, and Eden found herself sharing the wooden seat with the big farmer and his two youngest daughters while the back of the wagon was taken up with her luggage and a confusion of scuffling, wild-eyed children.

"Here, take this, dearie," Mrs. Cannon urged, pressing into Eden's hands a clean square of cloth filled with baked goods and an enormous wheel of cheese. "No tellin' what they'll be feeding you on that ship! I've been noticing you've precious little in your trunk to keep the cold away, too," she added, laying a second bundle into Eden's lap. " 'Twill be chilly so far north, even in June, so here's a shawl to keep you warm."

Without giving Eden time to protest or express her thanks, Mrs. Cannon then sternly admonished her giggling children to behave themselves and hastened back into the house. Taking up the reins, Mr. Cannon inquired heartily if everyone was ready and, amid a chorus of eager shouts, flicked his whip against the drafter's heels.

With a rattle of wheels the big wagon rolled onto the roadway, pasts fields of heather and sprawling coaching inns, on to the London docks and the last leg of Eden's long journey from India.

Chapter Eleven

From a tiny turret window that contained a single, age-frosted pane of glass, Eden Hamilton sat looking out over the towering chimneys and rooftops of the tall houses of Canongate, Lawnmarket, and The High—that crowded, bustling medieval section of Edinburgh's Old Town known as the Royal Mile. On the far end of Castle Rock sat Edinburgh Castle, as far removed from the exotic, marble-latticed palaces of India as the dark, cobbled streets below. It was raining, and the somber skies were the color of lead, spilling their contents onto a city that seemed covered by a misting pall.

"I don't think I'll ever get used to the rain," Eden said to the slim, red-haired girl curled in an armchair near the fire. "Or the cold! I never dreamed it could be this cold in the middle of summer!"

"The weather won't last," the girl assured her with a smile. "Why, tomorrow may be so sunny and beautiful you'll wonder if you've awakened in a foreign country."

I _am_ in a foreign country, thought Eden, yet did not say as much aloud.

Looking at Isabel's freckled profile in the glow of the flames, Eden felt a rush of protective tenderness. She had forgotten how small and delicate her cousin was, for Isabel had inherited not the Hamilton height, but the slimness and fragility of her red-haired mother, who had failed to survive the debilitating Indian climate after the effort of bringing her only daughter into the world.

It seemed to Eden that Isabel looked younger than her seventeen years, and more vulnerable than she remembered, but of course the shadows beneath her eyes and the unrelieved black of her mourning attire could well be responsible for that. She bent impulsively to embrace her, her wide skirts rustling, and Isabel's lips curved into a tremulous smile.

"I'm ever so glad you're here, Eden. Just knowing you were on the way home helped make Aunt Agatha's death more bearable for me."

Agatha Hamilton had drawn her last breath on the same day that Eden and Harriet Trowbridge had sailed away from Calcutta, and Eden had not been apprised of this shocking turn of events until the morning of her arrival in Edinburgh. Isabel had obviously been fond of the old lady, for she was far more quiet and subdued than Eden remembered, and her grief had been unpleasantly exacerbated by the discovery that the cozy townhouse in which the two of them lived had not, in fact, been owned by Aunt Agatha, and that an enormous debt of unpaid rent was owed the present landlord.

"Mr. Tybie has been ever so kind," Isabel had explained as the two young women sat in the warm parlor drinking tea on the night of Eden's arrival. "He knew very well Aunt Agatha didn't have enough money to pay the rent, and yet he allowed her to continue living here."

"But I thought—it seemed to me from your letter that Aunt Agatha was a woman of some means," said Eden with a frown.

"And so she must have been, at first. But she never married, and I expect her wealth simply dwindled away over the years. She was eighty-seven when she died, you know."

Isabel's eyes filled with tears at that juncture, for she blamed herself deeply for having been so blind to Aunt Agatha's penury. But how could she not have believed that all was well judging from the lavish manner in which her aunt had lived? There had been a dozen new gowns for Isabel every year, and frequent outings into the countryside in a hired carriage, and even a girl who came once a week to help with the cleaning, though Isabel wouldn't have minded doing it herself.

Seeing the tears that welled afresh in Isabel's brown eyes, Eden suspected quite accurately that her sensitive cousin felt very much responsible for the financial burden her presence had placed on Agatha Hamilton's shoulders. Yet she could do no more than point out with conviction that Isabel had certainly eased the intense loneliness of the old lady's life and brought her a great deal of happiness before she died. Surely that was worth a deal more than the negligible expenses Isabel had incurred?

Isabel had hesitantly conceded the point, yet Eden's mind was already moving on to other things. As kind as Isabel insisted this Mr. Tybie to be, he would clearly have no other choice than to sell the townhouse in order to recoup his losses now that the old lady was dead. Eden frowned as she turned her thoughts to the more practical problem of where she and Isabel were going to live. She did not care in particular for Edinburgh, finding it depressingly cold and damp and thoroughly lacking in character. Furthermore, she had taken an instant dislike to Mrs. Margaret Beasley, the live-in companion a sympathetic friend of Aunt Agatha's had provided Isabel, horrified at the prospect of the girl living all alone.

While Aunt Agatha had clearly possessed a staunch circle of friends, she had apparently never really embraced Edinburgh's lively social whirl, and Isabel had been too young and certainly too shy to do much socializing on her own. From the little her cousin had described of her life, Eden drew the conclusion that the two of them had led a very retiring existence, and perhaps it was a measure of Isabel's own dissatisfaction and unhappiness that she agreed with only a mere token of resistance to Eden's suggestion that they go elsewhere to live. But where?

"Bute is out of the question," Isabel said with surprising firmness when Eden broached the matter a day or so later. "Aunt Agatha took me there several years ago, and while she warned me that I'd not care particularly for Papa's side of the family, I wasn't at all prepared for how truly offensive I found them." A faint stain crept into her soft, freckled cheeks. "It's probably most disloyal of me to be saying that, but they were so rough and uneducated and not the least bit interested in anyone or anything other than themselves. Even Aunt Agatha's own brother went off deer hunting for the duration of our visit, despite the fact that he hadn't seen her for more than five years! I don't think they cared at all for me, and I quite understand why Papa and Uncle Dougal went away to India to make their fortunes!''

Upon further questioning, Isabel revealed that she could remember nothing at all about her mother save that she had been born somewhere in Ayr. The bleak likelihood that they had nowhere to turn became unsettlingly clear. That night, however, as Eden lay sleepless in her narrow bed, kept awake by the noisy drumming of rain on the gabled roof, she was struck suddenly with the idea of traveling north into the Grampians to seek out the Frasers.

''*Aunt Elizabeth's family?*'' Isabel had breathed the following morning, shocked by the temerity of her cousin's suggestion. ''Oh, Eden, we can't!''

''Whyever not?''

''Because—because your mother was disinherited or cast out of the family for some reason, wasn't she?''

''She left home when she was very young,'' Eden allowed.

''Then what makes you think her family will welcome *us?* Provided that we can even find them?''

''We'll simply have to wait and see what happens when we confront them face to face,'' Eden answered lightly. ''And as for finding them—at least I know my mother's maiden name, which is more than I can say of you. Oh, Isabel, please don't look like that! We'll come right back to Edinburgh if it turns out they're the least bit objectionable! Besides, what else should we do? Stay here while Mr. Tybie sells the roof over our heads?''

Dabbing at her eyes with a scrap of cambric, Isabel looked about the small room with its few shabby pieces of furniture and was forced to utter a soft laugh. ''You're right, of course. It won't do to stay here now that Aunt Agatha is gone, and I'd far rather seek out these mysterious Frasers than turn to the family on Bute for help. I must confess you took me by surprise, that's all. I'd forgotten how hotheaded and impulsive you can be. I suppose that's one thing about you that hasn't changed, has it?''

They smiled at one another, and then Isabel sighed and her eyes clouded with doubt. ''Still, I'm not at all certain I care for your suggestion, Eden. The Highlands are so remote, and the Frasers—''

''Oh, we'll probably find them to be truly despicable people,'' Eden interrupted carelessly. ''Papa told me once that Mother wrote Grandfather a letter when she knew she was dying, begging his forgiveness for whatever sin she had committed, and she never received an answer. I cannot imagine that anyone could be quite so hard-hearted, and to his only daughter at that!''

''I can't, either,'' Isabel said slowly, ''and that's why I cannot understand why you want to ask those people to take us in.''

''But I've no intention of going to live with them!'' Eden exclaimed with considerable surprise. ''Why do you think I said nothing about them to Sir William Cottington of the political service in Oudh?''

''Oh,'' said Isabel faintly. ''Then why—what is it you want from them?''

''Money,'' said Eden flatly, and her chin lifted in a manner that even Hugh Gordon would have had no trouble recognizing. ''I intend to see that they lend us enough to get us back to Lucknow.''

Isabel's eyes widened, and her breath caught on a gasp. ''Oh, Eden, I'm not at all certain—to *Lucknow,* you say?''

Eden nodded and proceeded to talk at length about the beloved city of her childhood, describing it in a manner that could not help but make the long-forgotten memories come alive for Isabel again. And having caught some of Eden's infectious enthusiasm, it was not at all surprising that Isabel needed little encouragement to make the momentous decision to accompany her. The two girls threw their arms about each other, vowing solemnly to permit nothing to stand in their way.

Regrettably, it proved far more difficult to actually act upon their plans. The elderly Mrs. Beasley, upon being told of their intentions, was sufficiently horrified to carry the tale at once to her employer. And Lady Charlotte Waring was a woman of stiflingly proper morals and considerable means who would not hear of dear Agatha's orphaned nieces returning alone to India to live. No, they must be placed at once in the care of their nearest relations on Bute, and in order to champion her cause she moved quickly to engage the backing of her nephew, a politically powerful Tory who had been sent to Parliament in Westminster only last year. As neither Eden nor Isabel were yet of legal age, he immediately proclaimed that it should not prove at all difficult to press them into traveling to Bute rather than into the remote obscurity of the Highlands or, God forbid, back to the wilds of India.

Fortunately for her cousin and herself, Eden was not exactly the shy, obedient sort of girl Lady Waring's nephew had expected. Not only did she refuse to defer to his demands, but she presented her own intentions and desires in so confoundingly inarguable a manner that he had no choice but to acquiesce. Lady Waring had quite misunderstood their intentions, Eden assured him innocently. Of course they had no intention of traveling alone to India. In truth they wanted nothing more than to inquire into the possibility of taking up residence with relations on her mother's side who lived farther in the north. Since there was certainly nothing illegal or improper about this particular request, Sir Graham Waring could not, in all honesty, refuse to grant them permission to go.

He was able, however—largely on the strength of his aunt's incessant posturings toward poor Isabel—to convince them to remain in Edinburgh long enough for him to write a letter of inquiry to Eden's grandfather and thus determine if the old man was in point of fact still alive. Eden agreed to his request only reluctantly and was not particularly surprised when the letter was promptly returned with the words "unable to deliver—addressee unknown" scrawled across the face of it. Fortunately she had already planned for exactly such a contingency, explaining to Isabel that, like a Rajput prince cornered in warfare, she intended to have several avenues of escape open to them. Isabel was not particularly enamored with the idea of openly defying Lady Waring and her formi-

dable nephew, yet she was equally reluctant to remove to
Lady Waring's cold and strictly regimented townhouse to
await their transfer to Bute, as seemed likely now that the
Frasers had been proven dead.

"But they aren't dead," Eden had assured her firmly.
"They've probably just gone elsewhere to live."

"How can you be sure of that?" inquired Isabel doubtfully.

"Because there were at least two brothers in Mother's
family," said Eden reasonably. "One of them, if not
both, must still be alive, and surely they would have
married and had children who are cousins of ours, don't
you think?"

Isabel wasn't at all certain of this, yet it was difficult
to argue with Eden's reasoning. Furthermore, since Eden
had somehow (she wouldn't say how) managed to learn
the name of the village to which Sir Graham Waring had
addressed his inquiries, there seemed nothing else to do
save pack their belongings and set out in the chill of the
dawn on a northbound posting coach.

Sir Graham, coming round to call on them later that
day, was taken aback to find the small house bare and a
note addressed to him propped on the mantel. Opening it,
he found a polite yet decidedly frank missive thanking
him for his efforts on the Hamiltons' behalf and regretting
their hasty departure. It had proved impossible to delay
any longer, Eden had cheekily written, as matters of the
most pressing urgency awaited them in the Highlands, and
surely Sir Graham and dear Lady Waring would understand?

"Damn that girl to hell," growled the portly Sir Graham, tossing the crumpled note into the barren grate, little realizing that he was not the first to express such
ill-tempered sentiments about Eden Hamilton.

Through the building of railroads and coachways, the
Scottish Highlands in the summer of 1861 were no longer
as remote as they had once been. Queen Victoria's well-
publicized summer holidays to Balmoral Castle had contributed greatly to the Highlands' growing popularity as a
vacation retreat and brought about a subsequent increase

in the number of inns and public roadhouses built to accommodate its burgeoning population of tourists. It had suddenly become fashionable among the wealthy English to travel north into the misty land that had, until recently, been viewed with disdain or, worse, with a shuddering revulsion by its southern neighbors.

Despite this sudden interest and the consequent modernization of what had been an admittedly primitive land, however, the rugged region encompassing the Grampians and the Great Glen, including Glen Tor, the home of Eden's grandfather Angus Fraser, was so desolate as to discourage the establishment of even a single posting inn. The roads that had been so conveniently laid out between Edinburgh, Stirling, and Braemar soon dwindled away to rugged sheep paths twisting through such torturous terrain that the last leg of Eden and Isabel's journey had to be completed astride hardy pit ponies with their luggage on primitive carts dragged from long ropes attached to the cruppers.

Though Eden was accustomed to spending hours in the saddle, the mincing gait of the small creatures proved exhausting for poor Isabel. They rode for the most part through misting rain and such icy cold that at night they were forced to sit for some considerable time before the warmth of an inn fire returned life to their frozen limbs.

They were immensely relieved when they arrived at last in the tiny village of Crairralsh and were informed by their guide that Tor Alsh, the Fraser stronghold, lay less than two hours away across the next mountain. They were given a room in the Cockade Inn, an ancient stone dwelling with soot-blackened rafters and surprisingly comfortable beds. The inn seemed to rise up out of the water of a deep, icy loch in which the mountains and the turbulent sky mirrored themselves with dizzying clarity.

It was Eden, secretly concerned by her cousin's pallor, who suggested the following morning that she ride alone to Tor Alsh. She would be back before nightfall, and Isabel would doubtless benefit from a day of rest here in the village. Isabel had readily agreed.

Pulling on a thick pair of gloves and wrapping a woolen muffler tightly about her throat, Eden set off with a local lad to guide her, spurred on by the innkeeper's assurances that Angus Fraser was "to the best o' me kennin' vurra much alive, if no a wee bit ill, an' sair pleased, I ween, to be receivin' sich bonnie visitors."

The dark, mountainous land and its sturdy, helpful people had made quite an impression upon Eden. Accustomed to the endless stretches of Rajasthan's dun-colored plains, she could not understand why these close, towering mountains should give her the same feeling of freedom and unending vastness, and yet somehow they did. There was unending beauty here as well: in the dark bloom of the heather on the wide stretches of moor, and in the dank bogs through which peat-colored streams churned and splashed before surging away into deep, secretive chasms. And always the mountains surrounded them, dotted at times with herds of sheep, their peaks lost amid the swirling clouds.

It was early afternoon when they came at last to the edge of a great moor that cut a green swath like an unfurled ribbon across the valley floor. The mist had lifted, and pale sunlight filtered through the clouds, illuminating in a riband of silver the swift-moving stream that plunged through its center.

"Tor Alsh," said the guide with a trace of native pride, and pointed a stubby finger toward a gray stone house resembling a hunting lodge nestled on the side of a heather-covered slope. Smoke curled lazily from chimneys flanking the main block of the house, and from the oast houses and outbuildings surrounding it.

"Some of the finest horses ever seen hae been bred here," he added. " 'Tis wha' the Fraser name be known for. Did ye no ken, miss?" he asked with obvious surprise, observing Eden's blank expression.

"No," she said honestly.

"Will ye be wantin' me to come wi' ye, miss?" he offered, but Eden shook her head and thanked him gravely.

Standing before the worn oak door with the wind lifting the ends of her traveling cloak, she knocked loudly and a moment later found herself looking into the pale eyes of a woman who bore not the least bit of resemblance to the portraits Eden had seen of her mother. This, then, could not be one of the family, and Eden guessed that she must be a housekeeper or some other servant in the Frasers' employ.

No, said the woman, making no move to open the door more than the width of her shoe would allow, Angus Fraser was not at home, for he had died unexpectedly last winter, and she couldn't for the life of her understand why the fools in Crairralsh hadn't thought to tell her that. Her manner was as hostile as her expression, and because she clearly expected the girl to take her at her word, she was caught quite unawares when Eden boldly pushed past her into the hall and said:

"I'm sorry, I don't believe you. Would you kindly take me to him?"

The woman stared at her, frozen with incredulity, yet even as she opened her mouth to speak, an imperious female voice came from the top of the oak-paneled landing.

"Whatever is going on here, Mrs. Walters? I thought I'd given orders—" Her words broke off in an instant as her gaze fell on Eden's upturned, interested face. She gasped, and her hand flew to her lips; then, with a quick, nervous rustle of her wide skirts, she hurried down the stairs and into the raftered hall. Here her disbelieving stare took in Eden's lovely, heart-shaped face, the wide, full mouth, and the blue eyes that were fringed with curling black lashes.

"You! You cannot be—"

"I am Eden Hamilton," Eden said with calm dignity. "Elizabeth Fraser's daughter. I've come from India to see my grandfather. Is he here?"

The woman called Mrs. Walters made a startled gesture with her hand, but the dark-haired, imperious creature silenced her with a glance. "Yes, he's here, but I'm afraid he's been terribly ill. We don't, in fact, expect him to recover, and I hope you can forgive Mrs. Walters for attempting to keep unwanted visitors from his door. Had she known who you were—"

"Aye, Miss Hamilton," the housekeeper breathed, and bobbed a clumsy curtsy. "I'd hae let ye in!"

"A letter was sent informing you of my arrival," Eden said suspiciously. "It was—"

"We return all mail addressed to Angus Fraser," the dark-haired woman interrupted not unkindly. "Nothing is to distress him, you see. His heart—"

"Please, I should like to see him," said Eden through lips that were oddly stiff. She felt afraid all of a sudden with that inexplicable, illogical fear of the unknown and was filled with the trepidation of knowing she was about to meet the very man who had cast her mother—his only daughter—forever from his house.

She was led into a bedroom on the upper landing in which the heavy drapes had been drawn across the windows to effectively block the daylight. In the bed in the center of the room lay an old man, his white hair falling across the pillows; Eden waited by the door while the woman crossed to him and spoke quietly in his ear.

"What's that?" Eden heard him whisper in a voice that was no more audible than the dry rattle of leaves. "Elizabeth's daughter? Here in my house?"

The woman bent over him again, and the wasted figure on the bed responded with startling vehemence: "No, I don't want to see her! Send her away, send her away, I say!"

The woman straightened with a rustle of flounces and turned an apologetic face to Eden's. For some reason the pity in her expression unleashed a surge of fury within Eden. Striding forward, she peered down into the sunken, parchment-colored face and said hotly:

"I don't think it at all fair of you to refuse to see me, sir! I've come all the way from India, and I'm cold and tired and hungry, and the least you could do is acknowledge my presence!"

There was a gasp of disbelief from both the dark-haired woman beside her and Mrs. Walters, who had lingered in the doorway, yet Eden paid not the least bit of attention to them. The nearly transparent eyelids had opened slowly and with obvious effort, and Eden was startled to find herself gazing into a pair of eyes as darkly blue as her own.

Angus Fraser focused upon her with difficulty, yet after a long moment his bluish lips curved, and a wheezing chuckle erupted from the depths of his laboring lungs. A clawlike hand reached out to take Eden's wrist and pull her close.

"A beauty, just like your mother," he said with great effort. "What's your name, lass? Eh? What's that? Eden? *Eden?*" His hand fell away from hers, and for a moment he lay slack-mouthed and breathing heavily, but as the dark-haired woman moved to go to him, he waved her away.

"She wrote me but two letters in all those years, your mother did," he said at last, every word punctuated with a labored breath. "The first came from England—said she'd spent the happiest summer of her life with friends somewhere in the country. I don't remember where. Went boating on a river, she wrote me, I do remember that. If she ever had a daughter, she said, she'd name her after that river—the Eden, it was. I'll never forget . . ." His words trailed away.

"And the second?" Eden prompted, her voice shaking. "The second came from India telling you she was dying, didn't it, sir? Why did you never answer her?"

"I was too proud," Angus Fraser confided, and Eden was dismayed to see tears well beneath his eyelids. "Too proud, and I've lived a lifetime with the regret. They're all gone, you ken: Tarquin and Malcolm and Lizabeth—"

"Hush, Father," said the dark-haired woman, moving quickly to his side and casting a warning glance at Eden. "You must rest now. You're very tired."

"Aye," Angus Fraser agreed with a heavy sigh, and was silent for so long that Eden thought he had fallen asleep. Yet as she turned away from the bed she heard him say roughly: "Janet, tell the lass she's to stay. Elizabeth's daughter . . . I want to talk to her again."

"Later, Father," Janet soothed, tucking the blankets about his thin body. "She'll come see you later, I promise."

In the downstairs study, where the pale sunlight fell on age-burnished oak flooring, she gave Eden a long, searching look. Aware that some sort of apology was expected on the score of her behavior, Eden merely returned her gaze with cool dignity and inquired calmly: "How long has he been like that?"

"Since last winter."

"What's wrong with him?"

"Nothing but the effects of old age, I'm afraid. Perhaps your being here will do him some good after all. Mrs. Walters," she said as the portly housekeeper appeared in the doorway, "see that Miss Hamilton's things are brought inside. You'll be staying with us for a time," she added to Eden in a tone suggesting that she was accustomed to giving orders and having them obeyed. "And I suppose I should call you Eden," she put in when they were alone again. "We are related, after all. I am your aunt, Janet Sinclair Fraser."

Eden regarded her dubiously. "My aunt?"

"I was married to your mother's younger brother, Malcolm. Your mother had two brothers," Janet explained, for it was obvious from Eden's wary expression that she knew little indeed about the family into which she had just made such a dramatic appearance. "Malcolm and Tarquin. I was Malcolm's wife. He died last year."

"Excuse me, mistress," said Mrs. Walters from the doorway, "there be no luggage to take in."

"Oh, that's because I didn't bring any," Eden explained, and proceeded to enlighten her aunt as to Isabel's existence and the whereabouts of their belongings. Though Janet Fraser's face hardened into lines of disapproval at the realization that Tor Alsh was to receive yet another unannounced visitor, she ordered a cart dispatched at once for Crairralsh and saw to it that Eden was given a comfortable room at the far end of the second floor. There she could wash up and rest before supper.

Once alone, Eden stared about the high-ceilinged room with its dark wood paneling and heavy, mullioned windows. The furniture was plush and certainly abundant, the bed an enormous four-poster hung with brocade drapes. A heavy earthenware pitcher and washbowl stood on the dresser, and a massive fireplace of carved granite blocks filled the entire wall across from it. It was a cluttered room, dark and somewhat uninviting to Eden, who was still accustomed to the cool, spare chambers of an Indian palace.

She stood in front of the window, her skirts rustling softly in the stillness. Below her a gravel drive flanked by low stone walls angled away toward the moors. A small grove of rowanberries grew near the carriage house, otherwise the grounds were devoid of plantings. Eden could hear the faint baaing of distant sheep and the splash and murmur of an unseen stream, and suddenly, inexplicably, she found herself hungering for the sounds of India—the singsong call of a muezzin, the braying of conches in the temples, the beating of tom-toms.

She should be happy. She had come home to the land of her parents' birth and found herself in possession of a family she hadn't even dreamed existed. But the thought merely served to tighten the band of pain about her heart, and as she stood and looked out at the heather-covered mountains, she saw instead the vast, windswept plains of India, and poignant loneliness swept her breath away and robbed her of the ability to shed so much as a single tear.

Eden and Isabel Hamilton's arrival at Tor Alsh had the unexpected yet welcomed benefit of bringing about a swift and astonishing recovery in Angus Fraser. Between the old man and his newly discovered granddaughter there sprang an instant, unlikely affection. Angus quickly found that he could lavish upon the girl who resembled his dear Elizabeth all the love and attention he had bitterly regretted denying her mother, a cure that proved far more successful in rousing him from the incipient pull of death than all the combined medicines.

Eden was intelligent, witty, and outspoken, and as she sat on the edge of his bed talking to him of her life in India, she was easily able to coax him into swallowing bowl after bowl of the bracing broth he had been turning away before. With the return of his appetite new color flooded his hollow cheeks, and strength returned to his wasted frame. Mrs. Walters, Tor Alsh's plump, cheerful cook, who had at first frowned upon Eden's arrival, could scarcely conceal her pleasure.

"The auld master ne'er had it so well," she confided complacently to her sister. "Not since his bairns died, ye ken. 'Tis hopin' I am the lass be stayin', and wee Miss Isabel, too."

Isabel, too, had fallen readily under the beguiling spell of Tor Alsh's rugged grandeur. Poor Isabel had never known what it was like to be young and gay and to laugh with companions her own age, and though she clung with fierce loyalty to her memories of Agatha Hamilton, she found an unexpectedly deep fulfillment in her renewed friendship with her cousin Eden. There was also Janet's sixteen-year-old daughter, Anne, a plain but amiable creature one could not help but like, and Isabel would have been quite content with that much alone if Tor Alsh hadn't begun to command its own place of affection in her heart. The bedroom Isabel had been given, for instance, was so far removed from that which she had shared with Aunt Agatha in Edinburgh as to bring to mind the spacious privacy of the queen's own chambers in Holyrood Palace. The manor house itself, ancient and regal with its dark oak furnishings and raftered halls, appealed to Isabel in a manner that the hot, high-ceilinged rooms of her father's plantation house in Ceylon had never done.

Though Isabel could claim little more than the connection of marriage to the Frasers, she felt curiously, inarguably, as if she had come home.

Lifting her teacup one morning at breakfast, she turned her gaze to the window. As her eyes came to rest on a dark-headed man emerging from the stables, she blushed furiously and looked quickly away. Davie Anderson was Angus Fraser's stablemaster, and Isabel had met him by accident only yesterday. She had wandered alone into the big, raftered barn and, rounding a darkened stall, had bumped squarely into him. Embarrassed, she had pretended an interest in the enormous horses that Angus Fraser bred for a living, and Davie had obliged her with a brief recitation of their history.

"Tor Alsh has been breeding blooded drafters since the fourteenth century, miss," he told her in his charming Highland dialect. "Legend has it Robert Bruce liberated Scotland at the Battle of Bannockburn astride a Tor Alsh drafter. They were called destriers in those days and were bred to carry the hundreds of pounds of armor worn to protect themselves and their riders. Nowadays, of course, they aren't ridden anymore. 'Tisna practical, though they be braw workers behind the plow.''

His gentle burr deepened with affection as he paused before a nearby stall to stroke the muscled neck of a big chestnut gelding. Isabel, who would rather have died than display her fear, had bravely put out her own hand and was rather astonished when the vicious-looking animal made no attempt to bite it off. She had looked up to catch Davie Anderson smiling at her and had been consumed by a wave of embarrassment, knowing he had clearly guessed her thoughts. Without another word she had lifted her trailing skirts and fled, yet their brief encounter had lingered in her mind.

The sound of voices from the drive below brought Isabel to her feet. Looking down, she saw that Eden had come out of the house dressed in a close-fitting habit of dark gray tweed and carrying a whip in her gloved hand. Her fair hair was confined in a net at the nape of her neck, and Isabel felt a tug of something curiously like envy as she watched her cousin slip her foot into the stirrup Davie was holding for her. The top of Eden's head came barely level with the drafter's sloping back, and yet she swung into the saddle without a moment's hesitation, chatting leisurely with Davie as he bent to adjust the girth. Eden, of course, was not at all afraid of Tor Alsh's drafters.

''Mornin' to ye, Miss Hamilton.''

Startled from her thoughts, Isabel's chin came up with a jerk as the sound of Davie Anderson's voice filtered to her through the heavy panes of glass. Looking down, she saw him lift an arm in greeting and smile at her before limping back to the stable with one of the collies at his heels; the limp, as Isabel had learned, was the result of an accident suffered in his childhood.

Oh! thought Isabel on a gasp. Whatever have I done? It was obvious that Davie had thought she was watching him, and by now it was far too late to open the window and explain. As quickly as that, the morning was all but ruined for her.

Chapter Twelve

Turning down the long, winding cart trail that led across the moor, Eden gave the Clydesdale his head, enjoying the feel of the brisk wind against her cheeks. The morning had dawned misty and cool, yet the sun was burning off the clouds as it climbed higher into the sky, giving the heather-covered slopes and the wide, open moorland a brilliance of color Eden had never dreamed possible. Bluebells nodded in the tall grass, and bracken ferns uncurled their heads in the damp copses beneath towering larches. Innumerable birds sang in the trees or soared overhead, and a pair of lithe red does bounded gracefully away as Eden's approach startled them from the rocky bank of a stream.

Clytie, Eden's mount, seemed to be enjoying himself in equal measure, and Eden made no effort to check his stride as they swept across the length of the glen and into a deep, densely grown stretch of forest. Here the sound of his hoofbeats was muffled by a layer of pine needles, and the sunlight filtering through the tall trees threw up shadows that gave Eden the impression she had plunged into a passageway of dark, impenetrable green.

How different this was, Eden could not help thinking, from galloping along the rocky banks of a *nullah* with her nose and mouth covered by a puggari to protect her from the clouds of choking dust!

It was a mistake to think of India. India was a world away and more than a lifetime removed from the isolated existence led by the Frasers of Tor Alsh. Grandfather Angus, Janet, Isabel, and Anne . . . those were the people she must think of now, not Jaji, the Begum Fariza, or the

Rajkumari Krishna Dai, or even Hugh Gordon, who was somehow as irrefutably bound to her memories of India as her adopted family in Mayar.

Damn him, Eden thought, as she always did whenever his image rose unbidden to her mind—which it had been doing with annoying frequency of late. She had been surprised and infuriated to discover that she actually missed him—no, not missed him, she corrected herself angrily, just wished at times that she might see him again because—because—

"Blood and fury, I don't even *know* why!" Eden said aloud, and furthermore, the thought was an appalling one. She was *glad* that they had gone their separate ways and that the probability of seeing him again was more than remote. Even the likelihood of a chance encounter between them in Lucknow had dwindled to nothing, for Eden was not entirely certain how long it would be before she returned to India now that her grandfather was making such a remarkable recovery. She couldn't bear to leave him just yet, not when he had asked her to stay. Isabel, too, seemed content to remain, and Eden couldn't bring herself to make her cousin unhappy. Besides, as much as she might long for India, she herself could not deny a certain fascination with Tor Alsh and its small but impressive breeding farm. Davie Anderson, though capable and determined, was clearly overworked, and Eden had secretly been toying with the idea of asking her grandfather's permission to take over some of the responsibilities from him.

That Angus Fraser was proud of her horsemanship Eden knew, and she herself derived a curious satisfaction from riding an unschooled animal such as Clytie, who was in actuality bred to pull heavy plows and not to obey the commands of a woman on his back. All of the big but gentle animals in the stone stable were a challenge to her, and she had been further intrigued by the stud books and brood mare lists her grandfather had shown her: records entered in neat, even columns on page after page of yellowed ledgers, some of them dating back to the fourteenth century.

Her uncles, Davie Anderson had already told her, had been planning to introduce Percheron blood into the Tor Alsh line, and it was on a voyage across the Channel to France with a pair of prize breeding fillies that they had been drowned in a freak winter storm. Eden had been caught up by the stablemaster's enthusiastic lecture on the proposed cross-breeding and sufficiently curious with the results as to dream of delaying her departure for India—at least for a time.

"And while you've been daydreaming," said Eden aloud, lifting her head and looking ruefully down the long avenue of firs before her, "you've managed to lose your way."

Without any proper cues from his mistress, Clytie had cantered in an erratic path through the forest, and Eden drew rein now uncertainly as they emerged at the edge of an unfamiliar valley. It was smaller by half than the one in which Tor Alsh stood, yet one of undeniably scenic beauty. A waterfall plunged in a foaming path down the sheer granite face of a mountain into a loch as clear and dark and deep as the tunnel of trees she had just left behind. Ringed by larches and silver birch, the shores of the loch seemed untouched by man—until Eden's eyes traveled higher, to a flower-covered meadow upon which stood a castle of impressive proportions. It was obviously not a remnant of feudal times, for the traditional battlements and parapets were flanked by towers that seemed intended to complement the symmetry of the structure rather than fulfill some ancient, archaic purpose of protection. Furthermore, there was no evidence of crumbling walls or long-ago plundered keeps, but rather an air of well-tended refinement enhanced by neatly tended lawns and flower-filled gardens.

Clytie's hooves rang hollowly as he crossed an arching stone bridge into an inner courtyard. It had not really been Eden's intention to inquire of the castle's inhabitants the way back to Tor Alsh, for she doubtless could have found it herself. Yet she was admittedly curious about these neighbors of whom the Frasers had mentioned nothing and interested to see what sort of person would appear at the door in response to her summons. Perhaps a handsomely kilted nobleman or a blue-blooded chatelaine of imposingly regal demeanor?

Eden smiled at the foolishness of her thoughts, yet the smile froze on her lips as the iron-braced door swung inward to reveal the most unlikely person she had ever expected to encounter in this remote corner of Scotland: a slim, dark-skinned man in loose-fitting cotton trousers, his black beard neatly groomed and his head swathed in a turban of brilliant gold silk. A Hindu!

For an endless space of time Eden could only stare at him, incredulous, and the bland look in the Hindu's black eyes glimmered with amusement and something very like resignation. Apparently he was quite accustomed to the indelicate stares of unsuspecting memsahibs, yet a moment later it was his turn to start in violent disbelief as Eden, recovering herself with admirable effort, placed the palms of her hands together in the traditional Hindu manner of greeting a respected elder.

Schooling his face with equal speed, for he was, after all, a mere servant in the household, the Hindu inquired in polite, faintly accented English if the young mistress wished an audience with his master. Whereupon Eden astounded him a second time by addressing him in fluent Hindustani, the quality of which was normally exhibited only by Indian ladies of excellent family.

"Thou art of Hind, sahiba?" he was betrayed into blurting.

"Oh, yes. I am of the household of Malraj Pratap Gaswarad," Eden said at once, "the rajah of Mayar, in whose palace I spent the years of my girlhood."

And such was the impression she made on him that the Hindu led her at once into the presence of his master, a breech of protocol that was astonishing in itself, for few visitors, if any, were ever admitted into the upper chambers of one Major-General Sir Hamish Blair.

"I—I'm sorry," Eden stammered with considerable consternation as she was shown into the private study of richly appointed oak in which a wizened, white-haired old man with luxurious drundeary whiskers sat reading near the fire. He was casually attired in slippers and a dressing robe of deep red silk brocade, and Eden could feel a blush of embarrassment rising to her cheeks.

"I believe your bearer must have misunderstood me, sir. I wanted only to inquire the way back to Tor Alsh. I didn't intend—"

Her words were promptly waved away with an impatient hand. "Sit down, girl, sit down. Dundhoo was absolutely right in bringing you here. I take it you're Angus Fraser's granddaughter, eh? Been curious to meet you." He chuckled asthmatically as his interested gaze roved over her. "You've your mother's looks, I ween, and she was a great beauty in her day. No milk-and-water miss, either, and I suspect you're the same, eh? Eh?"

"You—you knew my mother, sir?"

The elderly gentleman chuckled reminiscently. "I'll say I did! Had the pleasure of dancing with her at her coming-out ball when she was barely seventeen. Bonnie as a sprig of heather, and all the lads in the glen head over ears in love with her. Now what in hell was I doing here in Glen Alsh that time of year?" A bony forefinger tapped restively against the arm of his chair until, abruptly, his expression cleared. "Oh, aye, I was home on leave. Been wounded in the Afghan war, you ken, though I couldn't wait to get back to India. Wasn't until a year or so later, when I was already back in Lahore, that I heard the lass had contracted a *mésalliance* with one of the Douglas lads. Bad blood, the Douglases, and here you Frasers'd been feuding with them for a hundred years or more. Not surprising Angus lost his temper. Slow to anger, you ken, but dangerous once he did." Major-General Sir Hamish Blair broke off with an annoyed frown. "I'll be damned if I can remember what happened to your mother after that. It was years ago, and my memory ain't what it used to be. Must've married the Douglas lad, I ween, though you said you were a Hamilton, eh?"

"My mother never married him, because Grandfather sent her away to live with relatives in the Lowlands," explained Eden, who had herself heard the tale only recently from Janet. "And the Douglas boy you mentioned rode after her, only to break his neck when his horse fell in the darkness. Mother was unable to forgive my grand-

father for that, and so she ran away to England to the
home of some friends. Grandfather in turn cut her out of
his will, and she was eventually forced by circumstance
to take a position as a governess."

"Aye," said the major-general, nodding his head. "I
do remember something about that."

"The man who gave her employment happened to be
a director of the East India Company," Eden continued,
"and once his children were old enough, he sent for his
family to join him in Lucknow. My mother was asked to
go with them. That's where she met and eventually married my father."

"Then it was a happy ending for the lass, after all,"
said the major-general contentedly. "A pity Angus was
such a proud old bastard. Wouldn't yield an inch once his
wishes were crossed, though he should've given the bairns
his blessing instead of carrying on the way he did. Might
have prevented the poor Douglas lad's death if he had.
Though I suppose that's neither here nor there now, eh?
'Tis years in the past and long since forgotten."

He fixed Eden with an approving eye. "Heard his
health has improved of late. I'll wager you're to thank for
that. Here, sit in the light so I can see you better, there's
a good lass. Eyesight ain't what it used to be, I'm afraid.
Why don't you tell me a wee bit about yourself?"

Eden, in fact, told him considerably more than she intended, and for the space of an hour she and the elderly
gentleman engaged in a lively exchange that both of them
enjoyed. Major-General Sir Hamish Blair had spent nearly
forty years in India as a career soldier, and was of a mind
and a schooling that Eden, born into an Indian military
garrison, knew and understood. Both of them were
pleased to discover how much they had in common, and
since the major-general's command of the Hindustani language was still excellent, Eden was enchanted to converse with him. Dundhoo, carrying in a tray of
refreshments a short time later, was pleased to observe
how animated his elderly employer appeared.

"Did you ken this bloody beggar refused to part from
my side even after I was pensioned off?" inquired the
major-general of Eden, his voice filled with gruff affec-

tion. "Didn't give a damn that I was going back to England and that he'd be robbed of his caste by crossing the Black Water with me. I suppose living in Scotland these eight years past has turned him into a right proper Brit, eh, Dundhoo?"

"If the sahib so claims," Dundhoo intoned solemnly, though Eden was familiar enough with the nuances of expression on an Indian's face to see that the major-general's fondness for the Hindu was returned in equal measure.

"Oh, no, this ain't my home, lass," Sir Hamish hastily corrected her when the conversation eventually moved to the imposing castle in which he resided. "Belongs to my nephew, the earl of Blair. Bad-tempered fellow, and I must admit I'm sair glad he's gone away from home so much. I prefer to be on my own, you understand, and he's got a way of making this place seem damned small and close whenever he's in residence. Eh? What's that? Sheep, lass. We here at Arran Mhór raise sheep, and you can always find Lord Blair in the mills in Glasgow, or in the offices of his textile firms in London, anywhere but here at Arran Mhór. Prefers a warmer clime and warmer lasses, if you understand my meaning."

Eden did, and could not prevent a trace of color from creeping to her cheeks. She had already decided that Major-General Blair was an outspoken and somewhat outrageous old man, yet she had taken an instant liking to him, a feeling that was apparently reciprocated given the warmth with which the old man bid her farewell.

"I'll have a groom take you back to Tor Alsh," he said, and made no move to relinquish the hand she held out to him. "But only if you'll be promisin' to come back."

Eden promptly gave her word, and ten minutes later she was cantering down a wide lane leading along the shore of the loch with an Arran Mhór groom riding behind her. Glancing over her shoulder as the turrets of the castle slipped from view, Eden felt her heart fill with an unexpected surge of happiness. She had ridden away from Tor Alsh plagued by feelings of indecision and uncertainty, and now she was returning with a little bit of India to warm her. It was enough for the time being, she decided with a faint smile. More than enough.

"The Blairs of Arran Mhór?" Janet's voice had taken on an uncharacteristic sharpness, and the teapot nearly slipped from her grasp as she straightened abruptly in response to her niece's query. "You can't mean that you—you didn't by chance meet the earl of Blair today, did you?"

"No," said Eden, puzzled by her aunt's reaction. "I take it he wasn't even there, for Sir Hamish mentioned that he spends considerable time in London." She proceeded to describe her visit to the castle while her aunt, relaxing visibly, continued to pour tea.

"The Blairs are an ancient Highland family," Janet explained at last, "though the first of them was English, a Norman nobleman who marched from Yorkshire with Edward the Second to crush the rebel leader Robert Bruce. Bruce himself, you see, was at first aligned with the English king, and it was only later that he decided to take the crown of Scotland for himself. Like Bruce, the first Blair eventually renounced his fealty to his English sovereign, and later all his worldly goods, in order to see Bruce crowned at Scone. For that, and for distinguishing himself in the Battle of Bannockburn, Bruce presented him with an earldom and the lands bordering Tor Alsh."

"Legend has it Robert Bruce came to Tor Alsh himself to select the destrier he was to ride into battle," Anne added dreamily. "It's said he fancied the area so well that he bestowed it upon Blair as a special mark of favor. The Blairs and the Frasers have since intermarried a good deal over the centuries."

"That's enough, Anne. Finish your dinner," her mother said, again with that same sharpness to her tone, and Eden looked at her curiously. Aunt Janet rarely lost her composure or spoke short-temperedly to anyone. Could it be possible that her daughter's words had caused her a measure of discomfort, perhaps because she harbored some secret hope for a betrothal between Anne and Sir Hamish's titled and apparently unmarried nephew? The prospect was intriguing, for the little Sir Hamish had said about the earl had nonetheless hinted at a gross debauché, or at the very least a man of considerable appetites, both for women and for life. It seemed unlikely that he would ever turn his interests toward kind-hearted yet admittedly plain little Anne.

I'll have to ask Isabel what she thinks about that, Eden thought, for though she was fond of Anne, she couldn't resist deriving amusement from the thought of a union between her plump, timid cousin and the supposedly worldly earl of Blair.

"Personally I'd not have dared leave you alone in his company thirty-odd years ago," Angus Fraser told Eden upon hearing of her encounter with his elderly neighbor later that evening. "Complain though he will about that nephew of his, Hamish was something of a rake in his own day, too. Had an eye for bonnie women and a taste for expensive wines. It runs in the Blair blood, I ween."

"But you don't mind my visiting with him now?" Eden inquired anxiously.

Angus laughed and patted her hand. "Do as you please, lass. I just want to see you happy."

Surprisingly enough it was Davie Anderson who expressed open disapproval of Eden's unsquired visit to Major-General Blair. The two of them were in the process of examining the leg of a stallion who had injured himself in the pasture the night before when Eden, catching sight of Davie's expression, broke off abruptly in her description of yesterday's visit to Arran Mhór.

"What is it? What's the matter?"

"I wish ye'd no go over there," Davie said simply, though a flush had crept to his thin cheeks.

"Why not? My grandfather doesn't seem to object to Sir Hamish's company, and I don't see why you—"

"Och, it isna the auld general," Davie interrupted. "It be His Lordship what needs watchin'."

Eden's brows rose. "The earl of Blair? But he isn't even in residence."

"That doesna mean he willna show up without warnin' this day or the next. 'Tisna right you should be found there alone should he return. Or," he added, turning abruptly away to apply a bandage soaked in ointment to the stallion's cut leg, "if Miss Isabel happens to be with you."

"I suppose you're right," Eden agreed after a moment's silence, concealing with supreme effort the amused twitching of her lips. "I shall make it a point not to involve my cousin in any unexpected encounters with the notorious earl of Blair."

Lord Blair, however, did not deign to show himself in the days and weeks that followed, and Eden rode over to Arran Mhór as often as time would permit. She enjoyed her visits with Sir Hamish, who was, she suspected, rather lonely, and since he rarely spoke of his nephew, Eden soon forgot about him altogether. Indeed, the major-general seemed far more content to reminisce about India and show Eden the medals and battle souvenirs he had collected during the course of a long and brilliant career.

When he grew tired of the past he would talk to Eden of sheep and wool. The enterprise, begun with a mated pair of Cheviots presented to the third earl of Blair, had evolved over the years into an astonishingly successful business. In the past twenty-five years alone the Blair holdings had expanded sufficiently to encompass six thousand acres in Scotland and additional land in the great wool centers of England's West Country and included the establishment of offices in Glasgow, London, and, formerly, in India.

Whenever the weather proved pleasant and his arthritic joints did not plague him, Sir Hamish would lead Eden out into the paddocks or along the winding sheep walks and talk quite knowledgeably about a business in which, he often claimed, he had very little interest. Arran Mhór's extensive herds were managed by a pair of hardworking brothers Lord Blair himself had hired, and there was little for the old gentleman to do, yet Eden noticed that Sir Hamish, despite his protests to the contrary, was very much aware of everything that went on about him.

Eden was rather startled to make the discovery that she was equally as interested in Arran Mhór's sheep as with the breeding of Tor Alsh's Clydesdales. This heretofore unrealized bend toward livestock propagation bemused her considerably. She would never have imagined a year ago that she would one day spend most of her waking hours mixing liniments and hot bran mashes for ailing brood mares or slog in heavy boots through the byres in order to watch the McKenzie brothers dip their sheep.

Inexperienced as she might have been, it was obvious that she had been born with a natural flair for husbandry, and the men who at first welcomed her presence with polite tolerance soon came to appreciate her help. Eden found that she relished the hard work and the long hours spent in the fields, deriving from both a satisfaction she could not have imagined in another day and age. The idle life whiled away in the scented rooms of an Indian zenana no longer seemed real to her, and she was often moved to wonder how she could have considered herself contented there.

Her appearance, too, had begun to reflect the changes in her life: gone were the overblown crinolines with their wide, impractical hoops that had seemed so appropriate for the hot, languid days in Delhi. She wore nothing but loose skirts and unadorned blouses, and her hair was more often than not looped up in simple braids. It was doubtful that Hugh Gordon would have recognized her now, yet in some inexplicable way, perhaps because she was happy, Eden had never looked more beautiful.

Toward the end of August Angus Fraser announced unexpectedly that he intended to travel to Inverness to attend a livestock auction, and did Eden wish to accompany him? Eden did, and with them went Isabel and Anne and a half dozen mares who, having turned up barren during the breeding season, were to be sold. Angus, who several months ago had not even possessed the strength to leave his room, spoke enthusiastically throughout the course of the journey of the bargains he intended to drive and of the saddle horses he wished to purchase for his granddaughters. Both Eden and Isabel expressed a deep interest in the town of Inverness itself, never having visited this ancient capital of the Highlands before, and Anne could talk of nothing but the woolens and heavy silks she planned to add to her winter wardrobe.

All in all it was a gay procession that, three days later, rumbled into town, and most of the pedestrians who passed them on the road turned their heads to smile at the Frasers' high-wheeled cart, their attention caught by the bright expectancy on those young, lovely faces.

Inverness lay brooding under a leaden cover of clouds, and mist obscured the hills that tumbled in layer upon gray-green layer down to the shores of the loch. The auction grounds were muddy, and most of the crowd was dressed in heavy gear, yet business was brisk, and Angus found it difficult to negotiate the lumbering cart through the throngs of men and horses.

"I daresay they'll be eager to rid themselves of their stock before the rain begins," the elderly gentleman observed. "I hope we'll have similar luck."

Regrettably they did not, for they had sold no more than three of their mares before the swollen skies opened up into a torrential downpour. While Isabel and Anne took refuge in the milliner's shop, Eden dragged the hood of her traveling cloak over her head and clung stubbornly to her grandfather's arm.

"Let's see if we canna purchase a few well-bred mounts for you and your cousins," Angus said jovially when the last of his mares had finally found a new owner.

"Shouldn't we think about going home?" protested Eden, who was herself chilled and wet. "You must consider your health, Grandfather."

"Nonsense! A little rain never hurt anyone, and I'll na stand accused of permitting my grandchildren to ride plow horses for lack of better mounts. Ah, there's a bonnie pony for your cousin Anne. The chestnut with the white stockings there. I'll wager she has a wee bit of hunter in her. Come along, lass, let's see what she's worth."

Eden had already discovered that her grandfather possessed an extraordinarily forceful will, a trait that had come into evidence more and more with the improvement of his health and the subsequent return of a startling amount of energy for a man of seventy-two years. She had learned that there was little sense in arguing with him when he had set his mind to a particular purpose, yet since she did indeed fear for his health in the cold, slanting rain, she intended to see that the business of purchasing saddle horses was quickly concluded.

"Why don't you buy her, Grandfather," she suggested, "while I see to a mount for Isabel and me?"

Angus agreed, and in possession of a handful of pound notes, Eden left him. Her attention was caught almost immediately by a long-legged thoroughbred hunter being auctioned in the next ring. Liking his looks and seeing no evidence of unsoundness, she joined in the bidding, though the competition was by no means intended for novices. Undaunted, Eden bid coolly and carefully, and eventually there was no one left to challenge her save a gentleman in rain-soaked oilskins who stood obscured by the crowd on the far side of the ring.

The crowd was clearly entertained by the battle of wills that unwittingly ensued, yet Eden had no intention of recklessly mishandling her grandfather's money. Just when it appeared that she would have to back down, her opponent unexpectedly withdrew from the bidding, and her palm was slapped by the auctioneer in the traditional gesture of an accepted sale.

Flushed with pleasure, Eden went into the ring and took the big animal's halter, speaking soothingly as he snorted and sidled uneasily. The crowd dispersed in search of new entertainment, and only the animal's former owner remained behind, counting his money and assuring Eden that she had purchased "a rare ane, indeed."

Eden smiled her agreement, and above the steady roar of the rain she heard someone say behind her:

"Congratulations, mistress. You bargained quite shrewdly."

"Thank you," said Eden warmly, turning to the tall man in the oilskins. As she spoke she looked up into a face that was all but obscured by a dark, dripping hood. Suddenly she froze, and her heart seemed to skid to a halt.

"I would have continued bidding but for the fact that I'm only a temporary resident in the area," the man went on, seeming not to notice Eden's appalled silence. "It would be a shame for such a magnificent creature to stand idle for most of the year, wouldn't it?" He smiled down at her, and as his eyes fell on the small, white face beneath the sodden brim of a woolen hood, he stiffened abruptly. For an endless moment he stared back at her, his own expression mirroring the shock and disbelief clearly written on Eden's face while the rain continued to fall upon them and the last of the crowd slipped away.

"My God," said Hugh Gordon in a voice Eden hadn't known he possessed. "What are you doing here in Inverness?"

The words were a barely audible breath: "I came for the auction. I've been living in Glen Alsh."

"*Glen Alsh?*" Incredulous, Hugh seized her by the arms. "That wouldn't by any chance be at Angus Fraser's, would it?"

Eden found she could only make a slight, affirmative movement with her head. Hugh released her abruptly, turning away so that she could not see the expression on his face.

"How—how did you know?" she inquired at last through lips that were painfully stiff.

"Because I happen to live close by, at Arran Mhór, which I'm sure you've heard of. . . . Now why in hell are you looking like that, damn it? Didn't I tell you once before that I've too many titles to suit an honest man? Surely Angus must have spoken of me? The earl of Blair?"

The breath passed through Eden's lips in a muffled gasp, and it seemed to her as if a wave of hot, incredulous horror was washing up and over her. Without another word she backed away from him and then turned and fled. For a long moment Hugh stared after her, unmindful of the water that trickled cold and uncomfortable down his neck.

"I understand Lord Blair is in residence at Arran Mhór," said Isabel the following evening, looking round the table with bright expectancy. "No one could talk of anything else when Mrs. Walters and I went down to the village."

"He's probably come for the harvest," said Angus when Janet observed that it was rather late in the year for the earl to be making an appearance.

"Usually he arrives in time to open the dancing at the midsummer ball," her daughter added. "What a shame he didn't come in time to hold it this year."

"The midsummer ball?" echoed Isabel with interest. "It sounds terribly romantic."

"It is," Anne assured her. "The Blairs have held that same ball for hundreds of years, and some of the guests travel all the way from England just to attend. An enormous bonfire is lit in the garden at midnight, and all of the villagers and crofters are invited."

"I wonder if he'll still decide to have one this year," said Isabel dreamily, "owing to the fact that it's nearly September? Will we be invited, do you think?"

Her innocent query gave rise to a low laugh from Janet. "I'm afraid you'll find no invitations on your doorstep, dear, provided Lord Blair decides to hold the ball in the first place. They're nearly as difficult to obtain as a private audience with the queen."

"Who was denied an invitation four years ago because the guest list was already filled," Anne added, smiling. "Oh, of course the matter was straightened out eventually," she explained at Isabel's disbelieving gasp. "Lord Blair was *quite* apologetic and said it was only because he hadn't known that she and the prince consort would be in residence at Balmoral that year. Imagine," she concluded on a giggle, "the audacity of the man to say as much to our queen!" She turned to regard her grandfather with undisguised envy. "You'll be invited, won't you, Grandpapa? They always ask you, and yet you never attend."

"At my age there's deuced little pleasure to be found in watching overweight and tortuously corseted matrons making fools of themselves on the dance floor," said Angus disagreeably. "Hand me another of those bannocks, will you? There's a good lass."

"And there's little sense in discussing the point," his daughter-in-law added sharply. "There hasn't been a midsummer ball in years, and it's doubtful that Lord Blair will hold one now. Why should he, after all? Anne, if you're finished, you may bring in dessert. More tea, Father, or would you care for a pint of ale?''

Eden, who had been markedly silent throughout this lively exchange, asked abruptly if she might be excused. Though Isabel would have liked to accompany her, Eden brushed past her and out of the room as though unaware of her presence. There was an odd, tight look about her mouth, and Isabel wondered fleetingly if the earl of Blair had something to do with it. But that was absurd, of course. Eden had never met the man before, so why would a discussion about him seem troubling to her?

It was a question Eden herself did not care to answer, yet one that afforded her a singularly sleepless night. At six o'clock she was up and dressed and standing in the chill gray of morning, waiting for a groom to saddle her newly acquired hunter. The Rao-sahib, as Eden had named him, seemed to resent the intrusion of a rider upon his back, yet Eden was in no frame of mind to tolerate his unruliness. By the time they had left the fields behind them and were sweeping across the open moorland, they had reached an agreement of sorts, and Eden ventured at last to give him his head.

The air was sharp and cold, and a layer of hoarfrost lay scattered across the heather on the higher elevations of the mountain slopes. Eden's mount seemed to find the run invigorating, for he lengthened his stride until the wind fairly sang in Eden's ears and the ground passed beneath his drumming hooves in a blur. She was breathless and laughing when she reined him in to a trot at the edge of the forest that separated Tor Alsh lands from Arran Mhór's, yet the smile died from her lips when he pricked his ears and whinnied softly.

Lifting her head, Eden saw that a man had emerged from the dark stand of trees ahead of her: a man in a woolen vest and buckskin breeches. Although he had pulled his cap over his eyes to prevent the rising sun from shining full on his face, Eden knew at once who he was. She pulled quickly on the off-side rein in an attempt to turn the Rao-sahib around, yet Hugh had seen her and lifted his hand in greeting. There was little Eden could do save draw rein and wait politely until he had crossed a small stream to her side.

"Good morning, Miss Hamilton. I see you haven't given up any of your habits. Still abroad before the dawn."

"You look to have been riding yourself," Eden observed, studying his grass-stained attire with a suitably grave expression.

Hugh smiled wryly. "And so I was, until the mount I purchased at auction yesterday threw me and bolted for home."

He looked up as Eden's clear laughter rang through the air. She was dressed in a riding habit of gray woolen with a green-and-blue Fraser plaid draped for warmth across her slim shoulders, and it occurred to him suddenly that she could easily have passed for a native Highlander. Her shining hair was rolled into a modest chignon, and a white cockade was pinned in a jaunty fashion to the peak of her cap. The brisk air had whipped lovely color into her cheeks, and laughter had set her blue eyes glowing.

Abruptly Hugh turned his attention to the hunter, who stood quietly beneath his mistress's hands. "Perhaps I shouldn't have let you take this one from me. What did you name him?"

Eden told him, and a slow smile curved his lips despite himself and warmed the pale blue eyes that continued to study her intently. Oddly disconcerted, Eden tightened her hands about the reins and the Rao-sahib stirred restlessly.

"Why did you not tell me?" she blurted, though that was not at all what she had intended to say. Her face was no longer glowing and alive but drawn and strained with some undefinable inner tension.

"My dear girl," said Hugh, understanding her instantly, "why should I enumerate my many titles for everyone I meet? Surely you would have accused me of bragging?"

"Yes, I probably would have," Eden agreed slowly. "But you knew I was returning to Scotland—"

"To Edinburgh," he corrected, "which is many miles and, you'll doubtless agree, worlds removed from this place. As it didn't seem likely that we would ever meet again, I saw no reason to divulge personal details concerning my . . . other life.''

Oddly hurt by the remark, Eden said defensively, ''But you're not really a Blair!''

''Ah, but my mother was, and it was the general opinion of her family that she married far beneath herself when she became the wife of James Fitzwilliam Gordon, a minor staff sergeant of Highland artillery. And no one save my mother was particularly disappointed when he was killed years later on the battlefield of Ferozeshah. We came to live at Arran Mhór when I was nine, and regrettably, or perhaps fortunately for me, I happened to be the only male in the Blair family to survive infancy. I was assigned the heraldic title of twelfth earl of Blair when my grandfather died fifteen-odd years ago. The Blairs,'' he concluded blandly, ''have never been known for their longevity.''

''Except for Sir Hamish,'' said Eden without thinking, and her eyes widened at a sudden thought. ''Oh! Was it Sir Hamish you went to visit in Lahore the first time you came to India?''

''It was.''

Eden gazed at him wonderingly, for a great deal about his past had suddenly come clear to her, and she found it difficult to comprehend the odd twist of fate that had brought them both to this place.

''If only he had told me his nephew was—was a Gordon,'' she whispered.

''Would it have made a difference?'' Hugh inquired sharply.

''It might have,'' she allowed. ''And you, Your Grace?'' she demanded tartly. ''Would it have mattered if I'd told you in Delhi that I was the granddaughter of Angus Fraser of Tor Alsh?''

''My dear girl,'' Hugh said with an infuriating laugh, ''there's no point in answering that, is there? You are here, and I suppose we'll have to make the best of it. I expect you'll be pleased to know that I rarely extend my visits to Arran Mhór beyond a fortnight or two. I'll be gone before you have the opportunity to grow tired of me."

"Oh!" said Eden indignantly. "That isn't what I meant, and you know it! Why is it that you always—" She broke off and clamped her lips tightly together. She was not about to argue with him, though the mocking laughter in his eyes was so vexing that she very nearly forgot herself. She should have known that he would have the advantage of her once again, even standing there bareheaded and disheveled with his finely tailored breeches muddied after being thrown from his horse.

In an arctic tone she pronounced that she hoped his stay would be a pleasant one and regretted that it seemed unlikely they would see one another again. "We're awfully busy at Tor Alsh with the harvest," she explained, "and of course I'm certain you've neglected your affairs at Arran Mhór long enough as it is."

"Of course," he said gravely, and bid her farewell in that pompous manner of his that made Eden long to strike him with her whip. For a moment her gloved hand tightened longingly about the carved bone handle, then she wheeled the big hunter about and took off at a hand gallop across the moor, filled with a fury and resentment she made no attempt to analyze.

"I don't want to hear another word about Arran Mhór or your perishing Lord Blair!" she flared at poor Anne when her cousin unwisely chose to bring up the topic of their much discussed neighbor the following evening. Anne, who had raced eagerly into the study, where Eden was bent over a confusion of paperwork, stopped short in her tracks, her skirts swirling about her.

"Eden!" protested Isabel with soft reproach from her chair near the window.

"I'm sorry," said Eden, though she was not the least bit contrite. "It so happens that I am fatigued to the extreme with talk of the Blairs, and I don't wish to hear another word about them, thank you."

"Then I'll simply not tell you my news," threatened Anne with a childish quivering of her lower lip.

"Oh, come, what is it, Anne?" inquired Isabel kindly, laying aside her embroidery and casting a disapproving eye at Eden.

It was clear that Anne was bursting to tell someone, and she instantly forgot her hurt at Eden's brusqueness. "We've been invited," pronounced Anne, her voice trembling with sudden excitement, "all of us, not just Grandpapa, to the midsummer ball at Arran Mhór! A servant just brought the invitation round, and Grandpapa says all of us might as well attend, seeing that Lord Blair has decided to hold it after all. Isn't it grand? Mama says I'm to have a new ball gown if one can be finished in time, and of course you and Eden are to have them, too."

"Provided we are going," said Eden stiffly. "Which I am not."

Seeing the astonished looks on both her cousins' faces, she added tartly: "I have no intention of attending such a silly ritual, and besides, there's far too much work to be done here at home." With uncharacteristic energy she gathered up the sheafs of paper and swept stiffly from the room.

Chapter Thirteen

"Good evening, Miss Hamilton," said the earl of Blair, bowing politely over Eden's gloved hand. "It is indeed a pleasure to see you again, though I must confess I am continually amazed at your ability to cross effortlessly from one world into the next."

Eden lifted her chin, and the eighteen yards of taffeta that made up the skirts of her ball gown rustled sharply over the hoops of her crinoline. "Were you expecting me to make an appearance in farhi pajamas and a _choli?_"

Hugh's eyes glinted. "Either that or in a patched skirt and manure-spattered boots, which is how Simon McKenzie chose to describe you."

Eden stiffened and, detaching her hand calmly from his grasp, moved on into the ballroom. She was accosted almost immediately by Anne, who had preceded her in the reception line and was burning to discover what the earl had said to her. Eden responded evasively, her brow furrowed with annoyance, wishing she hadn't deferred to her grandfather's wishes by making an appearance at the midsummer ball.

From all indications it was going to be a glittering affair. Though it was scarcely nine o'clock, the ballroom was filling rapidly with guests, the women flaunting gowns of breathtaking magnificence while the men arrived attired in formal black or in the fabulous colors of numerous Highland regiments. Some of the women fluttered tartan ribands and were accompanied by husbands in kilts and plaids that proclaimed their fealty to various clans, yet for the most part the assembly was English,

209

guests of the earl, who, according to Anne, had traveled all the way from England to attend.

"I expect you've already heard that he's known as the duke of Roxbury there," said Anne, eyeing the tall figure of their host as he bowed over the hand of an imperious dowager. "I understand he inherited his title from a distant uncle, though the family ties are obscure. Of course everyone here still thinks of him as Lord Blair, but isn't it romantic to have so many titles? I simply don't know whether to address him as 'Your Lordship' or 'Your Grace.' "

"I find nothing the least bit romantic about a man who gains his position and wealth through the untimely deaths of rightful heirs," Eden pronounced tartly.

Anne's hand flew indignantly to the modest fichu covering her bosom. "Oh, now that is unfair of you, Eden! Lord Blair works very hard to manage his estates and is most deserving of them! Why, he spends most of his time traveling between London, Somerset, and Arran Mhór, and Grandpapa once told me he even goes to India on occasion, though no one is really sure, for he is so vexingly uncommunicative with his family. I doubt even Sir Hamish knows where he is at any given moment."

"I'm not at all surprised that he prefers to keep his affairs private considering his reported reputation," replied Eden shortly, deciding to say nothing at all to Anne of Hugh Gordon's involvement with the India political service. Anne was already behaving alarmingly like a besotted mooncalf and did not need to be supplied with further proof of Lord Blair's romantic virtues. "Furthermore, you'd better stop staring," she advised, "or His Grace is bound to notice."

Blushing hotly, Anne swept away without another word while Eden turned to greet Sir Hamish, who had been coaxed into making a brief appearance in the ballroom to welcome his nephew's guests. The scarlet regimental uniform he wore bristled with medals and military orders, and he cut such a dashing figure that Eden would not permit him to part company with her until he had promised her a dance.

"Cheeky as your mother," he informed her with a laugh, then eyed her slowly up and down. "And twice as bonnie, I'm thinking."

Eden's wide skirts were looped up at intervals with ropes of tiny seed pearls, which were also scattered through the netting that confined her smoothly knotted hair. The shimmering blue of her taffeta gown made the blue of her eyes seem all the more deep, and there was a youthful dignity to the tilt of her head that appealed greatly to the approving major-general.

"I'll be back to claim that dance, lass," he promised, though he hadn't really intended to stay downstairs overly long. Reluctantly he bowed over her hand and removed himself to resume his post at the duke of Roxbury's side.

Though Eden had at first been adamant in her refusal to attend the midsummer ball, she was surprised to discover as the evening wore on how much she was actually enjoying herself. Not only did Hugh Gordon keep his distance from her, he did not deign to glance even once in her direction, and with that most troublesome worry stilled, Eden could almost forget his existence and take pleasure in the company of his other guests. Apparently she was not the only one to do so. Pausing to catch her breath in a lighted alcove after a boisterous Scottish country dance, she saw her cousin Isabel leave the floor surrounded by no less than half a dozen hopeful partners. Smiling shyly, Isabel shook her head to indicate that she could not possibly decide between them, and Eden thought how fetching her cousin looked in pale purple tarlatan, her red curls looped up in a charming coronet. Even plain, plump Anne, dancing with a remarkably handsome young man of obvious English extraction, appeared flushed and lovely in the glittering candlelight.

Dressed in a gown of imposing puce velvet shot with black, Janet Fraser roamed the periphery of the dance floor keeping a watchful eye upon her daughter and nieces. Though she was obviously pleased by their apparent success with the masculine set, she could not shake her deep disappointment at the fact that Lord Blair had not chosen to dance with Anne.

"I do not think he ever bothers to dance with any-one," she confided to Eden in an unsuccessful attempt to soothe her frustration. "Of course it's understandable, given the fact that as a bachelor he really has no place to be entertaining on such a grand scale to begin with. Still, it's such an ancient tradition and so widely popular. Anne *does* look fetching, does she not? I cannot understand why he won't offer to lead her out for even a simple courtesy dance, considering we have been neighbors for so many years!"

She sighed and frowned and observed that it really was most rude of him, since a host should mingle with all of his guests, not just spend time with his business associates, as he seemed to be doing.

Janet's complaints seemed to be borne out by the fact that His Grace had spent the past half hour in conversation with a gray-haired gentleman near the arched doorway leading down into the elegant entrance hall, entirely oblivious to the carefree guests waltzing nearby.

In point of fact, however, Hugh's conversation had moved away from business matters some time ago and had turned to a discussion of the present assembly, which his companion, Sir Fitzroy Ross, considered markedly worthy of mention. It astonished him, he confessed, that although Arran Mhór did not possess a hostess to lend an aura of respectability to the evening, and Hugh had failed to make even a minimal effort to provide one in the form of an elderly aunt or a distantly related chatelaine, this seemed not to have stopped even the most fiercely conventional matrons from attending.

"It's obvious your wealth and position far outweigh the rather outré nature of the gathering," the elderly banker observed with a chuckle. "I'll warrant convention doesn't matter a fig to any mama desperate enough to parade her daughter before the highly sought after duke of Roxbury."

"Please, don't offer me a lengthy diatribe concerning my desirability as this season's catch," Hugh warned, bored. "I had to endure enough of that in Calcutta and Delhi, and I'm damned tired of it."

"Then why hold a ball to begin with?" inquired Sir Fitzroy with considerable surprise.

Hugh's shoulders lifted. "I'm not entirely certain. Perhaps a misplaced sense of duty. It *has* been a Blair tradition for hundreds of years, after all, and the last four of them have seen me in England tying up that bloody Roxbury inheritance."

"Still consider that a millstone about your neck, eh?" inquired Sir Fitzroy with interest.

"I'd rather it had been left to my half cousin William," Hugh said honestly, "despite the fact that he has the intelligence of a half-wit and the business acumen to match."

"The task of running Arran Mhór alone involves enough work to daunt the most industrious of men," agreed Sir Fitzroy, who had been banker to the Blair family for over a half a century and knew more about the business than anyone save Hugh himself. "And inheriting a duchy replete with dissatisfied tenant farmers, not to mention the floundering existence of Gordon and Blair, which the sepoy rebellion should have destroyed in its entirety rather than leaving you to grapple with the decision of whether or not to rebuild—" He broke off abruptly and fixed the duke with a fond yet frustrated eye. "Why do you do it, Hugh? Why can't you just leave well enough alone and settle only those affairs that will keep you from an early grave?"

"Do I seem that close to an untimely demise?" Hugh inquired with amusement. "Faith, I hadn't realized I was so badly overworked."

Sir Fitzroy frowned as he took in the duke's tanned, unlined face and the whipcord leanness of his body in the tailored black coat. "Fit as the devil himself, damn you," he growled, "and I'd have considered myself immeasurably blessed if I'd had half your bloody looks in my youth. No, it ain't that what worries me—not now, at any rate. But you're going on thirty-three this year and driving yourself harder than those cocky young clerks at m'bank, and I assure you they're hungry bastards who keep their ambitious eyes constantly on my salary and position! Do yourself the favor, Hugh: divest yourself of a few of your holdings, marry a lass of good family, and take the time to enjoy yourself a wee bit. Life's too short; God knows it's taken me a lifetime to discover that!''

''I'll consider the matter,'' Hugh promised with a suspicious degree of gravity.

''Bah! You're a damnable liar, and we both of us know it!'' Fearing that he was working himself into unnecessary agitation—a state expressly forbidden him by both his physician and his long-suffering wife—Sir Fitzroy turned his attention back to the dance floor, where his gaze fell inadvertently upon a slim girl in an elegant blue ball dress who was dancing with an officer of the Forty-Second Highland Regiment.

''Now who in hell is that beauty there?'' he barked. ''I don't believe I've seen her before.''

''That's Angus Fraser's granddaughter,'' said Hugh obligingly.

''Ah, so that's the Hamilton lass. I've heard of her, of course, though I hadn't suspected she'd look so much like her mother. Elizabeth Fraser was a beauty, too, you ken.''

''Perhaps, but I'm willing to wager that Miss Hamilton's temperament is mainly her father's,'' said Hugh dryly, and proceeded to explain to the interested Sir Fitzroy the rash courage with which Colonel Dougal Hamilton had met his death in the beleaguered, outnumbered, and hopelessly entrenched Lucknow residency.

''I imagine Angus is quite fond of her, eh? Made a remarkable recovery after her arrival, I understand, though I'm not surprised that he declined to attend your little gathering tonight. Never was much on socializing, Angus was, even at university.''

''Ah, that's right. The two of you studied in Edinburgh together, didn't you?''

''Aye, and what bloody little innocents we were!'' Sir Fitzroy chuckled reminiscently. ''Edinburgh was like the forbidden city to us in those days, though Angus never did come around to feeling completely at home there. Always called it an evil exile from Tor Alsh, I recall. By God, I've never met a man who clings more fiercely to his land, even for a Highlander! It must be killing him to know he's losing the place."

"What's that?" inquired Hugh with a sudden frown between his eyes.

"Financial woes, of course. Damnable mountain of debts made all the worse by the deaths of his sons last winter. Though their steward's an able fellow I've my doubts he'll be able to pull them back into the clear."

"I hadn't realized," Hugh said slowly.

"Well, by God, you should have!" said Sir Fitzroy energetically. "A large portion of their debt is owed to Arran Mhór for both the purchase of land and for several loans underwritten freely and perhaps a bit too readily by my bank at the coaxing of your uncle, the major-general."

"I've never had reason to criticize Hamish's decisions," said Hugh with a shrug. "He's managed the estate for years in my absence, and I cannot see his lending money to an old friend as a cause for alarm."

"I'm well aware of Sir Hamish's share in the family wealth, Hugh," said Sir Fitzroy crisply, "but what you're saying is precisely my point! If you would only spend more time in Scotland and involve yourself more in the Blair business, you'd be aware of what's been going on. Och, I'm not accusing Hamish of mismanagement—he's as shrewd as they come. But there are times when decisions should be made solely on the basis of their financial feasibility, not on the weight of their sentiment."

"Meaning I'm a cold-hearted bastard who wouldn't take the Blairs' ancient friendship with the Frasers into account?"

Sir Fitzroy did not return Hugh's smile. "Precisely. Hamish Blair and Angus Fraser have been friends since they were wee lads, and that's why this is one instance in which his reasoning prowess seems to have given way to foolish—perhaps even dangerous—sentiment."

"You make it sound as if there's some urgency to the situation," said Hugh with a frown.

"There is, damn it! The Frasers cannot possibly meet their payments, and I am attempting at all events to prevent a serious and consequential strain on the liquid assets of Arran Mhór—and the Northwest Highland Bank.''

''Then you should have notified me earlier.''

Sir Fitzroy's face became alarmingly red above his high, tight stock. ''I've sent a dozen letters to Somerset in the past year alone, and you've yet to respond personally to a single one! I've received nothing but assurances from that objectionable solicitor of yours, Highbee—Hillowby—''

''Higbee,'' Hugh said helpfully.

''Higbee, yes, blast your eyes!—that I'm to continue as always, and that His Grace should be pleased to look into the matter once he finds the time to pay a visit to Scotland!''

With rising indignation Sir Fitzroy became aware that Hugh was not fully attending him but had turned his head to regard with interest the belated arrival of a couple being divested of their trappings in the hall below by a bowing Dundhoo. Both of them were dressed in the first rank of fashion, the gentleman middle-aged and in possession of a bored, aristocratic air, the woman past the first bloom of youth yet still arrestingly beautiful in a ball dress of lavender tulle over white glacé, the billowing flounces edged with black silk and banded with chains of pearls. Her features were smoothly patrician, her glossy black hair glinting in the candlelight, and Hugh turned back to Sir Fitzroy with a grin.

''I agree that the matter requires closer attention, but I'm afraid now is not the time. If you'll excuse me? I must welcome the Wintons. I wasn't expecting them.''

Turning heel, he strode down the stairs, and Sir Fitzroy Ross had no choice but to concede defeat. Muttering beneath his breath, he cast his eyes despairingly to the ceiling, where the rafters were lost in the gloom, quite oblivious to the music and laughter that floated brightly about him.

At midnight the skirling of a bagpipe summoned the guests outside to view the lighting of the traditional midsummer bonfire. It was a pleasantly warm evening, for a period of unusually fine weather had descended upon the Highlands with the waning of summer. A new moon was rising into the blue-black depths of the sky, and the wind blowing through the glen was sweet, containing no breath of the chill of the winter to come. In the quiet garden the masses of late-blooming roses gave off a heady scent, and the ladies in their wide, bell-like skirts gave the impression of being scores of inverted flowers as they poured talking and laughing onto the lawn.

Aunt Janet had at first intended to return home before the lighting of the bonfire, not at all certain that she approved of such an outlandish ritual. It would be extremely difficult to keep a maternal eye upon Anne, Eden, and Isabel in the darkness, and she was further alarmed by the discovery that the Blair servants and numerous local crofters and villagers would be permitted to view the festivities from a distance. Concerned that the mood of these uncivilized people might become boisterous, she had been in the process of rounding up her charges when Hugh Gordon had appeared through the throng of chattering guests and inquired with mock disapproval if she intended to leave before the culmination of the evening's events.

Janet was instantly mollified at finding herself the object of the earl's undivided attention—no, she must remember that he was a duke, now, she told herself with a delicious shiver—and she had assured him that they would be delighted to remain, watching with breathless anticipation as he took the time afterward to speak quite personally to Anne. In her excitement Janet failed to remark that he exchanged no more than a brief, polite greeting with her daughter before turning to display an inordinate amount of interest in Isabel Hamilton.

"It is indeed a pleasure to meet you, Miss Hamilton," Hugh said gravely, taking Isabel's small hand in his and speaking to her in a tone that even the listening Eden had never heard before. "I regret that we were unable to exchange no more than a word or two in the reception line."

"Oh, it—it's quite all right. Everyone was in such a hurry," stammered Isabel, the darkness inadequately concealing the flush of embarrassed pleasure that crept to her cheeks. "It was—it was kind of you to ask us, Your Grace."

Hugh's white teeth flashed in his most charming smile. "The pleasure was entirely mine, Miss Hamilton. I confess a certain curiosity to seeing for myself what lovely granddaughters Angus had acquired. Mrs. Fraser? If you would see that your party keeps under those trees there? I would not wish any of you to be overcome by the smoke."

Janet breathed her thanks as Hugh left them, and no one seemed to notice that he had not acknowledged Eden's presence even once. No one, of course, except Eden herself, who suspected strongly that the snub had been deliberate.

Well, I don't care, she told herself stubbornly, following her cousins into the glade of trees the duke had indicated. Yet there was a curious ache in her heart as she thought of the gentle, almost tender tone with which Hugh had addressed Isabel and how it compared to the half-irritated manner in which he always spoke to her. Quite suddenly she had had enough of everything: the ball, the Blairs, and especially the twittering, giggling whispers of her cousin Anne. When the dried kindling that had been gathered into a huge heap on the sloping front lawn crackled into life to the accompanying cheers of the spectators, Eden slipped away unnoticed into the darkness.

She knew her way well enough by now through Arran Mhór's extensive gardens, and she did not hesitate as she ran lightly across an arching bridge that led to the grassy banks of the duke's well-stocked trout stream. Here the roar of the crowd was no more than a blot of sound against the warm, murmurous web of wind and water, and Eden sighed gratefully as she leaned her head against the trunk of an ancient sycamore and closed her eyes. How good it felt to be alone! She didn't think she had had a moment to herself since the duke's invitation had arrived at Tor Alsh, not with Anne and Janet scheming and planning what the three of them were to wear, and as for the ball itself . . .

"I wish I'd never come," said Eden aloud, "no matter what Grandfather said!"

She did not know how long she stood there fighting the irrational and entirely absurd impulse to cry before she became aware of the fact that she was no longer alone. There was a snapping of tree branches behind her, and Eden, whirling in alarm, hastily retreated. Perhaps she was not quick enough or the white blur of her skirts gave her presence away, for suddenly she found herself being seized from behind, her arms pinioned to her sides and her chin painfully captured in a rough grip.

"Whatever are you doing? Let me go!" Eden demanded, too indignant to feel frightened.

"A petticoat, by God!" gloated a coarse voice redolent with the smell of whiskey. "Fancy stumblin' on a wee bint alone in the darkness, eh? Were the dandies no' to yer likin', lass? Ne'er fear, you've found yersel' a willin' ane the noo!"

Without warning a hot, wet mouth came down on hers, and Eden found it impossible to cry out or to struggle against it. Gasping for breath, she attempted to fight her way free, panting and flailing uselessly until, with unexpected violence, she was wrenched away and pushed backward against the trunk of the tree. Struggling for air, she stood swaying and gasping until, suddenly, Hugh Gordon's face was there before her, a face she scarcely recognized because of the rage that disfigured it.

"You little fool!" he ground out furiously. "What in hell did you think you were doing?"

Eden could say nothing in her defense or even speak at all because the wild pounding of her heart had yet to still. She could only stare up at him with her mouth open and her breast heaving. Hugh uttered an oath as he saw the lingering shock in her eyes and, without turning his head, spoke curtly in Gaelic to a pair of hovering shadows. Eden heard the sound of a brief struggle and then the crackling and snapping of branches as something very large was dragged away through the underbrush.

"What—what will they do to him?"

"Does it matter?"

"I'm not sure. I wasn't—he didn't—"

"I'm well aware of what he was trying to do," Hugh interrupted through compressed lips, "and you, Miss

Hamilton, should have known better than to leave the
grounds alone while half the village—''

"Please," Eden whispered, and put her hands to her
throat. For the first time Hugh saw the purple bruises that
marred the soft flesh there. A killing rage seemed to ex-
plode within him, for those cruelly telling marks bore
home to him the harsh reality of what had nearly happened to her. Whatever he had intended to say to Eden
was suddenly swept away in a tide of helpless anger, and
his hands moved to lift away the trembling fingers that
clung about her throat.

"By God, if he had harmed you—'' he whispered
hoarsely, and his hands moved again to sweep back the
shining hair that curled in disarray about her face. The
moment he touched her something leaped between them,
something that had first flared into life during that long-
ago confrontation in the *mardana* gardens of Malraj's
palace. Suppressed and vehemently denied, it had shown
itself in Hugh's driving anger at the thought of what another man had nearly done to her, and now it blossomed
once again fully blown at his touch—beyond comprehen-
sion, beyond all denial.

With a groan Hugh pulled Eden against him and, lowering his head, kissed her with a desperation born of that
same anger. Oddly enough Eden felt none of the fear and
disgust that she had experienced upon being kissed in a
similar fashion only a moment ago. This was Hugh,
Hugh, not some drunken ruffian from the village, and for
a long, long moment she clung to him, returning his kiss
while the warm, dark night, the shouts of the revelers,
and the crackling glow of the flames faded into nothing.

Then Hugh's hands moved once again, for he could no
longer prevent or even deny the inevitable. Deliberately
and urgently he stripped away the magnificent ball gown
as though it did not exist, and the whalebone hoop fell
onto the grass and the cool night breeze caressed Eden's
naked skin. Hugh's lips moved against the hollow of her
throat, and his hands, strong and very sure, took possession of her slender body.

"Sweet, so sweet," he whispered against her cheek.
"I didn't mean for this to happen—''

Yet both of them knew it to be a lie, for there was no longer violent desperation in his touch or his kiss, but a warmth and tenderness that burned through them with an increasing delight. Eden's lips were soft and eager and incredibly sweet beneath his, and the shining waves of her unpinned hair fell about him, caressing his skin like the touch of a lover's persuasive fingertips.

Lifting Eden against him, Hugh felt her breasts brush his naked chest and felt, too, the shiver of desire that fled through her. He laid her back gently into the grass, knowing he could wait no longer.

"*Mo cridhe*," he whispered, and the Gaelic term of endearment was as much a caress as the touch of his hands, "I fear I cannot prevent hurting you—"

Eden's arms tightened about him in response, and she pulled his head down so that her lips could trace the contours of his hard mouth. The innocence of her offering filled him with delight, and as his own need overwhelmed him, Hugh's hands moved for the last time to take Eden's hips between them and roll her beneath his hard, waiting body.

There was a moment of stabbing pain for her, yet it quickly ebbed away into the glory of a touch she had never before experienced, a touch that burned its way through every nerve and fiber of her being. Hugh moved within her and their bodies melded and Eden shivered and arched against him, straining to make him that much more a part of her. A groan of agonized bliss rose softly from him, and he drove deeper inside of her, moving again and again until Eden shuddered and gasped in helpless transport and felt him surge against her while the very essence of her being seemed to flow into his.

How long they lay there afterward neither of them could say, yet gradually, inevitably, the reeling world stilled, and they found themselves left warm and intimately locked together. Hugh drew away from her at last and rolled onto his back, staring up at the star-dusted sky feeling incredibly relaxed and entirely content, and when he moved to pull Eden into the crook of his arm she came to him willingly. For a long time neither of them spoke until Hugh laughed unexpectedly.

"This has to be a damned sight better than engaging in interminable arguments, don't you think?"

"Perhaps we should have done it sooner," Eden agreed gravely. "We might have spared ourselves a great deal of trouble."

Hugh came up on one elbow to gaze down at her. "Oh, God, Eden, if you only knew how long I've wanted—" But he did not finish what he meant to say. His words were lost against her lips as he kissed her, and everything else was swept away in a rising tide of passion.

Suddenly, an arctic female voice broke through the sweet silence surrounding them:

"*Really*, Hugh! Must you sate your desires upon common village wenches? Supposing she's poxed?"

Eden's heart went still, as still and rigid as the rest of her. She did not move as Hugh slowly turned his head.

"Oh, it's you, Caroline," he said carelessly. "Toss me that shirt there, will you?"

The woman named Caroline obliged, though the expression on her lovely face indicated clearly that she would have preferred to strangle him with it. Turning back to Eden, Hugh lifted her lax body against his and slipped the shirt over her shoulders. There was something infinitely reassuring in his gentle, unhurried manner, yet Eden would not look at him, and her face was remote and stiff and very white in the starlight.

She knew, of course, who this woman was; everyone in the ballroom had seemed to know Lady Caroline Winton, and within the space of ten minutes following her dramatic appearance, Eden had learned everything she cared to know about her. While no one could quite agree on whether or not Lady Caroline was the duke of Roxbury's current mistress, everyone concurred that she had certainly been his favorite *paramour* in the past, and her unexpected presence here in Scotland had given rise to endless speculation.

Eden had listened in silence to all those furtive, giggling whispers and had looked with envy upon the raven-haired creature whose perfectly proportioned features and graceful carriage in the magnificent ball gown made her feel hopelessly coarse and inadequate by contrast. She had watched Hugh take Lady Caroline's hand in his, had seen the look on his face as she turned a dazzling smile upon him, and she had turned away with a dreadful, sinking sense of despair. Yet nothing, *nothing* Hugh Gordon might have said or done could equal the humiliation and despair she was experiencing now, nor deepen the pain that seemed to shrivel her heart and bind her throat until it was all but impossible to breathe.

Incredibly, Hugh seemed quite indifferent to her hurt and careless of causing her more, for after shrugging unhurriedly into his pants and reaching down to pull her to her feet, he said blandly to Lady Caroline, "This is Miss Eden Hamilton of Tor Alsh, Caroline, not a common wench from the village. Lady Caroline is an old acquaintance from Somerset," he added, turning briefly to Eden. "I don't believe you've been introduced."

"How do you do?" murmured Eden through stiff lips, for there seemed nothing else to say. Nothing, in fact, seemed real to her any longer save the shame and despair that was washing like a hot tide over and through her. She did not see the glow of appreciation that briefly lit Hugh's eyes at her reply, nor feel the strong fingers that for a moment closed about her own.

"You'll be interested to know," Hugh added, turning back to Lady Caroline with a suspicious twitching of his lips, "that Miss Hamilton is not a mere diversion of mine. She is going to be my wife."

In the stunned silence that followed, two pairs of eyes were suddenly upon him: one wide and incredulous and brimming with hot pain, the other cold and calculating and equally disbelieving. Although the color had all but drained from Lady Caroline Winton's face, she was able, with a quick, sharp rustle of her wide skirts and a toss of her elegant head, to recover an appreciable measure of her composure.

"I must say you surprise me, Hugh," she said somewhat breathlessly, "but then, you always do." She drew another deep breath and attempted to smile, though it was obvious that she was in the grip of a fierce fury. "I—I expect felicitations are in order. Hugh, Miss Hamilton, I congratulate you—both of you.''

Then she was gone, vanishing into the darkness and leaving a tautly strung silence in her wake.

"I'm sorry," Hugh said at last. "I would have given anything to prevent that."

Eden said nothing, for it was doubtful that she even heard him. Her face was set in a dreadful, silent stare, but in the next moment the rigid look in her eyes gave way to incredulous anger.

"How *could* you?" she breathed. "How could you stoop to something so—so utterly preposterous?"

"My dear young woman, I was not being preposterous. I was being perfectly earnest. Clearly we have no other recourse than to marry in order to prevent her tearing your reputation to shreds."

Shocked disbelief crept over Eden's face at his bland words, his even blander expression, and Hugh barely managed to hold her hands as she hurled forward to slap him. Briefly, she fought him, her panting breaths loud in the stillness, then abruptly she went slack. Her head bowed and fell to Hugh's shoulder, and he could feel the trembling of her body through the thin material of his shirt.

"It couldn't be helped," he said softly. "Nothing else I could have said or done would have prevented her carrying the tale—greatly embellished, I might add—back to the ballroom. And I'm afraid there really is no other way to protect you other than to make you my wife."

"How very noble of you!" Eden said bitterly. "Am I to have no say in this? Suppose I care nothing about my reputation or what that—that creature chooses to think?"

"There is still your family to consider," Hugh pointed out, suddenly curt. "Angus is old and his health uncertain. Do you think he cares equally little for the Fraser name?"

"He loves me," Eden insisted passionately, "and he would never—"

"He is still the same man who cast his own daughter from the house for a similar transgression," Hugh reminded her unkindly.

"Perhaps so, but that doesn't mean I have to marry you! I don't have to stay in Scotland at all if I don't wish to! I could go back to India, to Lucknow or—"

"And if there should be a child?"

Eden's body went rigid with shock, and this time when she tried to struggle free of his hold Hugh released her at once. She retreated a step and stood staring up at him with her small hands a white blur at her throat and her eyes wide and filled with a numb, disbelieving anger. Looking at her, Hugh felt a wrenching pain like a blow to his heart, yet when he moved unthinkingly toward her she drew sharply away.

"I still wouldn't marry you," Eden said, her voice shaking with emotion. "Not even if there was a child. I won't accept your charity or your pity, Hugh Gordon! I'd rather be dead!"

Pushing past him, Eden stooped to collect her discarded clothing. The cumbersome ball dress and stiff, billowing petticoats made quite an armful, and she struggled frantically to gather them against her. Hugh stood watching her, his face entirely expressionless, knowing better than to offer his help.

With tightly compressed lips Eden retreated behind a mass of rhododendrons and pulled off Hugh's shirt, tearing the buttons in her haste. Her limbs felt weighted, her body numb, as she completed the difficult task of dressing alone. A sobbing gasp was wrenched from her as she accidentally ripped one of the long loops of seed pearls adorning her skirts and watched the shining beads scatter in the grass.

"It's only a gown, Eden," she whispered to herself, struggling against the absurd tears that rushed to her eyes. "It isn't important—truly it isn't."

But it was the gown itself that was to prove her undoing. Examined in harsh daylight the following morning by Janet as she carefully hung it away, its smears made by grass stains, a ragged tear running along the seam of the bodice—as though it had been removed in haste by an utterly careless hand—could not be missed. Janet's heart grew still at the sight of it, for she had not failed to hear the disturbing rumors that had been whispered on the grounds of Arran Mhór last night, rumors that had seemed thoroughly unlikely and unwarranted and incredible to her—until now.

Waiting until her father-in-law had retreated to his study and Mrs. Walters had bustled out into the kitchen, she went slowly downstairs into the breakfast room. There she showed the gown to Eden and asked a single question.

Eden said nothing for a long, long moment. She merely looked at the gown in her aunt's work-worn hands and then up into Janet's white, anxious face.

"Yes, Aunt Janet," she said calmly, "I'm afraid it's true."

Chapter Fourteen

Hugh and Eden were married in the kirk of St. James, an ancient stone chapel in which the Protestant reformer John Knox had once made an impassioned speech to the parishioners of the glen, and in which Mary Stuart, beautiful, high-spirited, and ill-fated queen of Scots, was rumored to have spent a night in hiding after her escape from Lochleven Castle.

The wedding was, by design and of necessity, a simple affair, involving none of the pomp and ceremony that by rights should have surrounded the nuptials of a duke of the realm. While Aunt Janet had envisioned a glittering observance in Westminster Abbey followed by a formal reception at Roxbury, the duke's ancestral estate, Eden would have none of it. Her grandfather would never withstand the strain of such a long journey, she had argued, and the kirk of St. James had seen the union of countless generations of Blairs—surely sufficient in itself to recommend it. Outside of the family few guests would be attending, and Eden saw no reason to make a lavish spectacle of the sham and mockery that was to be her marriage to Hugh, yet this she did not say aloud, and her thoughts and her heartache she kept entirely to herself.

Behind the bright anticipation that glowed in her eyes and the enthusiasm with which she obliged the delighted Janet, Isabel, and Anne on the subject of planning her wedding gown and trusseau, Eden's thoughts were her own, and even Hugh, who rarely saw her these days, could not begin to guess at them. Yet the strain of pretending, of showing her eager family the expectant face of a happy bride-to-be, eventually began to take its toll, and when Sir Hamish Blair paid a rare visit to Tor Alsh he was genuinely shocked by her appearance. Eden seemed to have aged, and the quick, nervous gestures of her hands when she spoke were not at all natural for her. She was pale, and there were shadows beneath her eyes; those same vivid blue eyes that had always looked so boldly into others were now clouded with wary uncertainty.

Hugh was away in Somerset settling his affairs, Sir Hamish had come to tell her, but of course he could be trusted to return in time for the wedding. The old gentleman was clearly enjoying the uproar that had swept through his household with the first posting of the banns in the church. Even the vague breath of scandal that the formal announcement of engagement had not quite managed to still was something to be savored, and Sir Hamish fielded the discreetly worded questions of his neighbors and friends with all the aplomb of a diplomat. Hugh had always been the subject of unprecedented gossip and rumor, so why should there be anything the least bit conventional in the public's acceptance of his sudden decision to marry? Though he had his own ideas as to why his nephew had chosen Eden Hamilton, Sir Hamish kept them to himself, and it was not until he visited The Tor and saw for himself what the slow-crawling days since the midsummer ball had done to her that he experienced his first qualms of doubt.

Eden, however, was as pleased as ever to see him and during the course of his visit displayed enough of her usual composure to send Sir Hamish back to Arran Mhór feeling quite in charity with the notion of a wedding.

"A striking couple," he said to Dundhoo during supper that night, "and perfect for each other. Hugh's a lucky devil."

"I am pleased for the miss-sahib," agreed Dundhoo, who genuinely liked the girl. "There will be much joy in this house after the *shadi*."

"And brawling," pronounced the major-general thoughtfully around a mouthful of succulent squab.

"*Brawling*, sahib?"

"Aye, indeed! I've yet to see people change overly much once they're wed, and both of them are far too vigorous and stubborn to convince me they'll always live peacefully together. Like sparks off flint, Dundhoo, mark my words. Sparks off flint!"

Regrettably Sir Hamish's prediction was to prove only too accurate inasmuch as Eden's next confrontation with Hugh was concerned. Unable to tolerate any longer the tumult precipitated by the selection of material for Anne's and Isabel's bridesmaid dresses, she had left the house in something of a temper one morning and ridden the Raosahib at a hard gallop across the moor.

It was nearing the end of September, and a crispness in the air gave hint of the winter to come. The larches in the copses below were golden yellow in contrast to the brilliant blue of the sky, yet Eden saw none of their beauty or that of the masses of late-blooming flowers growing in the warm reaches of the meadows around her. She saw nothing before her save an image of Hugh's lean face and the half smile that had played at the corners of his mouth when he had told Lady Caroline Winton of their forthcoming marriage. She had felt then as she did now: angry and helpless and hating him for the fact that it was a sense of duty and honor that had prompted him to redeem her tattered virtue in this manner—honor and duty, not love.

If he had indicated to her with only a single sign or word that perhaps he loved her a little— But Hugh had not done so, and later he had merely bowed over her hand and kissed it in an impersonal fashion after her grandfather had given his glowing consent to their engagement. Eden had seen him only once or twice after that and always in the company of her aunt or someone else from the household, for Janet was adamant on the score of preventing further scandal.

Hugh had known, of course, what was going on in Janet's mind and had not made any effort to hide his amusement. Yet his behavior toward Eden was as remote and exemplary as Janet could have wished, and it was not until Sir Hamish Blair's visit to Tor Alsh that Eden first heard of his departure for Somerset. Hugh himself had not bothered to tell her he was leaving, nor had he taken the time to bid her farewell. If it hadn't been for the night of the midsummer ball, in fact, they could easily have been the same coldly distant protagonists of old.

Eden's heart contracted as it always did whenever she thought of that night, and as always the memories rose unbidden before her despite how she struggled against them. Hugh's lovemaking had awakened within her a need and a desire for him she hadn't dreamed she possessed, and though she hated herself for it, she could not deny the fact that he had gotten into her blood, become a part of her so that she could never again think of him, or look at him, without a breathless, loving cramping of her heart.

Quite suddenly and much to her annoyance, Eden's eyes filled with tears. Her vision blurred until the mountains and the sky swam together, and a pair of women who had been cutting peat on the moor ahead of her were suddenly no longer two, but three. . . .

Dashing the wetness from her cheeks, Eden lifted her head and saw that the number of laborers was still the same, but that the third was not a woman at all. It was a man, dark-headed and dressed in tall boots and riding trousers. She blinked and looked a second time and saw that it was Hugh. He was leaning against the low stone wall with his cap in his hand talking to the pair of women while his horse grazed nearby. Though he had doubtless recognized Eden some time ago, he did not acknowledge her until she had drawn rein beside her.

"Good morning, Miss Hamilton," he said finally, taking the Rao-sahib by the bridle and speaking to her in the same offhand manner in which he had always addressed her when they had been in India together. It was, Eden thought miserably, as though the enchanted evening of the ball had never existed, as though their wedding did not loom less than a week ahead of them.

"When did you return to Arran Mhór?" she inquired, peering past his shoulder to watch with feigned interest the laboring of the peat cutters on the moor behind him.

"Last night. I would have been back sooner, but it was snowing in the upper passes above Kingussie. My horse barely made it through." Hugh glanced down at Eden's hands, which were gloved and curled tightly about the reins. "Did you receive the ring I sent you?"

Eden's cheeks stained pink. "Yes, thank you," she whispered, but she was thinking not of the delicate band of gold with its cluster of diamonds and sapphires that adorned the third finger of her left hand, but of the impersonal and hastily scrawled note that had accompanied it. It was as if Hugh, preoccupied with other matters, had been impatient to send it off, and Eden could not help wondering what had occupied his time during his stay in Somerset. She knew that Lady Caroline Winton and her husband resided in an estate whose borders touched Hugh's, and she could not help but wonder if he had made a point to see the dark-haired beauty.

Her breath caught painfully at the thought, and the Raosahib sidled and snorted as he experienced an unexpected jerk on his bit. Hugh tightened his hand about the bridle and looked sharply into Eden's averted face. Frowning, he said:

"The ring is to your liking, I hope? It was once my mother's betrothal ring, yet if you find it too tawdry—"

"*Tawdry?*" Eden echoed incredulously.

"My father was not a man of exceptional means," Hugh continued coolly, misconstruing the reasons behind the sudden paling of her face, "though I imagine you're well aware that you're marrying an exceptionally wealthy one. Had you perhaps envisioned something on a grander scale?"

For a moment Eden was too shocked to reply. The fact that he could ask that of her when in truth she had been delighted with the beautiful ring and touched to learn it had once been his mother's hurt her immeasurably. She did not know what she could possibly say in her defense and wondered with a sense of sinking despair if she had not been mistaken after all in deciding to go through with this marriage. Perhaps she had been wrong in thinking that the intimacy they had shared when he had made love to her meant that he cared for her. Perhaps their lovemaking had mattered no more to him than if the woman in his arms had been Lady Caroline Winton or even the gaudy actress Camille Severance. The carnal act was different for men, Eden suddenly recalled the Begum Fariza saying in her placid, accepting way. One must never take their passions too seriously, for they were quickly sated and eager to look elsewhere for diversion.

Eden looked down into the face of the man who was soon to be her husband and saw before her a stranger's face, coldly handsome and utterly remote. Instinctively her hand tightened about her riding whip, and she brought it down quickly and savagely, though not fast enough. Hugh's fingers closed tightly about her wrist, and she gasped and let the whip fall useless to the ground.

"I'd almost forgotten about that temper of yours," Hugh remarked grimly. "However civilized you may appear, it would be wise of me to remember that there is still a great deal of the Rajput in you."

"You have no right to accuse me of—of fortune-hunting!" Eden flared. "If you want your bloody ring back, then take it, though I'll be damned if I accept another!"

Hugh released her at those words, and Eden snatched her hand away, rubbing her wrist and gazing down at him with dangerously brimming eyes.

After a moment Hugh said softly, and as though he had been considering the matter quite seriously, "No, I don't believe I'll be taking it back. I've a feeling I'm going to enjoy our marriage, Miss Hamilton, at least inasmuch as I will soon have the legal right to beat that tiresome arrogance out of you."

For a moment Eden glared hotly back at him, white and rigid, then she wheeled the Rao-sahib so savagely that the big animal reared on its haunches. Digging her heel cruelly into his flank, she sent him galloping headlong across the moor, unmindful of the startled stares of the peat cutters behind her.

Eden saw nothing of Hugh in the slow-dragging days that followed, though she grappled often with the impulse to seek him out and demand an apology for what he had said to her. Yet she did not, for that would not only be foolish but utterly unthinkable: he would only laugh at her. Still, the bitter taste of that unpleasant confrontation stubbornly remained. In time the notion of marrying him became so reprehensible to her that she began to ponder how best to escape gracefully from her promise to do so. Pride forbade Eden from begging her grandfather to annul the engagement, and regrettably she could not run away, for the first storms of autumn had come early that year, and the Grampians and the passes south were already inaccessible beneath a heavy blanket of snow. In the final analysis there was nothing left for Eden to do save go through with the wedding ceremony with as much of her pride intact as possible, and this she did by promising herself that she would make Hugh Gordon's life equally as miserable as he had vowed to make her own.

When the time came at last for Eden to take her place in the kirk beside the man she had given her word to marry, she did so with a pale face that was fortunately hidden beneath the heavy gauze of a flowing white veil. The morning had dawned cold and uninviting, and a bitter north wind rattled the single stained-glass window high overhead. The lighted candles shivered in the draft, and the minister's voice was often drowned out completely by the gusts as he read aloud the marriage sacraments from a worn leather Bible.

Coming to stand before the altar, Eden saw the scene before her as something that was not, could not, be real. She might have been any one of the spectators seated in the shadowy pews behind her, and when she repeated her vows her voice seemed curiously detached and remote—as though it belonged to someone else.

Eden started visibly when she felt Hugh take her hand and slip a heavily hammered gold ring upon her finger. Staring down at it with a frown, she grappled with the momentary impulse to tear it from her hand. Lifting aside her veil, Hugh saw her thoughts clearly in the expression on her face, and a flicker of amusement—or was it something else?—appeared briefly in his eyes. Then his mouth closed upon hers, and there was nothing tender in his kiss or in the hand that pressed tightly against the back of her neck, but something that was very much like anger. And when he drew away at last, leaving her shaken, a slow smile curved those same lips, and his eyes looked deeply into hers.

"You're mine now, Eden," he said so softly that no one else, not even Isabel who stood close beside her, could hear.

The minister spoke again, and Eden felt Hugh take her by the hand and turn her around. She caught a glimpse of numerous smiling faces: of Aunt Janet, wiping her eyes with a scrap of lace, her grandfather nodding approvingly as he leaned heavily upon his stick, and Sir Hamish beside him grinning and muttering complacently beneath his breath. Then they were outside, where the icy wind plucked at the wide skirts of her wedding dress and threatened to tear the veil from her head. Raindrops splattered onto the worn stone walk, and a sea of faces was clustered around her, offering congratulations and blessings in what seemed nothing more than a meaningless babble.

A covered carriage festooned with garlands of white ribbon and heather stood waiting on the road that cut across the open moor, and Dundhoo, gorgeously attired in purple and scarlet, made a great show of opening the door for them. Hugh lifted Eden inside and took the seat opposite her, and she was glad for her long train of *moiré gothique* and the wide-spreading skirts of white-flounced tulle that prevented him from sitting beside her.

The narrow road was lined with well-wishers, and Eden waved dutifully and smiled, yet as the carriage wound its way higher through the glen and the turrets of Arran Mhór became visible amid the trees, the spectators thinned, and Eden let her gaze drop to the hands in her lap. She frowned as she stared down at the heavy ring that bound her until death to the man seated opposite her, and when she glanced up at Hugh from beneath her lashes she found him staring out the window, his expression unreadable.

She was vastly relieved when the carriage rumbled at last into the courtyard at Arran Mhór. Turning his head to look at her, Hugh could not help but laugh as he saw the bewildered expression on her face in response to the number of servants who lined the steps waiting to welcome them.

"I've never seen them all assembled in one place. I hadn't realized there were so many. . . ." Eden's words trailed away into appalled silence as it dawned on her that she was now the countess of Blair, and that the household of Arran Mhór was hers alone to oversee and manage.

"There is also the estate in Somerset," Hugh reminded her, stepping out of the carriage and turning to help her onto the ground. "I trust you haven't forgotten that you are now the duchess of Roxbury?"

"No, I—I haven't," Eden said, and flushed hotly as a cheer rose up from the gathered servants at the sight of her. It was interspersed with cries of "Kiss 'er, Your Lordship!" from the bolder of the men, and Hugh, grinning, lifted aside Eden's veil and obliged.

It was a surprisingly tender kiss, containing none of the violence of that earlier one in the kirk. When he released her at last he was smiling unexpectedly.

"Shall we go inside, Your Grace?" he inquired amiably, and, tucking her hand beneath his arm, led his wife up the steps and into the great hall of the castle.

They were permitted no time alone for the remainder of that long and momentous day. As small as the wedding might have been, the reception was everything Aunt Janet could have wished for. There was music and dancing, a lavishly prepared feast, endless bottles of champagne and wine, and barrels of ale and mulled cider to soothe the parched throats of the revelers. The air of festivity and celebration was unmistakable; the great, raftered hall fairly pulsed to the glitter and pomp and the unending web of talk and laughter.

Most of the guests were fellow Scots, clan chieftains bristling with eagle-feather appointments, silver-bladed dirks and cairngorm brooches, their ladies wearing floor-length plaids representing numerous clans. Far more boisterous than the stiflingly proper English who had ventured north for the duke's midsummer ball, these gruff Highland men drank heavily and ate with gusto, danced eagerly, if not a bit shyly, with the new duchess of Roxbury, and performed in her honor the intricate steps of a Highland sword dance.

Eden found herself feeling remarkably at home with these fierce, towering men and their unpretentious wives. Several Highland regiments had been stationed in Lucknow when Eden had been a girl, and she had never forgotten the Gaelic she had learned from them and from her father. Their delight was obvious as she addressed them haltingly in their native tongue, and they were heard to remark approvingly among themselves over Roxbury's choice for a bride.

Throughout the course of the evening Eden found her eyes drawn time and again to Hugh. She found it remarkable that he could look so entirely at ease in the formal black of his wedding attire, he who was more accustomed to the khaki and whipcord breeches favored by India hands. Seeing his smiling, sun-browned face in the glow of the candles, she was filled with an inexplicable ache of longing—for what? Perhaps for the plains of Rajputana and the vast, unending land that had been her home—and Hugh's—and for the first time she was compelled to wonder what this strange new life together would hold for them. Would he take her back to Delhi, or would they reside here at Arran Mhór, or perhaps in the refined beauty she imagined his Somerset estate to be?

Strange that she had never considered the matter before or imagined what it would mean to spend the rest of her life in the company of this man. Eden wondered, not without considerable doubt, if any happiness lay in store for them. Remembering their hurtful exchange on the moor last week, she could not help but feel that neither one of them would ever come to terms with the other.

"So pensive, my dear?" Hugh inquired, leading Eden away at last for an obligatory waltz.

"I was thinking about the future—our future," she admitted honestly.

There was a moment of silence. "A suitable subject for one's wedding day," Hugh conceded at last. "Were you perhaps pondering the prospect of our happiness together?"

"Yes, I was," said Eden slowly, "and wondering if we would ever have any."

Hugh's mouth hardened, and he looked sharply into those wide blue eyes that were so innocent and wary and grave. "Why on earth shouldn't we be happy together?" he demanded brusquely.

Eden could only make a slight, negative movement with her head, and the unspoken despair of that simple gesture merely served to anger him more. Though Hugh said nothing, his expression grew remote, and there was nothing in the least gentle in the strong hand that tightened about her waist. They did not speak again, and as the evening wore on Hugh was seen to spend less and less time in the company of his bride and more in the anterooms with their offerings of cards and male companionship.

"I cannot tell you what a wonderful evening this has been," sighed Janet, seeking out her niece some time later. "I must admit that I had my doubts about a great number of things, but Lord Blair—His Grace—has been such an exemplary host, and so charming to the family!" Her hands fluttered. "I still cannot quite believe I am related by marriage to a duke, and of course Anne's chances for making a splendid match have been so greatly improved! You will allow her to visit, won't you, dear?" she inquired, suddenly anxious. "In Somerset, I mean? I've often dreamed of introducing Anne to English society, though I had no idea how to go about it. Now that you— What is it, dear? Are you feeling unwell?"

"No. I'm only a little tired, I think."

"That's quite understandable," Janet murmured, patting her niece's lax hand. "It's been quite a day for you, and perhaps I shouldn't be bothering you with such trivial matters. But you will consider it, won't you?"

"Consider what?" inquired Eden vaguely, her gaze roving the crowded ballroom as though searching for someone.

"Why, asking Anne to Somerset. I've just been saying—"

"I'm not at all certain if His—if Hugh intends to return there," Eden interrupted.

Janet gave a startled laugh. "But of course he will! Why wouldn't he? Do you think he intends to settle here in Glen Alsh simply because he's taken a Scots bride? I daresay Arran Mhór has never held the same worldly appeal for him that England has. How can it?'' Her eyes turned to the duke, who stood deep in conversation with a charmingly attired and quite lovely lady near the doorway. ''He's not at all the sort of man to while away his time raising sheep in a remote Highland glen.''

Janet turned back to her niece, her expression suddenly filled with concern—and an inkling of understanding. ''Are you having second thoughts, love? I assure you it's only natural. You've married a very wealthy man, and a highly public one at that. As the duchess of Roxbury I fear your life will never be the same.''

''Yes,'' said Eden slowly. ''I'm coming to realize that.'' She turned her head and smiled brightly. ''But of course there isn't any reason why Anne—why all of you— can't come to see me in Somerset. I'm sure Hugh will be delighted.''

Her gaze turned back to the lovely woman smiling up into Hugh's face, and Eden excused herself abruptly. She had no idea, of course, whether or not Hugh would welcome her family to Somerset. She had no idea, in fact, if she herself was expected to accompany him there once he left Scotland for the winter.

''Well, I don't care,'' Eden told herself stubbornly. She had no desire to leave her grandfather or Isabel, and if her new husband intended to force her to bid farewell to those at Tor Alsh, then she would simply tell him that she was going back to India, and not to Somerset, to live.

The lamps and candles had burned low by the time the carriages bearing the last of the wedding guests rumbled away into the darkness. Eden stood on the steps with Hugh beside her, watching silently until they had vanished down the long, tree-lined avenue. Once inside again, she found the glittering hall deserted save for yawning footmen and that curious air of emptiness and sad neglect that always seems to pervade a ballroom whenever the guests have gone home. Eden stood silently in the doorway surveying the empty bottles and glasses, the gay decorations that now hung askew, the flowers that had begun to wilt in the huge vases on the refectory table. The talk and laughter, the music and the wildly applauded speeches, had given way to a stillness that seemed as cold and empty as her heart.

Frowning a little, she turned to find Hugh leaning against a nearby table watching her. Without speaking, she walked past him and went slowly upstairs to the apartment that was to be hers now—hers and her husband's. The long train of her wedding gown trailed behind her, and she walked somewhat unsteadily, hesitating a long moment in the dark corridor before opening the door.

A lamp burned softly beneath the window, and the covers on the enormous bed had been turned back invitingly. There was a sleepy-eyed maid to help her undress, blushing and curtsying and explaining shyly that His Grace would be occupying the adjoining bedroom, and did Eden wish for anything else before she retired?

"No," said Eden tiredly, and was glad when the door closed behind her and she found herself alone.

It was quiet now, and Eden drew back the drapes and leaned her forehead against the chilly glass. Above the dark silhouettes of the mountains the stars sparkled and glittered far brighter than they had ever burned over the dry, dusty plains of Rajasthan. She could hear the distant murmur of the trout stream that surged into the loch below the castle grounds and then the sound of the door latch clicking softly. She turned slowly and saw that it was Hugh.

She regarded him calmly, revealing none of her doubts and fears. Hugh returned her gaze without speaking, recalling of a sudden how often he had dreamed of having Eden appear before him with her hair unbound and her slim body wrapped in nothing but silk. Dreamed of it, yet never imagined that she could look so impossibly beautiful with her chignon unrolled and her carefully brushed hair hanging below her hips in a curtain of shining gold. Her eyes were a dark, incredible blue, and that lovely red mouth he ached to kiss was turned down at the corners in a grave frown as she looked back at him.

"Are you tired?" he asked.

"A little."

Hugh grinned at her in response but did not speak. Instead he set down the glass he had been holding and came to stand before her. "I had the feeling," he said at last, "for a few moments there in the kirk, that you would have cheerfully cut my throat to escape marrying me. Or would you have preferred poison? Isn't that the most popular of Rajput methods?"

He saw Eden's eyes widen with uncertainty and wariness and realized with a sudden pang of wrenching tenderness that she was frightened. Of what? Surely not of the marriage act? How could she fear something that had caused both of them such piercing pleasure? She had not feigned her response to him that night, Hugh was sure of it. He smiled unknowingly at the memory and again saw that startled, uncertain look cross her face. It dawned on him then that she had no idea he was teasing her, and a surge of anger swept through him at the realization.

"My God," he said hoarsely, "you didn't really think you were marrying such an ogre, did you? Surely I couldn't have given you the impression that our life together would be so terrible, did I, Eden?"

But he did not wait for an answer. Instead he slipped his hands about her waist, groaning a little as her warm, scented body came into contact with his. Slipping off the silk dressing gown, he lowered his mouth to hers, never knowing that his kiss was more of an affirmation of his feelings than words could have been; that the touch of his mouth and his hands had swept away the doubts that had been plaguing Eden as surely as he stripped away her garments and left her naked and unashamed before him.

"I was afraid you had not—that you didn't . . ." Eden's words trailed away on a breathless gasp as Hugh touched her naked breasts. His hands moved, and with it the earth and all existence seemed to move as well, and he lifted her into his arms as she melted against him and laid her on the bed.

The mattress sagged beneath his weight as he leaned down to cup her face with unsteady hands. "Eden," he said gravely, "we are man and wife. I swore before God today to cherish and keep you. Surely you must know by now that I am a man of my word."

It was certainly an unconventional declaration of love, if it could be called any such thing at all. But for Eden, gazing up into the harsh face above her that was softened now by the glow of the lamp, it was enough, more than enough. Something hot and tight within her seemed to ease, and she held out her hands to him and smiled.

Hugh's lips curved in response—that devilish smile of old that washed clean the doubts and hurts and disappointments of the past. Sliding his hands along the length of her hips, he pulled her close, loving the feel of her naked body against his. He had some considerable experience of women, yet Eden's slim loveliness and the unabashed innocence she exhibited in her desire to learn and experience all that he had to offer made everything seem infinitely new and delightful to him. Hugh knew as he looked into Eden's passion-darkened eyes that here was a woman of endless enchantment, a rare treasure that fate had been kindly disposed to make his alone, and as he touched her, his hands and his lips were softened with a rare tenderness and wonder.

Hugh entered her slowly, savoring the moment of ultimate possession, and his touch awakened within Eden a fierce yearning to make him a part of her. Opening herself to him, she felt him draw back, then fill her again. Her hands slid to his hips, pulling him closer, coming alive under the power of his pleasuring.

"Sweet, so sweet," Hugh whispered in her ear. "Eden—"

"Hugh—" she gasped at the very same moment, yet neither of them finished what they had intended to say. There was no need for words, only for touch and sensation and the building of a wrenching, bittersweet passion. The feeling expanded, and Eden gasped aloud as she felt Hugh surge against her. Waves of passion bore them aloft to a dizzying climax where she clung to him, swept away by his touch, and both of them were lost.

Chapter Fifteen

That autumn of the year 1861 was to prove a glorious time for an ever-wealthier, ever-expanding British empire. Even remotest corners of Scotland were beginning to reflect the prosperity of Queen Victoria's growing dominations: the notorious Sutherland clearances with their mass exodus of Scots to America had come to an end, and Scotland was enjoying a political expression it had not experienced since the signing of the Treaty of Union. Though linen, and then cotton, was by far the largest mainstay of a reawakened economy, wool had by no means lost its importance, and those Scottish estates that had been given over during the clearances to the raising of sheep found themselves growing increasingly prosperous.

Arran Mhór was no exception, and Hugh Gordon was both surprised and bemused by the work entailed in managing his ever-flourishing herds of sheep. He had originally planned to leave for Somerset long before the winter came, yet it was growing increasingly obvious to him that he could not neglect the estate as readily as he had done in the past. Furthermore, there were other, more compelling reasons to prompt him to delay his departure time and again, one of them being his wife.

Hugh did not need to look at Eden to see that the loneliness that had caused her such pain both after her father's death and later in Delhi was gone. Her blood ties to the Frasers had quickly shown themselves to be far stronger than the friendships she had forged in the close-knit though intrigue-ridden courts of the zenana in Mayar, and he was reluctant to remove her so soon from the loving circle of her newly discovered family.

Furthermore, it was growing increasingly doubtful to him that Eden would even agree to accompany him to Somerset, for she seemed far more content these days than Hugh had ever seen her. There was a serenity and a glow about her that was in sharp contrast to the restless, rebellious creature Hugh had first encountered in Rajasthan, and he wondered often as he watched her laughing and chatting in halting Gaelic with his servants, or playing chess with Sir Hamish with a vengeance that fully equaled the old gentleman's, how he could ever have considered her a fitting wife for the dissolute rajah of Mayar. There was good Scots blood in Eden, more so than anyone familiar with her Indian background would have suspected, and Hugh doubted that she would find a similar measure of contentment in the stuffy regimentation that dictated life on his Somerset estate.

But I myself must go, Hugh told himself, lying in bed one night with the wind moaning against the glass and the embers popping sleepily in the grate. I'll go after Christmas, he decided, gazing down at the sleeping profile of his wife. Or perhaps after New Year's.

But already he was thinking of the winter storms that would savage the glen on the heels of the new year, wondering if the mountain roads would be passable and if it might not prove advisable to wait until spring.

Eden murmured softly in her sleep, interrupting his train of thought, and Hugh turned and took her gently into his arms. She sighed and snuggled closer, and Hugh could feel her body slacken as she sank deeper into sleep.

I'll consider it tomorrow, he decided, bending his head and letting his lips trail through the waves of silky hair at her brow. Or the day after, or perhaps next week. . . .

Barely six hours later he was up and dressed and sipping tea as he waited for his horse to be brought round from the stable. A cold blue dawn was fingering the sky to the east, and Sir Hamish, who had appeared downstairs after the brief night's sleep characteristic of old age, rubbed his hands together and complained of the cold.

"Can't take it like I used to, you ken. It's India I'm hungering for, lad: the heat and monsoons and the winters on the Northwest Frontier. I vow they never chilled a man to the bone the way the cold does here. Saw that wife of yours ride off from my window a half hour ago on that ill-tempered beast of hers," he added, changing the subject abruptly. "It won't do to let her tear about the countryside alone, especially not at this hour. Not decent, I say."

"Trust me, Uncle," said Hugh with a faint smile, "Eden is quite capable of looking after herself."

The major-general eyed his nephew sharply. "Damn," he said reflectively, "if I don't believe you've fallen in love wi' her, Hugh. Not like you to let a woman enjoy so much free rein. Not like you at all."

Hugh shrugged his shoulders, his expression enigmatic.

"I'll wager you weren't counting on that when you smuggled her out of Mayar," Sir Hamish prodded shrewdly. "Eh? Eh?"

Hugh regarded the elderly gentleman with an indulgent eye. "You're an incurable romantic, sir, despite that cut-and-dried military air of yours."

"India's to thank for that, lad! Couldn't have happened otherwise, not after a lifetime spent amidst such seductive beauty."

"Don't you mean beauties?" Hugh inquired with a knowing grin.

"Aye, them, too," said Sir Hamish defensively. "Wouldn't have done at all for an officer and a gentleman not to have a few of 'em tucked away in the *bibi-gurh* behind his bungalow." He stared down into his coffee with a faraway expression, and presently he sighed and observed that the glorious old days of company rule had certainly been the finest of his youth, and if he were twenty years younger, or perhaps even ten, nothing could prevent him returning East on the very next steamer.

"Take my advice and keep that girl firmly in hand," he added as Hugh set down his tea cup and shrugged into his coat. "A spirited creature like that needs a firm hand on the bridle."

"I'll do my best," Hugh promised, "inasmuch as Eden will permit me."

Five minutes later he was cantering across the frost-brittle grass, his breath clouding in the cold, crisp air. The ghostly light of dawn had given way to a pale rose that flared on the horizon while the last of the stars glinted ice blue and clear above the shadowed mountains. Light glowed from the window of a solitary croft and was eventually lost from view as Hugh turned down the long avenue of trees leading from the castle grounds to the sheep pens.

Even from a distance he could hear the barking of the dogs and the agitated baaing of sheep. Crossing an arching stone bridge, he drew rein near the whitewashed byre to watch Simon McKenzie direct the tallying and division of the winter herds. The pens were already teeming with ewes, and a lone figure was culling those that were barren with the aid of a rough-coated border collie that ran slinking and yapping amid the jostling, panic-stricken animals. A thin cloud of steam hung like smoke above the pens, and the scent of damp wool and manure was pungent in the chill air.

"We'll hae them counted and turned oot afore noon, Your Grace," said Simon McKenzie, coming to stand beside Hugh. He was middle-aged and soft-spoken, his shoulders bowed prematurely by a lifetime of hard work. Yet there was an indefatigable sense of pride about him and a gentle good humor: the invariable stamp of the Highland Gael.

"Her Grace be cullin' 'em fast as we can sort," he added with an approving nod in the direction of the pens.

"Who?" inquired Hugh with a sudden frown between his eyes, for he had not been attending his steward with his full attention.

Simon gestured again toward the pens, and Hugh turned his head and looked at the lone worker he had assumed to be one of McKenzie's sons. At that moment a shaft of sunlight, fingering the lip of the mountains, bathed the pen in brilliant light and illuminated a woman's slender body and a woman's lovely, heart-shaped face, and Hugh looked again and saw that it was Eden. She was wearing a heavy woolen cloak over a skirt of blue worsted and thick work boots that were caked with mud. Her fair hair was rolled and pinned tightly to her head in the manner of a Highland maiden—or a common milking girl—and Hugh, who had never expected his wife to appear before him like this, found himself thoroughly taken aback.

"It's often she's been helping us here in the byre," Simon McKenzie explained, and retreated a hasty step as he caught Hugh's eye. "Did ye no ken, Your Grace?"

"No," said Hugh grimly, "I didn't."

He opened the gate and went to stand before her, feeling angrier than he ever had in his life and at an absurd loss to explain why he should. Perhaps it was the sight of Eden laboring in the pens like a common field hand or the words of Hamish Blair coming back to haunt him, though when he had first heard them earlier that morning he had been inclined to dismiss them as being of no consequence.

Eden turned at the sound of his steps, an expectant light leaping in her eyes, yet the moment her gaze met his her welcoming smile faltered and froze on her lips. Though Hugh said nothing at all she seemed immediately aware of his anger.

"What is it?"

"What in bloody hell do you mean dressing like a lowly harpy?" Hugh inquired, answering her question with one of his own.

Hot color flared to Eden's cheeks, and she raised an unconscious hand to the wayward curls at her temples. "I'm sorry," she said hastily, "I can understand why you wouldn't approve of my attire, but—"

"*Your attire?* What about the rest of you?" Hugh gestured angrily at the milling sheep and the dog that crouched panting at her feet. "Is this the sort of pastime one expects from a duchess?"

"Would you rather I had taken up needlepoint?" inquired Eden calmly.

"Among other things, yes."

"So that I might become one of those—those colorless, swooning aristocrats who spend their days eating sweet-meats and grooming their spaniels?" Eden challenged, thinking with an unexpected twinge of Lady Caroline Winton. "Obviously those are the sort of women you seem to prefer!"

She saw Hugh's mouth harden at her words, a sign of annoyance that merely served to exacerbate her own temper. "Really, Hugh, you have no right to deny me a life and interests of my own! There's no harm in my helping Mr. McKenzie with the herds, and I certainly won't turn into a peasant simply because I enjoy working like one! Furthermore, it's incredibly boorish of you to think along those lines, and I must say that snobbery is one thing I never expected from you!"

She turned her back on him and walked away with the dog trotting behind, leaving Hugh to grapple with conflicting urges: to take her into his arms and kiss that angry frown from her mouth, or to turn her over his knee as though she were nothing more than an unmanageable child in need of a sound thrashing.

"I ought to do both," he growled, swinging into the saddle and riding away at a gallop. At the moment, however, it seemed wiser to do nothing, because he wasn't entirely certain which impulse would seize him once he touched her. Wife beating was certainly not in his line, despite the fact that he had once informed Eden how much he would relish the opportunity, and at the moment he certainly didn't want to kiss her. Reward that tart dressing-down of hers with a show of affection? Not bloody likely!

The remainder of the morning was given over to attending matters of estate, and it was long after teatime before Hugh returned to the house, mud-spattered, hungry, and still quite out of charity with his recalcitrant wife. His temper was little improved upon discovering from Dundhoo that the memsahib had ridden over to Tor Alsh to visit her family and had left no word as to when she would return.

Prowling the elegant rooms with an expression that was forbidding enough to intimidate even his unflappable servants, Hugh was finally routed by the major-general, who observed peevishly that he couldn't possibly concentrate on his chess game while his nephew paced the floor like a caged Bengal tiger. By God, it wasn't often that Dundhoo deigned to sit down with him at the board, and couldn't Hugh take his ill-tempered mien elsewhere before his concentration went completely by the wayside?

Ten minutes later Hugh was to be seen riding hell for leather down the drive in the direction of the loch road leading toward Tor Alsh. Sir Hamish leaned back in his armchair and fixed his bearer with a glinting eye. "Didn't I tell you? Like sparks off flint, the two of 'em! Sparks off flint!"

"It does not bode well for the Huzoor and his wife to find discord so soon after their *shadi*," the worried Hindu ventured to observe.

"Nonsense! Perfectly healthy for the two of 'em to fight! Keeps the marriage alive, and as for Hugh—deny it if he will, but I'll wager my last shilling he's in love with the girl. Never seen a woman get under his skin that way, and I wouldn't— Blast your eyes, you dark-skinned bastard!" he raged in the next breath as Dundhoo took his bishop in an uncalculated move, and his nephew was instantly forgotten. Squinting at the elaborate chess set, the major-general muttered and cursed beneath his breath and eventually moved a pawn, observing ill-temperedly that it had clearly been a mistake of enormous proportions to teach his bearer the rudiments of the game.

"I will pour another cup of tea for the sahib," offered Dundhoo soothingly.

"You'll do no such thing," snapped the major-general. "You'll sit right there until you've made your move. Oh, all right, go ahead and bloody well serve it if you insist, but I want more whiskey in it this time, eh? Eh!"

It was a very flustered Mrs. Walters who hurried into the cream-and-gilt parlor at Tor Alsh to announce the unexpected appearance on their doorstep of the duke of Roxbury. Visitors of such import rarely called upon The Tor, and Mrs. Walters wasn't at all certain how to address him as she showed him inside. Her work-roughened hands shook as she hung away the woolen mantle he extended, betraying her agitation.

"Sit down, Hugh," said Angus Fraser, exhibiting none of the awe that seemed to have incapacitated his housekeeper. "Mrs. Walters will be fetching a wee dram to chase awa' the chill. I take it you've come after Eden? You've just missed her, I'm afraid. She left the house na ten minutes ago."

"Was she on her way back to Arran Mhór?" inquired Hugh with a frown.

"She didna tell me, nor did she stay overlong." The faded blue eyes that were so startlingly like his granddaughter's peered at him shrewdly. "Had a disagreement wi' her, did ye?"

It was a question of inexcusable impertinence, yet it was Angus Fraser who had asked it, and Hugh merely regarded the elderly gentleman with a somewhat rueful smile. "Something like that, yes."

"Can't say I'm surprised," Angus pronounced dourly. "If it was a docile wife you'd been wantin', then you should hae brought an Indian lass hame wi' ye. I've heard Hamish speak often enow of their obedience and devotion to their menfolk."

"I may yet come to regret that I did not," Hugh agreed, his rueful smile deepening appreciably.

"Ah, bah," said the older man, dismissing the topic with a shrug. He was secretly pleased, however, to take note of the fact that the gravity in the younger man's tone seemed largely contrived: proof that his willful granddaughter had obviously married a man equal to the task of taming her.

Settling back in his chair with a sigh, he savored the malt whiskey served by Mrs. Walters and said nothing more on that score. A companionable silence fell between the two of them, and Hugh, who had never lost his taste for good Highland malt despite his many years in India, sipped appreciatively while his eyes idly roved the room. He had not been admitted to the study at Tor Alsh in a great while, and it was oddly comforting to see how little had changed. The worn Jacobean furniture, the heavy carpets, and the brooding collection of oils in their dark oak frames had not been moved, and even Angus Fraser, though older now and certainly distressingly frail, seemed an integral part of the memories of Hugh's past visits.

Still, something did seem different to him, and after pondering the matter for a moment in silence, his expression cleared, and he observed aloud that the pair of Wilkies that had always graced the wall opposite the fireplace had been replaced by other, less striking works.

"Janet had them taken down while I was ill," Angus explained. "She's never liked them, you ken. Thought them out of keeping with the room's decor, though they happen to be the most valuable in the house. Eh? Oh, probably up i' the attic, though I've na thought to ask after 'em. Will you be havin' another dram?"

"Thank you, no," said Hugh, rising. "I want to get home before dark. I hope you'll give Mistress Janet my best."

"I'll do that," Angus promised. "It's annoyed she'll be that she's missed ye. And Anne, too. Especially Anne! Gone awa' for the afternoon, they have, and as for Isabel—" He frowned and searched his memory with obvious effort. "Canna remember if Isabel went wi' 'em or na. Quiet lass, you ken, and sometimes I forget where she's gang to."

Turning up his collar as he stepped out into the chilly yard, Hugh heard the sound of light, running footsteps behind him and had just enough time to step out of the way before a cloaked figure came hurrying around the corner of the house directly in his path. It was a young woman carrying a basket of freshly gathered eggs, her features partially hidden by a fur-trimmed hood.

"Good afternoon, Miss Hamilton," Hugh said politely, and was unprepared when Isabel, jerking up her head at the sight of him, retreated a hasty step.

"Oh!" she exclaimed, hot color flaring to her cheeks. "Your Grace, I didn't see you! If you'll excuse me, please—"

Lowering her head, she pushed past him and vanished into the house, her abrupt departure hinting more at despair than rudeness. Hugh stood for a moment staring after her, frowning thoughtfully and wondering why Isabel, who had seemed so charmingly shy and sweet to him at the midsummer ball and again at his wedding, should become so distraught at the mere sight of him. Had Eden been influencing her impressionable cousin with improbable tales concerning her foul-tempered husband?

The likelihood in no way pleased him. Mounting his horse, Hugh rode off across the windswept moor with an expression that was equally as forbidding as his anger. "Damn the lot of Hamilton women!" he muttered to himself.

By the time he had reached the long stretch of fir-dotted forest separating Tor Alsh land from his own, however, his temper had largely faded, replaced by a puzzling and entirely unfamiliar feeling of helplessness. He had indeed, he acknowledged to himself, behaved like a dreadful boor to Eden that morning; even worse, like a snob— a detestable, class-conscious patrician with that lofty air of superiority Hugh himself so disliked and openly condemned in others of his rank. Of course he did not object to Eden's helping Simon McKenzie with the sheep. In fact, he was inordinately pleased by her refusal to play the role of a languishing chatelaine, a "colorless, swooning aristocrat," as Eden herself had so aptly termed it.

Hugh's mouth softened into a smile, for he could name a dozen or more such women without giving the matter undue thought, and though some of them had been indisputably charming and quite lovely, he had tired of them all with astonishing speed. In truth he far preferred the rather unconventional and endlessly refreshing behavior of his spirited wife. Why, then, hadn't he simply told her that? Why had he lost his temper over something that in truth mattered very little to him?

"For God's sake," Hugh said aloud, addressing the swiftly lowering sky and the mountains that rose vast and dark and brooding before him, "maybe she's right, and I *am* nothing more than an unmitigated boor!"

Smiling wryly at the thought, he clattered into the darkened courtyard and handed his lathered horse over to a groom. Upon making inquiries of the housekeeper, he discovered that Her Grace had arrived home a half hour earlier and had asked that a supper tray be sent to her room. The fact that Eden obviously did not wish to dine with him was not lost upon Hugh, and his expression was not at all pleasant as he mounted the stairs to their apartment.

I'll have to apologize to her, of course, he thought, not without a measure of reluctance, wondering how Eden would receive such a startling and unexpected disclosure from him. Yet if he knew anything at all about his wife, it was that she was not a vindictive creature, and that an apology, honestly made, would not—could not—be accepted by her with open scorn. Or so he hoped. . . .

The drapes had been drawn across the windows, and only a single lamp burned on the sitting room table. It was not like Eden to keep the room quite so dark, yet Hugh did not puzzle long over this, for the moment he stepped inside he found himself assailed by an entirely unexpected scent of exotic incense. It was a scent he had long since become familiar with—a scent as intricately woven into the fabric of the East as the sights and sounds of India itself, and one that caused him to halt on the threshold as a host of memories overwhelmed him.

"Sandalwood?" said Hugh aloud. "Eden, what the devil—"

There was a rustle of silk and a movement from behind him. Hugh whirled sharply and was checked by a voice that spoke softly in Hindustani:

"Do not ask unnecessary questions, sahib. Is it not enough that we are here alone?"

Through the dim lamplight Hugh found himself confronted by an Indian girl, her body encased in a flowing sari of rose-colored silk. Her features were hidden by a gold-trimmed veil—all but the eyes, those incredibly deep blue eyes, made bluer by the shadows of the room and the soaring ceiling beyond her. There was a teasing light in those lovely eyes, a look of invitation that gave the lie to the momentary hesitation he had been quick enough to notice when he had first turned to face her.

"To what do I owe such an honor, sahiba?" Hugh inquired, his lips twitching. He stood quite still as she moved closer, unwilling to believe that she had forgiven him so readily, afraid to hope that Eden had seen through the blunder he had made that morning and recognized the emotions lying beneath it for what they truly were.

"There is really no need for thee to ask," she said softly. Her voice was low and husky, her breath warm against his cheek. A pair of slim arms wound themselves about Hugh's neck, and he turned and lifted aside the veil to find Eden's lips only inches from his own. Taking her into his arms, he pulled her slim body against the length of his.

"Eden," he whispered, "I want you to know—"

"Hush," she breathed, leaning closer until her lips brushed softly, provocatively, against his. "Have I not said there is no need for words?"

Then her fingers were in his hair, drawing his head down to hers, and it was true: there was no need for anything but the shadowed silence that surrounded them and the feelings and passions that rose at the kiss to blot out all sensation and thought. . . .

It proved to be a night of unclouded loving, of a passion that transcended even the bliss of their wedding night and bound them irrevocably, inarguably, to one another. Lying in the crook of Hugh's arm with the night paling beyond the frosted windowpanes, Eden knew what it meant for the first time in her life to be deeply and completely happy. She stirred and sighed and felt Hugh's arm tighten about her, turning her body so that it lay intimately against his where she could hear the steady beat of his heart beneath her cheek.

"It will be morning soon," he observed, listening to the crowing of a cock as the dawn gathered strength and the dim light within the room changed subtly from indigo blue to gray.

Another dawn—only one of many that Eden had witnessed in her young life, and yet it seemed to her as if this particular one was like the very first of all: fresh and new and infinitely enchanting. Of a sudden a thought occurred to her, and she drew in her breath and felt Hugh's hold tighten about her.

"What is it, *mo cridhe?*"

"I was just thinking," she admitted slowly. "You'll be leaving soon, won't you? To go back to Somerset?"

"Have you no intention of coming with me?" Hugh asked lightly.

"How can I?" she whispered despairingly. "Somerset is so far away, and Grandfather's health—"

Hugh silenced her with a finger to her lips and, coming up on one elbow, gazed down at her intently. "I wouldn't dream of going without you," he assured her gruffly. "Angus's health should improve once the winter is over, and I see no reason why I can't wait until then."

Eden's eyes widened. "Then—then you won't be going for a time?"

"No. I'll just put it off until warmer weather."

Seeing the patent relief in her eyes, he gave a low laugh. "Am I to understand that you would be despondent over my absence?"

And Eden, who perhaps only a few hours ago would have been hesitant to admit such a thing, wound her arms about his neck and sighed. "Yes."

Hugh laughed again, a laugh that was no longer teasing but filled with an odd note of wonder. Pulling her to him, he kissed her roughly, and it was as if all thoughts and words were once again and instantly swept away by a rising tide of desire.

For Eden the days that followed brought her a happiness the likes of which she had only imagined in dreams. Every morning she awoke from the deep sleep of utter restfulness to find Hugh beside her, and after a leisurely breakfast made all the more delightful by their teasing and laughter, she would ride with him across the cold, snow-dusted moors to inspect his winter herds and the sprawling borders of his land. Together they paid numerous visits to his shepherds and his crofters, with whom Eden was learning to converse more fluently in their native tongue— the soft, lilting Gaelic that was so difficult to master. They would all of them smile at her shyly and receive her warmly, not only because she spoke their language and seemed to understand their ways, but also because she was so young and lovely and so obviously in love.

Often the storms of autumn would prevent them riding out altogether, and on occasion days would pass before the howling wind abated and the sleet and snow would cease to fall and they were no longer cut off from the rest of the glen. To Eden, who had grown up in the crowded, noisy world of a rajah's zenana, the quiet and solitude proved a novel experience—and a source of constant wonder. She could not have explained why she should feel so utterly content to spend day upon day without once setting foot outdoors—she, who had always chafed at restrictions and the inability to go where she wished and do as she pleased. Yet this was no longer the life she had known, a life she found she no longer wanted, and what did it matter to her that the elements raged fiercely without when it was so warm and peaceful and quiet within?

In the evenings Eden and Hugh would work together in the lamplit study, Eden helping him as best she could with his endless reams of paperwork or simply sitting in an armchair near his desk talking quietly with him while Sir Hamish, who had taken of late to joining them, would bow his grizzled head over his own books and smile contentedly to himself. And afterward the long, still, blissful nights enfolded them—nights that, however cold or storm-tossed and raw, provided a haven of warmth and sensation and love. There was never any need for Hugh or Eden to put into words what needed no expression, it blossomed between them at a touch or a glance and never failed to send them drifting into sleep feeling rapturously happy and content.

"There is a visitor to see you, memsahib," said Dundhoo, appearing in the sitting room one overcast morning.

Eden, who had been watching the raindrops slide down the mullioned windows with a dreamy expression, turned and smiled somewhat guiltily. "Who is it, Dundhoo?"

"It's me," said Isabel distractedly from the hallway, brushing past the Hindu to halt before her cousin. Casting a swift glance about the pleasant room, she inquired passionately, "He isn't here, is he?"

"No," said Eden at once. "He's ridden out to the sheep pens for the morning. What is it, Isabel? Has something happened?"

"Perhaps I should take the miss-sahib's cloak," suggested Dundhoo politely.

"Yes, thank you," said Eden with considerable relief, observing the pool of water spreading on the carpet at Isabel's feet. "And please fetch another cup of tea for my cousin." She waited in silence while the bearer withdrew, frowning a little as she studied Isabel's white, anxious face. Never had her cousin looked quite so agitated before, and a sudden thought struck a blow of fear into her heart.

"Grandfather! Has anything—"

"Oh, no, he's quite all right," Isabel assured her quickly. "He doesn't even know I'm here, and he must never, never find out."

"Why not?"

Isabel laced her fingers nervously together and hesitated a long moment before blurting: "I couldn't stay away any longer, Eden! I had to speak to you, I *had* to. You're the only one who can make him stay! Please, Eden, you must speak to—to your husband! You must make him understand—"

"Isabel, wait a moment," Eden interrupted helplessly. "I'm afraid you're not being very clear. Make who stay? And where? Here at Arran Mhór? Who is it you're talking about?"

"Davie," said Isabel on a breathless gasp, and suddenly her face crumpled and she began to cry.

"Davie?" Eden echoed, bewildered. "Do you mean Davie Anderson? Tor Alsh's steward?"

Isabel nodded, a scrap of lace held to her lips as she gulped and struggled to control her tears. "He's—he's leaving for Glasgow tomorrow morning, and nothing will make him change his mind! And it's all His Grace's— your husband's fault!"

"Hugh's? Why Hugh's? You must tell me what it is he's done, dear. I confess I'm completely in the dark."

The tale, as told by Isabel in a largely garbled fashion, involved the decision of Tor Alsh's steward to accept a position at one of the millinery factories that were cropping up with astonishing speed in Glasgow's everexpanding industrial quarters. Not only were the hours long and the pay incredibly poor, but Isabel had heard talk of the appalling hazards facing the workers, conditions that would assuredly prove doubly dangerous to Davie, given the fact that he was crippled. She could not bear the thought of him throwing away his youth and his health in a dark, airless factory, and surely Eden could do something to prevent it? She must!

"I still don't see what I can do," said Eden gently. "If Davie has made the decision of his own free will—"

"But he hasn't!" cried Isabel passionately. "It's all because of the money Grandfather Fraser owes Arran Mhór! Davie says the only way Tor Alsh can meet its loan payments this winter is if he takes another position, and the factory in Glasgow was the only one that would hire him."

"That's taking things a bit to the extreme, isn't it? Surely Grandfather could request an extension if he found himself short of money this time of year?"

"No!" cried Isabel in alarm. "Your grandfather knows nothing about this, and he must never find out! Janet is convinced the shock would kill him and—and I'm afraid she's right."

"So am I," said Eden slowly, and there was a sudden lump in her throat as she thought of the kindly old man who had come to mean so much to her, and of how frail and precarious his health remained, despite his arguments to the contrary. She was silent a moment, considering Isabel's words, and then she said in a brighter tone: "I cannot see that there is much to worry about. Hugh will assuredly agree to wait until the financial situation at Tor Alsh improves, and Davie need only—"

She broke off as she saw the look of dreadful, dawning realization that crossed Isabel's face. "What is it?" she demanded sharply.

"You don't know, do you?" Isabel said in a whisper.

A cold band of fear seemed to tighten about Eden's heart. "Know what?"

Isabel stared down at her hands and said quietly and matter-of-factly: "Tor Alsh is on the verge of bankruptcy, Eden. The way Janet explained it to me, there is little left of the family holdings that haven't been turned over to some bank or another, or soon shall be."

"That—that doesn't seem possible!" exclaimed Eden after a moment of stunned silence. Not Tor Alsh, with its acres and acres of land and its impressive barns and paddocks, and the rambling manor house with its valuable furnishings and appointments! The Frasers couldn't possibly be in debt, not while maintaining such an imposing air of genteel wealth and respectability—could they?

"It seems your grandfather borrowed an inordinate amount of money over the years without the knowledge of your uncles, money that was used for buying up land left over from the clearances, and for new equipment and brood mares and the like. His intention was to improve the breeding stock at a time when demand for workhorses hasn't been particularly strong, and the loss of those fillies in the Channel last winter didn't help things, either." Isabel's expression was bleak. "I suppose we should be grateful for one thing: he doesn't seem at all aware of what he's done."

"And of course he must never find out," Eden agreed. "I believe you're right in saying he could never withstand the shock."

"Poor Janet has been going mad trying to keep all those creditors at bay," Isabel continued unhappily, "and your grandfather from learning the truth. Do you remember the letter Sir Graham Waring wrote to him from Edinburgh? The one that was returned unopened? It was Janet who sent it back thinking it was just another demand for payment. Anne told me yesterday that her mother has sold most of her jewelry and some of the family paintings, but it isn't enough, and every day the chance increases that someone will come from the bank in Inverness—or Fort William or Edinburgh—demanding to see your grandfather personally."

"Perhaps Hugh could persuade them to wait," said Eden slowly, "or even extend The Tor a new line of credit. I would imagine he has enough money to do so. Would you like me to ask him?"

Isabel's pale face brightened instantly. "Oh, would you, Eden? Really, he only needs to give us more time so that—so that nothing will change at The Tor, at least until the spring foals are auctioned off. Davie—Mr. Anderson—says he's expecting a good crop, and perhaps there'll be enough money to pay the bills then.''

"I'll do my best,'' promised Eden. "And please don't worry. I'm certain Hugh will be happy to help.''

But several hours later Eden was not at all sure she had been right in making such a claim, for when she confronted Hugh at last in the warm, sunlit study, she found herself facing not the tender husband she had come to know so well, but a man who had inexplicably became a stranger:

"Absolutely not,'' was all Hugh said once Eden explained the situation to him. "I can't possibly consider canceling Angus Fraser's debts for him, not now or ever, and that's the end of it.''

Eden stared at him incredulously, and Hugh, turning from the sideboard where he had been pouring himself a brandy, said sharply, "There's no need for you to look like that! Though I sympathize fully with your grandfather's plight, there's really nothing I can do for him.''

"I find that hard to believe,'' said Eden stiffly, "when Arran Mhór holds most of the notes against Tor Alsh to begin with.''

"Not Arran Mhór, Eden, the Northwest Highland Land Bank.''

"Of which you and Uncle Hamish happen to be principle shareholders,'' countered Eden, whose memory was excellent and who had not forgotten the long discourses the major-general had held for her concerning Arran Mhór and the fortunes of its wealthy owner, the earl of Blair.

"That still doesn't mean we can pull strings as we see fit,'' Hugh told her, frowning at her. "Other investors are involved here, many of whom don't even reside in Scotland and who would certainly not be inclined to show sympathy to an elderly Scotsman who cannot meet his payments simply because he borrowed too freely from them.''

It was a quite telling point, but Eden refused to acknowledge as much. "There must be something you can do to help! Perhaps a loan through another bank or a personal one that—"

"I'm sorry, Eden," Hugh said evenly. "I'm not Croesus, and even if I were, I could not afford to pour so much ready cash into an obviously failing enterprise."

"A failing enterprise?" Eden echoed incredulously. "Is that how you see it? We're not talking about business or profits or investments here! This is Tor Alsh—Grandfather's home, his life! Surely you aren't going to turn your back on him like this, are you? It isn't fair!"

Fair? thought Hugh with a stab of despairing anger. What did Eden know of being fair, asking something of him that she must know he could not possibly grant her?

"I'm sorry," he said tersely, "but there's nothing I can do save speak to the bank directors. And I can assure you now it will be a waste of time."

"Thank you," said Eden through rigid lips, "but I suppose that won't be necessary. I'm sorry to have troubled you."

"Eden, wait," Hugh began, but she was already gone, her flounces rustling stiffly as she swept from the room. For a moment Hugh stood gazing angrily after her while the light of the dying day painted the room in a wash of rose and lavender.

"Hell!" he said violently, draining the contents of his glass in a single swallow and setting it savagely aside. Collapsing into a nearby chair, he sat for some considerable time without moving, his face hidden in his unsteady hands.

Chapter Sixteen

"He is, of course, being entirely unreasonable about this," pronounced Sir Hamish Blair energetically. "Why, he's known Angus Fraser for most of his life, and now that the two of them are related by marriage it doesn't seem possible that he refused to help. Bad blood there, I've always said. Gordon blood, you ken, and they've always been a clan of damned feudalists and alarmists. Bah!"

"It's your move, Uncle Hamish," said Eden softly.

"Eh? What's that? Och, all right, lass, though I've a feeling your heart's na in the game tonight."

"No, it— Of course it is," Eden insisted.

"Nothing else to do on a night like this, anyway," Sir Hamish decided. Drawing his shawl over his shoulders, he cast a shuddering glance at the heavy drapes that rustled in the draft. An icy wind howled against the windowpanes, and frozen sleet rattled the glass, and he was grateful for the fire that crackled in the grate. The cold seemed to seep into his very bones these days, and he despaired of feeling warm again until spring.

The study door opened quietly, and although he and Eden had been studying the chessboard with apparent concentration, both of them turned quickly. But it was only a footman come to lay another log on the fire, and after he had withdrawn, the suffocating silence descended once more. To Eden the ticking of the clock on the mantel and the incessant tapping and rattling on the glass began to grate on her nerves like a violin string drawn overly taut, and she checked with difficulty the impulse to hurl the chess set across the room. It had been a most trying day, and she for one would be glad to see it end—but for the nagging reminder that with every passing hour the roads were growing progressively worse and possibly preventing Hugh's return home.

Eden's breath caught on a painful constriction, for she hadn't wanted to think of Hugh, and yet it seemed that she had thought of little else during the past few, slow-crawling days. Hugh, who had been so remotely polite to her when he had taken his leave, explaining that he would be gone for a time and that she needn't worry. . . . But he had not told her where he was going, and she had indeed worried about him with a nagging uneasiness that robbed her of sleep and of the ability to do little more than roam the high-ceilinged rooms of Arran Mhór in restless frustration.

"I've no idea where he's gone," Eden had told Isabel only that morning during a brief visit to Tor Alsh. "He said nothing of his intentions to me, and I didn't ask."

She had not been able to bring herself to tell Isabel that she no longer dared make inquiries of her husband simply because she wasn't at all certain that he would deign to answer her. The chill that had sprung up between them during their unpleasant confrontation in Hugh's study had expanded to arctic proportions over the last few days, and Eden had despaired of bridging the chasm between them. Furthermore, she could not understand his indifference to her grandfather's plight, and once again she was forced to ask herself if perhaps she had been wrong in thinking he cared for her. Surely if he did, he would not have dismissed so callously and completely her plea to save Tor Alsh from ruin.

"Oh, Eden, I cannot believe he could be as heartless as that!" Isabel had protested when Eden had related something of that painful interview to her, and her words had unwittingly echoed Eden's own unhappy thoughts.

It was obvious that Isabel herself was far from happy these days, and Eden did not need to inquire as to the reason. Davie Anderson had departed for Glasgow some time ago, and the soft light that had glowed on Isabel's pretty face whenever she spoke of him was no longer there. In fact, she had not deigned to mention him at all, but in her silence was the heartache that she could not bring herself to put into words.

How dreadfully hurtful being in love can be, Eden had thought, riding home on the moor road a short time later. It had never occurred to her before that being in love did not always necessarily mean one was happy or immune from pain. Strange, for she had always believed, whenever she had chosen to consider the matter, that anyone in love must surely be far removed from those heartaches and miseries that afflicted common mortals.

"Perhaps it depends on whom you love," said Eden aloud, "and perhaps some men are simply harder to love than others." But she was not thinking of Davie Anderson or of Isabel. . . .

"It's your move, lass," said Sir Hamish unexpectedly, his voice serving to pull Eden's thoughts back to the present. Staring down at the chessboard, Eden frowned and bit her lip, then shook her head and pushed away from the table.

"I'm sorry, Uncle, I cannot seem to remember which piece I intended to move. Would you mind dreadfully if I went up to bed? I'm very tired."

"Of course not, my dear," said Sir Hamish gruffly. "Sleep well."

Eden kissed his cheek affectionately, then paused in the doorway as his voice addressed her from behind: "Do you ken if Hugh's expected home tonight?"

"No," said Eden after a brief pause. "I haven't the faintest idea."

Her bedroom was chilly despite the fire blazing in the hearth, and for some reason the cold and uninvitingly empty bed served to underscore Eden's deepening sense of loneliness. Seating herself near the fire, she stared unseeingly into the flames, frowning and wishing that she had accepted Isabel's invitation to spend the night at Tor Alsh, for surely her cousin's company would have been preferable to the chilly gloom of her deserted apartment. If only Hugh—

But Eden would not let herself think of Hugh, and she thrust the image of his browned, smiling face away from her with a violence that was almost pain. No, she would not think of Hugh or try to remember when, in fact, he had last smiled at her or laughed with her or when they had last talked softly together as she lay in his arms after a night of loving. Even if he did come home tonight, it was doubtful that he would seek her out, for the door separating their bedrooms had remained closed these many nights past, a coldly immutable sign of the hopelessness of the present situation.

Eden fell asleep at last, sitting fully clothed in the armchair near the fire, and such was the state of her exhaustion that she did not hear the footsteps in the hallway several hours later or the creaking of the door as someone entered the adjoining bedroom. A light flared briefly, then was gone, and she could not know that Hugh, who had returned half-frozen after a hellish ride of some forty miles, had stood for some considerable time by the narrow door that separated their rooms, feeling indecisive for the first time in his life, before turning away to shed his dripping clothes and retire to bed.

Not until the dawn had given way to a sullen, overcast morning of scuttling clouds and gusting rain did Eden appear downstairs and learn from Dundhoo that the Hazrat-sahib had returned sometime during the night and that he had ridden out again before first light with McKenzie-sahib. And though she willed herself to accept the news in a calm and noncommittal fashion, Eden could not prevent a feeling of breathless hope surging within her. Surely, surely now that Hugh was back all would be well, and they could at last mend the impassable gulf between them.

But Eden did not see Hugh again until the swift-lowering darkness had given way to impenetrable night and the unused supper dishes that had been laid out for him had long since been cleared away. She herself had eaten almost nothing despite Sir Hamish's quite vocal disapproval, and afterward she had whiled away the dragging evening hours with a pretense at reading.

At nine o'clock the chimes on the mantel rang their dutiful passage of the hour, and an ember in the fireplace exploded noisily, and something within Eden seemed to snap. Sending the book hurling across the sofa she came swiftly to her feet only to whirl as the door opened and

Hugh entered the salon. It was obvious that he had not expected to find her there, for he halted abruptly at the sight of her. For a long, taut moment they stared at one another, then Hugh stirred and went to the sideboard, where he poured himself a brandy. Not until he had drunk a healthy measure did he turn again to face her, his features composed.

"You look tired," blurted Eden, although she had been intending to say something entirely different. Her voice shook a little despite her efforts to steady it. "Are you all right?"

"Nothing that a good night's sleep won't cure," Hugh told her in an unexpectedly expressionless tone, and Eden, hearing it, felt something that had begun to expand joyfully within her heart shrivel and die.

"Then perhaps you should retire."

"Oh, I intend to." Hugh looked down into her face, and suddenly it was his turn to speak sharply. "You haven't been feeling unwell yourself, have you? You look pale, and Dundhoo tells me you've been eating very little."

Eden made a slight, negative movement with her head. "No, I—it's only because I've been worried—"

"Worried?" Hugh interrupted, frowning. "About what? Certainly not about me? I should think you know me well enough by now to realize that I can take care of myself tolerably well."

"But you've been gone for days, and you didn't tell m—you didn't tell anyone where you were going."

The light that had sprung unnoticed to Hugh's eyes at Eden's expression of concern died abruptly as he chose to put his own interpretation upon the meaning of her words. "Ah, so you've been curious about my whereabouts," he observed with a dry smile. Turning his back on her, he carefully set aside his empty glass. "I assure you there was no reason to lose sleep over my absence. I merely rode to Inverness to speak to several of the directors of the Northwest Highland Bank, exactly as I'd told you I would."

Eden said nothing, struggling with the tears that clogged her throat, knowing she couldn't bear the humiliation of shedding them before him. Oh, why did he have to be so mocking and hateful? She had been so anxious to see him, and now—now she only wished that he would go away and leave her alone.

"Don't you want to know what they said?" Hugh inquired finally.

"If you wish to tell me," Eden whispered.

"Actually," Hugh informed her with a shrug, "they said nothing at all, for I never even spoke to them." Catching sight of Eden's expression, he laughed harshly. "There was no need to, I'm afraid. Sir Fitzroy Ross, the bank director, obligingly made Tor Alsh's books available to me, and one had only to glance at them to see how hopeless the situation really is."

"I can't believe that!" said Eden stubbornly. "You have to be inventing, and it's only because—"

"Inventing?" Hugh echoed disbelievingly. He came to stand before her, looking down at her with his eyes narrowed and his mouth thinned into a grim line. "I cannot believe your puerile grasp of reality," he said at last. "Any business, even a long-standing, successful one like Tor Alsh and its Clydesdales, can go under if it's debted far too heavily. And your grandfather, I'm afraid, over-extended his credit years ago. If he had diversified, or perhaps invested in some other— Oh, bloody hell, where's the use in explaining this to you? You won't believe anything but the evidence of your own eyes. Just because your grandfather isn't dressed in rags and there's still plenty of food on the table and a closetful of new ball gowns for Isabel and Anne—"

"No, it isn't that," Eden said stiffly. "Isabel already told me that Aunt Janet was forced to sell a number of family heirlooms, and she isn't the sort to do something like that unless the situation has become truly desperate. It's the fact that you refuse to do anything to help them because you've already judged the situation as being entirely hopeless. It's—it's cowardly and craven of you, Hugh, and I'm wondering if you are really anything at all like the man I met in India."

A heavy silence settled in the wake of her words, and Eden, lifting her head and seeing the expression on

Hugh's face, bit back a dismayed gasp. She hadn't really intended to say that, hadn't meant to turn the topic of discussion from Tor Alsh's plight to an underhanded and entirely unjustified and unfair attack on his character. Yet the words were out, and despite the fact that she had not meant them, they had been regrettably, irrevocably uttered, and there was nothing she could now say to undo them.

Hugh was regarding her with grimly compressed lips, and something hurtful caught Eden by the throat, for in all their heated confrontations he had never looked at her quite in that manner before. Yet even as her own expression softened unconsciously and she reached out her hand to him, he inclined his head and said in a hard and final voice:

"I believe you're right, Eden. We each seem to have made a grave mistake about the other."

Walking past her, he opened the salon door with a jerk and left her. A cold blast of wind, spiraling down the chimney, caused the flames in the hearth to flare bright blue and a draft to sweep through the room, setting the drapes to rustling and the door to blowing shut with a soft, decisive click behind him.

"Eden, lass. Eden, are you awake?"

A hint of gray was creeping into the blackness beyond the drapes that Eden had neglected to shut the night before, and when she opened her eyes she wasn't entirely certain for a moment where she was. Then her vision cleared, and she climbed quickly out of bed. The room was bitterly cold, and she shivered as she crossed to the door and opened it.

"Don't make a sound, lass," cautioned Sir Hamish as she stepped aside to admit him. Peering past her shoulder, he whispered, "Is Hugh with you?"

"No," said Eden, too astonished by his unexpected appearance to feel embarrassed by the impertinence of his question.

"Good. Get dressed, then. I've the carriage waiting round front. Quickly, now!"

"Where is it we're going?" inquired Eden with a frown.

"To Inverness, of course. Hugh ain't the only one i' the family what has the final say on how our money's spent! If the shoe were on t'other foot, I ken Angus'd do the same for Arran Mhór. It's that banker Ross we need to see. He'll not refuse his help like that bloody nephew of mine! Bah!"

"Oh, Uncle Hamish, are you certain that's wise? If Hugh says there isn't—"

"We're wasting time, lass," the major-general interrupted imperiously. "Will you be coming or no?"

"It's a long way to Inverness," Eden reminded him doubtfully, "and very cold."

"I've whiskey and extra blankets in the carriage. Dress warmly and you'll be comfortable." He fixed her with a baleful eye. "Well, then? Am I to go alone, or will you come wi' me?"

"I'll come," said Eden at once, and dressed quickly, shivering with cold and indecision and wondering if she shouldn't take it upon herself to awaken Hugh, who might have better luck in persuading his uncle to abandon this impulsive scheme. But the thought of confronting Hugh so soon after last night filled her with reluctance. She left moments later by way of a side door leading to the courtyard, dragging the hood of her cloak over her curls and fighting her way through the teeth of the wind.

Sir Hamish, she saw at once, had carried out his preparations for the journey with the forethought of a well-laid military campaign. Heated bricks wrapped in blankets warmed the interior of the carriage, and a reed basket placed on the opposite seat held the makings of an enormous breakfast as well as the major-general's daily requirement of Highland malt. Dundhoo, who would most assuredly have protested his master's decision to embark upon such a trip, was noticeably absent, and it was a wool-muffled groom who helped Eden up into the carriage and closed the door behind her.

The graying dawn gave way eventually to an even bleaker morning, and by the time the carriage rumbled through the ancient feudal lands of the Menzies and the

MacPhersons, the tattered clouds overhead had gathered into a sullen mass hinting of snow. It was cold in the carriage despite the blankets and the warm cloak Eden had wrapped about her, and the wind buffeted them unmercifully as they crossed the wide open moors so that the vehicle swayed and shook and the horses were forced to lean hard in their traces.

"It willna be like this much longer," Sir Hamish remarked encouragingly. "Once we cross Rannoch Moor the roads will improve and we'll make better time."

But he had not counted on the weather, and they had not crossed half of that wide, desolate open space before a flurry of falling snow began to stream from the sky. The wind screamed while the gradually thickening flakes coated the vehicle and forced the horses to a crawling walk.

"Don't you think we ought to turn back?" inquired Eden, peering worriedly out of the window. The road was fast disappearing beneath a layer of white, and she could see no sign of human habitation anywhere on that desolate moorland. Indeed, it had been some considerable time since they had passed through a village or seen so much as a single, isolated croft, and it was difficult for Eden to shake the unsettling impression that they had crossed to the very end of the earth.

Sir Hamish chuckled in response to this and assured her that there was no cause for fear, no cause at all! A wee bit of snow was common this time of year, and the horses and the coachman were quite accustomed to traveling through it. But perhaps the fury of the storm was greater than he had anticipated, or perhaps the driving snow blinded the horses sufficiently to prevent them following the lie of the road, for not half an hour later the carriage, rumbling dangerously close to the edge of the roadway, struck hard against an outcropping of stone and lost a wheel.

Eden, who had been dozing on the padded seat, was thrown against the wooden bracings of the door with sufficient force to momentarily lose consciousness. It was the cold and the anxious voice of McNeil, the coachman, that finally aroused her. Opening her eyes, she found the vehicle leaning at a precarious angle and McNeil doing his best to pry open the door.

"I canna open it, Your Grace!" he called in to her at last. "You'll have to climb through the window if you can. Is Sir Hamish unharmed?"

"Aye, I'm all right," came the major-general's rather irritated voice from somewhere beneath a pile of blankets and the overturned remnants of their breakfast.

With the coachman's help they exited through the window to stand shivering and silent before the wreckage of their vehicle, wondering with no small measure of dismay what they ought to do now and trying their best to hide their fears from each other. It was McNeil who suggested at last that he unhitch the lead horse, which was saddle broken, and ride to the nearest village for help.

"That'll be Kirkcaldie," said Sir Hamish with a thoughtful nod. "Na more than six miles across the braes. Aye, we'll wait here. It seems the best we can do."

And so they installed themselves as comfortably as possible back within the cramped confines of the leaning carriage while the coachman swung himself onto the bare back of one of the horses and, taking off at a hand gallop, was quickly lost in the driving snow. Eden was thankful that she had taken the precaution of donning her warmest dress of gray merino wool. Wrapped in blankets with her hands buried inside a fur-trimmed muffler, she felt surprisingly comfortable—discounting, of course, the unpleasant throbbing of the bump on her temple. Animated by a sense of adventure, she and Sir Hamish chatted companionably for a time, yet as the morning waned and the snow continued to collect upon the roof and the door of their carriage and McNeil did not return, they grew increasingly silent.

"I wonder what's keeping him?" said Eden at last, voicing aloud the worrisome thought that was foremost in both their minds. "Surely he should have returned by now?"

"The snow'll be slowing him down," guessed Sir Hamish, "and 'twill doubtless take time to round up a blacksmith and horses for us to ride."

He did not mention the possibility—increasingly likely, given the drifts that were whipping across the whitening landscape—that the coachman might have wandered off the road and lost his way. The mountains were no more than a blot of gray against the lowering sky, and it would be difficult for anyone, even someone familiar with the area, to maintain a grasp on his bearings. He did not say as much to Eden, however, although there was really no need for him to conceal his thoughts from her since that same possibility had already occurred to her with frightening certainty.

"Perhaps I should ride after him," she suggested at last, though the major-general instantly rejected the idea, supporting his decision with a host of inarguable observations:

"You'd only lose your way, lass. And despite how well you can handle horseflesh, I still wouldna trust you wi' those beasties McNeil left behind. Besides, you've no proper gloves, and your hands'll freeze on the reins."

He was probably right, Eden reflected reluctantly. Already her fingers were so frozen that she could barely feel them, and her feet ached with cold. Drawing the fur-trimmed collar of her cloak more tightly about her, she turned her face away and said nothing more. Perhaps they were just being overly worried in imagining that the coachman was taking far too long. Sir Hamish had neglected to bring his pocketwatch, and it was impossible to accurately guess at the passage of time without the sun to guide them; in this swirling grayness it could just as easily prove to be eleven o'clock as three.

Leaning her head against the padded cushions, Eden closed her eyes and wished for the luxury of sleep. Perhaps in that manner she could escape the terrible, penetrating cold and the thoughts of Hugh that came to her unwittingly and dragged at her heart with a sadly familiar ache. Perhaps, she told herself upon examining the matter with the bitter clarity of hindsight, she should have awakened him after all instead of agreeing to accompany Sir Hamish to Inverness. Yet where was the use in thinking about that? "What is written is written, and one cannot change what God has ordained,'' Fariza Begum, had always been fond of saying. Better to accept what could not be changed, Eden decided, than to fret and lament about what one should have done. And better still to close one's eyes and mind to the bitter cold and the moaning of the wind and dream of the warmth of the bedroom she had left behind. . . .

Raised in Rajasthan and accustomed to the sweltering heat of Indian summers, Eden was still a stranger to the chilling blizzards of northern latitudes and lamentably ignorant of the dangers of hypothermia—of falling asleep while the insidious cold, like silent death, crept unawares through the blood and the veins and the limbs of the body. Sir Hamish knew, or had once known, for he was no stranger to the harshness of the winters spent on the northwest Indian border, yet perhaps he had forgotten, or the cold and weariness had already sucked him down into apathy, for his chin had fallen to his chest, and the light, easy sleep of old age was already upon him.

Silence descended upon the tilting carriage, a silence made all the more complete by the snowflakes that continued to fall in a muffling layer over the windows and the trappings and the broken, off-side wheel. To Eden it seemed as if the cold were indeed being held at bay as she had hoped, for as she sank deeper into sleep she found her dreams taking her back to the sun-scorched plains of Mayar and the pleasing warmth and tranquillity of the zenana gardens. She could almost hear the gentle rustle of the *purdah* screens in the slight breeze and the laughter of the women as they gathered in the courtyard, preening like elegant peacocks in their jewel-spangled saris. She ran forward to join them with a glad cry on her lips, only to find herself being held back unexpectedly by a pair of restraining hands. Though she struggled against them she could not win free, and as she began to protest someone said harshly in her ear:

"For God's sake, Eden, stop it!"

It took Eden a moment to realize that the furious voice above her was not at all a part of her dream and that it was speaking to her in English, not Hindustani. It was a voice she had heard often enough in the past, yet never had it been in possession of such a driving intensity of anger, and when it addressed her again she recognized it suddenly and incredulously as Hugh's.

"You bloody little fool! Wake up before you freeze to death!"

Eden opened her eyes then to find his face hovering above hers, a face made almost unrecognizable by rage and impatience and something else, something that seemed very like fear, though what Hugh should be afraid of was beyond Eden's understanding. She could feel his arms about her, holding her hard against him, and realized with a sense of wonder that she was no longer cold, but warm, wonderfully, deliciously warm.

"What in bloody hell were you trying to do?" Hugh demanded savagely, seeing her eyes open at last, but Eden merely smiled at him.

She did not remember the long ride back to Arran Mhór or the anxious whispers of the maids who put her to bed, or, indeed, the examination by the doctor Hugh hastily summoned from the neighboring glen. Eden slept the sleep of total exhaustion, from which she did not awaken until the following evening, when the sky beyond her windows was ablaze with the purple of coming night, and the first stars flared above the glittering peaks of the mountains.

Except for a bruise on her temple, there was nothing to indicate that she had come very near being frozen to death in a crippled carriage high on a desolate moor, and Eden was inclined to dismiss the worried posturings of the maid who answered her summons for tea as bordering on the dramatic. It had been nothing more than an unfortunate mishap, after all, and now that it was over she was quite prepared to dismiss it entirely from her mind.

Perhaps for this reason she was not at all prepared for the tongue-lashing she was to receive from Hugh on the heels of her appearance downstairs—a charged confrontation that was to precipitate a great many changes in their lives, though both of them were as yet unaware of it.

"I cannot believe your limitless capacity for stupidity!" Hugh said immediately at the sight of her and with an anger that had apparently remained unabated since he had brought her back to Arran Mhór the day before. "Of all the crack-brained, idiotic schemes you've ever indulged in, this is undoubtedly the worst! What in God's name were you thinking of? Didn't it occur to you that it might prove dangerous to venture out into a snowstorm with only a groom and an old man to accompany you?"

His anger was certainly understandable, given the fact that neither Eden nor Sir Hamish seemed to have grasped how serious their predicament had been. The coachman McNeil had indeed lost his way in the howling blizzard, and it had been Hugh and half a dozen grooms from Arran Mhór who had arrived in time to pull the old man and the duchess of Roxbury from the carriage. Sir Hamish had suffered a severe case of frostbite, and the fact that it had taken considerable effort to revive him from the half coma into which he had slipped had unsettled Hugh more than he cared to admit. The thought that his wife might have suffered a similar fate, and the sight of the bruise that discolored her temple when she entered the study and lifted her face to his had understandably exacerbated an already badly frayed temper.

Yet perhaps it was unwise of Hugh to lash out at her without warning, for Eden, having no inkling whatsoever of the unpleasant bend of her husband's thoughts, had been unprepared for the shock and the hurt that cramped her heart at his unexpected outburst. She had secretly been expecting to mend the rift between them, her dreams fueled by the hope that the anger Hugh had displayed toward her on the moorland yesterday had been caused by concern for her that surely must mean he loved her. She had not been at all prepared for his blistering accusations or the unfairness of them and, stung, retreated behind an air of stubborn dignity that ended entirely the possibility of their communicating honestly with one another.

"I'm sorry," she said distantly now, "it was neither mine nor Uncle Hamish's intention to cause you any inconvenience. We were on our way to Inverness—"

"I know damned well what you were up to," Hugh interrupted furiously, "and I hope you realize that your impulsive, meddlesome behavior nearly cost both of you your lives! Dr. Cutcheon cannot vouch for Uncle Hamish's immediate recovery, given his age and the condition of his heart—'' He broke off as he saw the expression on Eden's face and, turning away from her, struggled to gain control of himself. "He'll be all right, of course," he said roughly, "though it's going to take some time. His feet and hands were badly frozen, and Dr. Cutcheon isn't at all certain he'll regain total use of his fingers."

"I didn't know," Eden whispered in horror. "I didn't think—"

"No, you never do, do you?" Hugh put in brusquely. "You've never been content to leave matters as they are! Always interfering and embarking on impulsive schemes that cause far more trouble than they're worth! If I had known that marriage to you would prove so endlessly tiresome—"

The frozen look on Eden's face gave way to one of wounded fury. "Don't you dare try to tell me you entered into our marriage with your eyes closed, Hugh Gordon! That's untrue and unfair, and something I never expected to hear from *you!*"

Hugh stood gazing at her for an ominous moment without speaking, wondering what he could possibly say to ease the tension in the air between them and defuse his own towering anger. He found himself wishing, too, perhaps entirely irrationally, given his present frame of mind, that Eden didn't look so heartbreakingly lovely and desirable to him, and that he wasn't so acutely aware of how close he had come to losing her. But it wasn't any use. He could not rein in his runaway temper quite so readily, not after yesterday.

"Yes, you're right," he said with cold finality. "It would be wrong of me to say I had no idea what I was getting into. It's a pity, actually, because it means there really isn't any excuse for such blind stupidity on my part, is there?"

And once again, and in a nightmare repetition of their last exchange, he wordlessly turned heel and left her.

Chapter Seventeen

"Oh, yes, I know exactly where he's gone," said Eden calmly. "To Somerset. He was kind enough to leave me a note this time, though he didn't bother to say when he might return."

Isabel's eyes opened wide. "To Somerset? In this weather? But why on earth—"

"Really, Isabel," interrupted her cousin briskly, "I haven't come to talk to you about Hugh. I wanted to ask you a few questions about something entirely different."

"Very well," said Isabel dubiously, and motioned Eden into the warmth of Tor Alsh's salon. "Janet and Anne are out," she explained, "and Grandfather Fraser is resting upstairs. You will make a point to see him before you go, won't you? It's been days since you were here last, and he's been asking after you." She hesitated, biting her lip, and then added slowly: "Perhaps you shouldn't mention to him that Lord Blair has gone to England. He'll only worry knowing you're alone in that big old castle."

Eden fixed her cousin with an amused look and gave an unexpected laugh. "Really, Isabel, I'm not at all alone! There's Sir Hamish and Dundhoo and the servants, and I certainly don't mind spending some time by myself. It's not as if Hugh and I were accustomed to—" She broke off abruptly, then finished quickly, "But of course I intend to visit Grandfather! Did you think I'd ride all this way through the cold without doing so?"

Isabel smiled her agreement, though the worried frown that had creased her brow at Eden's unexpected appearance on the doorstep at Tor Alsh did not fade. She was dismayed by Eden's casual disclosure that Hugh Gordon was in Somerset, for surely there must be something entirely untypical about a marriage in which a husband and wife spent so much time apart? Why, if she and Davie Anderson—

A hot wave of embarrassment washed over Isabel at the thought of Tor Alsh's former steward. She mustn't think of him, *hadn't* thought of him for days and days, in fact, and besides, it wasn't as though Eden looked particularly unhappy. Actually she seemed quite cheerful and relaxed and certainly looked undeniably beautiful in a gown of dark blue merino edged with figured jaconet, her golden curls arranged in a becoming coronet beneath a trim little hat of terry velvet trimmed with fur.

"Actually, I'm rather relieved that Aunt Janet and Anne aren't home," Eden confessed, "for they would undoubtedly wish to know why I'm here. And it would have been most curious, not to mention inexcusably rude of me, if I told them I wanted to speak with you alone."

Something in the forced light-heartedness of her tone gave Isabel pause. "What is it, Eden? Does it have anything to do with your grandfather's money?"

"In a way, yes." Seating herself near the fire, Eden drew off her gloves and began to speak in a low, calm voice. Wasting little time, she told her cousin of her memories of the Meerut massacre and the dawn of the Great Sepoy Mutiny. Of how her Hindu *ayah* Sitka had come to be murdered by a British infantry officer and of his reasons for killing her. It was a story she had never told anyone, not even Hugh, and Isabel, who had at first attended her with a puzzled frown, could not help but shed dismayed tears at the news of Sitka's death.

"She was always so very kind to me," recalled Isabel softly. "Sometimes I think she considered the two of us children of her own flesh and blood." Her warm smile faded abruptly. "And I simply cannot believe one of Colonel Carmichael-Smyth's own officers would do anything so brutal to her!"

"Can't you?" inquired Eden dryly. "It's amazing what men can be prompted to do by the lure of untold wealth."

"I suppose you're right," Isabel agreed sadly, and lifted bewildered eyes to her cousin's face. "But why are you telling me this now? Surely that isn't why you came, is it?"

Eden leaned forward to regard Isabel keenly. "Yes, it is. I wanted to ask you if you had any idea how that man might have found out about the existence of Uncle Donan's jewels."

Isabel did not need to think the matter over. Shaking her head, she insisted that she hadn't had the faintest notion that such a vast fortune in gemstones had been hidden away in the tobacco tin she had carried to Lucknow from Ceylon. No, she hadn't mentioned them to anyone—why should she?—nor had she seen the tin again after handing it over to Uncle Dougal. Yes, of course she had known that her father mined rubies and other precious gemstones on his estate, but she hadn't *dreamed* that he had managed to amass such a fortune.

"Then we really know no more than we did before," said Eden unhappily. "I had so hoped you might know something about this British officer who took them. He wasn't serving in any of the Meerut *pultons,* you see, for I made certain of that." She bit her lip and then threw up her hands in an unexpected gesture of defeat. "Bloody hell! I suppose it was mad of me to think we could find him!"

Isabel asked diffidently: "Does it matter so very much that we do? I mean, Sitka has been dead for over four years now. Surely it would be too late to bring charges against him after all this time?"

Eden turned her head to regard her cousin with open astonishment. "Oh, Isabel, it isn't that! It's the jewels, of course—your inheritance! How else do you think we can pay off Tor Alsh's debts and bring Davie Anderson back from Glasgow unless we find them?"

"Find them?" echoed Isabel, too shocked by the very idea to take note of anything else Eden said. "Why, that would be nearly impossible, wouldn't it? Even if you did know this man's name or where he might be now, you have no way of identifying them or proving they once belonged to us!"

"I've considered that, of course," said Eden crisply, "but I was hoping your father might have left a letter of appraisal or a document of sorts—" She broke off as Isabel shook her head, then added ill-temperedly and not a little hopelessly, "I certainly don't know what else we can do to help Grandfather keep Tor Alsh! Bloody hell! If I could just get my hands on a few of them, take them to the Chandi Chauk in Delhi to a certain trader I know—"

"Would you really go back to India to look for them?" inquired Isabel disbelievingly.

"But of course," said Eden calmly.

"Without telling Hugh?"

Eden's face set into an expressionless mask. "Hugh has told me often enough that he doesn't wish to be bothered with Tor Alsh's problems. Why, then, should I tell him anything about this? It's none of his business, after all."

Isabel made no answer, and after a moment Eden observed honestly, "I suppose I should have forgotten about those jewels a long time ago. But it just seems so terribly unfair that Grandfather and Aunt Janet stand to lose Tor Alsh while that—that monster is living the life of a wealthy *box-wallah* on the spoils of Sitka's murder!"

The two women fell silent, each of them thinking of the fortune that might have been theirs and acknowledging the bitter futility of their dreams. After a moment Eden sighed and came to her feet, her heavy skirts rustling. "I believe I'll go upstairs and visit with Grandfather. You don't suppose he's sleeping, do you?"

"No, I don't think so. Eden . . ." said Isabel hesitantly, following her into the hall, "I've never asked you—that is, I've always wondered, especially since your marriage to Lord Blair was so unexpected—" Her troubled eyes were on her cousin's face, and she blushed as she blurted: "Is all well with you? I mean, with His Grace gone to Somerset, I can't help thinking—"

Eden caught her breath against the impulsive words that welled like a tide of treacherous tears within her. If there was anyone she knew she could confide in, it was Isabel, whom she loved as a sister and who would never betray her heartache to anyone else. How good it would feel to unburden herself and confess that, yes, she had been wretchedly unhappy since Hugh had left Arran Mhór, and what did Isabel think she should do about it? Surely the love she and Hugh shared had not—could not have—been destroyed so easily! Yet the long years spent in the crowded confines of an Indian zenana, where privacy was always at a premium and gossip and betrayal not uncommon, had taught Eden to keep her own council, and the lessons had been far too well imprinted upon her young girl's heart to allow them to be so quickly abandoned.

"Why, no," she said instead, uttering a careless laugh. "There's nothing at all wrong between Hugh and me. Why should there be?"

"I'm sorry," Isabel countered unhappily, "I didn't mean—"

"Are you expecting someone, Isabel?" interrupted Eden without warning.

Isabel regarded her blankly. "Expecting? Why, no. What makes you think so?"

"Because I believe I hear a carriage coming up the drive."

"That can't be!" protested the startled Isabel, hurrying to the window. "Janet and Anne aren't due back until late this afternoon, and I can't think who else would be coming to see us." She inhaled sharply as she caught sight of a closed coach emerging from the short avenue of rowanberry trees leading to the front drive and turned to regard Eden with considerable alarm. "I hope it isn't anyone from—from the bank! I've no idea what to say to them!"

"I do," said Eden grimly.

They watched in silence as the carriage drew up at the doorstep and exchanged bewildered glances at the sight of the men who descended from it. They certainly couldn't be bankers, Eden decided, not dressed as they were in rough homespun and laborers' aprons. Furthermore, they did not seem to be particularly interested in the house, for they gave it only a hurried glance before turning and leaning into the deeply shadowed interior of the vehicle. By that time the coachman had jumped down from the boot and come round to help them, and Eden saw that they were lowering some sort of board onto the ground, a board that was intended to serve as a stretcher for the man who lay upon it: white-faced, gaunt, and as still as death.

She stared at it for a bewildered moment until she heard Isabel give a soft moan that was no more than a whisper of sound. "No, oh, no!" she breathed, and then she had wrenched open the door and was running outside, unmindful of the cold and the wind that clawed at her skirts and sent them billowing behind her.

Eden saw the man on the stretcher turn his head as Isabel approached, saw him attempt to speak, and recognized him in that moment herself, though it seemed impossible that she could do so. The man on the stretcher—haggard, feverish, and obviously racked with pain—bore no resemblance whatsoever to the one who had left Tor Alsh barely six weeks earlier, determined to earn his fortune in the mills of Glasgow.

At Isabel's direction Davie was carried upstairs and put to bed in Eden's former room, because Isabel would not hear of letting him stay in his old rooms above the stables, which were drafty and bitterly cold. They covered him with blankets, and Isabel hurried downstairs to fetch whiskey while Eden spoke briefly with the men who had brought him. Afterward she went into the kitchen and drew up a bowl of steaming broth to bring to Davie, not knowing what else to do for him.

She found Isabel sitting next to the bed, her face white and strained and filled with unspoken fear. Crossing the room with a nervous rustle of heavy silk, Isabel demanded in a whisper if Eden had sent for the doctor.

"One of the grooms has ridden round for him. It shouldn't take too long," Eden assured her. She peered past her cousin's shoulder to the still figure on the bed and tried not to let her own worry show, yet the words of the men who had brought him here haunted her.

"I'm hopin' ye willna mind our bringin' him, ma'am," one of them had said. "He didna wish us to, ye ken, but a mon ought tae be allowed tae die i' his ane home, shouldn't he?"

"You can't mean that," Eden had protested, shocked. "He isn't going to die!"

The two men had exchanged wordless glances and, declining an invitation to warm themselves before the fire, had been driven away in the carriage through the gusting rain. Now, as she listened to the sound of Davie's shallow breathing and saw the grayish tinge of his skin, Eden felt a knot of fear constrict her throat. That he was gravely ill was obvious to her, yet she had no idea how to help him beyond trying to keep him warm. Apparently Isabel didn't, either, and the nagging, helpless fear that filled both of them as they hovered near the sickbed was like a tangible thing in the room.

Fortunately Janet arrived home earlier than expected and long before the doctor had managed to brave the lashing wind to make his own appearance. Taking one look at the pale, frightened faces of her nieces, Janet set about immediately giving orders and sending to the kitchen for supplies. Tying a clean apron about her waist, she asked a terse question of Eden, who hovered in the doorway waiting to assist her.

"I'm not really sure," Eden responded at once, immeasurably calmed by her aunt's ready competence. "Eight or nine days, I think."

Her aunt's lips thinned. "The fools! And the fever? How long has he had it?"

"I don't know. It was the woman who owned the boarding house who finally called them, they said." Eden's voice dropped to a whisper, though they were alone in the room. "She told them she didn't want another death on her hands, and that they should take him away at once. Surely she couldn't mean—"

Janet made a contemptuous sound deep in her throat. "Oh, aye, she could. I've heard about those factories— death houses, they call them, though it isn't surprising, considering most of the workers are children, not yet ten years old. Standing in water twelve hours a day with nothing in their bellies and no bedclothes to warm them at night, it's enough to make one doubt the existence of God! . . . Ah, thank you, Isabel. Here, Eden, put this plaster on his chest. Careful, now, it's hot. Aye, that's right, wrap it tightly."

Not long afterward Dr. Cutcheon arrived, chilled and red-faced from the biting cold, and after examining the patient he was quick to pronounce that Janet had done everything she could for him, and that in point of fact there was little left for any of them to do but wait.

"Though it's my opinion the young man shouldna hae been moved frae Glasgow. Not i' this weather! Och, and the distance—" He frowned and shook his head, and from the look on his face there was little reason to believe that he held out any hope for Davie's recovery.

Eden wished Isabel had not been in the room when he had said that or that her cousin had not managed to draw the same, hopeless conclusion that the rest of them did. It was no longer a matter of idle speculation whether Isabel was in love with Davie Anderson—the truth had been there on her rigid face for all to see, mingled with an expression of such agonizing despair that it was obvious she expected him to die. And Eden, who not too long ago would not have understood the dragging ache of love or the numbing pain of losing someone dear, swore to herself that she would not permit Isabel to be hurt like that.

If he loves her, she told herself vehemently as she started for home a short time later, and if he lives—which he will!—then he should never have to go back to Glasgow!

To Eden's mind there was only one way of achieving that end: by paying off her grandfather's debts so that Davie could return to work as Tor Alsh's steward. Regrettably there was only one way she knew to keep those selfsame creditors at bay, however absurd the idea, however unlikely. If Hugh would not give her the money, and if the Northwest Highland Land Bank was not prepared to extend additional credit to Tor Alsh, then she would simply have to go to India to recover that stolen fortune in Hamilton jewels.

Returning to Arran Mhór in a somber frame of mind, she began at once to lay her plans, and the bleak, cold light of a new dawn was breaking on the horizon before she rose at last from Hugh's desk, where she had spent the night deciding on how best to set those plans into motion. . . .

Naturally Sir Hamish was hidebound to prevent her leaving, but Eden had expected as much and was prepared for his angry outburst.

"It ain't decent!" he choked, waving his fist energetically in her face as she sat quietly in an armchair beside his bed. "It ain't decent at all, I tell ye! The seas ain't safe this time of year, and you'll be gone eight months or more!"

"I shall return precisely in time to pay off Grandfather's debts," Eden pointed out, unperturbed.

"Provided you'll be able to find that dastardly fellow, who, I might add, won't hand over those jewels quite as willingly as you seem to think—if he hasn't sold them already!" Seeing the intractable look on Eden's earnest young face, Sir Hamish reached out to seize her wrist in an urgent grip. "The man's killed before, lass, you've told me so yourself. It willna be safe for you to deal wi' him!"

"On the contrary, I shall be more than safe, because I don't intend to deal with him at all. I'm not going to go about this in the same way I did before, you see. I intend to enlist the help of the Political Department, the council, even the British army if I must."

"And just what makes you think they'll be willing to help you, girl?"

Eden's chin lifted. "As the duchess of Roxbury I imagine my request will wield considerably more authority than any made by the daughter of a deceased colonel of India infantry."

Sir Hamish's face seemed to sag, for he knew that she was probably right—the government in Calcutta would not hesitate to do everything in their power to lend their assistance in this particular matter. Such was the stuff of British gallantry, and the fact that one of their own officers had been responsible for the crime would only serve to fire their passions more fully on the score of seeing justice prevail. Doubtless they would find that cursed fellow in the end, provided he was still alive, because Eden had not forgotten the cut of the military orders on his uniform, which shouldn't prove too difficult to trace, or the name of the lieutenant who had ridden into Meerut with him that day.

Looking into Eden's calm, composed face and seeing the determination in those lovely dark eyes, Sir Hamish was seized with the sinking suspicion that she just might succeed. "Och, lass, I'm not at all sure about this," he was nonetheless compelled to say. " 'Tis a long way to India, and I don't like the idea of your traveling alone."

A warmth of color flared to Eden's cheeks, for in his gruff, reluctant tone she could hear the acquiescence he would not put into words. "But I won't be going alone, Uncle Hamish! Dundhoo brought me a gazette from Crairralsh yesterday afternoon, and I've found a steamship sailing for Alexandria on the eighteenth of December. The passenger list included no less than four officers from various Lucknow regiments who will be traveling with their wives, and surely there must be one among them who won't object to offering me protection. Furthermore, I intend to wire Colonel Porter in Delhi to make arrangements for me to be adequately chaperoned from Calcutta, and I'm certain he can be counted on to see that the proper authorities are notified as to the reasons of my coming."

Sir Hamish found it difficult to protest such meticulously laid plans. She had plotted far too well, he realized, leaving not a single unbarricaded defense he could argue down, and there, if you please, was the danger in letting a girl grow into womanhood on a military garrison: there was always a chance that she might develop the clear, analytical mind of a military man—a dangerous weapon in the hands of a woman, b'gad!

"He should have sent ye home to England to grow up like the rest of your peers," observed Sir Hamish peevishly, "instead of letting you spend your days soaking up all that military claptrap from the soldiers in the lines."

"Who?" inquired Eden blankly.

"Your father, of course."

"My—my father?"

Seeing the bewildered look on her face, Sir Hamish leaned forward and patted her hand. "You go on and do

what you think best, child. I confess I don't like it a wee
bit, but then I suppose there's little else we can do to
keep Angus from being turned out of his house." He
smiled at her fondly, and presently the smile faded and
he heaved a dramatic sigh, lamenting gruffly the fact that
he had grown too old to accompany her.

Smiling in turn, Eden reminded him that it would be
like a homecoming for her. Bending to kiss his cheek, she
felt as if a great weight had been lifted from her shoulders. She hadn't really wanted to leave Scotland without
either his knowledge or his approval, though she had been
preparing herself exactly for that possibility.

But while Sir Hamish seemed to have no pressing objections to her plans, there were two conditions upon
which he stood firm and from which, in the space of the
next half hour, no amount of arguing on Eden's part could
sway him. For one thing, he would not permit Eden to
travel alone to London, nor would he hear of her sailing
for Alexandria without informing Hugh. Allowing a
young woman to journey across the length of Great Brit-
ain without a proper chaperone was unheard of in this day
and age, Sir Hamish pointed out crossly, and keeping
Hugh ignorant of her plans was likely to precipitate a reaction that he had no desire to witness.

"I'll not have you journeying halfway round the world
without telling your own husband, b'gad!" he said with
inarguable finality.

Janet Fraser, upon hearing of her niece's intentions, had
taken up the old gentleman's cause with equal vehemence, and Eden had been left with no choice but to sub-
mit to their wishes. Fortunately the first of Sir Hamish's
conditions was easily if not somewhat unexpectedly remedied in the form of Tor Alsh's housekeeper, Mrs. Walters, who admitted diffidently that she had always
dreamed of visiting London. As it turned out, one of her
sisters resided in Cheapside, and there seemed no reason
to Mrs. Walters's mind why she couldn't spend some time
with her after seeing Eden safely aboard the steamship
Lexingham Mews. Did Eden have any objections if she
were to come along? Naturally Eden did not. She was
quite relieved, in fact, to accept the housekeeper's offer.

Since the second condition could not be met without making a personal appearance in Somerset, Sir Hamish wrote at once to his nephew informing him of his wife's arrival, and posted it a full six days before Eden's own departure. That way, he had told her in a tone heavy with meaning, Hugh would know when to expect her, and there would be no chance of them accidentally missing one another.

"Of course, Uncle," Eden had said calmly, and went upstairs to pack her trunks.

On the day before she left, she rode one last time to Tor Alsh to bid farewell to her family. As expected, it was not an easy parting, for none of them had taken any pains to hide the fact that they did not approve of her decision. Yet inasmuch as Eden was now a married woman and had always been very much her own person, there was little they could say to change her mind. Eden was able to draw a certain measure of comfort from the fact that her grandfather seemed in excellent spirits when she left him and that Davie Anderson, though still appallingly thin and weak, was likely to recover.

It was raining when the cumbersome coach drew away from the doorstep of Arran Mhór, and it continued to rain throughout the long days that followed: cold, slanting rain that left the roads all but impassable and the bedsheets in the posting inns where they slept uncomfortably damp and cold. Mrs. Walters, voluble and enthusiastic at the onset, grew silent and anxious as the jolting, swaying, bone-jarring miles of their journey elapsed and was often moved to wonder aloud what momentary madness had forced her to give up the warmth of her cozy ingle back home.

Eden was herself far from cheerful these days, for she was plagued by continuous doubts as to how Hugh would receive her. Since he had had ample time by now to prepare for her coming, she could not help but hope that he was willing to attempt a reconciliation between them. They were not irrefutable enemies, after all, merely estranged, and since she had never stopped loving him, she refused to accept the possibility that Hugh's feelings for her might have changed. Surely they could settle their differences of opinion without jeopardizing the happiness they had shared? Eden was certain of it, and deep in her heart, scarcely felt or even realized, quivered the breathless, eager need to see him again.

Maddeningly, they were no more than eighteen miles from the borders of Roxbury when their lead horse cast a shoe, necessitating a delay of several hours in a steep little hamlet not far from the wild grandeur of the sea. By the time they were once again ready to depart, however, a dense fog had rolled in from the Bristol Channel, and the local smith advised them to think twice before continuing on their way.

"It be 'ard enow crossin' the moors when you can see the lie o' the land," he warned, "but the fog will be 'idin' the road sure as night. It won't be liftin' 'til morning, neither, I can promise you that."

He had suggested that they spend the night in the nearby inn. They had discussed the matter between them and, taking his advice, were gratified to find their rooms warm and comfortably furnished. Tired as she was, however, it proved difficult for Eden to fall asleep, so she sat for some time before the fire with her chin propped on her knees, listening to the dripping of the rainwater from the eaves and trying not to think of Hugh. It proved difficult not to do so, however, given that the end of the journey was so near, and it was not until long after the noisy crowd in the pub below had dispersed into the fog-shrouded night that she crawled at last into bed. Yet even then she lay staring with wide eyes at the blackness of the ceiling above, filled with a restlessness that made it all but impossible to sleep.

She was markedly silent as the coach pulled away from the inn the following morning, though judging from Mrs. Walters's talkative manner, her spirits had been vastly improved by a refreshing night's rest. The morning sun, burning away the skeins of lingering mist, revealed to them a land of singular beauty. Somerset was a county of ancient Norman churches, of sleepy villages, tumbling combes and rolling hills, and, despite the dreariness of winter, a contrast of vibrant colors. Herons picked through plowed fields of black peat, rivers surged across the moors and lost themselves in a wilderness of mud and marsh, and countless, colorful thatched cottages lay nestled beneath pollarded willows along the length of the roadside. Far in the undulating distance, against a gold and pearl and apricot sky, rose the lonely levels of the Mendip Hills and the lovely, wooded hollows that marked the beginnings of the borders of Roxbury.

"I warrant His Grace will be wondering what's become of us," Mrs. Walters remarked as the sprawling rooftops and battlements of the great house of Roxbury grew visible at last above a long avenue of lime trees. "Perhaps we should have sent word from the inn last night."

"I'm sure he's aware that the weather was responsible for our delay," Eden replied through lips that felt oddly stiff, and she did not speak again as they were driven beneath a tall gate of ornate wrought iron and into a long, rolling stretch of parkland. She could not know that the letter Sir Hamish had written to Hugh had never been received, that it had been lost en route through the sheer negligence of a careless postal clerk, and that Hugh did not, in point of fact, have the least idea that she was coming.

Eden's throat felt annoyingly dry as she descended from the coach and tipped back the hood of her cloak to peer at the soaring stone walls of the house of which she was now mistress. She would not admit to herself that she was feeling a little anxious and that an absurd light-headedness had taken hold of her because she would shortly be seeing Hugh. Dragging the hood of the cloak back over her head and squaring her slim shoulders, she mounted the long flight of steps and lifted the ornate knocker.

The astonishment of the manservant who answered her summons was rather unexpected, yet Eden did not notice. She was doing her best to appear outwardly composed while her heart was racing uncomfortably in her breast. Yes, the servant assured her politely, His Grace was indeed at home, and whom should he say was calling?

"His wife," said Eden calmly, and while the manservant stared incredulously, she brushed past him and stepped for the first time in her young life over the portal of her new home.

Chapter Eighteen

"There are three of them, there to the left beyond the trees. Do you see them?"

Hugh Gordon turned his head and peered through the spreading branches that made a dark canopy of leaves against the darker sky. A new moon was shimmering on the horizon, barely visible through the raveling veils of mist, and by its watery light Hugh could make out three shadows moving furtively toward the dense grove of beech that marked the northern boundary of his estate.

"I've no doubt their bags are stuffed with game," added his stablemaster darkly. "It's become something of an epidemic, Your Grace, but I haven't wanted to act without your authority."

"You did the right thing," Hugh assured him, and gave a thoughtful grin. "Two men on horseback could easily bring them down, don't you think?"

"They may be armed," the stablemaster warned, though it was obvious from his tone that the prospect did not daunt him. He was a grizzled old specimen of an earlier day and age, when poachers had been hung without trial from roadside gibbets to discourage others who might be similarly inclined. The fact that this particular trio had been making off quite freely with Roxbury game during the duke's lengthy absence had left him chafing with impatience to administer his own form of justice.

Hugh himself was not at all reluctant to work off some of his own restless energy by giving them chase. He could not remember when he had last had the opportunity to undertake something more challenging than sorting through a mountain of paperwork or listening to the endless excuses of his ever-anxious solicitors. Perhaps the exercise might even prove sufficiently tiring to provide him a good night's sleep, which, God alone knew, had been eluding him long enough of late.

Grinning to himself, Hugh drew a pistol from his saddlebag and examined the firing mechanism carefully before sliding it back into place. It would have startled him considerably had he known that his wife was at this very moment sitting before the fire of a posting inn no more than twenty miles distant, envying him the peaceful night's sleep she envisioned him as having. Hugh, however, was not asleep, nor was he thinking of his wife, and even if he had been, he would never in his life have supposed that she was not in Scotland but less than two hours from the borders of his land.

"Ready, Pierce?" he inquired softly.

"Aye, Your Grace."

Touching his heels to his mount, Hugh sent it crashing without warning through the underbrush. His grizzled stablemaster needed no further urging. Riding at a hard right angle through the thick avenue of trees, he sent the startled poachers scattering like frightened hares. Dropping their pouches, they attempted to scramble over the high stone wall that separated Roxbury property from public land, only to find their escape cut off by the duke of Roxbury himself, a long-barreled pistol held in his hand.

"No 'arm, zur!" cried one, lifting his hands high over his head. "On my 'onor we meant no 'arm!"

"Indeed," Hugh observed lightly, and addressed his stablemaster over his shoulder as the latter appeared on the scene: "They claim to be honorable thieves, Mr. Pierce. What do you make of that?"

"Pah! Not unless they happened to stumble across these in the fog." Pierce's wizened face was grim as he examined the contents of the leather pouches he had retrieved. "Looks like they've been using metal traps, the callous bastards." He spat contemptuously before him. "What's to be done with 'em, Your Grace?"

It was in Hugh's mind to have them taken at once before the magistrate. A few nights in jail might possibly show them the folly of their ways and discourage similar attempts. Yet as the moon rose higher above the barren glade of trees and the fog lifted momentarily, the weak light fell full on the frightened faces of the would-be thieves and revealed their unexpected youth.

Hugh's lips tightened, and he said curtly: "Let them go."

"Your Grace?" Pierce was visibly startled.

"I said, let them go. There's nothing to be gained by sending three beardless boys to jail, not when they were merely indulging in a bit of fun—or happened to be hungry." Observing the sorry state of their clothing and the hollowness of those youthful faces, Hugh was inclined to think that the latter was probably responsible. "Well, Mr. Pierce?"

There was little sense in protesting the order, and after a moment the stablemaster lowered the weapon he was carrying and turned his horse aside. For a moment the youths exchanged hesitant glances, then one of them bolted for the opening made by the retreat of Pierce's mount, only to draw up short as the pistol Hugh had not as yet withdrawn was thrust without warning into his face.

"I don't expect to hear any talk in the village about how easy it is to poach Roxbury land," Hugh warned him softly. "I've never been overly tolerant of pointless boasting, nor will I be quite so lenient the next time." His voice dropped even lower, becoming almost playful. "And I believe you've heard that I'm a man of my word."

There was a moment of silence, then the young man swallowed hard and nodded, and Hugh turned the pistol skyward. Needing no further encouragement, the three of them fled, the underbrush crackling in their wake. Turning in the saddle with a curious frown, the stablemaster thought better of speaking as he caught sight of his employer's expression. Neither of them said anything as they cantered back across the dark stretch of lawn to the stables, where Hugh dismounted and handed over the reins.

When in hell, he asked himself with unexpected weariness, crossing the deeply shadowed courtyard toward the house, would he ever see an end to the problems that threatened to deluge him every time he set foot on Roxbury land? His inheritance had proven more troublesome than he could ever have imagined, and he wondered if it wasn't some spiteful quirk of the old duke's nature that had made him decide to hand over his coronet and mantle to his nephew Hugh rather than his slow-witted, illegitimate son, William Winthorp Alston St. Brynne?

The St. Brynnes, from all accounts, had been something of an enigma when compared with the rest of England's ancient, aristocratic families. Hugh was inclined to believe, not without considerable support from Roxbury archives and the claims of knowledgeable historians, that a healthy measure of inbreeding had accounted for the streak of madness that tended to crop up from one generation of St. Brynnes to the next and which had, quite probably, accounted for the mayhem that continued to this day to seethe throughout the duchy. It was certainly no secret that the St. Brynnes possessed an exceptionally colorful past crammed with suicides, murders, courtly intrigue, and the like, though their courage on the battlefields of history had won them the lasting favor and friendship of nearly every English monarch.

It was Roland Marylebone St. Brynne, a staunch supporter of the Stuart kings, who had been presented the duchy of Roxbury as a mark of favor by Charles II after the exiled monarch's return to England in 1660. St. Brynne had always fancied the rich, heather-clad countryside of Somerset, and Charles readily annexed a portion of the medieval shire and presented it with full royal honors to his loyalist friend. Yet however quiet and unspoiled the pastoral beauty of Somerset, the neighboring duchy of Roxbury showed itself to be in possession of a paradoxical tendency toward upheaval and unrest—not unlike the Indian province of Oudh, Hugh had come to think these days with something of a wry smile.

It was Lady Penelope St. Brynne, marchioness of Alden and the only legitimate child of Hugh's uncle, the ninth duke of Roxbury, who had most recently exhibited a predisposition toward the infamous St. Brynne madness. Or at least this was the conclusion Hugh had been forced to draw upon examining firsthand the gross chaos that had irrevocably become his inheritance. It was Lady Penelope who had handled the matters of estate during her father's last illness, and who, against the better judgment of her family and ignoring the entreaties of solicitors, attorneys, and administrators alike, had single-handedly managed to run the ancient household and its sizable enterprises expediently into the ground.

Hugh had been fully aware from the first that he was inheriting little better than a colossal white elephant, yet bristling with impatience to return to mutiny-torn India, he had rashly and, in retrospect, probably unwisely left the estate in the hands of his solicitors. They had managed in his absence to enmesh themselves even more deeply into a myriad tangle of debts, legal suits, questionable business arrangements, and even acts of civil disobedience—these having taken place among Roxbury's overtaxed and understandably dissatisfied tenants.

There were times when Hugh was quite prepared to wash his hands of the estate and its appalling woes, and yet he found to his annoyance that he could not. For one thing, he had made a promise to his uncle who, though lying on his deathbed, had not been quite as senile as had been supposed, and who had remained sufficiently aware of the wretched condition of his holdings to realize that a cooler head and more capable hands than those possessed by his slow-witted, illegitimate son, William, were needed to save the St. Brynnes from ruin. There was also—all sentiment aside—the fact that Somerset had once been the great wool center of the West Country, and Hugh had been quick to see the advantage of uniting Roxbury's assets with those of Arran Mhór.

Nowadays, however, he was less inclined to view the union as a shrewd business decision than as a liability, for the very nature of its existence meant long months away from Scotland and no time at all for the pursuits that awaited him in India. Tonight's incident with those poachers had been merely another example of the long string of ridiculous annoyances that cropped up whenever he was in residence and prevented him devoting his energies to other, more legitimate problems—the most pressing at the moment and the one that had brought him to

Somerset to begin with being the question of Tor Alsh and its floundering finances.

Hugh's mouth twisted as he thought of Tor Alsh and, further, of Arran Mhór, and he found himself wondering unexpectedly if Eden was there and what she was doing at that very moment. Sleeping, most likely, as it was already long past midnight, yet Hugh instantly turned his thoughts to other channels, for he didn't want to imagine Eden asleep in the wide, comfortable bed the two of them had shared, or, indeed, think of her at all.

"Goddammit, how can I not think about her?" he asked himself with considerable frustration. One look at those ledgers in the offices of the Northwest Highland Land Bank had inarguably convinced him that there was nothing he could do to retain Tor Alsh in Angus Fraser's name, nothing short of selling a large portion of Arran Mhór's holdings—or Roxbury's—to raise the necessary cash, and this he was not about to do. It was not only an unsound business decision, as he had so unwisely (and admittedly unkindly) pointed out to Eden, but sheer folly, because there was no guarantee that the farm would manage to hold its own even after its debts had been settled. In this age of runaway mechanization, of a vast industrial revolution spreading rapidly across an ever-hungry empire, there seemed little need for the enormous, lumbering, uneconomical horses Tor Alsh had been breeding for the past three hundred years.

Furthermore, what would become of the farm after Angus Fraser's death? He had no sons to carry on behind him, and since poor little Anne was clearly terrified of the powerful creatures, Hugh could not imagine her assuming any sort of responsibility for them. And while Isabel Hamilton seemed genuinely enamored of Tor Alsh's steward (Hugh was not entirely unobservant on that score), it was doubtful that she was capable of taking over such a difficult business even with Davie Anderson's help.

Eden, of course, would not hesitate to do so, and she would doubtless administer the farm in the same efficient manner that she tackled everything else. She was not one to turn away from adversity or hard work, and there were no other women, and precious few men, of Hugh's acquaintance who possessed such driving tenacity and courage.

Eden—

Closing the door to his study, Hugh leaned his head against the padded brocade cushion of an armchair and tiredly closed his eyes. An image of his wife's face rose immediately before him, and for the first time in weeks he did not attempt to thrust it away. How many different expressions had he seen upon that lovely, heart-shaped face since he had first met her? Arrogance, uncertainty, pain, and despair had played regrettably often across those innocent young features, and yet the vision that always came to him more clearly than the rest was the memory of the gentle smile that curved Eden's lips when she had held out her hands to him that night in the sandalwood-scented darkness of her room, her eyes bright with passion, her features softened with love. He had held her slim body close and kissed her deeply and knew in that one moment with a conviction that robbed him of breath that she had never belonged anywhere else than there in his arms. . . .

Hugh sat up so violently that the chair creaked in protest, his mouth drawn tight with unexpected anger. It didn't seem likely that Eden would agree with that particular sentiment—not now, at any rate, while this impassable rift yawned between them. And it seemed further unlikely that the future would hold any sort of reconciliation, not as long as the question of Tor Alsh's fate stood between them.

"Damn it to hell," said Hugh aloud. How could he possibly do anything to change such a lamentable situation, when his time was constantly being taken up by irate creditors, dissatisfied tenants, incompetent administrators, and, lastly and most annoyingly, a band of troublesome poachers?

Staring into the fire, he turned his mind away from his wife and to the problem of obtaining working capital, and it was Gilchrist, his valet, who discovered him early the following morning asleep in the brocade armchair. The fire in the grate had gone out long before dawn, and since the chill in the room was considerable, Gilchrist could not prevent himself from shaking him anxiously, convinced that His Grace had caught his death of cold.

"I'm quite all right," Hugh assured him brusquely as he opened his eyes. Coming stiffly to his feet, he scowled at the elderly retainer and observed unpleasantly that a pot of strong coffee would be far more preferable than the old man's fussing.

" 'Twill be but a moment, Your Grace," the unflappable valet promised. Shuffling to the door, he added over his shoulder, "Oh, and Mr. Chapman be here to see ye. I've asked 'im to wait, and I've laid out fresh clothes. Will ye be wishin' a shave the first?"

"No. What the devil does he want? And what in hell is the time?"

"Six-thirty, Your Grace. If you'll remember, ye asked Mr. Chapman to ride out to the south end with ye to—"

"Yes, I remember. Tell him I'll be there in a moment."

Ten minutes later Hugh and the burly farm administrator were riding across the damp, misting moor, their destination the tenant farms and the homes of the estate workers that dotted the fertile landscape on the southernmost border of the estate. Here the men whose forefathers had tilled St. Brynne soil for hundreds of years awaited the opportunity of airing their grievances before him and submitting, at Hugh's own invitation, suggestions of how best to end their disputes.

The cool, crisp air and wide-open stretches of land that were welcomingly free of the cultivated, confining hedges surrounding the manor house proved ideal for a hard gallop and thus beneficial to Hugh's foul temper. Furthermore, he found it unexpectedly refreshing to put his own thoughts aside for a time and talk earnestly with this solemn collection of men. Their talk was a talk Hugh understood well, for he had come of age amid the sprawling byres and barns and pasturelands of Arran Mhór, which, for all its pageantry and splendor, was really nothing more than a working farm. Hugh's grandfather, the sixteenth earl of Blair, had devoted his life to the cultivation of the earth, and it was entirely possible that his pride and devotion for that same soil had been responsible for instilling similar feelings for the land in the heart of his young grandson.

For over an hour Hugh sat and listened to their earnest words about crops and harvesting, of the unfair burden of taxation and rent, of wives and children, and of the dwindling profits being eked from the land that made it so difficult to care for them. Hugh listened without commenting to each of them in turn and then spoke to them frankly, laying the blame for the estate's current difficulties equally upon his own shoulders as well as those of his uncle and "mad Lady Penelope," who had, to no one's real surprise, thrown herself from the towering limestone cliffs into the Ax River on the eve of her father's death.

By the time the morning sun had burned away the mist and cast its cool silver light across the hills and the heather-clad moors, Hugh had managed to lay before them a series of proposals that the men deferred to quite courteously. Returning to their chores, they found themselves filled with a renewed sense of optimism. The young duke, they all agreed, was far wiser and more fair than the old duke had been, and one could only hope that he would not return to India anytime soon and once again leave the estate in the hands of his incompetent administrators and solicitors.

It was nearly ten o'clock before Hugh completed his tour of the estate and, dismissing George Chapman, rode slowly back home. Turning down the tree-lined carriage drive, he lifted his head to peer up at the house, and a wry smile touched his mouth as the tall towers of Roxbury came into view. Like the ruins of the abbey upon which it stood, the manor house was built of honey-colored stone overgrown with ivy, an imposing edifice of numerous wings and crenellated rooftops, its inner courtyard enclosed on two sides by a cloister of square stone pillars. The colonnade was inhabited by pigeons and by a noisy congregation of martins in spring, while beyond the east wing stood the stables and granaries and the coach houses with their collection of carriages, wagons, and sleighs.

A pair of shaggy sheepdogs greeted Hugh as he rode beneath the gate carved with a ubiquitous escutcheon bearing the St. Brynne coat of arms and dismounted on the cobbles, where a groom hastened forward to take his lathered mount. A second groom was standing near the fountain watering a pair of leggy hunters whose gleaming stirrups still dangled from their leathers, and Hugh's brows rose questioningly at the sight of them.

"Sir Charles and Lady Caroline Winton have just arrived, Your Grace," the groom told him, catching the duke's eye.

Passing through a door at the far end of a long arcade, Hugh was informed by a footman that his guests had been shown into the withdrawing room. There he found Lady Caroline seated on the settee pouring tea for her husband and herself, the green-and-rose-colored chintz that dominated the room seeming to pale in comparison to the brightness of the yellow morning dress of French barège she wore. Her slim hands moved gracefully as she poured the tea into wafer-thin cups, and Hugh stood for a moment unnoticed in the doorway studying the long, white arch of her neck and the delicate sweep of dark hair at her brow.

She seemed quite a part of that elaborate, elegant, patrician room, as much so as her husband, Charles, who had not bothered to scrape the mud from his exquisitely tailored boots before entering—boots that had doubtless cost him the equivalent of a year's wages for one of his estate workers, yet which were so very important to a true sporting squire. The Wintons, thought Hugh rather cynically, were the embodiment of landed English gentry, and Priory Park, their home, was everything Roxbury was not: neatly and painstakingly cultivated and maintained, discerningly well run and staffed by a virtual army of snobbish servants in imposing canary-yellow livery. Sir Charles, as befitting any country gentleman of a serious bend, imported his own personal cache of wines and brandy from the Continent, kept a prize-winning collection of fighting cocks, and was the enthusiastic master of his own hounds—indeed, the Priory hunt was considered one of the finest in the West Country.

Having more money than he knew what to do with, and being ever-eager to expand his holdings, Sir Charles had been pressing Hugh for some considerable time now to sell him the large tract of land that meandered in a series of undulating green hills toward the border of his own estate. As arable land went, it was not particularly suited for farming, though a productive apple orchard had flourished for centuries in one of its pastoral little vales (Roxbury was well known for the quality of its cider), and the thatched stone farmhouses nestled in the middle of it provided a modest measure of rent.

Sir Charles, however, was not in the least interested in rent or agriculture. Unlike Hugh, the term "gentleman farmer" was nearer an insult than an appellation to him, and he was quite content to leave the management of his own granaries and cultivated acres to his small army of estate workers and his rather tyrannical administrator. No, what Sir Charles coveted, with much the same measure of greed displayed by an Indian *dacoit* after gold, was the stretch of river that wound along the gentle rises of bridle paths and sheep walks of that pleasant little dale, a river so rich in salmon that even the most notable anglers of the day vied fiercely for the opportunity to cast their lines within it.

While Sir Charles happened to be an avid fisherman himself, he was also remarkably pompous and ambitious and not at all unaware of the advantages of nurturing the friendships of the men who arrived annually at Roxbury for a week of salmon angling: members of Parliament, titled peers, and wealthy industrialists who drove hard bargains over port or brandy or cider in Roxbury's enormous library after the sun had set and their rods and reels and Wellingtons had been left outside the door. Even the Prince of Wales had asked—and been granted—permission to be included a time or two, and while Hugh had viewed His Royal Highness's presence with polite amusement, Sir Charles Winton had chafed at his own inability to host such a singularly influential guest.

Hugh was, of course, well aware of his neighbor's thoughts and the reasons behind them, and it had amused him for a time to entertain the notion of offering Sir Charles the rights to his river in exchange for the favors of his beautiful wife. Yet Lady Caroline had proven an easy enough conquest without her husband's knowledge, and Hugh had tired of her long before he had made the decision that he had no intention of giving the obnoxious Sir Charles what he sought.

Sir Charles, on the other hand, found it hard to believe that His Grace could not eventually be persuaded to change his mind, and his visits to Roxbury never failed to include broad references to the selling of that coveted stretch of water. While Hugh was inclined to find him both tiresome and remarkably lacking in finesse, it occurred to him suddenly as he entered the drawing room that Sir Charles was wealthy enough, and certainly greedy enough, to pay a great deal more for the waterway than he had originally offered. Certainly not enough to clear all of Angus Fraser's debts, but enough to warrant further consideration.

Hugh scowled to himself, generally disliking the idea of dealing with men of Winton's ilk, yet the possibility of raising ready funds was not to be discounted so quickly, and he certainly had no practical use for that particular stretch of land himself. Furthermore, it seemed that Sir Charles had come to Roxbury to once again remind his host of his offer, for the subject was broached almost at once, and he was able to sense immediately the subtle change in the direction of Hugh's thoughts. Measurably heartened, he did not linger, announcing instead that he would take the time to look the property over and that surely the two of them could arrive at a mutual agreement.

"Let's go, my dear," he said to his wife, obviously impatient to be off.

Lady Winton made no move to rise. "In a moment, darling. I'd like to ask Hugh something, if you don't mind."

"Certainly. I'll see to the horses." A contented smile crossed his ruddy features. "By God, it's a splendid day, isn't it? Roxbury, your servant, eh?"

"What is it you have in mind with him, Hugh?" inquired Lady Winton the moment they were alone.

Hugh cocked his brow at her. "In mind?"

Her lovely face remained composed. "Of course. The mere mention of that land has always bored you to distraction, yet now you're suddenly indulging Charles in a most unlikely manner. I'll confess it has me curious."

"My dear Caroline," Hugh said blandly, "I have no intention of playing games with your husband. We were obviously discussing a legitimate transaction of sale."

Lady Winton's white hand fluttered. "Oh, really, Hugh! I'm not as obtuse as Charles, you know. You've something more in mind than a mere land sale, and I'm all agog to find out what it is."

Hugh's lips curved, and he said maddeningly, "I'm afraid you'll simply have to wait and see." Turning his back on her, he helped himself to a cup of tea. "That isn't really what you wanted to ask me, is it?" he inquired after a moment.

"No, it isn't," said Lady Caroline at once. "I confess I am most curious about the continued absence of your wife. Doesn't she intend to join you at Roxbury for the winter?"

Hugh turned his head to look at her, and the smile on his face was no longer bland. "You've always made it a point to hit from the shoulder, haven't you, my dear?"

Lady Winton rose from the sofa amid a rustle of satin flounces and, laying her hand on his sleeve, stared intently into his face. Hugh could smell the subtle fragrance of lavender that lingered about her person and was unprepared for the rush of memories it evoked. Those lovely, liquid brown eyes were upon him, and her lips parted as she said breathlessly:

"You cannot possibly be happy with her, can you? I mean, considering the circumstances of your marriage and the fact that you are here without her?" Her fingers tightened about his arm, and she lifted her face to his. "Will you kiss me?"

For a moment, for a moment only, Hugh was tempted. That lovely, disturbing mouth was capable of a great deal of passion, he knew, and it had been some considerable time since he had taken his pleasure with a woman. But looking down into that upturned, pleading face, he had a sudden vision of Eden's face, equally lovely and certainly far more desired, and his lips curved into a smile that was no longer the least bit pleasant.

"Would that please you, Caroline? I thought we had tired of one another quite some time ago."

Lady Winton's long, curving lashes fluttered, and her eyes widened with startled indignation. "Oh!" she gasped. "How can you say that when you know—when you were the one who no longer wanted—Hugh, please . . ." Her voice grew low and husky with urgency. Insinuating herself closer, she tightened her hands on his sleeves and raised her mouth eagerly to his.

Hugh found himself engulfed in a tide of futile anger, and he reached up quickly to thrust her away, though regrettably not in time. He heard the sound of light, running footsteps in the hall and the door open, and, turning his head, he found himself staring into Eden's shocked face.

Chapter Nineteen

Lady Caroline Winton was a woman of considerable intelligence, and she had known Hugh Gordon far too long to contemplate even for a moment taking advantage of the situation that had suddenly presented itself. That Hugh had been unaware of his wife's arrival was obvious, and the shock on Eden Gordon's young face made it equally plain that she thought to have stumbled upon them in an intimate embrace. Caroline knew better than to encourage that impression, at least for the time being. Oddly enough, and somewhat unexpectedly, she found herself moved by an unlikely twinge of empathy as she looked into the younger woman's eyes. Dropping her arms to her sides, she stepped unhurriedly away from Hugh and smiled at Eden.

"Why, what a pleasure to see you again, Your Grace! I was just telling Hugh about the dinner party my husband and I are giving on Thursday, and of course we'll be expecting you." She put on her hat as she spoke and, tying the ribbons beneath her chin, moved casually to the door. "I hope you don't mind, but I was just on my way out. Charles is doubtless pacing the courtyard wondering what's become of me. We'll talk again soon, won't we?"

Then she was gone, her skirts rustling as she retreated down the hall. For a long moment neither Hugh nor Eden turned their wary eyes from each other until Eden said stiffly:

"Perhaps I should see to my things. The carriage is still waiting outside."

"Why don't you wait until your rooms have been prepared?" Hugh inquired in an equally expressionless tone.

304

He reached for the bell pull. "I regret it wasn't done sooner, but I had no idea you were coming."

"How could you not? Sir Hamish wrote a letter."

"Did he? I'm sorry, I never received it."

Swallowing hard, Eden made a determined effort to appear composed. "No, I can see you didn't."

Hugh stood staring down at her for a moment in silence, feeling frustrated and helpless and enormously angry all at once, and curiously ashamed of himself as well. What could he possibly say to her that would not sound like some thoroughly trite and meaningless excuse? It didn't seem likely at the moment that she would accept any explanations he cared to offer, and so he could only stand there and glower at her and wish that he had not been caught so completely off guard by something as utterly absurd and improbable as *this!*

"I believe I would like to go to my rooms now," Eden said at last. "I'm a little tired, and I should like to wash." Her voice shook despite her best efforts to keep it steady, and Hugh's brows drew together.

"You didn't by chance travel alone?"

"No. Mrs. Walters came with me. She intends to visit her sister in London."

"Somerset is rather out of the way for anyone wishing to go to London," Hugh pointed out.

Eden hesitated, then said calmly, "Yes, I know. But I'm going to London, too. I've reserved a berth on a steam packet leaving for Alexandria on the eighteenth of the month."

"Oh?"

She could not prevent a wave of color flaring across her face. "Yes. I—I'm going back to India for a time, Hugh. Your uncle thought it best that I come here to see you first."

"Did he?" The faint suggestion of a drawl deepened in Hugh's voice. "That was kind of him, though hardly necessary. A letter would have sufficed, provided, of course, that it reached me. Ah, well, I expect one cannot count on the mail these days, can one?"

"No," Eden said tightly.

"At any rate, if you feel the need to return to India, I see no reason why you cannot— Yes, what is it?"

"Excuse me, Your Grace." A maid stood in the doorway curtsying hesitantly. "You rang for me?"

"I did. Please see that Her Grace's trunks are taken up to her rooms. Oh, and make certain you only unpack those she directs. She will not be staying long."

Ten minutes later Eden found herself alone in a spacious apartment of gilt-and-cream brocade. She had dismissed the hovering maid and the footmen who had carried her trunks up the long flight of stairs and, seating herself on the edge of the bed, stared forlornly about her, biting her lip and trying hard not to cry.

"Well, what in God's name did you expect?" she asked accusingly of the reflection staring back at her from the looking glass. "That he would laugh? That he would be angry? That he would sweep you into his arms and beg you not to leave?"

The heavy train of her traveling gown rustled loudly as she crossed restlessly to the window and stood gazing out across the somnolent winter park with its barren elms and browned grass. She wished she had never come. Hugh had not been glad to see her. He had been extremely annoyed by her unexpected arrival, in fact. Had she walked into the room a moment later, Eden felt certain that she would have witnessed an impassioned kiss between him and Lady Caroline that would have rivaled any he had ever given his own wife.

She shut her eyes quickly on that unwanted vision, but the scene stubbornly played itself out in her mind, and with a gasp she crossed the room and wrenched open the door. She was not at all certain where she intended to go. She knew only that she must get away from here, away from this enormous, imposing house in which she was a stranger, in which it was clear she was not wanted.

"Excuse me, Your Grace."

Eden drew back, startled by the unexpected appearance of a maid in the corridor. "Yes?" she whispered, gripping tightly to the door.

"I'm to tell ye the meal's bein' laid on downstairs. 'Is Grace apologizes for the early 'our, but 'e's been out since dawn, you see, and 'e thoughts you might be 'ungry, too." She bobbed a curtsy and smiled. "I'm to show ye to the way, if you please."

"I—yes, just a moment."

When Eden appeared downstairs some ten minutes later she was still wearing the worsted-wool dress in which she had arrived, yet she had taken the time to pin a diamond brooch to its high, buttoned collar and to reroll her disheveled hair. She gave every appearance of being calm and composed as she took her seat at the long, linen-draped table, though Hugh had been observant enough to catch the momentary falter of her steps as she saw that the two of them would be dining alone.

Signaling the waiting servants, Hugh leaned back in his chair and inquired if she had found her rooms to her liking. Roxbury was an ancient estate, he explained, far older than Arran Mhór, yet since it had been recently modernized he trusted she had no complaints?

"No," Eden said quietly.

He seemed outwardly pleased. "I think you'll take to the countryside as well. Both Roxbury and Somerset are rich in history, you know. For one thing, you'll discover that the locals are devout believers in the Arthurian legend. In fact, most of them will try to convince you that King Arthur kept council with his knights right here in this very area."

He paused to sample the wine a footman had poured into his glass. Giving a brief nod, he leaned back in his chair and resumed: "You might be interested to know that the duke of Monmouth was defeated in Sedgemoor, which isn't too far from here. I'm certain you remember learning that the Battle of Sedgemoor was the last to be fought on English soil?" He frowned a little as he caught sight of Eden's expression. "Didn't they teach you English history at the garrison in Lucknow?"

"Yes—yes, of course. My father always said the duke of Monmouth was an inexcusably poor soldier."

Eden was rather startled when Hugh laughed at this, and she eyed him suspiciously over the arrangement of hothouse orchids that were between them on the table.

She could not understand his expansive mood or the motive behind it, and was wary of it.

"You seem very fond of this place," she ventured to observe at last.

Hugh frowned. "Do I?"

"Yes. And I wonder," she went on hesitantly. "Is this where you prefer to live? Of all the countries in which you own a house, I mean?"

Hugh did not answer immediately, and then he surprised her—and himself—by grinning unexpectedly. "You know, I'm not exactly sure."

It was true that he had grown into manhood in Scotland, and perhaps that should mean that he ought to feel more at home there than anywhere else. Yet that was not entirely true. The solitude of the Highlands had never really appealed to him, not, at any rate, in the same manner that the wide, open, arid plains of India had. Yet he could not honestly say that he would care to spend the rest of his life living in the East. He loved India, as well he should, having devoted nearly half of his lifetime to it. But his hesitation was due to something that had disturbed him ever since the first furtive whispers of mutiny had been carried to him by Baga Lal five long years ago— a nagging suspicion that had only seemed to grow increasingly obvious after he had returned to India and seen for himself the evidence of continued dissatisfaction among the natives of the Punjab, of Bikaner, of Oudh and Mayar.

Despite all evidence to the contrary—for most of the ruling princes of India's royal houses seemed largely content with their present lot—Hugh could not help but believe that the days of the British raj were irrevocably numbered. The rebellion had not succeeded in improving matters for the Indian people. The natives were still accorded lamentably few rights, most of them were as wretchedly poor as they had been before, and there was nothing to distinguish the present administering policies of the British Crown from the grossly unfair ones of the hated East India Company. Hugh was convinced that another bid for Indian independence was all but inevitable, and while it would probably not be as sweeping as the first, it would doubtless prove just as bloody and violent. To a younger, more ambitious man, the risks involved might matter little, as, indeed, he himself had once been careless of the danger, yet when one had a wife and a family to consider . . .

"I suppose a man in my position would find it preferable to remain here at Roxbury," Hugh said without warning and in a tone that was far more curt than the situation warranted.

Looking up at him, Eden felt a small shock flee through her. The harshness of his tone and the expression on his face were such that she could almost believe he was blaming her for that, though how could she possibly be responsible?

"And you?" he pressed unexpectedly. "Where is it you would prefer to live, presuming you had a choice?"

Eden opened her mouth to reply, then shut it abruptly without speaking at all. Where she would once have promptly answered "India," she found herself seized by a sudden and entirely unfamiliar feeling of indecision. Looking across the board at Hugh, she was conscious of a familiar ache in her heart and knew quite suddenly that she would never be free of her love for him or ever be happy again without him. Hadn't the last few lonely months proven the bitter truth of that? Even the glittering allure of India seemed to tarnish before her eyes when she tried to imagine herself returning there alone, so she said nothing at all in response to his question because it was wretchedly clear to her that she wouldn't care in the least where she lived—as long as the two of them were together.

"Well?" inquired Hugh after a moment.

"I'm really not sure," Eden whispered unhappily.

A muscle twitched at the corner of Hugh's mouth, and for a moment he regarded her in silence. Then he lifted his glass and said carelessly: "Well, then, perhaps you may come to find Roxbury to your liking, after all. The climate is certainly better than Scotland's, and of course London and its endless amusements are never too far away. Though I warn you that a true country squire rarely makes an appearance in the city if he can help it. You'll also find the countryside as beautiful as any the High-lands can offer, though the Mendips can never rival the Grampians in size or magnificence. But then we have the sea, and Exmoor and the Quantocks, and I imagine your Rajput upbringing will have prepared you quite well for the rigors of fox hunting.''

"It sounds quite lovely,'' Eden murmured, staring down at her plate.

Draining his glass, Hugh added with a shrug, ''But I suppose none of that really matters, does it? You're only going to be here for a few days.''

"I haven't—'' Eden began, but Hugh interrupted her by signaling for another bottle of wine, and the expression on his face suddenly became remote, precluding further conversation.

After lunch, at Hugh's invitation, Eden rode out with him through the park, and as the cool, clean wind whipped against her cheeks and the leggy animal beneath her hit its stride, Eden could feel something tight and painful within her heart begin to ease. It had been too long since she had galloped across a wide-open stretch of land, and far too long since Hugh had accompanied her. She had only to turn her head to find him bareheaded and tousled in the saddle beside her to recapture the content-ment the two of them had experienced riding for hours across the wide, empty heaths surrounding Arran Mhór.

Something contracted in her heart as she looked at him, and yet there was no denying that an impenetrable wall still existed between them. She glanced at his hands and remembered how they had drawn Lady Caroline Winton's slim body close, and she knew again the despair of re-alizing there was no way to penetrate the barricade sep-arating them. How foolish she had been to imagine that Hugh would not succumb to the charms of the lovely woman who had once been his mistress! Eden knew she could have forgiven him anything and everything: their disagreements, their estrangement, Hugh's refusal to lend money to her grandfather . . . any number of things, but not this. No, not this, not when he had made it clear that he didn't care at all if she sailed for India or not; not when he had, in fact, shown such open approval of her going.

If Hugh noticed the bleakness of Eden's mood, he did not comment upon it. Instead he took her on a protracted tour of the estate, noting its various points of interests in a detached manner he might have used in dealing with any casual acquaintance. He, too, was acutely aware of the coolness between them, and he cursed again the vagaries of fate that had led Eden into the withdrawing room at such a disastrous juncture. There was no point, however, in lamenting over what had happened, and he refused to dwell on the nagging reminder that things would doubtless have been far different if Eden had entered the room to find him alone. He would not acknowledge even for a moment the fact that he had been absurdly pleased to see her, nor would he permit himself to act upon the tenderness that filled his heart whenever he turned his head to see her there beside him.

In silence the two of them returned to the house, and it was Hugh who lifted Eden down from the saddle in the empty courtyard. His hands lingered for a moment about her waist, and as she lifted her face inquiringly to his, they found themselves looking at one another silently and with undeniable longing until a groom, hastening outside to lead their mounts away, stepped between them.

"I've ordered tea laid out in the salon," Hugh said with unwarranted curtness. "Will you join me?"

"Thank you, but I'm not hungry," Eden replied, stepping away from him and demonstrating an inordinate preoccupation with stripping off her gloves. "I'd prefer a hot bath in my room, if you don't mind."

"Of course," Hugh said politely. "You have only to ring for one."

It proved to be an endless afternoon for Eden, who found little enjoyment in spending the hours until dinner with nothing but her own thoughts for company. While her newly washed hair dried in the heat of the crackling fire, she busied herself writing letters to Tor Alsh and sorting through the contents of the trunks the maids had unpacked earlier that day. Eventually nothing remained for her to do but sit by the window staring distractedly into the park, thinking of Hugh and wondering what he would say if she were to confront him openly about Caroline Winton. Distasteful as it seemed, Eden was growing increasingly convinced that the subject must be brought out into the open, for there was no denying that it had hovered uncomfortably between them all afternoon.

Perhaps if I give him the chance to explain what happened, she thought, yet wondered in the next moment if there was really any need for explanations. What she had witnessed was nothing more than simple proof that Hugh had once again taken the lovely Caroline Winton to his bed.

"I can't bear it!" she burst out of a sudden, "I vow I cannot!"

Leaping from the window seat, Eden rummaged wildly through her belongings. She was going to confront Hugh right this minute, she decided, and insist that he be entirely honest with her concerning his relationship with Caroline Winton.

Eden put on a day dress of warm cream muslin that spread over billowing, sky-blue petticoats. Plaiting the heavy mass of her hair, she rolled it into a soft chignon and stood for a moment before the mirror, gravely studying the result. It was suddenly important to her that she look her best when confronting Hugh.

Directed by a servant to a salon at the far end of an oak-paneled corridor, Eden drew up short in the doorway, dismayed by the unexpected presence of two gentlemen in tight stocks and cutaway coats seated with Hugh before the fire.

"Oh," she said, extremely disconcerted. "I didn't realize you had visitors. Perhaps I should come back later."

She would have backed away but for Hugh, who had risen at the sight of her and now took her by the arm and led her inside. There was a gleam in his eyes as he gazed at her that Eden had never seen before: the look of an appreciative male confronted by an infinitely desirable woman. It was a gleam that was mirrored in the bold gaze of the first of the gentlemen to whom she was introduced, yet where Hugh's had had the effect of making her feel oddly breathless, Mr. Fred Abercromby's only served to make Eden's skin crawl uncomfortably. She found she had to fight the urge to snatch her hand away from the hot lips that bent to kiss it, and she was inordinately relieved when Hugh's second guest proved of a far more personable sort.

Sir Arthur Willoughby was long past his youth—thin, white-haired and taciturn—yet Eden found herself inexplicably drawn to him, and was delighted to learn that he had spent most of his life in India in the capacity of commissioner to a Rajput territory. His command of Rajasthani was still excellent, and upon discovering that the young duchess was similarly well versed, he could not prevent himself from addressing her in that harsh, guttural, yet oddly beautiful language. Eden had not conversed in Rajasthani since she had left Mayar, for even Hugh spoke it only passably, yet now the words fell nimbly from her lips, and an animated glow lit her features so that she looked disarmingly radiant and young.

"By God, you've found yourself a well-favored one, Hugh," commented Fred Abercromby in an enthusiastic aside to his host, yet quickly fell silent as he caught Hugh's eye. He knew that look, of course, and was compelled to hide his discomfiture behind a fit of earnest throat clearing and a hefty swallow from his glass.

Both gentlemen, Eden soon learned, had been invited to spend several nights at Roxbury, and during the course of the lengthy dinner that followed, she discovered that they had traveled from London to consult Hugh on business matters, a dull topic Mr. Abercromby in particular seemed loath to abandon. She was inordinately relieved when the time came to leave them to their port and cigars, and as she silently withdrew she heard Mr. Abercromby embark for perhaps the third time on a lengthy diatribe concerning several questionable investments he had recently made.

Seating herself in the salon with a sewing basket in her lap, Eden stared for some time into the fire, her mouth drawn in a grave line as she thought of the disastrous course the evening had taken. So much for her plans to speak privately with Hugh! It was obvious that he would

have no further time for her as long as his guests were
here, and on Friday, scarcely three days hence, she and
Mrs. Walters would be leaving for London.

Perhaps there isn't any sense in speaking to him anyway, Eden told herself unhappily. Hugh had said very little throughout the course of the meal, and hardly anything
at all to her, and Eden, suspecting that he had been ignoring her deliberately, had to bitterly admit that there had
really been no reason for her to come to Roxbury to see
him.

It was a mistake, she thought, and carried her unhappy
musings one step further: I should never have married him
to begin with. For that had obviously been the gravest
mistake of all—as had been the assumption that a man of
Hugh Gordon's lusty appetites could remain faithful to her
alone.

Midnight came and went, and still the murmur of masculine voices continued from the study, where Hugh and
his guests had withdrawn. Eden remained seated before
the fire in the adjacent salon, her hands moving carefully
over her embroidery, though her thoughts were far away.
A yawning footman, entering to inquire if Her Grace
wished another log placed on the fire, found her staring
into the distance with a distracted expression. He had to
address her twice before she looked around, blushing.

"No, thank you . . . Chisolm, isn't it?"

"Yes, Your Grace."

Eden's eyes went to the clock. "I think it's time I went
to bed. Hugh—my husband—is he still in the study?"

"Yes, Your Grace."

She hesitated, seeming on the verge of saying something else, then added quietly, "Thank you, Chisolm.
Good night."

His dignified mien softened a fraction. "Good night,
Your Grace."

Eden was relieved to find her bedroom invitingly warm,
and the shy chatter of the maid who helped her undress
turned out to be unexpectedly soothing. It wasn't often
that Eden enjoyed the companionship of her own sex, and
once the lamps had been extinguished and she was alone
in the wide, canopied bed, she regretted not having asked

her to stay a little longer. It was disconcerting to realize that she had no one to talk to, and she was suddenly filled with an unpleasant sense of abandonment. However absurd the feeling, she could not dismiss it. If only Isabel were here, Eden thought. But Isabel was miles away, and Mrs. Walters was undoubtedly deeply and enviably asleep by now and wouldn't take kindly to being disturbed.

Eden thought it doubtful that she herself would find any measure of rest that night since her mind and her heart were so very full. But she was young, her heart resilient, and it had been far too long since she had slept in a bed as comfortable as this one. In no time at all, it seemed, a great weariness crept over her. Her lids grew heavy, and she drifted at last into the sleep of complete mental exhaustion.

Some time later that night—Eden had no idea how long—she was pulled awake abruptly by the sound of the door latch clicking softly. A draft stirred the embers in the fireplace as she opened her eyes, and she gasped and came upright as someone sat down on the edge of her bed, causing the mattress to sag alarmingly. A hand touched her arm, and Eden jerked away, yet the scream that rose to her throat died there as a voice said gruffly in her ear:

"For God's sake, Eden, who do you think it is?"

"Hugh?" she breathed disbelievingly, and heard him laugh.

"It certainly isn't Fred Abercromby—or were you perhaps hoping it was?"

"Fred Abercromby?"

"Oh, come now, Eden. Surely you cannot be unaware of the way he was staring at you all night!"

Eden's astonishment turned instantly to anger, but she was permitted to say nothing more. Hugh's hands had found their way into her unbound hair, his fingers entwining themselves in the silky strands, turning her face to his. She was suddenly, breathlessly still.

"What is it you want?" she demanded unsteadily.

Hugh's answering laugh held an unmistakable note of regret. "Need you really ask, *chabeli?* After we've been apart for so many weeks?"

"I'm not at all sure. Not after—"

"Not after what?" he prompted when she fell silent.

Eden did not reply. She merely looked at him with a trace of apprehension in her eyes, and after a moment Hugh's hands fell away.

"I expect you're still thinking about Caroline Winton."

Eden stiffened despite herself as the other woman's name fell from his lips. "There's really no need to discuss her."

"Isn't there?"

"No."

"Are you so certain of that?"

Once again Hugh's hands were in her hair, turning her head so that she found herself looking deep into his eyes. She found she could not look away, and a lengthy silence stretched between them.

"You should know better than anyone that things are never as they seem," Hugh said softly at last. "That appearances can be deceptive, that the evidence of one's own eyes is not always reliable or indicative of the truth. Didn't your years in the zenana at Mayar teach you that?"

"Are you saying that I was mistaken about what I saw?" Eden asked defensively.

"You should know by now that I am not given to seducing married women in my withdrawing room," said Hugh, and his lips curved unexpectedly. "Unless, of course, they happen to be married to me."

His hands moved as he spoke, slipping the nightgown from her shoulders. His fingers entwined themselves in the strands of unbound hair lying against her skin, and Eden felt a shiver of longing flee through her. It had been far too long since he had touched her, far too long since he had looked at her with such hunger in his eyes. She found she no longer cared about his feelings for Caroline Winton; she forgot the coldness and restraint he had exhibited toward her since her arrival. She shivered again as Hugh's hands moved over her, destroying the barrier he had erected between them, closing the distance as though it had never been until nothing mattered but the warmth of his lips on hers, the feel of his hard body pressed against the curves of her own.

"Fred Abercromby was right," Hugh said gruffly into her hair. "You're far too costly to risk losing."

He turned his head as he spoke, and his lips caressed the line of her throat while his hands stripped away her nightgown. When she lay naked before him he pressed her back upon the sheets and boldly cupped her hips, his fingers hot against her flesh.

Eden moved seductively beneath him, craving the masculine touch of him, and he groaned and gathered her to him. Her thighs parted, and he took her, driving deep inside until he seemed to become a part of her. Eden sighed his name in response and flung her arms about his neck. Opening herself to him, she strained to draw him closer still. It seemed to her as if the past and present, as if all reality, faded and was lost as he moved against her. Nothing remained but the sound of their wildly beating hearts, the touch of his mouth on hers, the love for him that all but overwhelmed her as she soared and teetered and the climax swept her away to bright, bursting oblivion.

"It's entirely possible that Her Majesty will award Dundu Ali Khan the Star of India," Sir Arthur Willoughby said trenchantly over breakfast the following morning. "Of course, it will do nothing to disguise his humiliating loss of power since the days of the mutiny, though I imagine it will serve its purpose by outwardly strengthening his alliance to the British raj. In which case I suppose I should support it."

"Both the viceroy and the queen seem to have forgotten that Ali Khan ordered the butchering of a score of British guests attending a durbar in his palace on the eve of the mutiny," Hugh reminded him with a wry twist of his mouth.

"I suppose there's no better way to assure the loyalty of an unwilling vassal than to shower him with accolades," countered Sir Arthur with a shrug.

"It's a bribe, my good fellow, a bribe," Frederick Abercromby put in. "Royal India is being bought up with the price of meaningless knighthoods, though I suppose one could say that it isn't costing the government overly much, eh?''

''There's potential danger in that sort of reasoning,'' Sir Arthur remarked pensively, ''for the cost may account for bloodshed in the future. The British have yet to learn that Easterners place no value at all upon the concept of loyalty to a foreign monarch, though they are intensely, passionately loyal to the emperors of their own race. Bahador Shah is a prime example of their zealousness, for the desire to see him crowned emperor of India prompted the Indian people to join the sepoys in mutineering against us. For the first time in history Mussulman and Hindu were united in a common cause, and it is blatantly, dangerously wrong of us to assume that a coronet and a pretentious title will buy the same devotion to our queen. Don't you agree, Hugh?''

Hugh nodded. ''I assure you Ali Khan sees nothing wrong in accepting a British knighthood on the one hand while intriguing actively against our raj on the other. And when he and his numerous cohorts turn against the hand that feeds them—which eventually they must—we British will once again be caught entirely unprepared while our soldiers and our women and children die for our blindness and our arrogance.''

''Quite right,'' concurred the elderly Sir Arthur gruffly. ''It's happened twice now in the Afghan campaigns and four years ago in India, and yet the same disastrous mistakes are being made all over again.''

''And we are still profiting unfairly from them.''

''That is precisely why these self-serving English nabobs must be stopped!'' Mr. Abercromby said energetically, choosing to condemn the bribe taking he had so recently dismissed as harmless. ''We must set an example for the ruling princes, not give them the impression that we will tolerate insurgency discreetly, provided we profit from it!''

''I'm not certain the problem is as simple as that,'' ventured Sir Arthur somewhat impatiently, for he disliked Fred Abercromby intensely, thinking him both cowardly and officious and thoroughly lacking in a real grasp of the

Indian problem. "I would certainly agree, however, that—
Ah, Hugh, here is your wife, and looking exceptionally
charming, I might add! Good morning, Your Grace."

"Good morning," Eden responded, smiling at him
shyly as he bowed over her hand. At the same time her
eyes moved to Hugh, and her blush deepened as she
found his gaze upon her. Seating herself with a rustle of
silk, she lowered her head and stirred cream into her tea,
hoping no one had noticed her heightened color.

"I trust you slept well, my dear?" Hugh inquired politely.

"I—yes, I did." She lifted her head and could not prevent herself from smiling at him, and was rather startled
when he chose to return it with a smile of his own—one
that made her heart beat faster with happiness. All at once
she felt young and gay and free of cares, as if yesterday's
heartache—indeed, as if their entire unhappy separation—
had never been.

"We were discussing India, Your Grace," Sir Arthur
told her. "I understand from your husband that you yourself will be sailing for Calcutta in a few days' time?"

Eden's chin lifted with a jerk, and the aura of happiness about her dissipated like a candle snuffed out by a
cold, insidious wind.

"I'm quite certain Eden no longer intends to go,"
Hugh answered lightly.

"Oh, but I'm afraid I must," Eden said after a small,
unhappy pause.

"What's that?" Hugh's narrowed gaze was suddenly
upon her.

She toyed with her fork, her fingers trembling. "I'm
afraid I still have to go," she whispered at last.

"I take it you plan to visit relatives?" inquired Sir Arthur.

"No, I—" Eden broke off and wet her dry lips, and
heard Hugh say evenly:

"Come, my dear, why don't you tell them what you
intend? I confess I'm rather curious myself."

Eden met his piercing gaze unflinchingly. She wouldn't
have minded telling Hugh the story of her *ayah*, Sitka,
and of the theft of Isabel's jewels. But she could not pos-

sibly speak when that awful, mocking gleam had once again returned to his eyes, and certainly not when two strange gentlemen were listening.

"Excuse me," she said without warning, coming somewhat unsteadily to her feet. "I'm afraid I'm not feeling well."

Without another word she retreated to her room. How was it, she asked herself forlornly, that she could feel so utterly happy one moment and so completely miserable the next? Hugh's abrupt mood changes left her bewildered and uncertain, and she was forced to admit that the fragile fabric of their lives could not be mended quite as easily as she had let herself believe. Too many conflicts still existed between them, especially on the score of her going to India and the nagging question of Lady Caroline Winton—a question she had naively thought resolved in the dark, blissful hours of the night before.

Eden's hands twisted in the ruffled folds of her skirts. Why couldn't she simply confront Hugh openly about his possible infidelity and at least lay that particular matter to rest? After all, she had never been afraid to speak her mind before and had always been careless of any unpleasantries she might uncover. Yet now, haunted by the possibility that she might be losing Hugh, she found herself desperately afraid of the truth. If only she had confronted him that very afternoon instead of shrinking away from what she had seen like some cowardly, die-away creature! If only she hadn't let him make love to her last night, because then she would never have been reminded of how vulnerable she remained to his kisses and his touch. If only—

"Now, then, suppose you tell me why in hell you really are going to India?"

Eden's chin lifted with a jerk, and her eyes widened as she saw Hugh leaning against the door jamb watching her, his arms folded across his chest and his expression not at all pleasant. With considerable effort she held rein on her composure as he came inside and halted before her in the middle of the room.

"I was willing to indulge your nonsensical posturings on the score of your going when you first arrived," he told her before she could speak, "because I suspected you were only doing it to retain your dignity. You must agree that such a conclusion was not at all unlikely, given the unfortunate circumstances surrounding your appearance in my withdrawing room." A measure of mockery crept into his tone. "It was certainly a gesture worthy of admiration. Few women in your position would have conducted themselves so well."

"Thank you," said Eden stiffly. "Is that all you wished to say to me?"

Hugh's mouth tightened. "Of course not. I've since come to realize that you have been in earnest all along about sailing aboard the *Lexingham Mews,* and Mrs. Walters assures me you have the approval of my uncle as well as your own family to embark upon the journey."

He stood glaring down at her, but when Eden showed no inclination to speak he inquired with sudden violence, "For God's sake, tell me the truth, Eden! Do they think our marriage so intolerable that they would willingly permit you to return to India to escape it—and me?"

Eden's lips parted on a soundless gasp. "Is that what you think?"

"In God's name, why else would you go? Unless you have some foolish notion of finding the fortune there that has eluded you here thus far."

Seeing the frozen look on Eden's face, he burst out incredulously: "Good God! Surely you cannot—Eden, are you really so naive? Where in bloody hell do you propose to find that kind of money?" A sudden thought struck him and exacerbated his rising temper. "Not in Mayar, I hope? Malraj may be a wealthy beggar, but the price he'll extract from you may be more than you are willing to pay."

"Are you suggesting that I would—would sell myself to him?" Eden inquired through rigid lips.

"I'm not suggesting anything," Hugh told her brusquely, "but it is obvious to me—"

"No," said Eden distinctly, "I don't think anything is obvious to you! After all this time you still have no idea why I must return to Delhi, and you've never even cared enough to ask! If only you'd given me the chance to explain, instead of—'' She broke off suddenly and swallowed hard against a hot constriction that clogged her throat. ''Excuse me,'' she said stiffly. ''I don't want to talk about it now.''

There was a long moment of silence.

''Very well,'' Hugh said at last. ''I suppose I'd better be getting back to my guests.'' He came forward as he spoke and, taking her lax hand in his, bowed over it unexpectedly. As his tight lips touched her open palm, Eden struggled with the impulse to snatch her hand away. Not because she found his kiss repulsive, as Fred Abercromby's had been, but because she was overwhelmed by a fierce wave of longing.

Chapter Twenty

The annual December hunt was held at Priory Park the following morning, and it was inconceivable, despite Eden's protests to the contrary, that the duke and duchess of Roxbury not attend. The morning dawned bleak and raw, and the sweep of lawn upon which the restive horses milled was wet with rain. Eden was not unaware of the curious glances turned her way as she trotted up the gravel drive at Hugh's side, nor of the speculation and envy in the eyes of some of the women. No sooner had they appproached than Hugh found himself surrounded by a cluster of acquaintances, while Eden, who felt inordinately reluctant to meet them, fell back and eventually drew rein beneath an elm tree a short distance removed from them. Here she casually adjusted the long skirts of her habit, her face outwardly composed against the dripping gray branches.

"A pretty little piece, b'gad," remarked one of the huntsmen in an undertone to his scarlet-coated companion.

"Sits a horse like a man," the other replied, meaning it as a compliment. "Military schooled, I'll wager. Indian cavalry. Can't imagine where His Grace found such a prize."

"Can't you?" The other was clearly amused. "I vow you haven't considered Hugh's discerning tastes or his uncanny knack for attracting the prettiest bits of lace. Egad, those eyes! Never seen a darker blue. Probably put m'lady Caroline's nose quite out of joint, eh?"

A short toot on the huntsman's horn put an end to their exchange and quieted the field of chattering riders. The horses were stamping and blowing impatiently, their bits jangling in the stillness, and a chilly wind ruffled the barren treetops as a bevy of black, tan, and white hounds were released in the copse below and began to feather through the underbrush at the urging of their whippers-in.

"It isn't really the proper weather for picking up scents," Hugh remarked, halting beside Eden, who was watching their progress with interest. "If they don't have any luck here, they'll head over to the mill wood. Of course, it's always possible that they'll come up empty-handed."

Even as he spoke, however, a single hound gave voice from the field below them, and Hugh grinned in response. "Perhaps I'm mistaken. Wait, now," he cautioned as Eden's hands tightened about the reins, "it might only have been a rabbit."

But then another hound spoke, and suddenly the whole pack took up the chorus. Somewhere in the covert an unseen whip halloaed, and immediately the huntsman blew the unmistakable notes of the "gone away." Within a matter of seconds the grounds of the park became a mass of steaming, blowing, galloping horseflesh, and Eden would have been splashed with mud and left hopelessly behind if her mount hadn't leaped away in pursuit of Hugh's.

Hugh had described for her both the rudiments and the etiquette of fox hunting the night before, and Eden had been inclined to dismiss the sport as both affected and without purpose. Yet as the field thinned and the big hunters left behind the smaller ponies and cobs, she found herself gripped by a strange exhilaration. It required a considerable amount of skill simply to maintain her seat as her mount cleared the crumbling stone walls and wide ditches in their path, and there was an undeniable challenge in keeping the baying pack of hounds within sight.

A portly farmer, taking a hedge directly ahead of her, went sprawling into the mud when his gray cob refused, and Eden heard him shout a warning as her mount gathered itself for the jump. Then she was over and sweeping across a wide meadow, an image of his wide, astonished eyes accompanying her.

It's just like jumping the *nullahs* outside the fortress road at Pitore, Eden thought, and she turned her face to the overcast, tumbling sky and laughed for what seemed the first time in weeks, laughed simply and solely because she had forgotten how much she loved to ride like this across the boundless countryside.

"Have a mind now, Eden!" she heard Hugh call from behind her, and she had a brief glimpse of his worried expression before she was hurling over a stone wall overgrown with moss. Pounding up the track beyond it, she glanced over her shoulder to find him galloping in pursuit, and though the wind whipped strands of unruly hair in her eyes, she could not fail to see the open approval on his face.

"It would seem you *gora*-log have forgotten how well a Rajput can ride, sahib!" she called to him.

His reply held an answering note of laughter. "*Nahin*, lady! I had merely forgotten that my wife is nothing more than an impudent *chee-chee*, a half-caste in dire need of discipline."

"And who will discipline me, sahib?" taunted Eden. Her eyes were sparkling, and the wind had brought the color high in her cheeks so that Hugh was hard-pressed to remember when she had ever looked more beautiful.

"*Khabadar*—have care," he warned, "lest I take it upon myself to do so."

She would have responded in kind, for she was seized by a recklessness she had thought long forgotten, yet a water-filled culvert was suddenly before her, and she turned away to prepare herself for the jump. By the time she was safely across it, the rest of the field had caught up with them, and Eden saw Hugh cut back and veer far to the left in order to make room for the more uncontrollable horses among them.

The tightly packed field swept on across bleak hills, through farmyards where cows stood herded together by the fence and dogs leaped after them in barking pursuit. The skirts of Eden's habit were soon splattered with mud, yet she rode with a rash abandon that brought the color still higher to her cheeks and doubtless did much in the way of stilling the criticism of the more experienced women of the hunt, women who had already decided among themselves that the duchess of Roxbury was far too young and unskilled to prove equal to the rigors of the sport.

The hunt ended sometime later far beyond the borders of Priory Park as the fox, slipping into a covert of tangled brambles, escaped the clamoring, panting, exhausted hounds, and everyone agreed that it was time to turn back. Splashing through the muddy furrows of a recently plowed field, Eden looked for Hugh among the other riders. She had lost sight of him some time ago, but had been too caught up in the chase to notice.

It occurred to her that perhaps he might have taken a spill—a fate that had accounted for the loss of nearly half the field. She reminded herself sternly that Hugh was quite capable of looking after himself, and that he would not appreciate her womanish concern. Nonetheless she could not prevent herself touching her spur to her horse's flank, setting it trotting through the wet, heavy plough as she searched the bleak landscape for a sign of his mount.

"I understand this was your first hunt, ma'am," came an unexpected voice from somewhere behind her.

Turning her head, Eden smiled shyly at the elderly gentleman in the mud-splattered breeches who urged his mount to her side. "Yes. I wasn't at all certain I'd be able to keep up, but Vanity behaved himself marvelously." She stroked the chestnut hunter's lathered neck as she spoke, and beneath the brim of her derby her young face glowed.

"Hugh certainly keeps his horses fit," the gentleman agreed in an amiable tone, watching the big animal's response to the touch of that small, gloved hand.

Eden raised startled eyes to his. "Do you know my husband, sir?"

He chuckled. "Very well. Though I must confess we haven't exactly been seeing eye to eye of late. Local issues, you understand," he explained, seeing her puzzled look.

"I hadn't realized Hugh—His Grace involved himself in such matters."

"Oh, indeed. I assure you he's quite the public-minded fellow."

Eden thought this a decidedly curious pronouncement, but as the man did not elucidate and since she did not know him well enough to pursue the matter, she changed the subject by observing that surprisingly few of the original riders seemed to have stayed the course. Her comment clearly amused him, and he chuckled and said that the Priory hunt was always run in a hell-for-leather fashion simply because Sir Charles Winton was a puffed-up clod of an aristo who enjoyed seeing his fellow creatures lose their dignity by being pitched into the mud.

"An odd cove, I don't mind telling you, and I'm convinced there's a genuine mean streak in him." He broke off with a grin and peered keenly into Eden's face. "Dear, dear, listen to me, will you? I've no business speaking like that about our host, especially not in front of a lady. I haven't offended you, I hope?"

"No," said Eden simply, refraining from adding that Sir Charles had struck her in much the same way. Though she had only laid eyes on him twice—at the Midsummer ball at Arran Mhór and briefly today at the onset of the hunt—he reminded her inexplicably, yet in no small measure, of that officious, toadying servant Gar Ram, who had once sought her death in the hunting fields of Mayar.

"Do you know," said her companion unexpectedly, "I believe I like you, Your Grace. It isn't often I've come across a woman so refreshingly direct."

Eden found herself blushing and was filled with an absurd rush of gratitude toward this gruff, white-haired gentleman. It seemed an inordinate amount of time since anyone had said anything in the least bit kind about her, and she could not help smiling at him as though he had given her some delightful gift. "Thank you," she said shyly. "You are very kind."

Looking down into her face, which was soft and unguarded and defensively young, he was quick to see the loneliness and uncertainty there that so many others had missed. Reaching over to pat her hand, he said gruffly, "I'm not in the least bit kind, Your Grace, and you'll do well to remember that."

"I'll do my best," Eden promised, and a dimple appeared in the corner of her smooth cheek. "Will you not tell me your name, sir?"

"What's that? My name? Egad! Gladstone, William Ewart Gladstone, and I apologize humbly for my horrible manners. You must forgive an aging man his occasional lapses, though I fear they are becoming distressingly frequent. Ah, here's the main drive at last, and just in time, too. Hurry, child. It's starting to rain."

In the courtyard he bowed over Eden's hand and kissed it in full view and unmindful of the other riders. Smiling up at him, Eden remained oblivious to the startled looks this unexpected gesture of gallantry aroused and asked if he intended to join the rest of the field for the traditional hunt breakfast at Priory Hall.

"Regrettably not," Mr. Gladstone replied. "I'm leaving for London this very afternoon. But I shall be returning in a few weeks' time, and I trust I shall see you again?"

"Yes, of course," said Eden promptly. She had forgotten that she herself would be leaving Somerset on Friday and that she would probably not be coming back.

Dismounting in the stableyard, she turned her head and happened to see Hugh's bay gelding being rubbed down in one of the loose box stalls; she went quickly inside to inquire of the groom how long ago her husband had returned.

"O'er an 'our enow, Your Grace. Lady Winton's 'orse took a nasty fall on't third 'edge. 'Is Grace were obliged to brings 'er back. The tendon were pulled proper," he continued, indicating a leggy hunter being poulticed in a nearby stall. "Not usually like 'Er Ladyship, I'll tells ye true. She ain't what you'd call a reckless rider."

"No," said Eden quietly. "I imagine she isn't."

She was markedly silent as she withdrew into the house and repaired her disheveled attire in one of the anterooms before joining the other guests. Stepping into the withdrawing room, she spotted Hugh standing near one of the long buffet tables, a wineglass in his hand, listening with apparent absorption to a gesticulating narrative provided by Sir Charles. Yet Eden could tell immediately that

Hugh was paying his host little mind, for she knew him well enough to recognize that slight, distracted frown between his eyes. His attention seemed to be focused upon the doors of the withdrawing room as though he were waiting for someone, and as she entered Eden saw him lift his head and promptly set his glass aside. She could not prevent herself glancing over her shoulder, feeling certain that she would find Lady Caroline Winton behind her.

But there was no one.

A moment later Hugh had strolled across the room to join her, and at first he did not speak but merely looked at her, frowning a little as he always did whenever he was not entirely certain what he intended to say to her. Eden lifted her chin and met his gaze calmly, though inwardly she had steeled herself for what would undoubtedly prove an unpleasant confrontation. His words, however, took her entirely by surprise.

"Charles tells me you rode superbly, Eden. That's quite a compliment coming from him. No spills, then, I take it?"

"No." Her lips formed the words with difficulty, for she was wondering whether or not he intended to lie to her: "And you?"

"I was unable to finish the course myself. There was a refusal ahead of me which resulted in the animal's injury. I was obliged to show the rider back to the house."

"Yes. I've already heard about Lady Winton's mishap."

Hugh glanced down at her sharply, and his mouth tightened in response to what he saw there. "I've the feeling this may turn into an unpleasant scene," he observed after a moment. "Perhaps you would oblige me by continuing it in private?"

"There is no need—" Eden began stiffly, but Hugh interrupted her.

"Oh, yes, I'm afraid there is. You forget I'm quite familiar with that expression on your face."

Without another word he took her firmly by the wrist and led her across the hall. Opening a side door, he thrust her into a small salon where a single oil lamp burned on a table and cast a flickering orange glow upon the cluttered furnishings. Closing the door behind him, he turned to face her, and all Eden could think of as she stood rubbing her bruised flesh and glaring up at him was how well he seemed to know his way about the Wintons' home.

For a long moment Hugh did not speak, and when he finally did, his voice was hard and impatient: "I hope you are not going to accuse me of inventing Lady Winton's fall as a means of returning home with her alone? Don't you think I'm a little more discreet than that?"

"No," said Eden coldly, thinking of the scene she had interrupted several days ago in the withdrawing room at Roxbury.

Hugh's mouth tightened. "By God," he said softly, "perhaps I really ought to send you to Alexandria after all."

"Oh? How very good of you. I hope you haven't been entertaining the notion of detaining me?"

"No," Hugh said darkly. "Not anymore."

For a moment they looked at one another in silence, neither of them really knowing what to say next, both of them painfully aware of the irreversible path down which they were treading.

"Then I imagine we have nothing more to say to one another," Eden ventured at last, pointing out the obvious even as her heart was breaking.

Looking down at her, Hugh knew a futility more profound than any he had ever experienced. How could they have drifted so far apart that they could have come, without realizing it, to something like this? How could they stand here regarding one another with contempt when only last night—

But he would not permit himself to think about last night, nor could he bear to look at Eden now, finding himself almost hating her simply because she could look so heartbreakingly lovely and desirable even in a close-fitting habit that was no longer quite clean, her hair worked loose from its imposing chignon and curling softly about her temples, her cheeks still reddened from exercise and the cold winds of December . . .

Hugh turned away from her abruptly, and in the line of his stiff back there was something chillingly final. "If you go to India, Eden, I see no reason why you should come back."

She wet her dry lips and said slowly, "Yes, I realize that."

"And I think perhaps it might be better if we did not—"

But Hugh did not finish what he meant to say, for there came a sudden gust of wind from the outside corridor, and Lady Caroline Winton was standing on the threshold regarding them with no small measure of surprise.

"Oh! I'm sorry! Charles told me you were here, Hugh, but I assumed you were alone." She looked curiously from Hugh's dark countenance to Eden's rigid one. "I trust I'm not interrupting anything of importance?"

"Not at all," Hugh assured her. "Eden was just expressing her regrets on the score of being unable to attend your dinner party Thursday night. You see, she's leaving for India on Friday."

"And I was just explaining to Hugh that I see no reason why I cannot attend, provided we don't stay overly long," Eden put in evenly. "You wouldn't mind if we left early, would you, Lady Winton?"

The older woman's expression was more than a little startled. "No—no, of course not."

A faint smile played unexpectedly at the corners of Eden's mouth, a smile that had not shown itself for some considerable time. But because she was staring intently at a portrait above Lady Caroline's head, no one, especially Hugh—who would have recognized what it meant—could see it.

"It's entirely possible," Eden continued thoughtfully, "that I will not be departing for India on Friday anyway. Perhaps I won't be going at all."

It was difficult to say who was more taken aback by this unexpected disclosure: Lady Winton, who found it impossible to conceal her gasp of dismay, or Hugh, whose eyes narrowed as he took in the composed, unreadable countenance of his wife.

"Of course we would be ever so delighted if you chose to remain in the area," Lady Winton declared at last. "I've always believed that it simply isn't decent for a married woman to stray so far from home."

"Have you?" inquired Eden, regarding her with interest, and something in her expression brought a wave of color to the older woman's cheeks. For a moment she said nothing, her lips compressed in an effort to conceal her vexation. Then she gave a tight little smile and did her best to keep the edge from her voice:

"I suppose I should be getting back to my guests. Hugh, you won't stay away too long, will you? I know Charles will be wanting you to propose a toast for the stirrup cup."

Hugh inclined his head. "I'll be there in a moment."

"Before you go, Lady Winton—is that a recent portrait?"

Caroline's eyes went automatically to the canvas Eden indicated—a portrait of herself in a flowing blue *gros de chine*, which was illuminated clearly by a shaft of light from the open door behind her.

"It's very lovely," Eden continued. "I hadn't noticed it when I first came in."

"It isn't really hung to best advantage," remarked Lady Caroline with a forced laugh. "Charles insists I sit for a portrait every year, you see, and I never quite know where to put them. This one was painted last year. It's a Barrimore. Are you familiar with Barrimore, Your Grace? He happens to be one of the most revered painters in his field."

"I confess I know nothing about portrait artists," Eden informed her blandly. "In India one never had the idle hours required to sit for them."

Lady Caroline stiffened visibly, and her annoyance increased as she caught sight of the amusement in Hugh's expression. That the young duchess had scored a telling hit was vexingly obvious, and she thought it wise to remove herself at that juncture, before their enmity became openly acknowledged.

The door had barely closed upon her stiff back before Hugh moved forward to seize Eden by the arms and pull her toward him in a gesture that might easily have been mistaken for passion. Yet there was no mistaking the expression on his face or the barely suppressed violence in his tone.

"What in God's name are you playing at?" he demanded savagely. "You've changed your mind about going to India?"

"Yes," Eden admitted calmly.

"Would you mind telling me why?"

Eden's eyes were drawn once again to the portrait of Lady Caroline Winton that peered down at her with a trace of hauteur from its place high on the wall. "I've decided that it wouldn't be advisable for me to leave just now."

Hugh's eyes followed hers to the painting, and his countenance softened unexpectedly. "Oh, my dear," he said in a voice she had not heard him use in a great while, "you cannot possibly think—I give you my word that Caroline Winton is no cause for anxiety. While it's true that I cared for her once, that was years ago—a lifetime ago, in fact."

Eden said stiffly: "It's precisely because of her that I must stay. You see, those jewels she's wearing—"

Hugh interrupted her with a soft laugh that held an unmistakable note of tenderness of which he seemed unaware: "You cannot possibly think I gave them to her!"

"No. I know you did not."

Looking down into her rigid face, Hugh frowned, and the fond light died from his eyes. He was silent for a moment, then said slowly, "I think we are playing at cross purposes here. What is it you're talking about, Eden?"

But she merely shook her head and did not speak, and once again Hugh had the distinct and entirely frustrating feeling that she had withdrawn into some secretive place he could not possibly reach. His mouth tightened, and he turned away from her, grappling with a sudden rage that left him shaken by its violence. He did not speak—for what could he possible say to her now?—and the silence stretched interminably, inexorably between them.

When they returned to the withdrawing room several minutes later, they were walking side by side, Hugh's hand resting lightly beneath Eden's elbow in a gesture of husbandly affection; and yet they might have been standing a thousand miles apart, so complete and uncrossable was the distance between them.

"I must find a way to get into that house!" Eden told herself aloud, pacing the length of her darkened bedroom while the fire died in the grate and a chill crept into the air. "I must find out if she still has them—and how in the name of God she came by them!"

She was thinking, of course, of the rope of glittering rubies that had adorned the white throat of Lady Caroline Winton in the portrait by Barrimore hanging in the salon at Priory Park. Thinking of them, in fact, to the exclusion of all else, including the dismaying coldness displayed during dinner by Hugh, who had removed himself directly after the meal and had not chosen to make another appearance that night.

It had been nearly five years since Eden had last seen those rubies, and then only briefly, winking on a blotter on Colonel Carmichael-Smyth's desktop in Meerut. It was doubtful that she would have recognized them again but for the fact that they, and a similar handful of emeralds and diamonds, had been strung into a necklace at the time and had not been scattered loosely like the rest. Yet she remembered them quite clearly—so clearly, in fact, that a single glance at Lady Winton's portrait had identified them instantly as Isabel's.

Eden knew she could not be mistaken. It was not possible, for one thing, that another necklace could exist that possessed exactly the same number of stones in such a distinctive setting of heavily hammered gold filigree, or that the largest ruby, huge, dusky, and pigeon's-blood red, could possibly have been duplicated in size and shape by a different gemcutter.

I must find out where she got them, Eden thought again, and do so on my own, without Hugh knowing about it. But how do I go about making inquiries? Lady Winton would never acknowledge that the jewels were stolen, provided she even knows that they were—and I'm probably the last person on earth she would want to help in this matter. How, then, do I go about gathering proof that they are Isabel's? *How?*''

In the end the opportunity presented itself far more effortlessly than Eden could have imagined. Riding alone across the windswept moor the following morning, she found herself no more than a mile from the main gate of Priory Park when Vanity cast his left hind shoe. The mishap was entirely unexpected, as Roxbury's stablemaster had examined the animal carefully at the conclusion of the hunt and should have noticed that it was loose. Since Eden would not permit her horse to turn up lame, she had no other choice than to dismount and lead him up the drive to the Winton stable.

The head groom, a grizzled specimen in a worn leather apron, remembered her clearly and was quick to assure her that he would have the shoe replaced within the hour. As luck would have it, he explained, the blacksmith was just finishing up one of the horses that had participated in yesterday's hunt, and if Her Grace didn't mind waiting they'd set her own mount to rights in a moment.

''They bain't 'ome, Sir Charles an' 'is lady,'' he added politely, ''but I'm believin' they wouldn't 'ave cared to see ye standin' in the cold. Go on up to the 'ouse, and I'll 'ave one of the lads come for ye when't smith is through.''

And so Eden found herself being shown into a pleasantly sunlit salon and offered tea, which she refused. No sooner had the elderly retainer withdrawn, however, than she realized her mistake and cursed out loud, for it would have proven laughably simple to question the servant when he returned with her refreshments. This way, however, it seemed unlikely that anyone else would disturb her until Vanity's shoe had been replaced, and of course it simply wouldn't do for her to seek out the servants of her own accord and ply them with questions. Furthermore, while it was a tempting thought to steal into Lady Caroline's bedchamber and simply appropriate the jewels for herself, Eden knew better than to attempt any such thing. Perhaps in Mayar such behavior might be deemed excusable, but this was Victorian England, and she was the duchess of Roxbury, not the reckless youth Choto Bai.

In the end, and much to her enormous frustration, Eden was presented no other choice than to mount the newly shod Vanity and thank the stablemaster politely, her disappointment hidden behind a carefully composed mask. It was beginning to rain as she set the hunter trotting down the long avenue of trees, and she sighed unhappily and turned up the collar of her cloak. It seemed entirely unlikely that she would again find herself alone in the Wintons' house, and she could scarcely contain her annoyance at having let the opportunity slip so foolishly through her fingers. What on earth should she do now? She couldn't turn to Hugh for help—the thought in itself made her quail—and as for broaching the matter with either Lady Caroline or Sir Charles—

"I won't do it! I cannot! They will simply accuse me of being fanciful, or say that I'm coveting the jewels for myself, and Lady Caroline hates me enough to seize upon any opportunity to make me look foolish in Hugh's eyes."

Lost in thought, Eden had permitted her hold on the reins to slacken, and when she lifted her head at last she was startled to discover that Vanity had veered from the drive and was trotting blithely down a little used path that opened eventually upon a cluster of copper-roofed hothouses. She pulled sharply on the off-side rein and was about to turn him around when she heard, faintly above the murmur of the rain, the sound of someone singing.

It was a melody Eden had known since girlhood, and one that caused her breath to catch painfully in her throat, for she had not expected to hear it ever again. The last time she had heard it sung, in fact, had been during the searing heat of her last summer in Rajasthan, when all in the palace had prayed daily for the coming of the monsoons. It was the *Raga Megh*, the raga of the rains, sung in a faltering voice by a wizened old man plucking browned leaves from rows of potted ornamentals and humming to himself as he worked.

> Be festive, mortals. The sky is girdled
> with stars and the earth garlanded with
> flowers. Nature has decorated herself to
> seduce you in the season of the rains.

He was a Hindu of indeterminable age, and when Eden spoke to him from the doorway of the hothouse, he turned without haste to peer at her. Though she had addressed him in his native tongue, he seemed not at all surprised to find himself confronted by a slim English girl in a dark green riding habit, and his faded eyes regarded her with interest.

"Who are you, that you command the tongue of Hind so readily?" he inquired at last.

"I am called Eden. I was born outside Lucknow, in the garrison of the Fourteenth Bengal *rissala*," Eden explained. "Though I am English I spent the years of my girlhood in the palace of the rajah of Mayar."

"Ah. Then I take it you are the wife of Gordon-sahib."

"Know you my husband?" Eden inquired, startled.

He leaned upon his rake and regarded her with gentle amusement. "Many a night I have smoked the tobacco he has brought me from Hind, and thanked the gods that he is not too great a man to forget a humble servant. He has often brought me news from home, and the talk of my people, and carried letters to my family. Ai, I would say I know thy husband well."

His name was Ram Dass, Eden learned, and he had been born some sixty-odd years ago in a small village on the Northwest Frontier within sight of the mighty Hindu Kush. For most of his adult life he had served in various regiments of India Irregulars and had been pensioned off at last after being injured in a skirmish with rebel Pathans along the Afghan border. He had spent the years thereafter serving the sahib-log in various capacities, winding up eventually in the polyglot household of a British general in the unlikely role of *khansamah*—the household cook. It was a position Ram Dass found he enjoyed and for which he apparently displayed considerable talent. When the general, who had over the years developed a genuine passion for Indian cooking, retired his commission some eight months before the onset of the mutiny, Ram Dass was asked to return to England with him, an offer to which he promptly gave his acceptance.

Regrettably the general had died some two years ago, and Ram Dass, unable to find new employment, had reluctantly decided to return home. Fortunately Gordon-sahib, a frequent visitor to the elderly general's home in nearby Wells, had arranged for him to work at Priory Park. His days were largely idle, Ram Dass confessed, for the Wintons' fruit trees and ornamentals required little care, yet despite the fact that he had little to do and his new employers were far from ideal, he considered himself for the most part content.

"You do not care for the Wintons?" Eden inquired curiously.

"I do not wish to seem ungrateful," he said quickly, "but they are *Angrezis*, and do not understand the ways of my country as did the general-sahib. It seems to matter little to them that in Hind I was a *jemadar*, a soldier of rank. Here I am treated no better than the lowest of servants. *Ohé*," he added with a sigh, "I suppose even that does not really matter. Their own *nauker*-log are accorded no better."

"Are you saying the Wintons abuse their servants?" Eden asked, startled.

"Only when the sahib has been drinking too much, which thankfully is not often. I have been told, too, that he parts reluctantly with their wages, though the wealth he spends on himself and his mem is considerable."

Fortunately he himself was rarely found wanting, Ram Dass added, inasmuch as he lived most frugally, and he shook his head energetically in response to Eden's suggestion that he return to India to live.

"In my youth I took but a single wife into my home, and the gods willed that she died long before she could present me with the sons and daughters that should have brightened my old age. Indeed, there are few in my village who remember my name, and I would surely be reviled by Hindu and Mussulman alike were I to return, for I have crossed the Black Water and eaten of the sahib-log's food and so have polluted myself for all eternity. Here I have a small house of my own, and a dog and a goat to provide companionship, and the *nauker*-log of Winton-sahib leave me in peace. What more could an old man ask, hmm?"

They talked for perhaps an hour or more, Eden seated on a small wooden bench, her face alive and glowing against the rich, leafy green of the potted orange trees, while Ram Dass squatted on his haunches before her in the manner of a man from the hills. It was difficult to say which of them found greater pleasure in speaking once again the lovely, ancient language of Hindustan, but it was quite obvious that neither seemed concerned by—or even the least bit aware of—the vast differences in background between them.

"It is time thou wert leaving, my daughter," Ram Dass pronounced at last, coming stiffly to his feet. "Winton-sahib and his mem will be returning soon, and thou shouldst not be found conversing with a servant."

Surprisingly enough, Eden did not argue. She merely shook out her skirts and smiled at him, her face serene and peaceful for the first time in many, many days. In the doorway she paused to pull on her gloves. "May I come again?"

Pleased, Ram Dass inclined his graying head and stood watching as she mounted the stamping gelding and rode away through the misting rain.

He is just like Awal Bannu, Eden thought, turning up her collar against the rising wind, and for some reason the fact left her feeling far more cheered than she had been for days. To be reminded of India, to hear again the stories and the descriptions of the sounds and sights of what she had always considered to be her home, was like a balm to Eden's ravaged soul and an anodyne for the pain and loneliness she had suffered since Hugh had first left Arran Mhór.

It was a loneliness of a depth of which she had remained largely unaware—until she had found it unexpectedly eased by the acquisition of this delightful new friend. Not only had Ram Dass made her feel for a time young and gay and entirely free of cares, he had helped to remind her of many things she had forgotten, the least expected and yet perhaps the most significant being the fact that she had once been the pampered favorite of a powerful Indian ruler who had taught her the courage and clear thinking of a Rajput warrior.

It's almost as if I'd forgotten completely about that part of myself, Eden thought, and wondered how she could possibly have let "Choto Bai" slip so far away from her. For it had dawned on her that Choto Bai would never have permitted that opportunity in the Wintons' salon to pass by without acting. Suddenly Eden was determined not to behave in so cowardly a fashion again. Indeed, if she had suffered indecision earlier on the score of re- claiming Isabel's jewels, she no longer felt that way at all. Ram Dass's idle gossip had served to remind her that a good deal of India still ran through her blood, and that she was no chaste Victorian maiden who trembled at the thought of taking what was rightfully hers. And although Eden wasn't entirely certain how she was going to go about it, she knew that she was not about to fail—indeed, that she *could* not fail—in getting those jewels back.

Chapter Twenty-one

Hugh and Eden were driven to Priory Park in a closed carriage that afforded them little protection from the biting cold. The rain that had been falling since early morning had turned to snow that collected on the barren branches of the trees and swirled in great drifts across the open moors. Despite the rug thrown over her knees and the fur pelisse encasing her shoulders, Eden shivered as a blast of icy wind shook the carriage and rattled the drawn leather blinds.

"Cold?" inquired Hugh from the seat opposite her.

"A little," Eden admitted. She was aware that he had been watching her ever since the carriage had drawn away from the front door of the house, and she found herself rather disconcerted by it. She wondered what he was thinking, yet could see nothing of his clean-cut features in the dim light and was therefore unable to guess his thoughts. Still, she was not unaware of the fact that Hugh's behavior toward her had changed markedly ever since she had joined him in the hallway dressed for the Wintons' party. She could not help but hope, with a painful cramping of the heart, that perhaps it was because he thought her beautiful.

Indeed, beautiful she was, with that breathtaking allure rarely found even in a woman of striking looks, and certainly never in an average one, which Eden clearly was not. Her gown was completely white, an unconventional choice that had raised the eyes of the maids who had dressed her, and yet its simplicity and the cut of the satin overskirts and slim, flower-embroidered bodice enhanced her rare loveliness as nothing else could have done.

Hugh had regarded her for a moment or two in silence, his expression grave, and he had insisted upon handing her up into the carriage himself, his palm lingering at the small of her back. The intimacy of the gesture had not gone unnoticed, and Eden had shivered in response to his touch.

"We'll be there in a moment," Hugh told her now, his tone unexpectedly kind.

A tightness closed Eden's throat, and she did not trust herself to reply. She could not remember the last time he had spoken to her without sounding impatient or irritable—as though he were utterly weary of her.

In the glittering withdrawing room of Priory Park, Hugh remained by her side, although Eden had expected him to remove at once to the anterooms where the other gentlemen were avidly discussing politics over port and cigars. She knew that Hugh could be maddeningly charming when he chose, and she was hard-pressed to conceal her astonishment that he was being so with her now—he, who had calmly suggested only two days earlier that she need not bother returning once she left for India. He pointed out people she did not know, supplying her with anecdotes or amusing observations that left her, accustomed to his usual bored behavior in a crowded assembly, filled with wonder.

"I'm so pleased you postponed your departure for the East, Your Grace," Lady Caroline told Eden insincerely upon greeting her a short time later.

Eden smiled politely, though she was studying with interest the jewels Lady Caroline wore. An assortment of emeralds dangled from her ears and sparkled on her fingers, and although they were obviously costly, she knew unquestionably that none of them were Isabel's.

"I take it you'll be remaining at Roxbury for the winter?" Lady Caroline pressed on with ill-concealed dislike.

With an effort Eden drew her gaze away from the other woman's jewels. "I'm not at all certain. It depends on my husband."

Her words were greeted by a surprised look from Hugh, who gazed at her questioningly for a moment before turning to Lady Caroline and saying gravely: "Actually, it really depends on Her Grace. If she wishes it, then of course we'll remain."

Eden, daring to meet his probing eyes, felt something quiver hopefully within her heart. Could it be possible that Hugh was hinting at a reconciliation between them?

"Why, I believe there's Andrew Carstairs," Hugh suddenly said. "I've been wanting you to meet him, Eden. He's an old India hand, a former cavalry colonel, and the only John Company director to my knowledge who actively fought the annexation of Oudh. It's entirely possible that he could have single-handedly stemmed the rebellion if his voice had been heard by more than those incompetent fools who governed in Calcutta. Come along, I think you'll like him."

And Eden went, dazed by the attention Hugh was paying her and by the fact that he seemed, for once, entirely oblivious to the presence of the dazzling Lady Winton.

Colonel Carstairs turned out to be charming, and neither he nor Hugh left Eden's side until the doors to the dining room had been opened and the colonel requested—and was graciously granted—permission to escort her inside.

The table was set for twenty-five, and Eden, looking down the long board, saw Hugh being led to a seat between an imperious dowager on the one side and on the other a mousy sort of creature who blushed furiously when he addressed her. Eden could not stifle a smile, thinking how much he was going to suffer throughout the long-drawn-out meal in the company of a pair of women who seemed prepared to bore him no end. A fierce, possessive love filled Eden's heart as she caught Hugh's eye and a look of amused understanding flashed between them.

What an utter fool she had been to let something as insignificant as money come between them, Eden thought suddenly. While it was impossible to put a price on the immeasurable happiness Hugh's love had brought her, she had very nearly destroyed it for the cost of what was, in all honesty and in Hugh's own words, a worthless, failing enterprise: Tor Alsh. If she hadn't been so mulish, so immature and blind, she never would have insisted that

Hugh help her family to the exclusion of all else and in doing so come very close to compromising their marriage. She had been entirely wrong about that, and she would tell Hugh as much tonight—tell him everything, in fact, including the story of Isabel's jewels.

The discussions held during dinner proved both animated and interesting, yet Eden remained largely detached from them. Though she knew herself to be acting in a thoroughly shameless manner, she could not prevent her gaze resting time and again and quite blatantly on Hugh. His lean brown face seemed all angles and planes in the brightness of the lights, and she longed to run her hand through the lock of hair that fell negligently across his brow. She loved everything about him, and yet it seemed to her as if the dragging uncertainty of the past few months had only now fallen away so that she could see clearly again, and all she could think of was how much she wished that the two of them were alone this very minute at Roxbury and that Hugh was making love to her.

"—I daresay! Wouldn't you agree, Your Grace?"

Color flared high in Eden's cheeks. "I'm sorry. I'm afraid I was not attending."

"We were discussing Red Rory, Your Grace," Sir Charles Winton informed her affably, taking no offense. "A notorious highwayman who roved these parts a hundred years ago or more, robbing coaches and murdering the local gentry for the price of a few lifted baubles."

"Tonight is the anniversary of his death, you see," Mrs. Sophie Alexander informed Eden in a breathless whisper. She was something of an imaginative and overstrung creature, and it was obvious that the very thought of the long dead highwayman made her exceedingly nervous. "It's said his ghost makes an appearance every year in the home of one of his many victims, and Priory Park was the scene of one of his most fantastic robberies."

"Will we have to wait until midnight, I wonder?" inquired Eden with interest. Neither dead highwaymen nor the thought of confronting their restless ghosts could possibly perturb her—not after she had come of age in a country overrun by murderers and *dacoits,* and the far more ominous and secretive bands of *phansigers,* the buriers of the dead. Ghosts, decided Eden, whether real or imagined, couldn't possibly practice more unbelievable cruelties than had those bloodthirsty devotees of Thugee!

"Red Rory was shot and severely wounded here in this very room," Lady Caroline informed her guests dramatically. The remark elicited a gasp from Sophie Alexander, who turned immediately to the head of the table.

"That cannot be true! Is it, Charles?"

"Indeed it is," he replied, bored. "I only wish my great-grandfather had killed him on the spot. Took off with a fortune in family heirlooms, you know."

Poor Sophie's eyes bulged, causing her to bear an uncomfortable resemblance to a cornered rabbit. "Then— then it's entirely possible that he may show up here, isn't it?"

"Utter nonsense," someone else put in energetically. "Red Rory was hung by the neck just outside Wookey Hole, and if his ghost were indeed of the restless sort, it wouldn't go traipsing about the countryside. It would haunt the place where its mortal body died."

"Do you have that on good authority, Cecil, or is that mere speculation?" Sir Charles inquired.

Mr. Cecil Fallon chose to look indignant while the other guests laughed. A lively discussion concerning the nocturnal habits of ghosts quickly ensued, and Eden turned to her table partner and inquired interestedly:

"The Wookey Hole? What is it?"

"There are numerous caves throughout the Mendips, Your Grace," the gentleman seated beside her explained obligingly. "The largest is known as the Wookey Hole, though I've no idea how it came by the name. It's a series of chambers, actually, carved into the limestone hills by the Ax River, which flows underground at numerous points. Red Rory is said to have buried his goods there— an excellent hiding place, as the locals were afraid to venture inside."

Eden smiled. "Doubtless because they thought it haunted?"

"Yes, indeed. Legend has it that the Witch of Wookey was turned to stone at the mouth of the cave for insulting a powerful wizard, and that she continues to guard it jealously. Prehistoric man is said to have lived there as well, and to have shared his quarters with hyenas."

"It's barbaric to contemplate the likelihood that hyenas once roved our forests and parks," exclaimed Mrs. Alexander with a shudder, having overheard his casual remark.

There was a general burst of laughter in response to this, though the speaker merely looked bewildered until Sir Charles pointed out that the Somerset of some sixty thousand years ago bore scant resemblance to the lovely hills and moorlands of today. Mrs. Alexander rejoindered smartly that she didn't care at all how long the hyenas had been gone—the very thought of those ferocious creatures anywhere within the proximity of her home made her positively squeamish. Surely they had to have been far more dangerous than wolves and certainly far uglier, with their grinning mouths and hideous, loping bodies?

Her remark encouraged a number of narratives from those at the table who had traveled to India and could remember clearly their encounters with those slinking, elusive animals that are the scavengers of the dead.

"You yourself must have seen many wild hyena packs, Your Grace," remarked Cecil Fallon.

"Not to mention tigers," someone else put in.

"Indeed, my wife and I first met at a royal tiger hunt given by the rajah of Mayar," Hugh said from his end of the table.

All eyes went to Eden, who was immediately urged to provide a detailed description of that particular event. There were exclamations of disbelief from the ladies present, and Eden would have felt compelled to satisfy their curiosity by a further account of her years in Mayar had Lady Caroline not decided at that point that her young guest had monopolized the floor long enough. She rose with a rustle of silk, signaling that the ladies were to leave the men to their wine and cigars, and contrived to turn the talk into more general channels the moment the chattering group of women had entered the wi drawing room.

Eden took no offense at what she correctly perceived to be a deliberate effort on Lady Caroline's part to once again claim the lion's share of the attention. Given her reawakened feelings for Hugh, she had found it difficult to talk about Mayar without recalling their first encounter in the *mardana* gardens or the time he had kissed her on the night she had fled the palace. She had been aware, without really knowing how, that Hugh had been thinking of those things, too, and the manner in which his gaze had rested upon her as she talked had distracted and disturbed and excited her all at once.

It was a relief to find herself no longer the sole object of interest, and as the ladies turned to the more routine discussions of household management, incompetent servants, and recalcitrant children, she wandered unnoticed onto the balcony.

The night was clear and very cold, but Eden relished the solitude and found enjoyment in viewing the pinpoints of blue moonlight upon the fallen snow. The wind sighed through the barren elms, setting the branches to quivering and revealing the warm lights of the stables across the stretch of snow-covered lawn.

Against the frozen backdrop a figure moved, and Eden watched as it approached, recognizing the Hindu gardener Ram Dass.

"Good evening, Father," she called as he came nearer. "I trust thou art well?"

He was pleased to see her. He was, he explained, on his way back to his rooms after having spent the evening engaged in desultory talk with the various grooms and coachmen who had arrived with the Wintons' guests. Among them had been the Roxbury driver, and Ram Dass was eager to impart to Eden something of importance that a chance remark from the man had inadvertently revealed to him:

"I did not know when first we met that thou wert the daughter of Hamilton-sahib of the Lucknow garrison."

Eden stared into the Hindu's dark, upturned face. "Yes, this is true. Did Colefield tell you?"

"He mentioned that thou wert the daughter of a Colonel Hamilton of the company army. The name is not unknown to me."

"That cannot be! Art thou saying thou knew my father, Ram Dass?"

"Regrettably not. But a cousin of mine, a *havildar* in the Fourteenth Bengal, served him loyally for a number of years. I have heard much about thy father from letters sent me at the end of the mutiny: how my cousin chose to defend the Lucknow residency against his own kind, he and many others of thy father's *rissala*, simply because of the strength of their loyalty to Hamilton-sahib. I have heard that thy father was called a *burra*-sahib, a great man, among the Hindu soldiers."

"I did not know this," said Eden gravely. "I knew only that he was killed defending the residency and attempting to protect the wounded *Angrezis*, including many mem-log and *babas*, who were trapped inside."

"Ai, this is true. The residency was besieged for a year or more, and while thy father was slain almost at the onset, my cousin and many other Hindus chose to remain true to their salt until Campbell-sahib stormed the bastions and liberated Lucknow. It must be that the gods have favored us both by sending us here to *Belait* together, for now I may thank thee personally for my cousin's life, which thy father was instrumental in saving. We were boys together, and we have always been closer than brothers."

"I, too, am honored," said Eden softly. "For I have never heard this tale, and in its telling I have found a part of my father that might otherwise have been lost forever."

They smiled at one another in mutual understanding, and then Ram Dass sketched a brief farewell with his hand and left her. Eden stood staring thoughtfully at the dark line of trees that had swallowed him up until she became aware of the piercing cold and the fact that she was shivering.

Stepping back into the withdrawing room, which seemed all at once far too hot and bright and crowded, she found herself pounced upon without warning by a pair of stiff-backed matrons whose expressions indicated clearly that they had been engaged in some sort of private argument, the outcome of which was apparently to be decided by Eden herself:

"I wonder if you would be good enough to describe for us the attire of an Indian lady of family, Your Grace," began the imperious dowager who had been seated next to Hugh during supper. "Mrs. Challoner and I are in disagreement as to the degree of Westernization that British women have managed to introduce into the harems of the East. It is my firm opinion—"

"Oh, you and your opinions, Abagail!" interrupted Mrs. Challoner with a derisive snort. "Since when has anyone ever described to you a Mohammedan lady attired in petticoats and crinolines? You fancy yourself an authority on the East simply because Albert once owned a number of shares in the East India Company!"

"Really, Charlotte," protested the other in arctic tones, "I will not—"

"And furthermore, I'm not the least bit interested in colored women or their wardrobes, which I have always held to be disgracefully outlandish!"

Abagail Challoner (the two of them were sisters-in-law and well known throughout the county for their constant bickering and for the misery inflicted upon their unfortunate husbands) favored the younger woman with a quelling look. "Then whatever are we arguing about, you silly goose? You told me that you wished to confer with Her Grace on the subject of Indian attire, and naturally I assumed—"

"There, you see?" Charlotte Challoner said angrily. "You are always assuming and drawing the wrong conclusions simply because you never wait until I've finished speaking! What I wanted to ask you," she continued, turning deliberately to Eden, "is about the jewelry they wear. I understand that Indian ladies are accorded certain rank by virtue of the wealth they own. And is it true that an Indian maharajah will sometimes purchase a concubine for the price of her weight in diamonds?''

"I believe that was once the practice, yes," said Eden politely. "Though most of India's kings and princes have very little left them in the way of diamonds and gold. Over the years their wealth has been all but confiscated by the British—and that in exchange for interfering government officials, occupying troops, and unfair taxation. After the mutiny they were stripped even further of their ornaments, their land and their wealth to insure that their power was truly broken."

"Dear me," murmured the younger Mrs. Challoner, who hadn't been expecting such a heated reply.

Realizing that perhaps she had been a little unfair, Eden obligingly provided her with a detailed description of Prince Malraj as he might have appeared during a religious festival or a holy procession, wearing gold brocade silk pantaloons and a jewel-encrusted coat weighted down with heavy gold daggers. During state durbars, she explained, he often wore a necklace consisting of nine egg-sized gems representing the nine planets, in addition to a gorgeously plumed aigrette and a presentation sword of rubies, emeralds, pearls, and filigreed gold. As for the women—they were all equally fond of finery, though there was little occasion for them to display it, as they spent most of their lives in seclusion. Only the senior Rani, by virtue of her rank, was permitted to attend some of the more elaborate public affairs, and despite the fact that she had to sit behind a *purdah* screen, she never failed to drape herself in dazzling jeweled silks.

"It sounds like a most ostentatious display," Abagail Challoner observed with a sniff. "Small wonder the company chose to Westernize such frivolous people!"

"I'm not so certain that we are any different," remarked Charlotte unexpectedly.

Abagail Challoner's nostrils quivered with affront. "Whatever do you mean?"

"Only that we sometimes seem to indulge in such extravagant parades ourselves. Take Millicent Fallon's ear-bobs, for example. Don't you find them rather unsuitable for a simple dinner party? They're by far too heavy and large. See how she cannot turn her head without setting them swinging like pendulums?''

"Now there I cannot agree with you!'' her sister-in-law stated energetically. "Cecil Fallon is quite the devoted husband, and I can assure you that were Albert to present me with a similar gift, I would not hesitate to wear them anywhere!''

With difficulty Charlotte refrained from blurting the most obvious rejoinder on the score of Albert Challoner's tight-fisted ways, and perhaps her sister-in-law appreciated this act of gracious restraint, for after a moment of silence she added pensively, "Perhaps you are right after all. I sometimes cannot help but think that Caroline, for instance, spends Charles's money far too freely on baubles. Oh, I know she looks quite charming tonight," she added as both Charlotte and Eden turned to look at their hostess, "but there have been times when she has appeared in public tricked out exactly like one of those strutting Indian princes just described. Take that ruby necklace she owns. If it were mine, I would insist the larger stones be separated and worked into several smaller pieces, perhaps into a brooch or an armband. It's simply too vulgar as it is.''

Eden, who had been listening with an expression of polite interest to such unbelievably vapid talk, grew still, and when she spoke at last she forced herself to sound deliberately calm. "Are you referring to the rubies in the portrait of Lady Winton hanging in the salon?''

"Do you mean the Barrimore?'' Abagail asked. "It's not his best work, I must say, but then again I understand he can be terribly moody, which surely must influence the quality of his paintings. Still, it's considered a great honor to sit for him, and of course Caroline—''

"Please,'' interrupted Eden breathlessly, "do you know anything at all about those rubies?''

"Why, no, except that Charles presented them to her some time ago on her birthday.''

"She once told me they came from India,'' Charlotte added.

"Why, yes, I do believe you're right. How interesting for you, Your Grace, seeing as you've spent so many years in the East. Shall we ask her about them?"

"No," said Eden slowly. "No, I don't think that will be at all necessary."

Two hours later, as she stepped into the warmly lit entrance hall of Roxbury, Eden caught at her husband's sleeve and gazed into his face. "I think it's time the two of us talked, Hugh."

"I think you're right," he responded without hesitation.

He led her into his study where a single lamp burned on the low table and the dying remains of a fire cast its sleepy orange glow upon the paintings and books. There he closed the door and turned to her, thinking to himself that she looked unusually tired and distracted. She was standing with her back to him, her hands clasped in the folds of her wide satin skirts, and when she faced him, her expression was grave.

Hugh knew better than to press her into speaking. He had always been sensitive to her moods and could guess her thoughts with an uncanny accuracy that had often left him—at least in the early days of their acquaintance in India—filled with a sense of helpless frustration, even anger. He had not wanted any woman, especially Eden Hamilton, to affect him like that, and he certainly hadn't intended to fall in love with her. Yet the fact remained that he had. An intangible bond linked them—a bond that now made him inexplicably aware that she was prepared to speak of all she had kept hidden from him since Delhi.

Hugh looked down at his wife with an expression of infinite tenderness and concern. He was not by nature a patient man, and yet he could afford to be patient now. As maddening as Eden's reticence had been in the past, as much as he had despaired over the fact that she could shut a part of herself so completely away from him, he had never pressed her to reveal to him the heart of what was troubling her. Eden was not the sort of woman one could force against her will, and though he had wanted at times to shout at her and shake her, he had not. And he knew the moment her dark, solemn eyes came to rest upon him that he had been right to wait.

But it was impossible not to react with disbelieving anger to what she finally said:

"I want to talk to you about Caroline Winton."

For the space of a full minute there was utter silence between them while Hugh grappled with an overwhelming sense of unreasonable, irrational disappointment and anger. Unable to prevent himself, he exclaimed at last in a harsh and condemning tone, "Good God, Eden, I cannot believe you're still harping about that! I've told you before there's nothing between the two of us, and yet you insist on behaving like some jealous, possessive wife!"

Startled, Eden burst out, "That isn't fair, Hugh!"

"Fair?" His coldly level eyes burned into hers. "What do you know of being fair? For months now you've made impossible demands upon me concerning your grandfather's debts, and now you've chosen to jeopardize our marriage merely on the strength of some ridiculous scene you witnessed in my withdrawing room!"

"Which you've never bothered to explain," Eden pointed out defensively.

"What was there to explain?" Hugh asked brusquely. "Haven't I told you I no longer care for the woman? And I trust you remember that I am not given to telling lies."

"No, you are not," said Eden stiffly.

Once again the silence stretched interminably between them. To Eden it seemed a nightmare repetition of all the bitter confrontations of the past, and yet she could not permit this one to end as the others had: in angry silence and pain. She couldn't bear to go through that again, she told herself numbly.

Perhaps Hugh's thoughts were moving along the same lines, for Eden saw his set features soften a fraction as he became aware of the hurt and confusion in her own expression.

"My God, Eden," he burst out unexpectedly, "how can you possibly think I could even look at another woman after making love to you? Surely you must know there cannot be—there will never be—anyone else for me. As damning and impossible as that may seem!"

Eden stared up at him, her breathing suddenly stilled, and her eyes filled with a dawning, disbelieving wonder.

"By God, woman—" Hugh said gruffly, and then he broke off. "Come here."

And Eden came, feeling his arms close about her and draw her hard against him, feeling his mouth come down on hers and his fingers curve through her hair, tilting back her head so that he might kiss her more deeply. She sighed, and her body melted against his, and she knew a need and a want that matched his own.

"My dear, my love—" Hugh's voice was like a whispered caress, and his arms tightened about her, molding every inch of her slim body to his. "I cannot believe we always end up arguing when we should be making love."

"It needn't happen every time," murmured Eden.

"No, it shouldn't," he agreed, and although she could not see his face Eden knew that he was smiling. His hands were once again in her hair, turning her face to his so that he could kiss her again. In the next moment, however, he had lifted his head at the intrusion of a sound, only dimly heard yet nonetheless easily recognizable: the distant jangling of the outer bell.

"Now who the bloody devil can that be?" Hugh demanded, annoyed.

"Your pardon, Your Grace," murmured the elderly steward who shuffled into the room. "There's a messenger just arrived with an urgent dispatch from London."

"At this hour?"

"He claims he lost his way out of Wells shortly after dark and has only now managed to find the house."

"Very well. Show him in."

The dispatch proved to be a single, travel-worn letter delivered into Hugh's hands by a frost-chilled and obviously weary young man who accepted with relief Hugh's suggestion that he spend the night rather than attempt to negotiate the roads back to Wells.

"See that he gets something hot to eat," Hugh directed the steward who had waited to lead the young man away.

Turning the letter over in his hands, Hugh waited until the door closed behind them before breaking the seal.

Watching him read it, Eden saw a tightness appear about his mouth.

"What is it?" she asked worriedly.

"I'm afraid I must go out for a time," he told her curtly, reaching for the bell chain.

"At this hour?" she demanded.

"I'm afraid so. The matter is one of considerable urgency and cannot wait."

"Won't you tell me what it is?" suggested Eden. "Perhaps I might be able to help."

Hugh uttered a short laugh. "Would that it were true! No, I'm sorry, but it's something I must attend on my own. I shouldn't be gone but three or four days."

"Three or four days!" Eden could not hide her dismay. "Where are you going?"

"London."

Eden watched him crumple the letter and toss it into the fire, and a disbelieving anger filled her as she realized that he intended to say nothing more. She waited without speaking while a footman was dispatched to arouse Gilchrist, Hugh's valet, and see that His Grace's belongings were packed and that a horse was saddled and brought round to the front steps in ten minutes. Only when they were alone again did Hugh, looking around with a distracted frown, see her standing in the shadows and seem to remember her presence.

"I'm sorry, my dear, but I cannot prevent this."

Eden could feel the absurd sting of tears in her eyes. "I suppose it doesn't really matter."

He moved toward her. Afraid that he intended to touch her, Eden backed quickly away, and they stood looking at one another helplessly across the width of the room.

"I'm beginning to wonder if there will ever be any hope for us, Hugh," said Eden at last, and she could not keep the tremor from her voice. "It seems there are simply too many secrets between us."

"Damn it, Eden—"

But she was already gone.

A watery moon hung low on the horizon, and the cold wind lashed Hugh as he mounted his horse. Casting a last glance up at the house, his eyes went automatically to the single light that burned in a window high in the west wing.

Even as he watched, it abruptly went out.

Bringing down his whip with unexpected violence, Hugh sent the startled animal clattering across the courtyard, his cloak billowing wildly behind him.

It was not the London road down which Hugh turned his mount, however, but a little used cart trail that meandered west through the snow-covered hills. An hour later, he entered the small hamlet of Iselin.

On such a cold, uninviting night, it was not at all surprising that the single street of the village should be deserted, and by virtue of the lateness of the hour even the tavern was dark, although a small light burned on the stoop at the rear door of the coaching inn. Nothing stirred in the courtyard or the stables save a cat that slunk away at Hugh's approach, yet his knock was answered in a manner that suggested his arrival was not unexpected.

A white-haired man in a work-stained apron led him down a dark, drafty corridor with numerous twists and turns. At last he opened a creaking door that revealed a small dining room of the sort commonly reserved for better-paying guests. Here a fire blazed in the hearth, its warm yellow glow revealing the age-blackened rafters high overhead and a collection of pewter plates and mugs lining the rough-hewn oak mantel.

A single gentleman was seated before the fire, and the empty decanter at his elbow revealed that he must have been waiting there for some considerable time. His expression was quite affable, however, as he rose to greet the newcomer and gave the innkeeper to understand that another bottle of wine would not be unwelcome.

"What brings you back to Somerset so soon, Arthur?" Hugh inquired once he was comfortably installed in another chair and the innkeeper had uncorked a second bottle and left them.

The elderly gentleman, who had last visited Roxbury less than a week ago, shook his head with considerable gravity. "Fred Abercromby was taken in for questioning three days ago, Hugh. They've yet to release him."

"Good God! On what grounds?"

"On the strength of a telegraph received from Delhi containing evidence implicating him in last month's affair with Sidney Durlach. I came here as soon as I heard."

"The bloody fool! Has he said anything yet?"

"Not that I know of, though it won't be long before he does. You know him."

"Regrettably so."

"This is going to change our plans, of course. Force our hand, though I would have preferred to wait. What do you think we ought to do?"

Hugh was silent for a moment, toying with his glass and considering the possibilities. "Did you have the chance to speak to Gladstone before you left?"

"Unfortunately, no. It's all but impossible to get an audience with the man on short notice like this. Even if the matter *is* of considerable urgency."

"I suppose we'll have to go ahead as planned," Hugh said thoughtfully, "though I would have preferred a little more time myself. Are you in agreement, Arthur?"

"Quite," pronounced the other man energetically. "No sense in waiting until Abercromby ruins everything for us."

They talked for perhaps another hour, devising plans and stratagems and dismissing one after the other until the most obvious course lay clearly before them. Sir Arthur, who had been yawning discreetly throughout, fell noticeably silent at that point and stared for some time into the flames, his expression more than a little pensive. Presently he rose and stretched and observed that since there was little else to be done that night he might as well go to bed.

"Will I see you in the morning, Hugh?"

"Most assuredly, since I'll be spending the night here myself."

"Oh? Why not return home? It isn't that far, and surely your wife is expecting you."

"She thinks I'm on my way to London."

"London? It probably isn't wise to lie to her, my boy. She's far too intelligent for that, and I've always found that keeping secrets can be damned unhealthy for a marriage.''

"You may be right," Hugh conceded wearily, but he summoned the innkeeper and requested another bed be prepared. Then, as if Sir Arthur were not in the room, he drained the last of his wine and sat staring into the flames. There was an expression on his face that discouraged further conversation, and Sir Arthur, wishing him only the briefest of good nights, wisely withdrew.

The innkeeper, returning several minutes later to inform his guest that his room was now ready, found him leaning forward in his chair, the empty wineglass dangling unheeded from his fingers and his face hidden in his hand.

Chapter Twenty-two

The same pale sickle moon that had accompanied Hugh
Gordon's wild departure from Roxbury the night before
cast its dim light upon another rider who galloped with
similar abandon across the empty moorland. It had rained
throughout the day, causing the snow to melt and run in
muddy streams toward the sea, but shortly after midnight
the wind had picked up and dispersed the tattered clouds
so that the waxing moon and its companion stars sparkled
coldly overhead. Patches of snow lingered in the folds of
the upper hills and amid the rocks and tree roots lining
the roadside, but for the most part the ground was clear
of it and uncomfortably soft and wet.

The wildly galloping animal, splashing through the
puddles, slipped alarmingly, yet it was a surefooted beast
accustomed to the wet of a moorland winter, and its rider
knew better than to rein it in. Moments later a blast of
wind tore at his cloak and forced him to gather the long
folds against him. The material was sodden and splattered
with mud, but even in the weak light of the moon it was
possible to identify its intricate weave as the plaid of some
ancient Highland clan. A black satin vest, hobnail boots,
and gauntlets of heavy black leather encased the rider and
offered protection against the elements, and in the button-
hole of his vest, perhaps to soften the unrelieved severity
of his attire, was tucked a single blood-red rose.

At the top of a rise the rider jerked unexpectedly on
the reins and sent his horse plunging off the road and into
a dense stand of trees. Here he let his hold go slack and
allowed the animal to pick its own way along the uneven
ground. Presently they were skirting a high stone wall and

a lodgekeeper's cottage in which the windows showed black against the moonlight.

Not until they had reached the borders of a garden and saw the glimmer of light from the manor house through the swaying branches did the rider halt the weary animal at last. All was silent save for the sighing of the wind through the treetops and the blowing of his tired, winded horse. Lifting his head, the rider scanned the walls of the house before him, and in the moonlight his face was clearly revealed—a face that at first seemed as startlingly black as his attire—until he moved his head, and one saw that he was wearing a mask. His hair, too, was concealed by a strip of dark cloth and covered by a tricorn hat that was reminiscent of an earlier age, its severity softened by a white cockade that swung jauntily from the brim.

There was no mistaking the blue of the eyes that glittered behind the mask, however, nor the obstinate tilt of that pointed little chin. Flexing her fingers against the penetrating cold, Eden Gordon peered anxiously about her, wishing she hadn't left Roxbury quite so soon, as it now seemed obvious that she had come far too early.

Something stirred in the ornamental shrubs off to the left, and she rose quickly in the stirrups, but it was only a foraging animal that slunk away in alarm as it sensed her presence. Lowering herself back into the saddle, Eden drew the plaid cloak more tightly about her and, sighing, resigned herself to what would probably prove a long and uncomfortable wait.

As cold and nervous as she might be, however, she could not prevent herself from thinking back on the events that had led her here to Priory Park—a chain that had moved with disconcerting swiftness and had left her, even at this late a juncture, not entirely certain whether she was in control of the situation or whether she had merely been caught up in an inevitable tide of unlikely circumstance. . . .

Less than twenty-four hours earlier she had been breakfasting alone at Roxbury, trying her best not to think of Hugh and yet finding her gaze falling time and again on the empty chair across the long, linen-covered table. She had been wishing fervently that they hadn't parted on such unpleasant terms the night before and cursing the fact that fate was forever consigning them to endless interruptions and arguments every time they seemed on the verge of putting their differences behind them.

It isn't fair! Eden thought passionately, remembering with shameless longing the heat of Hugh's kiss and the thrill that had swept through her at his gruff confession that he desired no other woman—not even Caroline Winton. She had believed him then, though, cruelly, she could not help but doubt him now, and her throat ached with an overwhelming urge to bow her head and cry.

The footman who entered the room just then found her staring out into the misty park, her expression remote, the breakfast dishes sitting untouched before her.

"Here's a letter just arrived from Scotland, Your Grace," he told her, laying an envelope before her on the tablecloth. "Perhaps it's a bit of good news from home."

"Thank you, Chisolm," Eden said, taking no offense at his forward remark. She was fond of him, and he was right: the letter was from Isabel and would probably contain much to cheer her.

Yet it had done anything but that. Hastily dispatched from Crairralsh in the hopes of reaching Roxbury before Eden and Mrs. Walters departed for London, it contained a most dismaying disclosure: Angus Fraser had suffered a stroke that had left him partially paralyzed and incapable of normal speech. Though there seemed no readily explainable reason for it, Isabel could not help but wonder if the old man had not inadvertently discovered the extent of Tor Alsh's penury and had managed to guess the purpose behind his granddaughter's journey to India.

"Doubtless the shock was responsible," Isabel had written, "and his spirits as well as his health seem to have been affected, because he is certainly no longer himself. He hardly speaks to anyone anymore, not even Janet, and we are all trying hard to cheer him up—with poor results, as you can well imagine. Please hurry back as soon as you can," Isabel had begged at the conclusion of the letter, the words heavily underscored to indicate her urgency. "While it seems unlikely that his condition will worsen, it will doubtless not improve until you return."

She had added a postscript containing the fervent hope that Eden would find the jewels quickly, and that they would prove of sufficient worth to settle their debts, and she pleaded with her not to worry, as her grandfather was receiving the best medical help available in the glen.

The letter had fallen unnoticed from Eden's fingers, and she had sat for some considerable time before the window, seeing nothing but the image of her grandfather's proud, beloved face before her and feeling a numbing emptiness in her heart. After a moment, however, she rose to her feet, her mouth a tight line of determination. Crossing the room, she rang the bell, and the footman who answered her summons was dispatched at once to the stables to see that a horse was brought round for her.

Eden had ridden away from the house with a reckless disregard for safety that had astonished the grooms and left her mount blowing painfully for air when she drew rein at last before the largest of the glass hothouses belonging to Priory Park's extensive ornamental gardens. Ram Dass had met her outside and listened expressionlessly to her breathless words, and afterward he had been silent for so long that Eden had taken up the reins and turned away, certain that he was unable, or perhaps unwilling, to help her.

What she had asked of him was quite preposterous, after all. One simply did not enlist the aid of a trusted servant to steal a priceless collection of gemstones from under the very noses of his employers. Yet despite her urgency Eden had considered the matter quite carefully and had felt sufficiently convinced of the elderly Hindu's dislike of the Wintons to risk taking him into her confidence.

In that, at least, she had not been mistaken. While Ram Dass had no particular quarrel with the vast majority of sahib-log he had encountered in the West, he had never cared in the least for the Wintons, despite the fact that he had spent the last four years in their employ. In his honest opinion they were both of a character strongly reminiscent of the irresponsible *Angrezis* who had come to India merely to indulge in life-styles of appalling excess and whose behavior and intolerance of Indian ways had ultimately sewn the seeds of discontent that had sprung full blown into mutiny.

In considering Eden Gordon's unhappy tale, there was little doubt in his mind that the girl spoke the truth. And if it were indeed true that Winton-sahib's possession of those particular jewels was in some way responsible for the death of an innocent Hindu woman, however long ago or however indirect Winton-sahib's involvement, then Ram Dass was prepared to do anything he could to help.

Hai mai, but what he could offer was pitifully little! He was old, he explained with considerable regret, and his eyesight was failing, and the damp winters of the northern latitudes had left him so stiff of joint these few years past that he was no longer capable of much physical activity. How could he possibly be of any use to her?

Eden had assured him that she required nothing more from him than to locate the whereabouts of the jewels and to let her know when he thought it would be the best time to attempt taking them. Ram Dass had given his solemn word that he would look carefully into the matter, and Eden had ridden back to Roxbury in a fever of uncertainty. Only two days ago she had dismissed out of hand the idea of simply stealing Isabel's jewels, yet now it appeared that she had no other choice, not if she wanted to get them back in time to help her grandfather. And she must act quickly, before Hugh returned, for she had no illusions on the score of what he would think of her plans. It might even prove, Eden reflected with a sinking sense of dismay, to be the final act to drive them apart forever.

It then occurred to her that perhaps she ought to wear a disguise. That way she was increasing the likelihood of fleeing undetected in the event she were seen, and no one, including Hugh, would suspect her involvement in the theft.

Ironically, it was Charles Winton who supplied Eden with her disguise—Charles, who had spoken of the long dead highwayman, Red Rory, and the fact that his ghost was wont to make appearances on the eve of the anniversary of his death.

Only this year he shall be a night or two late, Eden decided the moment the idea occurred to her. She was, after all, quite comfortable with the notion of masquerading as someone else. Hadn't she played the part of Choto Bai long enough and well enough to deceive even a man like Hugh Gordon? And as for protecting herself in the event someone spotted this long dead apparition and unwisely chose to challenge it—hadn't her Rajput upbringing left her skilled in the use of *bundooks*, of firearms? Nor was she particularly afraid of being caught—not if Ram Dass could provide her with a detailed sketch of the upper stories of the manor house and the most likely location of Lady Caroline's jewels.

It's just a question of not making any mistakes, Eden argued with herself with ever-increasing confidence. No one on earth, after all, could possibly suspect that Charles and Caroline Winton of sleepy Somerset county were about to be robbed by a ghost, and Eden was certain that as long as she kept her wits about her, nothing could go wrong.

Indeed, in the end it had proven ridiculously easy. She had not been home a full two hours after her wild ride to Priory Park before Ram Dass sent her a message in carefully worded Sanskrit to the effect that the Wintons would be dining out at the Fallons' estate the following evening, and if one could draw any reasonable conclusions based on their visits in the past, he considered it unlikely that they would be returning home before three or perhaps even four o'clock in the morning.

Their absence usually left the servants with little to do, which naturally resulted in a slackening of their vigilance. In conclusion, Ram Dass saw no reason why Eden could not ride over to the house tomorrow night, provided she was prepared to move that quickly. If she would meet him by the gate leading into the herb garden shortly after midnight, he would make certain that she got into the house undetected. The rest, he had concluded solemnly, was up to her and to the gods.

Something stirred in the bushes off to Eden's left, causing Vanity to snort uneasily and jerk her own thoughts back to the present. Peering intently through the dark margin of trees, she drew a long breath of relief as she saw Ram Dass emerge into the clearing. Making a sign that she was to follow him, he disappeared again in the direction he had come, and Eden, leaving the horse tethered to a stout branch, quickly followed.

They did not speak until they reached an arching portal beneath the eaves of the kitchen. Ram Dass stood studying her for a moment in silence. "Aiee," he said at last in a tone of amused approval, "if I did not know better, I would think that thou wert truly the spirit of a long dead *Angrezi budmarsh.*"

"Let us hope no one else sees me," Eden replied grimly, "for it is meant as a precaution only."

"Then let me tell thee what it is thou must know. It is unwise to linger here."

He had seen Winton-sahib's carriage drive away from the house nearly two hours ago, and though he had not ventured inside since then for fear of arousing unwanted comment, he felt fairly certain that most of the servants had withdrawn to their quarters or gathered in the kitchen for a forbidden pint of ale.

"It is always that way with them," he assured her, "and none will have any reason to enter the memsahib's rooms until her return. Thou wilt find no one in the corridors and halls, yet even though it is doubtful anyone will see thee, go quickly. There is little time to waste. I will wait here for thee, and protect thee as best I can. But remember there is little indeed that I can do."

Eden heard his teeth chatter as he finished speaking but could not be certain if it was out of fear for her or because of the penetrating cold. Unconsciously she reached out her hand to touch the pistols tucked into the wide sash at her waist—Hugh's pistols, which she had removed from his study little more than an hour ago. Feeling their reassuring weight beneath her gloved hand, she lifted her chin and indicated that Ram Dass was to open the door.

It was very still and cold in the walkway, and Eden's heavy boots resounded loudly on the flagstone floor. She fled quickly up the dark flight of stairs Ram Dass had indicated, hesitating only briefly at the top, where a light showed between the uneven boards of paneling, and she heard the subdued sounds of murmured voices and laughter. The scent of cooking oil lingered strongly here, and she guessed that she was just outside the kitchen and that Ram Dass had been right in suspecting that the servants gathered there whenever their employers were gone.

Opening a door leading off to the right and making a series of dizzying turns, Eden soon found herself in the long corridor she recognized as the one leading to the Wintons' withdrawing room—and the salon in which she had first seen the famed Barrimore hanging on the wall. A vision of the painting came to Eden's mind, and a cold determination consumed her as she clearly pictured Isabel's rubies fastened about Caroline Winton's white throat.

She crossed the imposing entrance hall and mounted the spiraling staircase. The few wall sconces that remained lit in the hallway below threw her shadow against the wall in monstrous, exaggerated relief, yet Eden ignored both it and the possibility that the sight of it would instantly alert anyone entering the hall to her presence. Her hand resting lightly on the butt of Hugh's pistol, she ascended to the landing and strode unerringly down the dim corridor.

Ram Dass had described for her as best he could the location of Lady Caroline's apartment, and Eden had no trouble at all in finding it. Leaning open the door so that the weak light could fall across the threshold, she crossed without hesitation to an ornate armoire and took out a small padded box that was cunningly concealed in the false bottom of one of the drawers. She did not waste time in pondering how Ram Dass had discovered its whereabouts when it seemed likely that only Lady Caroline and her personal maid knew of its existence. Yet it seemed entirely probable that the elderly Hindu, having been born and raised on the Afghan border and trained as a soldier, was no stranger to the art of observation—or even thievery.

The box was locked, of course, and the key nowhere in evidence. Eden had expected it to open easily with the small metal file she had brought for that purpose, yet she was dismayed to find that the clasp was sturdier than supposed and that no amount of prying would open it.

Though she hadn't planned at first to take anything other than Isabel's jewels, it seemed unwise to linger, so she thrust the entire box into her waistband and, shutting the armoire doors, quickly left the room.

She was feeling light-headed and absurdly breathless as she stepped down into the entrance hall. Her heart seemed to be pumping in furious rhythm with the rapid rise and fall of her breath, and she forced herself to walk slowly, although the urge to run was all but overwhelming. A scant fifteen paces remained until she reached the doorway that would lead back to the herb garden and Ram Dass; fifteen paces, then fourteen . . . thirteen . . . ten . . .

A man's laugh, low and filled with mocking amusement, assaulted her suddenly in the absolute stillness.

It had come from a closed door off to Eden's right, and she froze instantly as a hot tide of incredulous horror washed over her. She knew that laugh, had heard it often enough to recognize it at once, and yet her frozen mind refused to believe the evidence of her own ears. It wasn't possible—it couldn't be . . . *Hugh!*

He had lied to her! He was here at Priory Park, not in London, and Eden could think of no other reason why he should be here in the middle of the night except for one— the obvious one that occurred to her with the swift pain of an unexpected blow to the heart. She put out a groping hand and leaned against the door, breathing heavily and trying to gather her wits about her.

Blindly, she stumbled toward the steps, and it seemed to her as if the darkened corridor were suddenly filled with a gray, swirling mist, though it was only the tears that blurred her vision. A sob tore from her throat, and at the sound of it she began to run—only to land hard against an impenetrable object that was suddenly there in her path. Dully, through the veil of tears that welled behind her mask, she looked up and saw that it was a footman, a muscular specimen who seemed curiously unsurprised by her presence.

"Well, well," he said slowly, "what 'aves we 'ere? An 'ighwayman from the looks of it. You're not thinkin' of makin' off wiv the master's riches, are you, little man?''

His hand snaked out and grasped her arm as he spoke, and it was not until his fingers bit painfully into her flesh that Eden awoke to the danger. But by then it was far too late, for the big fellow had seized her roughly by the collar and was dragging her away.

Eden, hampered by her cape and by the arms that entrapped her, could do no more than struggle ineffectually until she was thrust roughly through a doorway and released. Shaken and breathless, she lifted her head to find herself standing before none other than Charles Winton himself, though she could not imagine what he was doing here when he had supposedly left the house hours before.

''Found 'im out in the corridor, sir. Don't know where in 'ell 'e come from.''

Eden looked up into Sir Charles's pale eyes and for a moment experienced a dreadful, sinking shock, certain that he recognized her. But he was merely studying her masked face with a mixture of disbelief and amusement, and after a moment he turned his head and inquired:

''One of your ideas, Hugh? I'll confess it's novel, though rather useless, wouldn't you say?''

''I assure you I'm not in the least responsible, Charles. Never seen the fellow in my life.''

At the sound of that unaffected voice Eden's head whipped around, and she smothered a gasp seeing Hugh lounging in an armchair. His legs were crossed comfortably before him, and he seemed entirely oblivious to the men at his elbow—burly footmen, who were, incredibly, armed with revolvers. At Hugh's right, wearing an expression that was not nearly so composed, sat Sir Arthur Willoughby, though Eden scarcely acknowledged his presence. A primitive fear took hold of her, and she tried to check the furious pounding of her heart, certain that everyone in that small, silent room could hear it. She had no idea what was transpiring here, but the armed footmen, the black anger in Hugh's eyes, and the grimness about Charles Winton's mouth served to tell its own dreadful story.

"Come, come, now," said Sir Charles in a voice that Eden had never heard him use before and one that was all at once not even remotely amused, "someone must be responsible for this. I agree it isn't in your style, Hugh, but then again he must have been sent here deliberately. Mayhew, bring the bloody devil to me. Let's see who it is behind that foolish mask."

Eden shrank instinctively away as the burly servant reached for her. Looking over his shoulder, her eyes met Hugh's across the room, and she saw the shock and the grim whiteness that settled over his features as their glances met and held. Then he was out of his chair, the movement taking everyone by surprise, and the servant Mayhew gave a startled grunt as he found himself unexpectedly seized by the throat.

"Go on! Get out of here!" Hugh grated, shoving Eden aside.

The sound of his voice seemed to release everyone from the paralysis that had gripped them. Immediately the room was filled with the sound of trampling feet and shouting voices, and Eden pushed herself free of the footman's hold and groped instinctively for her pistols. The unbelievable crash of a firearm sounded just as she drew the weapons from her waistband, and Eden, panic-stricken, saw Hugh still struggling with the servant, apparently unharmed. Abruptly another shot followed, then another, this one accompanied by a dreadful scream of pain.

Whirling, Eden watched, horrified, as Sir Arthur Willoughby staggered toward her, the front of his vest stained with gushing blood. Meaningless words gurgled from his throat, though somehow, instinctively, Eden sensed that he knew who she was—and that he was urging her to flee. With the last of his strength he reached out his hand to push her away, then sank to his knees, his clutching fingers leaving a trail of blood on the hem of her cape.

"Eden, look out!"

The voice was Hugh's. Through a haze of swimming lights, Eden lifted her head and saw a footman rushing toward her, all but stumbling over Sir Arthur's fallen body in his haste. Raising her pistol, she fired quickly, and astonishment spread across his homely features as he staggered and fell. Then someone seized her arm and all but jerked her off her feet, and amid another crash of gunshots she felt herself being pulled out into the darkened corridor.

"This way, quickly!" a rough voice urged in her ear, and then she was stumbling down the long flight of steps and out into the night, where the cold air hit her like a blow across the face.

"Cover your eyes," the voice commanded. In the next moment she was thrust into a thicket of prickly thorns that scratched her fiercely and clawed at her clothing. She did not think to struggle or protest, however, for she had known instinctively, despite the darkness and even without hearing that terse command, that it was Hugh beside her, and she obeyed him instantly and without argument. The branches crackled and snapped into place behind them. Through that sound came the shouted order from Charles Winton as he stepped outside:

"Caretaker! Loose the dogs, damn you! Loose the dogs!"

Instantly lights blazed in the stables, and from the direction of the kennels came the eager clamoring of hounds. Eden felt Hugh's hand tighten about her arm, dragging her through the darkness.

"Hurry, for God's sake! They'll tear us apart if they catch us!"

"They—they wouldn't! Sir Charles would never—"

"The hell he wouldn't! They've been trained to kill on command, and Charles has no use for us alive. You've given him the perfect alibi for murder."

"I don't understand. Hugh, what is it? Why—"

But Hugh had no time to waste answering. Behind them came a sound that made the hair rise on Eden's scalp in a wholly primitive fear: the baying of a dog as it caught its quarry's scent. She knew instinctively that these were not the friendly hounds belonging to the Priory hunt, but the enormous mastiffs that were kept isolated in another part of the kennels.

The heavy boots Eden wore were not made for running, and it was all but impossible to see because her mask had slipped and hung askew over her eyes. She clung blindly to Hugh's arm—only to feel it being torn away without warning as her cloak tangled in a confusion of thorns and jerked her to a halt.

"Hugh!"

He was already beside her, tearing at it with his hands, but it would not come free. By now they could hear the dogs crashing through the underbrush behind them. Then something crackled in the bushes off to their left, and a man emerged into the clearing, his eyes wide and alarmed in his white face. Ram Dass, his breath coming in short gasps, instantly took in the situation.

"Here, sahib. Cut her loose, quickly!"

There was a knife in his hand, a long, curved knife of the sort commonly used on the Afghan border, and Hugh wasted no time in taking it. With one slashing motion he cut the cape and Eden, abruptly freed, went down on her knees in the mud.

"There are fresh horses for you," Ram Dass added, pointing. "Go quickly now. Quickly! I will try to turn the dogs."

"No!" Eden gasped. "Ram Dass, you cannot!"

"They will not harm me," he assured her. "They know who I am."

"Come on," Hugh said, and brutally pulled her away.

The horses were tethered near the gate separating the tangle of wild shrubs from the cultivated neatness of the herb garden. Both of them were snorting nervously and rolling their eyes at the scent of the approaching dogs and the terrible, primeval baying that seemed to echo more loudly the closer they came. Speaking to them quietly, Hugh managed to unloop the reins and fling Eden up onto one of the saddles. He vaulted into the other, dug his heels into the animal's sides, and leaned across at the same time to bring his hand down smartly on the flank of Eden's mount. Seconds later they were speeding through the trees and toward the moonlit expanse of open road.

"Where are we going?" Eden cried as they emerged from the long avenue of stately oaks and turned not toward Roxbury's border, but north, in the direction of the sea.

"It's too dangerous to head for home," Hugh shouted in response. "They'll know right away where we've gone."

"But surely they wouldn't dare pursue us all the way to Roxbury!" Eden protested, white-faced at the prospect.

"Yes, they would. Listen!"

Even above the drumming of their own mounts' hooves and the rush of cold night air that tore through their clothing and wailed shrilly in their ears, Eden could hear a faint pounding from somewhere behind them. Risking a quick glance over her shoulder, she saw at least four horses turn down the moonlit roadway in pursuit, the black shadows that were their riders leaning low in the saddles as they settled in for the chase.

"Keep your head down and stay out of the line of fire," Hugh warned. Eden felt quickly in her waistband for a weapon, but the pistol she found there was spent, and she must have dropped the other one without noticing during their flight from the house.

"Give that to me," Hugh ordered grimly, following the movement of her hand. "We'll have no further heroics, Red Rory. Is that clear?"

Eden handed it over without argument; then, suddenly remembering the place where that notorious highwayman had died, she caught her breath and gasped out: "Of course! The Wookey Hole!"

She turned quickly to Hugh, but there was no need for explanations, for he understood her instantly. The matter, in fact, was settled by no more than a single glance between them, and Eden followed as Hugh sent his horse plunging into a dense stand of trees at a right angle to the road and set it galloping across the open moor.

They rode as if the furies were behind them, careless of the dangers presented by the rocky ground. Fortunately Ram Dass had selected their mounts with care; they were unquestionably the finest in the Winton stable and exceedingly fresh by virtue of the fact that they had taken little exercise since the Priory hunt. And as terrifying as their escape might be, Eden could not help but feel a strange sense of exhilaration creep through her blood as the ground passed beneath her in a blur.

Leaning low in the saddle, she crooned encouragement into the ear of her mount, the remnants of her cape fluttering madly behind her. Hugh, too, seemed affected by a similar madness, and when by chance their eyes met, Eden saw the white flash of his teeth in the darkness and knew that he was feeling as she did. Their pursuers seemed to have fallen back, cast into confusion by their unexpected turn from the road, and to Eden it was almost as if she were once again back in Mayar riding under the tutelage of the old rajah himself, who had drilled her for hours on the Rajput art of eluding anything and anyone on horseback.

But their confidence and high spirits could not last. Their horses were winded long before the land began to turn uphill and the level moors gave way to torturously twisted tracks of limestone outcroppings and straggling clumps of heath. They were forced to slow to a walk and let the weary animals find their own way, while behind them the pounding of hoofbeats picked up again.

Eden was not consciously aware that the exhilaration of the ride was suddenly gone. She knew only that she was feeling very cold and tired and that her teeth were chattering uncontrollably. She glanced over at Hugh and wished that she hadn't; he was no longer smiling, and there was no mistaking the grimness of his expression.

They halted at last in a small clearing ringed by trees that were twisted by age and honed by the winds of countless icy winters. Here Hugh dismounted and loosened the girth so that his tired horse could blow. Coming around to Eden's side, he lifted his arms to help her dismount, and as she slid into them, the sole of her boot caught in the stirrup. She lost her balance and fell hard against Hugh. She heard him grunt in response, and her heart seemed to stop at that seemingly insignificant sound. When he set her aside she did not turn away but peered anxiously into his face, and her breath caught painfully as she noticed for the first time the whiteness about his mouth.

"Oh, God, Hugh, you're hurt! Why didn't you tell me?"

"It's nothing," he said harshly, but Eden reached out and put her arms about him, and a quiver fled through her as she felt the warm wetness that seeped through his vest.

"Hugh—" she whispered, but he caught her elbow and whipped her about.

"It's nothing, I tell you! Just a wing from a stray bullet."

"But surely you cannot—"

"We've a long climb up to the cave," he interrupted curtly. "We'd better hurry."

Yet the progress they made was torturously slow. They were forced to walk on foot and lead the horses behind them, for it proved impossible to see in the darkness, and Hugh could not be certain as to the exact location of the cave. While it would have been a simple enough matter to negotiate the rutted path in daylight, he could not dismiss the possibility that he might be leading them in the wrong direction or, worse, toward some unseen danger: an open well or fissure, or the steep banks of the Ax River that flowed in foaming cataracts onward to Cheddar Gorge, and down which an unsuspecting horse and rider could easily plunge to his death.

The horses, accustomed to roaming the level, grassy grounds surrounding Priory Park, were nervous on the uneven footing of loose stone and shale, and they threw up their heads whenever a gust of wind rattled the dry heath beneath them. While Eden could guess at the agony Hugh was suffering, she knew there was nothing she could do to help him. She could only follow stoically behind him, her head bowed against the wind and her cheeks wet with silent tears.

They found the cave at last, though neither of them were at all certain how they had managed it. The moon that had provided them with sufficient light during their whirlwind flight across the moors was hidden now behind a bank of clouds that had been driven inland from the sea by a fierce, keening wind. While Eden was relieved to step inside the cave and so escape the biting elements, she was dismayed to discover that it was not the warm, wind-sheltered haven she had envisioned, but a stifling black hole that was bitterly cold and damp.

"I'm sorry we can't build a fire," said Hugh, feeling her shiver as he took the reins from her. "They'd find us the moment we did. Wait here while I tether the horses."

He was back a moment later, and by then Eden's eyes were sufficiently adjusted to the blackness to make out dimly the drawn features of his face. She stared up at him anxiously. "You don't really think they'll come after us, do you?"

Hugh merely grunted in response, but Eden caught urgently at his sleeve. "What did you mean when you said I'd probably supplied Sir Charles with the perfect alibi for a murder?"

Hugh's shoulders lifted in a shrug. "Only that the authorities will probably accept his explanation as to how Arthur Willoughby and I came to be shot accidentally by a thief breaking into his home—a thief cleverly disguised as a long dead highwayman."

Eden's lips felt painfully stiff. "You cannot honestly believe he means to kill you!"

"Sir Arthur was shot in cold blood, wasn't he?" Hugh reminded her grimly.

"But you—you are his neighbor and friend! It doesn't seem possible that anyone would dare— What is it you've done to him, Hugh? Why does he want you dead?"

Hugh could hear the fear that trembled in her voice and paled her cheeks so that her face was no more than a dim oval against the dark walls of stone. Yet he knew that her fear was not for herself, and he turned his head away because he found it impossible to look at her any longer.

"I imagine we both have quite a bit of explaining to do, don't we?" he inquired lightly.

"Yes," Eden whispered. Reaching out her hand to touch him, she felt him draw imperceptibly away from her. Although the gesture was entirely unexpected she knew instantly why he had done so.

"Hugh, your arm!" Her eyes were suddenly bright with anger. "You must let me look at it!"

"I told you it was no more than a flesh wound."

"Is it?" She rolled back his sleeve and probed the sticky wetness of his arm. Though she could not see the wound in the darkness, she suspected that it was a deeper gash than Hugh would have liked her to believe, and that it must have bled considerably during the hard ride across the moors. The fact that it was bleeding no longer should have relieved her, yet she felt nothing but an irrational, driving anger at him. She unwound the scarf from her head, ripped it into two strips, and bound them tightly around his arm. Perhaps Hugh sensed her anger or was by now too weary to protest, for he said nothing at all as she worked but merely leaned his shoulder against the outcropping of rocks and watched her through the darkness.

"I must be slowing down in my old age," he said at last and in an obvious attempt at humor that tore at Eden's heart. "I was certain I had managed to keep out of the line of fire when I went after that oafish flunkey who grabbed you. Apparently I miscalculated."

Eden could feel the prickle of tears in her eyes and an old, familiar ache close her throat and wondered why she had never realized before just how deeply she loved him. She would have gone to him then and sensed that he would have taken her into his arms at once and held her close to his heart, but he lifted his head at that moment and laid a warning hand on her wrist.

"What is it?" she whispered.

He did not answer, and Eden, aware that he was listening to some sound she herself could not hear, moved restlessly. Instantly Hugh's fingers tightened, and suddenly Eden, too, heard something that caused her heart to contract within her breast: the metallic clink of a horseshoe on stone.

"Stay here," Hugh said into her ear, his voice so low that his breath barely stirred the tendrils of hair curling against the nape of her neck. "I've got to go after the horses. They'll give us away if they make a sound."

He was gone before she could protest, pausing only long enough to press his pistol into her hand. Endless moments later Eden heard him return leading both mounts behind him, their hooves wrapped in strips of cloth from clothing he had torn. Though they balked at first at being led deeper into the dark interior of the cave, it must have been that they suddenly caught the scent of water, for all at once they threw up their heads and surged forward eagerly. It was fortunate that they did so, for Hugh knew enough to take heed of the inherent warning in their behavior and feel his way carefully along, otherwise he probably would have plunged into the unseen waterhole that opened up suddenly onto the path.

As it was he managed to hear the telltale plopping of pebbles into water on time and drew back sharply. Releasing the bridles he let the horses find their own way by scent, and as he made his way back toward the mouth of the cave, he heard them drinking noisily. Rejoining Eden, he took the pistol from her.

"I'm going to wait for them at the mouth of the cave. It may be that I can take one or two of them by surprise."

"I'm going with you," said Eden at once.

"For God's sake, Eden, are you mad?"

"No," she said slowly. "You've got two pistols there, haven't you? Let me have one of them."

"No. You'll stay right here while I—"

"I wager I'm as good a shot as you are," she reminded him quietly. "Perhaps even better."

For a long moment they looked at one another in silence, the air between them charged with something very like hostility. Yet Hugh knew there was really no need for further argument. He remembered clearly that Eden had brought down considerably more sand grouse during their journey across the plains of Rajasthan than even the most experienced of the native *shikari* who had ridden with them. He had hunted sand grouse himself on occasion, and they were elusive creatures, far more difficult targets than the unsuspecting men pursuing them up the hillside.

"Very well," he said at last, "but you'll stay well back and obey my orders. Is that clear?"

Eden nodded, yet still Hugh's fingers closed relentlessly about her arm.

"Your word on that?"

"Yes," she said quietly. "I promise."

Looking down into her face and seeing the calm trust in her eyes, Hugh felt his heart contract almost painfully. Then, abruptly, he released her arm and took up Ram Dass's knife. He signaled to her to follow him and that there was to be no more exchange of words between them. Despite his own marksmanship and Eden's undisputed skill with firearms, Hugh knew that their best chance of survival lay in remaining undetected. He could not be certain how many men Charles Winton had brought with him, but in all likelihood he was more than desperate and would see to it that the two of them were hopelessly outnumbered. Their chances, actually, were less than slim, but Hugh would not permit himself to dwell on that fact.

What is written, is written, he thought suddenly to himself, and was startled that those particular words should spring unbidden to his mind—he, who had spent most of his life among the followers of the Hindu faith and not among the worshipers of Islam. Yet for some inexplicable reason they strangely reassured him; he could not believe that fate had brought Eden to him on this night merely to die.

Checking the pistol's firing mechanism once again, he lifted his head much like a preying tiger testing the air and abruptly went rigid. Something was moving in the darkness below him, something that was taking considerable precaution not to let itself be seen.

Slowly Hugh eased himself down on his stomach and steadied the weapon in his hand. He would not fire until he had at least one of them in his sights, and after that . . . A grim smile played at the corners of his mouth. After that it was all in the hands of God. *Insh'allah*. What is written, is written.

He settled down to wait.

___ Chapter Twenty-three ___

There were four of them—at least that was the number Hugh could make out moving up the hill, keeping well to the shelter of the scattered rocks and trees. They had left their horses behind them and were proceeding slowly on foot, and it must be that they were careless of detection or believed their quarry farther away, for they made little effort to keep their voices low. It was, Hugh thought grimly, a misjudgment that would cost at least two of them their lives.

Less than two minutes later a dark head poked inquisitively from behind a boulder directly below him, and Hugh waited until the man had risen to his feet and exposed himself as a better target before taking aim.

There was a howl of pain and the shadowy figure disappeared amid a tangle of limbs, only to be replaced by another whose quickly discharged weapon sent a ball hurling perilously close to Hugh's head. As he primed his pistol, another shot came unexpectedly from somewhere off to his left, followed immediately by a hair-raising screech and then silence.

Good girl, Hugh thought exultantly, but in the next moment both his optimism and the silence were shattered by an unexpected fusillade of shots. Incredibly, it seemed to be coming from behind him, and Hugh ducked low as a bullet whined past his ear. It was instantly obvious to him that someone was shooting at him from the hillside above.

Only when he heard a series of hoarse yells and realized that men were scrambling from all directions did he understand how seriously he had underestimated Charles

Winton's driving desperation. Coming to his feet, he slid breathlessly down the loose shale and found Eden still crouched within the protective embrasure where he had left her.

"Come on," he said to her, his voice crackling with urgency. "The entire valley must be crawling with men!"

Pulling her along behind him, he ran panting uphill, keeping to the treeline and the rocks that afforded at least a modicum of protection. His arm was tightly about her as he shielded her with his body, and they had almost reached the mouth of the cave when a shout went up behind them: "Look! There they are! Fire, damn y—"

The words ended on a gurgle as Ram Dass's knife hurled through the air and imbedded itself in the speaker's throat. There hadn't been enough time to take careful aim, and in such utter darkness it had been difficult to locate his target, but Hugh needed no further encouragement than the sound of the nauseating bubbling with which the shouted words died to take Eden by the arm and drag her by force into the blackness of the cave.

Where less than an hour earlier it had seemed to Hugh a coldly unwelcoming place, now it was a refuge, a veritable haven of endless chambers in which the two of them might hide. But for how long? Sir Charles had undoubtedly sent back to Priory Park for reinforcements who could quarry them effortlessly by the sheer force of their numbers. The chance of being rescued, furthermore, was nonexistent given the fact that Hugh and Sir Arthur had, of necessity, conducted their visit to Priory Park in secrecy. No one knew where they were, and if any of the trusted footmen at Roxbury did happen to think of their master at all this night, they would believe him in London still and not besieged and fighting for his life in the dark confines of a limestone cave absurdly known as the Wookey Hole. Perhaps Ram Dass—?

But Hugh did not want to think about the remote possibility that the elderly Hindu might be able to help them. Not now, not when he needed to keep his wits about him and urge Eden on as fast as was safely possible down this dark, impenetrable corridor of stone. He had forgotten entirely about the presence of the well and the wandering horses, and it was Eden who drew back in sudden alarm.

"Hugh! There's someone ahead of us!"

Drawing up short, he set her quickly behind him, and for a moment he stood motionless, although he could hear no sound save the steady drip of water and the moaning of the wind from the direction they had come. Then, unexpectedly, he gave a low laugh, and Eden could feel the rigid muscles of his arm grow slack about her.

"It's only the horses. Come on, they'll let us pass. Mind your step. There's a waterhole here somewhere, and I've no idea how deep it is."

His voice threw up numerous echoes from the unseen rocks, and as the sound faded and died away, it was immediately replaced by another: a low, vibrating murmur that at first defied all description until suddenly, terrifyingly, both of them recognized it for what it was—voices, a great number of them, that were headed their way. Hugh heard Eden's breath catch on a gasp, and his arm tightened about her.

"Come on, love. We'd better go."

Eden clung to him as they hurried down the dark corridor, unmindful of the bruises she received as they bumped time and again against the unseen walls of stone. She could feel the urgency in the arm that held her and did her best to keep her own fears under control. Yet she was afraid, desperately afraid, for she knew that Hugh was seriously weakened by the loss of blood from his wounded arm, and she did not know how long he could continue this maddened pace.

The cave, they soon discovered, wound deep into the hillside and consisted of numerous chambers and side caves. The possibility of never finding their way out again occurred to Hugh, but the dangers seemed far less threatening than the men who followed in pursuit.

They had not gone very far down a branching side tunnel when he realized that the others seemed not to have followed them. The voices that had pursued them relentlessly were inexplicably gone, and as he slowed to a walk and then halted, he found that he could no longer hear any other sound save Eden's breathing. Pulling her to him, he pressed his fingers lightly against the back of her neck in a warning that she was to remain still. Obeying him willingly, Eden leaned against him, far too weary to question his intentions. Above her bowed head Hugh's eyes were fixed upon the corridor down which they had come as he strained to listen for the telltale sounds of pursuit.

"I think we've lost them," he said at last, and could not prevent a measure of elation from creeping into his voice.

Eden made no reply. Her head had drooped to his chest, and Hugh could feel the shuddering effort it cost her to draw every breath. She must be on the verge of total collapse he thought.

Feeling his way along the uneven stone, he came upon a small side cave whose narrow opening assured him that no one could squeeze inside without a goodly amount of noise, and that he would have the advantage over anyone attempting to do so. It seemed as good a place as any to stop.

"Sit down," he said softly to Eden. "We'll rest here for a while."

Eden needed no further encouragement. Sinking down onto the soft sand, she closed her eyes and leaned her head tiredly against the hard stone wall. Eventually she opened her eyes and saw Hugh pacing restlessly.

"Does your arm hurt very much?" she ventured to ask.

"No."

"You're a poor liar, Hugh Gordon."

Unbelievably, she heard him laugh, and then the sand whispered softly as he seated himself beside her. "I confess it didn't bother me too much earlier, though I think it's getting stiff now. How about you?" he added with sudden concern. "Do you feel better now that you've had the chance to rest?"

"Oh, I suppose I'll manage, though if you really must know"—she leaned toward him and whispered conspiratorially—"these boots are giving me bloody awful blisters."

Hugh was speechless, unable to find the words to say how much she amazed him. No other woman would have attempted to make light of such a desperate situation or followed him so calmly through the nightmare blackness of an endless cave while armed men pursued them with murderous intent. She was a woman like no other, this enchanting creature who had become his wife, yet Hugh found he could not bring himself to say as much. There were simply no words to describe how he felt. He could only tighten his arms about her and draw her more closely to him; Eden sighed, and the tension ebbed from her body as she laid her head against him.

They lay together for some time in silence, feeling curiously at peace despite the fact that both of them knew this was merely a respite from the harshness of reality.

"Would you mind telling me what you were doing in Charles Winton's house dressed in that ridiculous highwayman's garb?" Hugh finally broke the silence.

"I thought it was a rather clever idea myself." Eden laughed.

"Perhaps it was," Hugh agreed after a thoughtful pause, "inasmuch as no one seemed to recognize you."

"But you did. At least, I thought—I wasn't certain—"

"I knew who you were the moment I saw those blue eyes behind that mask. And yet I couldn't believe it at first. That's why I didn't take advantage right away of the distraction you provided. Perhaps," he added bitterly, "Arthur Willoughby would not have died if I'd acted sooner."

"Oh, no, Hugh, there's nothing you could have done to prevent that! There were so many of them, and you were unarmed, and—" Eden's voice broke. "Remember, they shot you, too. You could have died just as easily."

He felt the shudder that went through her as she spoke and drew her hard against him. Presently, she leaned her forehead against his cheek and answered his question by telling him things she had never told him before: of the murder of her *ayah*, Sitka, during the massacre in Meerut, of the theft of Isabel's jewels and her own hopeless quest for them in Delhi, and of the fact that she had discovered them at last, unbelievably, in the possession of Lady Caroline Winton of Priory Park. Lastly, she told him how she and Ram Dass had conspired together to steal them back and how she had happened to stumble across the footman who had brought her into the room in which he and Arthur Willoughby were being held.

It was an amazing tale to Hugh, who had never possessed even an inkling of knowledge concerning its existence, and quite long in the telling. When Eden fell silent he did not speak but held her close and tenderly stroked the silky hair that tumbled across her brow.

"My God," he said at last in a voice that was gruff with emotion, "why didn't you tell me all of this before? Never mind, I can well imagine. My behavior toward you in Delhi certainly didn't encourage confidences, did it? Though I feel I must defend myself by saying that I'd never come across a woman who angered me quite as much as you did. But I think that was simply because I'd made the mistake of falling in love with you."

Eden said nothing, yet Hugh could hear the quick, startled intake of her breath, and he smiled to himself in the darkness.

"And after we were married," he continued slowly, growing sober once more, "it must have seemed to you that I was hell-bent on your grandfather's destruction. Eden, I swear I would have helped him if I could have. That's why I came here to Roxbury, though I'm afraid—"

"Hush." Eden's fingers pressed softly against his lips. "It doesn't matter. I understand."

He knew that she meant it, and a fierce tenderness welled up inside of him. Turning his head, he kissed her. It was a kiss that was, for once, entirely devoid of desire, and yet so filled with longing that both of them were left dangerously breathless when Hugh lifted his mouth from hers.

"And what about you?" Eden asked. "What were you doing at Priory Park? You were supposed to be in London. I thought at first that you and—"

She broke off abruptly, for there was no need to tell Hugh that she had at first suspected him of conducting a clandestine affair with Lady Caroline Winton. Without any real amazement she realized that the likelihood no longer troubled her—that it didn't matter at all, in fact.

She would never doubt Hugh's feelings for her again. She knew, as surely as if she had been able to peer straight into his heart, that she was completely, irrevocably, a part of him, and the feeling left her curiously at peace with the image of the woman she had once thought to be her rival.

"I take it you never intended to go to London," she said without any measure of anger or reproach in her voice. "It was Sir Charles you went to see, wasn't it? Will you tell me why?"

"You'll be surprised to know," Hugh answered gravely, "that your cousin Isabel's jewels are partly the reason. Oh, not just her jewels alone, but others, a great many others, as well as Mughal artifacts, money, firearms—Charles Winton dealt in all of them, I'm sorry to say."

"Are you saying he was a black marketeer?" Eden asked incredulously.

"Only the pawn of one, though he happens to be very ambitious. That's why Sir Arthur and I were there tonight—because overly ambitious men are prone to making mistakes."

"Do you mean you were attempting to entrap him?"

Hugh nodded.

"But why? What is it you wanted from him if he is as insignificant as you say?"

"A name. The name of a man in Delhi known only as 'the Angling Cove.' Have you ever heard the term before?"

Eden shook her head.

"It's Cockney. It means a receiver of stolen goods, and as such this particular fellow has become the most influential man in Delhi's black market."

"Catching him sounds like a matter for the Delhi authorities or the military police," Eden observed with a frown. "Surely there was no need for you to get involved?"

"No. At least not until it became apparent that the Angling Cove was accepting bribes in the way of gold and jewels from various Indian rulers, who contributed them in the belief that they were amassing funds for another uprising against the British raj.''

"*An uprising?* Oh, no, Hugh! I won't believe it!''

"I'm afraid it's true. At first we thought it was a plot planned by some of the senior wives of disaffected maharajahs. It isn't any secret that most of them intrigue actively against the British from the throne rooms of their zenanas. And it seemed entirely inconceivable that any white man would conspire deliberately against his own kind, not after the atrocities committed in the fifty-nine uprising. Yet after traveling to Mayar and speaking to Lala Dayal, I was handed irrevocable evidence that someone in Delhi, an Englishman, no less, was responsible.''

"And you've since found out who it is?''

Hugh's mouth tightened. "Yes.''

"Who?''

"Do you remember Sir Percy Meade?''

Eden frowned. "I'm not certain. It seems I ought to know the name, and yet . . .'' Abruptly her expression cleared. "Yes, of course. The *Moti Mahal,* the Pearl Palace! I attended a ball there with the Porters.'' Her eyes opened wide. "But he seemed such a harmless little man!''

"An unassuming fellow,'' Hugh agreed, "and perhaps that's why he managed to escape detection for so long. He and Charles Winton happen to be related, however, and it wasn't difficult to draw some obvious conclusions once the connection was made. We lacked only the evidence that Charles was acting as a front for Sir Percy, evidence we would have gotten tonight if the arrest of Fred Abercromby hadn't alerted him to the fact that someone had grown suspicious and was attempting to set a trap for him.''

"I find it hard to believe that an Indian maharajah, that any Indian, in fact, would trust an *Angrezi* with his prized valuables—or the plans for another rebellion,'' Eden said slowly, still thinking of Hugh's disturbing revelation concerning the situation in India. "Not after the secrecy with which the Sepoy Rebellion was carried out.''

"Ah, but Sir Percy knew better than to deal with them directly. He was aided by Ranjit Ali Singh, a Delhi nobleman who originally resided in the Pearl Palace and was supposedly related by blood to the last king of Oudh. It isn't entirely clear whether or not Ranjit Singh was aware that Sir Percy was in fact selling the jewelry abroad and keeping the profits for himself. We only know that he was found in a ditch in the Kudsia Bagh not too long ago with his throat cut from ear to ear.''

"Perhaps a *dacoit*—''

Hugh shook his head. "It doesn't seem possible. Singh was a Brahmin, and it would have been an unspeakable sacrilege for another Hindu to take his life.''

"Then you think Sir Percy had him killed? Because he found out too much?''

"It seems likely.''

"And Sir Charles? How does he figure into this, as a front?''

"The stolen goods were shipped to him from Delhi, and it was up to him to see that they were sold here in England and elsewhere on the Continent. I wouldn't be surprised if Miss Isabel's jewels found their way out of India in a similar manner.''

"And when Lady Caroline took a fancy to them, she was simply permitted to keep them,'' guessed Eden bitterly.

"It seems that way,'' Hugh agreed. "I imagine we'll never find out how they fell into the hands of Sir Percy Meade. Not unless I can make some inquiries in Delhi and Meerut about the officer who stole them. I'd personally like to find out how he discovered their existence, and we can certainly arrange to see that he's punished for your *ayah*'s death. Provided, of course, that he survived the mutiny and is still alive.''

"Or that we are, too, come morning.''

"Yes,'' said Hugh after an appreciable silence, and the fact that he respected her too much to make an attempt at false assurances filled Eden's heart with a fierce love for him.

"There may still be hope yet,'' he told her. "If we stay where we are, they may not find us, and I've the feeling that they won't linger long past first light. Too many people pass by this way, and the presence of so many men is bound to cause comment.''

''I don't mind staying here,'' Eden assured him. In fact, she far preferred the quiet of this dark cave to their frantic flight down those endless tunnels of stone. It was warmer here, and dry, and she was content to lie in the curve of Hugh's arm listening to the steady rise and fall of his breathing beneath her cheek and know that for the time being both of them were safe.

But a persistent question continued to nag at her, and after a long interval of silence she could not prevent herself from asking it.

''How did I get involved?'' Hugh echoed. ''I assure you it was not my original intent. When I agreed to journey to Mayar and investigate the rumored plot against the British raj, I never dreamed it would lead me back to Somerset and to Charles Winton, Roxbury's closest neighbor. Apparently no one else did, either. Not until the queen, who was alarmed by the prospect of another uprising in India, requested that the secret service look into the matter. Sir Arthur, one of her London chiefs, asked for my help. And of course I couldn't refuse.''

''No, I suppose you could not,'' Eden agreed without any real surprise. She thought she detected a trace of amusement in his tone as he continued.

''Naturally the best course to take was to make it appear as if unmitigated circumstances had prompted me to turn to Charles for financial help. He has always suspected me of being in something of a monetary quandary, which isn't too far from the truth, I suppose, when one considers the deplorable state of Roxbury's fortunes.'' A trace of self-derision had crept into his voice, but he merely fell silent and chose to say nothing more on that score.

''So you acted as a go-between for Mr. Abercromby and Sir Charles,'' Eden prompted.

''Yes. Our intent was really twofold, however, in that the board of control and the foreign secretary were demanding to see the Angling Cove caught out once and for all, while the prime minister was mainly interested in Fred Abercromby's arrest. That was why Sir Arthur was asked to step in—because he knew how best to achieve both ends without jeopardizing either situation. He was a good man.'' Hugh's voice was flat with bitterness. ''It's a bloody shame we lost him.''

Eden, who had thought Frederick Abercromby a rather unpleasant but innocuous enough individual, was puzzled by this particular disclosure. ''I don't understand why Lord Palmerston himself would be interested in Mr. Abercromby's arrest. Not if he was guilty of nothing more than buying stolen Indian jewelry.''

''Not jewelry,'' said Hugh softly. ''Rifles. He has made a vast fortune supplying arms to Irish insurgents.''

''Rifles?'' Eden echoed, puzzled.

''Abercromby serves in Westminster, Eden, and recently came under suspicion for secretly supporting the Young Ireland Movement, which is agitating for the repeal of the British union. Since there is always a great need for arms among rebels, it was obvious that both Charles and Fred Abercromby would benefit mutually from a business association. Charles, you see, didn't confine himself solely to selling goods for his Delhi cousin.''

''But Hugh—*arms!* Surely you could have—''

''There was never any real danger,'' Hugh assured her. ''At least we never expected it. I was only to introduce the two of them, you see, and Sir Arthur, posing as an interested third party, was to take care of the rest.''

Eden was silent, considering what he had just told her. Presently she said, ''You mentioned earlier that Mr. Abercromby had been arrested. Was that supposed to happen?''

''No, it was not. But some overweaning, ambitious fool of an official in the C.I.D. obviously couldn't wait to take credit for the affair and had him taken in for questioning. Sir Arthur traveled to Roxbury at once to let me know what had happened, but by then it was too late. The alarm had been given. Even as we arranged our final meeting with Sir Charles, he had already been informed of the arrest, though the devil knows how he found out about it.''

''So he was waiting for you—you walked right into a trap,'' said Eden.

"Like inexperienced schoolboys," Hugh agreed. "We must have been brought into his study at about the same time that you met Ram Dass out in the garden. Charles and his henchmen were obviously far too preoccupied with us to think of searching the house for others. Perhaps," he added flatly, "you might have gotten away if that half-wit Mayhew hadn't seen you."

Hugh fell silent, wondering with a spasm of helpless anger how he could possibly have blundered so blindly into Charles Winton's trap. Yet in truth the fault had been neither his nor Sir Arthur's. Charles Winton had possessed more connections and greater power than either man—indeed, than anyone—had suspected, and it would take more long weeks of investigation by a number of men before the names of several prominent officers in both the C.I.D. and the Foreign Office were implicated. . . .

"And so it was Lady Winton who went alone to the Fallons for dinner," said Eden slowly, "while her husband remained behind, ostensibly suffering the effects of some last minute illness of which even Ram Dass was unaware. Do you think she knew?"

Hugh shook his head. "Charles is far too careful to involve his wife in anything as dangerous as arms running. It's entirely possible that she also knew nothing about the deals made in Delhi, despite the fact that she is in possession of Isabel's jewels. She is not a woman governed by a prudent tongue, and Charles wouldn't dare take unnecessary risks by apprising her of his . . . hobbies."

An image of Sir Charles playing the affable host came briefly to Eden's mind and was just as quickly dispelled by the unpleasant memory of the ugly expression on his face when he had ordered his footman Mayhew to unmask her. "I would never have suspected Charles Winton of being an arms runner," she whispered, and added with a sudden catch in her voice, "Or of trying to kill you, either! Mr. Gladstone said he was an evil man, and I imagine he was right."

"Gladstone?" Hugh queried with a start of surprise. "You don't mean William Gladstone, do you?"

"Yes. I met him at the Priory hunt. He seemed a very pleasant man, and we became friends of sorts. Now, why on earth are you laughing? Do you know him? He said he knew you."

"William Gladstone," Hugh informed her disbelievingly, "happens to be one of the most influential speakers of our time. I wouldn't doubt that he'll be elected prime minister one day, and he'll be a damned good one, too. As for his character—it's a known fact that he doesn't think too highly of the female species. I'm surprised that he was civil to you, and you should take it as a rare compliment that you can call yourself his friend. No," he added after a thoughtful pause, "I'm wrong about that. I suppose it shouldn't surprise me at all that you managed to charm him out of his usual bad humor."

"Perhaps he only likes to pretend that he is dour and unkind," suggested Eden. "Though he did say some rather unpleasant things about Sir Charles, and mentioned that the two of you didn't often see eye to eye. Oh! He couldn't have been—was he talking about this arms affair? Did he know—?"

"Yes, he certainly did. And I can only hope that he acted quickly upon hearing of Abercromby's arrest and sent assistance here to Somerset."

"It may be far too late for us by the time it arrives," said Eden softly, and the bluntness of her words hit Hugh like a savage blow to the heart.

"You mustn't talk that way, my love. Sir Charles and his men must have given up the chase, otherwise they would have found us by now." Hugh's voice was urgent with the need to convince her. Drawing her down even tighter into the circle of his arm, he put his lips to her ear and added softly: "We're safe for the time being, Eden, I promise you. Rest now. We'll move on in a little while."

Eden said nothing in response, merely turned her head against him and tiredly closed her eyes. Silence settled over the tiny cave, a silence that lengthened and grew slowly into a tangible vacuum in which every drop of water falling from the surrounding walls and every displaced stone rattling onto the sand from some unseen crevice overhead seemed magnified beyond endurance. Yet they were normal, reassuring sounds that contained no hint of danger, and gradually, their taut nerves began to relax.

Eventually Hugh became aware of Eden's quiet, even breathing and realized that she had fallen asleep. Though he himself was weary beyond belief, he knew he could not afford the same luxury, and he was grateful for the pain of his wounded arm, as it helped keep him awake and reasonably alert.

The minutes ticked by, and when he found that he could no longer tolerate the stillness or the prickling of his numb limbs, Hugh set Eden gently away from him and got to his feet. Feeling his way to the mouth of the cave, he held himself still and listened.

It seemed inconceivable to him that Charles Winton had given up the chase so soon, and he knew that he and Eden could not have managed to elude his men quite so easily. A vague feeling of uneasiness, some whispered instinct of survival, warned Hugh that the night and its devil work were not yet over, and he chafed at the helplessness caused him by Eden's presence, for he could not possibly leave her here alone while he slipped off to investigate the comings and goings outside of the cave.

He knew, of course, that she would not prevent his going if he were to awaken her and tell her that he must. Yet he knew, too, that his conscience and his heart would not permit him to abandon her in this dark, stuffy embrasure that possessed all the makings of a lethal trap. For perhaps the first time in his life he found himself helpless to make a rational decision, and the realization filled him with a curious sense of despair.

Hugh turned and slowly went back inside. He stood for a moment looking down at her, his expression a mixture of frustration and tenderness. He wished he was not so deeply aware in that moment of how very much he loved her, and that she did not look so wrenchingly young and fragile. In the dim light he could see the shadows of exhaustion beneath the dark lashes fanning her cheeks and the scratches on her face. Her sleep was so deep that she did not even stir when he reached down to brush away a strand of silky hair that spilled across her brow.

Dressed in close-fitting breeches and a man's black vest, she reminded him in no small measure of the Indian youth Choto Bai. Memories came tumbling back to him in a tangled profusion of images: the cocky creature in the scarlet turban who had challenged him for the first time in the desert of Mayar, the spirited girl who had annoyed and taunted and delighted him in the moon-drenched darkness of a Delhi garden, the woman who had raised her trembling lips to his and shared a kiss that had been like no other before in his life . . .

Quite suddenly the driving restlessness within Hugh was gone, and the indecision that had filled him with such angry despair was replaced by a certainty that needed no expression. Every one of those memories was as much a part of Eden as she herself had come to be a part of him. His place was here, at her side, and if they were indeed destined not to survive this night, then at least the two of them would die together.

"Good God!"

It was a whispered expletive that was wrenched from him with the force of an unexpected blow. What on earth had he been thinking? Here he was admiring the face of a woman who, not less than ten minutes ago, had been sleeping in such utter darkness that he had been unable to make out so much as a single one of those lovely, haunting features! He had been so wrapped up in his thoughts, so oblivious to everything but his own agonizing indecisions, that he hadn't even noticed that a soft, graying light had crept into the cave and subtly dispersed the gathered gloom.

It seemed to him as if the very air smelled different. A faint breath of wind, actually no more than a draft, stirred the grains of silver sand beneath his feet: a new wind that seemed to him to herald the inevitable passage from darkness into light. The cave walls that had given him the illusion of being so suffocatingly close throughout the night were also beginning to take subtle shape, and as Hugh watched, the contours of the rocks grew more and more distinct until they assumed the pale, unmistakable colors of the coming dawn.

Hugh removed the pistol from his waistband. There was not much left in the way of ammunition, but he took his time nonetheless in loading the weapon before bending to touch Eden on the shoulder.

"Come, *chabeli*," he said softly as she stirred and those dark eyes opened to peer into his face. "It's morning and time for us to go."

He helped her to her feet and watched with a feeling of grave tenderness as she attempted to repair the damages of a night spent sleeping in the sand. Lifting and twisting the heavy tangle of her hair, she pinned it as best she could to the nape of her neck and then slapped the dust from her breeches. Raising her head, she looked at him for a moment in silence, and then a faint smile curved her lips.

"Where to, sahib?"

Grinning, Hugh gestured toward the mouth of the cave, where the dim light trembled and made clear the fact that the world beyond could not be far away.

"Outside, my love. Where else?"

Chapter Twenty-four

The world into which Hugh and Eden emerged after long hours spent in suffocating darkness was one of incredible beauty and grandeur—or so it seemed to them—and served to raise their flagging spirits as nothing else could have done. Below them the land stretched away beneath endless skeins of rising silver mist, and the dawn sun that was creeping over the distant ridge of hills painted the heather and the meadows and the dark margins of the forest in a glorious wash of winter colors: lavender, gray, gold, and green.

Eden, watching as the strengthening light drove away the darkness and paled the lingering stars, thought that she had never seen anything more beautiful than the sleepy hamlets and dales of Somerset visible amid the folds of the distant hills. Unmindful of the cold and the uncomfortable dampness of her clothing, she looked long and lovingly at the sprawling scenery below her.

Hugh, who had been studying the landscape below with equal interest but for entirely different reasons, was thinking that they must have emerged from some obscure tunnel on the far side of the Wookey Hole that no one else seemed to know about. He could not otherwise explain how they came to find themselves alone on the hill, for he was certain that Charles Winton had not yet abandoned his pursuit of them.

"The light will grow stronger, love. We'd better go while we can."

"Where?" she inquired in a whisper.

"Home."

Her eyes widened. "Back to Roxbury?"

His lips twitched despite himself. "Can you think of a better place?"

"What if Sir Charles is waiting for us?"

"There are ways of getting inside the house if it's being watched," Hugh assured her. "Ways that Charles Winton knows nothing about. And the household will not simply stand by and do nothing to help us."

Yes, they would be safe at Roxbury, Eden decided, and found herself filled with a sudden yearning for the tall, ivy-grown structure that, until this moment, she had never really thought of as her home. Yet now she longed for it as a child might long for the close, protective arms of a parent.

It would be difficult returning to Roxbury, Hugh knew, not so much because of the distance, but because they had no horses, and the terrain provided little cover from the men who were doubtless still hunting them on the far side of the cavern. They would have to proceed slowly, and on foot, and exercise an extreme caution in avoiding detection, at least until they had reached the sheltering line of trees in the valley below.

Neither Hugh nor Eden were daunted by the prospect as they discussed it between them. It was enough that they found themselves once again in the open air and free of the uncertainty afforded them by the crippling darkness of that damp, airless cave. And both of them had spent too much time stalking wild game in the arid hills of India not to be unfamiliar with the rudiments of stealth.

"I'll take this route, here," said Hugh at last, pointing out a path directly below them, "and I want you to follow the riverbed. There's more cover that way, and it'll be safer if we travel alone. Here." He extended the pistol as he spoke, but Eden shook her head.

"Take it," he ordered sternly. "You can always use it to signal me in the event you get lost."

"I've no intention of getting lost," Eden informed him tartly, but she took it, and as their hands met, their eyes locked as well, and they stood and looked at one another in a long, silent exchange that needed no words. Then Hugh's voice became deliberately impersonal as he described where they should meet. Moments later they parted.

Though the distance to Roxbury was no more than several miles if one proceeded in a straight path across the moors, it took Hugh and Eden the greater part of the morning to cover it, for they were forced to follow the meandering lines of the river and the uneven margins of the forest. Hunger and the increasing discomfort of blisters slowed Eden's progress by a significant degree, but she was sufficiently driven by her fear for Hugh's safety to push onward with stoic calm. Her hunger could always be appeased later, once they were safely back at Roxbury, and as for the blisters—a thick padding torn from the remnants of her cape and wrapped tightly about her heels helped ease the pain. Hugh's wound could not be so readily remedied, and an unreasoning fear grew within her that the exertion of walking so far, and through such endlessly rough terrain, might prove too taxing for him.

Eden would have been alarmed to discover exactly how justified her fears could be. . . .

Hugh was not at first aware that he had developed a fever; it only seemed to him that the pale winter sun felt unusually warm as it filtered through the ancient trees in the cool of the forest, and that he felt absurdly weak after having negotiated a distance of less than two miles. He was in possession of a raging thirst that remained unslaked despite how often he bent to quench it from the clear depths of a spring, and he found himself obliged to rest for longer periods of time whenever he stopped beside those damp hollows of icy, bubbling water.

"Must be getting old," he thought, and was startled to find that he had muttered the words out loud and that his tongue felt too swollen and thick for his mouth. Flexing his injured arm and feeling the white-hot pain that threaded through the corded muscles, he paused to lean unsteadily against the trunk of a tree and passed a shaky hand across his eyes.

Good God, he couldn't afford to fall ill! Not now, for Christ's sake! Eden had cleaned the wound as best she could and bound it well, and there was no reason at all why he should be suffering the onset of side effects from an infection.

Perhaps I simply *am* getting old, Hugh decided, or I've made the mistake of marrying a woman who has aged me prematurely. He smiled at the thought, yet it was a wry smile that ended in a grimace of pain. Lowering himself to the ground, he rubbed his aching temples and closed his eyes against the sunlight that suddenly seemed too harsh and bright.

He would rest for a moment, he decided groggily, and then be on his way. He had come quite a distance and made good time, after all, and Eden would not yet be awaiting him. Besides, it was undeniably pleasant to sit here in the cool of the morning and rest his head against the moss-grown roots of a tree and think of her, and there certainly was no harm in delaying his arrival at Roxbury for just a few minutes more. . . .

It seemed like hours before Eden, having given up waiting at their rendezvous point and running half-blind with panic through the forests, found him at last. Her heart seemed to stop altogether, and she dropped quickly to her knees beside him. She found that she could scarcely rouse him, and the heat of the fever that consumed him terrified her.

"Hugh!" she whispered urgently, pulling at his sleeve. "You must get up! We cannot stay here!"

He finally opened his eyes to look at her, and she could have wept with relief because, though clouded with fever and pain, his gaze was steady, and he seemed to recognize her. She helped him to his feet, and he stood swaying and frowning down at her, noticing the tears that had dried on her cheeks and the scratches she had endured while plunging through the underbrush in search of him.

"Eden, your face—"

"It doesn't hurt," she assured him, and caught again at his sleeve, swallowing hard as she felt the terrible heat of his body and the fear that cramped her heart in response. "Hugh, we must get away. There are men on horseback patrolling the grounds of the estate. We can't let them find us."

He looked at her, only half comprehending what she said, and she spoke again, urgently. "They're armed with guns. I saw them myself. Where shall we go?"

"We could head for the village, or—or one of the tenant farms," Hugh said slowly, forcing himself to think, though his brain seemed not to want to function anymore.

"We can't. It's too far for you, and doubtless they're being watched, too." Eden's voice broke on a dry sob of despair. "They've got the estate surrounded. I couldn't get any closer than the lodgekeeper's cottage. If only there was somewhere else to go! Somewhere where they wouldn't think to look for us. You need rest, and the attention of a doctor and—" She broke off abruptly and regarded him with an expression that was suddenly, touchingly eager. "Wait, I know! Come with me, Hugh, come, please—"

He did not have the strength to argue. His wounded arm and his head—his entire body, in fact—seemed to him a single throbbing nerve of unendurable pain, and were it not for the supporting hand Eden placed beneath his arm, he did not think he could have gone anywhere at all. How long they walked, and what direction they took, seemed utterly immaterial to him. The fever was mounting, and already the sharp line between reality and delirium was beginning to blur.

Around them the forest was cool and very still, and the sunlight penetrated only dimly through the dense canopy of pine. Yet Eden seemed to know exactly where they were headed, for she turned unhesitatingly down a barely discernible foot path that had perhaps been made by the deer who roved the estate in numbers and sought water from a nearby stream, or tenant farmers who had, before the building of proper roads, once hauled their wares to market across Roxbury land. It was an area that was at best only vaguely familiar to Hugh, who rarely had time to venture into places inaccessible on horseback, yet he remained sufficiently alert despite his fever to take note of the small stone marker they passed some fifteen minutes later, a marker half-hidden by the tangled root of an ancient silver beech and one he instantly recognized.

"Good God!" he exclaimed, drawing to a halt and turning to regard Eden with uncomprehending eyes. "We're on Roxbury land! What the devil are you about, woman? You told me the place was patrolled! If someone should see us—"

"Hush," said Eden quickly, for Hugh's words were slurred and unsteady, and that, as well as the feverish brightness of his eyes, frightened her far more than the fact that his voice had risen alarmingly and could easily be overheard by anyone chancing by. "There's a place I know of not too far from here. I think—I think we shall be safe there, but you must come with me now. Hugh, trust me, please."

Her voice had dropped to a whisper as she spoke, and there were tears in her eyes. Looking down into her white, anxious face, Hugh was overcome by a wrenching tenderness that blotted out his own pain and weariness. His hand cupped her cheek for a brief moment in what might have been a wordless apology or an unspoken declaration of love.

"Go on, then, *chabeli*. I wouldn't dream of not following you."

Ten minutes later they crossed a fallen log spanning a muddy expanse of marsh and came upon a hut made of stones crudely packed together with earth and moss. The ground was cold and damp and green with lichen, and the hut stood in a small hollow just beyond the silvered trunk of an ancient oak, so well hidden that even Hugh, who had ridden this way on occasion and surely must have passed within twenty feet of it, had remained wholly unaware of its existence.

Eden, however, seemed no stranger here. Opening the wooden door, she led him across to a small cot and insisted he lie upon it. There was an earthenware pitcher on a crude table nearby; she offered it to him, and Hugh drank deeply. The water was not fresh, but it soothed the parched rawness of his throat and tongue.

"This place," he said, setting the pitcher aside and looking about the tiny room with its packed dirt floor and the heavy matting covering the single opening that served as a window. "What is it? How the devil did you find it?"

Eden's lips curved. "I'm told it was once used as a hideout for some of Somerset's more notorious highwaymen. Perhaps Red Rory himself once hid here. And I found it quite by accident."

"You shouldn't have been riding through this part of the estate to begin with," Hugh countered, seeing no humor in the situation. "It isn't safe, what with the bogs providing such treacherous footing. Supposing your horse had turned up lame, or you'd been thrown?"

"I had nothing better to do than explore the grounds," Eden answered lightly. "You were gone so often, you see. And I really did stumble upon it by accident."

"That's how she found me, too, Your Grace," came a voice from behind them.

Hugh's head whipped around, and he reached reflexively for his pistol, forgetting that he had given it to Eden. He heard her give a small, glad cry and watched incredulously as she hurried across to take a young man in rough homespun by the arm and pull him toward the cot.

"This is Tom Parker, Hugh," she told him breathlessly. "He's become . . . well, a friend of sorts. Oh, Tom, I'm so glad you're here! You'll help us, won't you?"

She was visibly startled when Hugh gave an unexpectedly harsh laugh, his eyes having come to rest on the younger man's face. "Still poaching on my land, son?"

A wave of color flared across Tom's thin features. "Not anymore, Your Grace."

"Yet I see you haven't given up trespassing."

The boy swallowed hard. "I'm supposing that's true, Your Grace. But I ain't doin' no 'arm comin' 'ere. I just likes to be orf by myself from time to time."

"Do you?" Hugh inquired darkly. Turning to Eden, he added, "I want you to know that I caught this young fellow leaving Roxbury land with a pouchful of illegal game not too long ago. I must have been mad to let him go unpunished. And you say he's a friend of yours?"

She nodded somewhat uncertainly.

"I suppose I shouldn't be surprised."

"Hugh, please," Eden whispered with a catch in her voice, and his heart softened because he could not find it in him to rebuke her just now. He held out his hand to her and wondered, surely not for the first time, if he was ever going to understand and come to terms with the unpredictable child-woman who was his wife. He felt her cool hand slip tremulously into his, and a raw, helpless ache seemed to close his throat. What he should have been, of course, was angry—entirely, utterly, unappeasably angry, and yet he found that it no longer mattered to him that Eden should have made the acquaintance of one of the poachers he and Pierce had hunted down on Roxbury land not a fortnight ago.

Good God, had it really been only a fortnight ago? No, not even that, for Eden herself hadn't been at Roxbury longer than a week. Hugh shook his head and tried to make sense of everything that had happened in the course of those short seven days, things that suddenly seemed entirely senseless to him—the murder of Sir Arthur Willoughby, for instance, and the fact that he and Eden had been forced to spend the night in a cave, and lastly and most worriedly, the fact that Roxbury was surrounded like some besieged feudal castle by Charles Winton's men. . . .

"Must do something about that," Hugh decided thickly, struggling to his feet. But it seemed as if his body were no longer prepared to obey the commands of his brain, and after a moment he fell back dizzily, exhausted by the struggle of simply attempting to move.

"Tom, you must help him," Eden whispered, grasping the lapels of the young man's coat. "He needs a warm bed and dry clothes and—and a doctor."

Tom looked at the half-conscious man who lay shivering on the cot behind her. "We can't move 'im now, Your Grace. It's too dangerous. Not just for 'im. For you, too."

"Then you've seen those men at the gates?"

Tom nodded. "My cousin wot works at Priory Park told me wot 'appened last night. I figured this ud be where you'd come to 'ide." He frowned down at her. "Wot be they wantin' from you?"

Eden told him, speaking in a low, urgent tone, watching the disbelief and anger that crossed his face in response.

"There must be some way to get help," Eden concluded desperately. "The police or the local magistrate—"

"'E wouldn't be of no 'elp," Tom informed her darkly, being more than fleetingly familiar with the self-serving, interfering, elderly magistrate who practiced such execrable law in the nearby town. "None of 'em ud be— the police, neither, I mean. Not seein' as they got themselves buried deep in Master Winton's pockets. Everybody knows it, though there's few 'oo'd come right out and say so. We'd be better off doin' something on our own."

"We?"

"Aye. Me and a few of the lads I know."

Eager color flamed in Eden's face, and she forced herself to speak steadily. "Then you'll help us, Tom?"

"That's wot I comes 'ere for," Tom said simply. " 'Is Grace did me a good turn once. I ain't forgot that." He grinned unexpectedly and patted her hand. "Now don't you worry. It ain't so bad. Just give me a bit of time, and I'll comes up wiv something. I always do."

But in the end it was Eden who came up with a plan— Eden, who had grown up under the influence of a Rajput maharajah and who had unknowingly learned to think and act exactly as that crafty old warrior might have done— and Eden who had taken to heart a comment made half-jokingly by a hastily summoned acquaintance of Tom's: "Know what? We ought to storm the bleedin' 'ouse ourselves! Just like we was in the bloody army. . . ."

Hugh did not recover consciousness until well into the afternoon. The brief winter day was already drawing to a close when he opened his eyes at last, and the shadows fell long across the floor of the hut. A blanket had been thrown over him, and his wounded arm had been crudely but carefully bound, and though he felt absurdly light-headed and weak, he realized that his fever had broken. Turning his head, he saw that he was alone, and he frowned and came up on one elbow, calling for Eden, his voice unconsciously harsh because of the sudden fear that drove him. There was a rustle and a movement in the corner, and Hugh relaxed, thinking she was safe.

But it was not Eden who came to stand beside the cot, but an impossibly bent and shriveled old woman who regarded him keenly and with no small measure of interest.

"Awake, are ye, zur? Didn't think it ud 'appen so soon. Cares for water, do ye, zur?"

"Where the devil is my wife?" Hugh demanded, and was startled to discover that the forcibly uttered words were no louder than a whisper.

"Don't be worryin' after 'er, zur. Ast me to looks out for ye, she did. Didn't want to at first, I'm believin', but I told 'er I've nursed plenty o' sick 'uns in my day, and I'm o'er past eighty. Tom Parker's me grandson," she added with a trace of pride, and her eyes gleamed in the myriad folds and wrinkles that crisscrossed her face. "A good lad, an' I knows wot yer did for 'im. Only right to return the favor now 'Is Grace be needin' 'elp. That's wot I tolds 'im, zur."

Hugh had closed his eyes and fallen back onto the cot, and when she finished at last with her ramblings, he inquired again, without bothering to look at her but in a tone that clearly indicated he expected an answer, "Where the devil is my wife?"

"Gone away wiv me Tom," answered the old crone simply, and began to smooth the blanket that covered his body. She gave a frightened gasp as his hand closed unexpectedly about her wrist, and she swallowed hard as she looked down into a pair of eyes that were no longer clouded with fever but disconcertingly hard and bright.

"I don't rightly know where they've went, Your Grace," she said in a frightened whisper. "All Tom ud say is they was on their way t' 'ouse. I don't know what they're plannin' to do."

She fell back as Hugh released her and came unsteadily to his feet. Without another word he stumbled from the hut, and she stared after him, rubbing her wrist while tears of resentment glimmered in her eyes.

The wrought-iron gates that guarded the front entrance of Roxbury stood open, and a sentry on horseback paced restlessly before it. Lights glowed in the lodgekeeper's cottage beyond, and Hugh felt certain that it was occupied by Charles Winton's men. Daylight was fading, but a greenish-blue glow lingered on the western horizon and afforded sufficient light for him to see the expression of boredom on the face of the guard who trotted his mount up and down the gravel drive.

They're getting cold and hungry and tired of waiting for me, he thought, and, indeed, not a half minute later the approach of other men on horseback prompted him to pull back into the thickets, where he had no trouble over-hearing their disgruntled exchange. None of them appeared particularly pleased with their duties, and a few of them had begun to question the wisdom of waiting through the night when it was obvious that Hugh Gordon was elsewhere by now—probably halfway to London, as popular opinion seemed to have it.

Other men soon emerged from the lodgekeeper's cottage, lending their voices to a host of similar complaints, and Hugh was wondering how best to make use of their obvious disgruntlement when Charles Winton rode up.

"I would suggest that you men return to your posts," he ordered them.

One of the bolder of the malcontents spoke up from the crowd: "Can't see as it'll do much good, sir. Roxbury's no fool. 'E won't come round 'ere when 'e finds we're waiting for 'im."

"On the contrary," said Sir Charles with an unpleasant smile. "I know Hugh Gordon better than any of you. The very fact that his home is besieged will be enough to draw him out."

You bastard, thought Hugh, and felt a surge of rage pack him by the throat—because he knew that what Winton said was true.

"Perhaps," Sir Charles continued after a thoughtful pause, "you men might find the task more to your liking if I were to place the sum of fifty pounds on Hugh Gordon's head.''

There was a murmur from the crowd, for it was a startling sum, and someone called out enthusiastically: ''Dead or alive, sir?''

Charles's lips curved. ''Any way you please, Mr. Mayhew.''

Now there was a fellow with whom he had an unquestionable score to settle, Hugh decided grimly. It was regrettable, in fact, that he didn't have a pistol on him at the moment, but then again cold-blooded murder would accomplish little save revealing his hiding place to Sir Charles and his men.

Crawling deeper into the thickets, he stretched out on his stomach and mentally reviewed a list of Roxbury's neighbors, trying to decide who among them might prove willing to help him. Sifting and discarding names with unsettling speed because he could not be certain of their relationship with Priory Hall, he settled at last upon Major Edgar Chiverton, a crusty old curmudgeon who had fought his last battle at the Crimea and who would assuredly prove eager to take up his sword and lance one more time for a worthy cause.

Somerset, Hugh had reflected on many an occasion in the past, was littered with the aging relics of British army campaigns, and while he had frequently viewed the fact with no small measure of cynicism, he was suddenly glad for the number of retired officers in his midst. An old, enthusiastic India hand like Edgar Chiverton would not hesitate to pick up arms against an enemy of the empire, b'gad!—even if it *was* his long-standing neighbor Charles Winton, and doubtless he'd have no trouble rounding up a veritable pack of other army graybeards whose aim would still be steady.

But Edgar Chiverton lived in Dorling Heath, and Dorling Heath was six miles distant. On foot it would take Hugh the better part of the night to get there, for he was not so reckless as to ignore the fact that he was absurdly weak from fever and the loss of blood. He wasn't certain that he could manage the distance, and in the back of his mind, nagging him even more so than the unpleasant throbbing of his wound, was the question of Eden's whereabouts. He certainly couldn't leave without finding her. In fact, he ought to take her with him, for she'd be safe in Dorling Heath, a sleepy little hamlet tucked beneath the shadows of the Mendip Hills where Charles would never think to look for her.

I should have taken her there in the first place instead of coming here, Hugh thought, and felt a surge of anger at the realization that in his dazed, feverish state he had probably made a serious blunder.

His thoughts were broken off without warning by a shout that came through the darkness from somewhere beyond the grounds of the estate. The shout was repeated, and this time he could not doubt what he heard, though he could scarcely believe it:

"Ready, all! Advance!"

A bugle shrilled, the notes harsh and discordant as though its player was badly out of practice, and Hugh watched, incredulous, as the roadway beyond the dark margin of trees was suddenly transformed into a seething, thundering mass of horseflesh. In the dim light it was difficult to tell how many of them there were, but there was no mistaking the strict formation and the position of each rider, or the glint of starlight on freshly polished arms.

A cavalry charge.

Hugh had seen enough of them to recognize this one at once, but his disbelieving mind would not accept what he was seeing. It was improbable, impossible! He must be suffering the onset of some fever-induced delirium. There in the lead was old Andrew Carstairs, a former colonel of the Twelfth Calcutta N.I., and a man normally so bent by gout and rheumatism that he was forced to walk with the aid of a cane. Though the colonel's faded uniform bulged at the seams and his whiskers whipped ludicrously about his cheeks, his seat was impeccable, and he brandished his sword with all the hot enthusiasm of a youth riding into his first glorious campaign.

Behind him and a little to his right, leading a band of wildly whooping outriders, came Eden. She had tied Red Rory's mask about her face once again and was carrying a musket from which two strips of cloth flapped like he-

raldic banners: the plaid of the Frasers and the crisp, unmistakable colors of the Gordons. She passed so close to
Hugh's hiding place that he could see the dark blue of
her eyes behind the mask, and as she swept past him he
was up and running, fear and fury lashing him on like a
white-hot brand.

A cavalry charge was undoubtedly the last thing the
denizens of rural Somerset ever expected to see, and
judging from the reaction of Sir Charles's men it was
nothing that any of them cared to experience. There were
shouts of alarm and a mad thrashing of dimly seen figures
as the lot of them scattered like panicked pea fowl. It was
Sir Charles—plunging his horse between them to cut off
their escape and exhorting them at the top of his voice to
fire, fire!—who prevented them from fleeing into the
darkness.

Yet not all of them turned to run. Some stood their
ground or reined in their horses to look. Quickly seeing
that the attackers were nothing more than elderly men and
unskilled laborers from the village and tenant farms, they
lifted their weapons and opened fire, sending a furious
crackling of shot into the oncoming crush.

Hugh reached the roadway just as a riderless horse
came hurtling past, and he seized it by the bridle and attempted to drag it to a halt. He felt the shock as the
bandage about his arm tore free, and the panicked beast
neighed frantically and swerved. Hugh hung on grimly
and, running alongside it, managed at last to haul himself
onto the crupper.

A moment later he was in the saddle, digging in his
heels in an effort to bring the lathering beast under control. The reins were sticky with the blood that poured
freely from his arm, but Hugh scarcely noticed. Leaning
low, he sent the animal hurling forward, swerving and
threading his way between the other riders in a frantic effort to reach Eden.

A shot whistled past his cheek, and a horse galloping
close to Hugh's left flank stumbled and went down. His
rider collapsed amidst a tangle of limbs, and Hugh
reached across and managed, more by luck than any measure of skill, to snatch his weapon as he fell. Jerking it

to him, he recognized the familiar weight of a shotgun beneath his hand and flicked open the chamber to make certain it was loaded. It was not a particularly maneuverable weapon, but he had nothing else, and he was determined to make best use of it.

"Close up! Close up, damn you!" old Carstairs was roaring from somewhere in the lead, and, incredibly, the line of madly galloping horses moved closer together, bearing down on the wide-open gates in a seething mass of pounding hooves and wildly yelling men. Winton's men charged out to meet them, firing as they went, and for a brief moment Hugh felt as if he were looking down some long, narrow tunnel at a fantastic scene that could not be real.

But it was, and if he needed further evidence of the danger, he had it when he spotted Eden and a small detachment of riders careening forward to take the oncoming horsemen by the left flank. The advance was carried out in pukka light cavalry style, a bold maneuver she could only have learned at the knee of some brilliant cavalry officer who had served with her father.

"Damn you!" Hugh cursed beneath his breath, not really knowing at whom his fury was directed, and lifted his gun.

A chorus of yells erupted from both sides as they met and clashed amid the wild plunging of the frantic horses. Hugh rose up in the stirrups, the shotgun cradled against his cheek, and a man who would have fired a pistol point-blank at his wife jerked and spun out of the saddle. Eden's head whipped about, and their eyes met and held, but Hugh was not at all certain she recognized him.

"Get back!" he shouted, cupping his hands in order to be heard above the confusion. "Get out of the line of fire!"

But Eden turned away, and Hugh could not know if it was because she hadn't heard him or because she had chosen simply to ignore him. Grinding his teeth together, he dug in his heels and urged his horse to a hand gallop. At that same moment another man broke unexpectedly from the press and charged toward Eden, pistol brandished, and a low moan of anguish rose in Hugh's throat because his weapon was empty, and he knew he could not reach her in time.

It was Colonel Carstairs who was instrumental in saving Eden's life: arthritic old Carstairs, who had unhesitatingly offered his services upon hearing for himself what all the fuss at Roxbury was about, and who had insisted on carrying his clanking, cumbersome cavalry saber despite the fact that his palsied hand could barely lift it. In the grip of battle fever, however, he seemed twenty years younger, and the hand that wielded the pitted weapon was surprisingly steady. He had discharged his aged musket some time ago, yet when he, too, turned his head and saw the danger for the young duchess, he rode forward with a piercing yell. The saber moved in a sweeping arc, and Charles Winton's body was jerked from the saddle, its partially severed head lolling grotesquely.

Hugh did not even bother to check his horse's stride at the horrible sight. Guiding the animal with his knees, he pushed his way through the confusion and had just managed to reach Eden's side when it stumbled unexpectedly. Jerking up on the reins, Hugh realized at once that it had been hit, but by then it was too late, and he was unable to prevent himself being hurtled over its head as it sank beneath him. He felt a moment of weightlessness, then jarring pain as the ground rushed up to meet him. Landing full on his wounded arm, he heard the bones snap, and in the next instant darkness closed about him.

Chapter Twenty-five

"*Ohé!*" wailed Ram Dass, twisting his hands together in genuine agony. "*Ohé,* I have killed the Hazrat-sahib!"

"Be still, will you? Good God, Your Grace, can't you make the fellow stop his bloody caterwauling?"

Wordlessly Eden left her place at her husband's bedside and crossed the room. "He lives, Ram Dass," she said quietly, laying her hand on the Indian's arm. "And the hakim is skilled. He will not let him die."

"An *Angrezi* hakim!" Ram Dass said scornfully. "What does he know of medicines and healing? The fever is very bad. See how he speaks to himself as if beset by demons!"

Eden turned her troubled face to the bed, where Hugh lay muttering to himself and thrashing feebly while the doctor held his arm still and hovered over him with a grave expression. "I do not think—" She swallowed hard. "I do not think he will die. It is only because he has lost so much blood."

"And that is because I shot his horse from beneath him," Ram Dass lamented. "It is my fault that his arm is broken and that his life now lies in the hands of the gods."

Eden said nothing. That Ram Dass genuinely despaired of Hugh's recovery was obvious, and she wondered if perhaps it would not have been better to prevent him from entering the sickroom. But he had been waiting outside the door all night, and she did not have the heart to send him away.

Wearily she turned her head and saw the harsh winter sunlight falling in brilliant bars between the half-opened drapes. With a small shock she realized that the dawn had come without her being aware of it. She could scarcely believe that the doctor had only been here for little above two hours. It seemed like days, weeks, a lifetime since the storming of Roxbury's gates, and yet it had only been last night.

Eden herself had seen Ram Dass fire the shot that had accidentally felled Hugh's mount, but she had not known just then how badly he had been hurt. Even Ram Dass had not realized at first what he had done. He had appeared on foot at the outside of the gate just as the opposing sides had met and clashed, and it was the battle cry that had sounded from his throat—a Pushtu battle cry like those that had echoed on the Afghan borders since the long-ago invasions of the Mughals—that had drawn Eden's head about. He had been carrying an ancient *jezail*—God alone knew where he had come by it—and Eden had seen the bright spurt of exploding powder as he discharged it into the crowd. His aim had been good; he would have hit Charles Winton at the same moment that Colonel Carstairs's saber felled him, yet Hugh's horse, stretched out in a gallop, had taken the shot in the neck.

Even before Eden reached her husband's side, Tom Parker was already there, lifting up Hugh's head and cradling it in his lap. They had fashioned a stretcher from the door of the lodgekeeper's cottage and carried him up to the house while Colonel Carstairs saw to the disarming of Charles Winton's men. It was not the glorious surrender the old man had envisioned, for with the death of their master the fight had largely gone out of them, and they seemed willing enough to obey Carstairs's commands.

Hugh regained consciousness only once: when they had laid him on his bed and their unskilled handling had badly jostled his broken arm and caused him sufficient pain to drag him back to agonized awareness. He had looked up through the waves of throbbing scarlet mist to see Eden's face above his, so white and grave and frightened that he had not recognized it at first. But then his vision had cleared and with it, for the moment, his memory. He had taken her chin in his hand, his grip surprisingly firm, and said the rasping words that haunted her still:

"I can't forgive you for this, Eden. I'm sorry, not ever."

Dr. Theodore Blakeney had arrived a few hours later to find the house ablaze with lights and considerable unrest and confusion still hovering inside and about the grounds. Yet up in the west wing where the injured duke had been placed, there was nothing but somber silence to greet him. A white-faced servant showed him upstairs, and he had curtly sent away the others who hovered anxiously in the doorway. He was nearing eighty, and his once burly frame had been bent and withered by the damp and cold of countless English winters, yet he was still a figure of unquestioned authority within the community, and they had obediently withdrawn.

Eden alone remained while he set Hugh's badly broken arm and sewed together the ragged edges of the gaping wound, ending the terrible bleeding at last. As he removed the strip of cloth that had been knotted around a broken stick and bound above the elbow and the still pulsing wound, he had remarked with approval that it had doubtless served to save His Grace's life, and who in the household had known enough to fashion such a crude yet effective tourniquet?

"I did," Eden had said quietly, and the elderly doctor had turned his head and really looked at her for the first time. He could not say that he cared in particular for the young duchess of Roxbury's attire—she was wearing riding breeches and boots like a man—but then again he was old and admittedly out of touch with the times, and if such was the current fashion . . . Besides, there was something in the still young face that appealed to him, and she followed his terse directions gravely and without question, a trait one did not often find in untrained medical laymen in general and flighty young women in particular.

"You have had medical training, Your Grace?" he inquired with a sudden show of interest.

Eden shook her head. "I grew up in India."

"Ah," he said, for the simple comment served to make a great deal clear to him. The medical conditions in India were unbelievably bad, judging from the descriptions of those colleagues of his who had journeyed there or had been mad enough to actually attempt to set up a foreign practice within the country's borders. Untold diseases flourished in the glittering golden cities of the East, and India was littered with the graves of English babies and hapless mothers who had not been able to survive the rigors of birth in that cruel, unclean, and squalid land.

Taking the untold hardships of Indian life into account, it shouldn't have surprised Theodore Blakeney that a young woman like the duchess of Roxbury had learned to stanch wounds and assist in setting broken bones with a skill he found lamentably lacking in his own trained assistants.

"So you are Hugh's Indian bride," he had said, his tone deliberately conversational, and for the first time he allowed a smile to play across his tired, serious face.

Eden had gazed up at him with wide, confused eyes, and he had smiled at her again.

"I've known your husband for many, many years, Your Grace. Even before he came to live at Roxbury. I had a medical practice in London, in the West End. Lived there for twenty-three years before retiring home to Wells. Our paths crossed from time to time. He's a fine young man, you know."

"Yes," Eden whispered, her throat aching, and she had turned away so that he could not see the sudden, childish trembling of her lower lip. Surely Hugh must be out of danger now that the doctor had relaxed and become so unexpectedly gregarious?

But half an hour later Dr. Blakeney no longer felt inclined or even able to indulge in cheerful gossip. He no longer said anything at all, in fact, for Hugh's fever had abruptly returned, and in the doctor's handling and sudden silence there hovered the dreadful certainty that Eden could not bring herself to put into words.

"He will not die," she repeated to Ram Dass. "The hakim says he is strong—stronger than most men. It is only a question of time."

"As you wish, my daughter," Ram Dass replied solemnly, but it was obvious that he did not believe her, and, grief-stricken, he left the room.

Eden turned her face to the wall and, pressing her knuckles to her lips, wept silently and helplessly.

"Perhaps you should retire, Your Grace."

A gentle hand was on her arm, and she turned and looked up into Theodore Blakeney's sympathetic eyes.

"I'm certain you haven't slept all night, and though I don't mean to sound disrespectful, you look as if you need some rest."

Eden pushed the hair from her eyes and, accepting the handkerchief he offered, wiped the tears from her cheeks. Actually she hadn't slept for two nights now, but she was not about to admit as much to the doctor. She had no intention of leaving until Hugh was out of danger, and perhaps the doctor sensed as much, for he gestured to a nearby chaise and suggested that perhaps she might like to rest there for a while.

"You'll be here with him should he need you," he pointed out, and it was the truth of this remark and the fact that she was feeling admittedly weary that convinced Eden to give in.

Incredibly, she did fall asleep, her eyes closing even before Dr. Blakeney had managed to unfold a blanket and lay it across her. She did not stir as the daylight brightened and the sun crawled higher and higher across the wintry heavens, nor did she notice when it began to wane at last and the sky was painted a fiery wash of apricot and gold, then palest rose, finally the deep indigo blue of night, and the lamps at Hugh's bedside were lit one by one.

By then a number of people had come and gone in the corridor without, exchanging whispered comments with the doctor through the half-opened door. Some of them had not been pleased upon being turned away, but the good doctor had been adamant, and the scowling visage of Roxbury's formidable housekeeper, who had come upstairs to lend her assistance, was enough to daunt even the most determined of men.

When Eden awoke at last the night had ended and another dawn had broken on the horizon; she had slept round the clock without even being aware of the passage of time. Though she was furious that Dr. Blakeney had not bothered to awaken her, she forgot her resentment the moment she slipped off the chaise and touched Hugh's forehead and knew that the fever was gone. He slept deeply, unaware of her presence, and her heart contracted as she studied his thin face, recalling Dr. Blakeney's comments concerning the fact that he might never fully recover the use of his broken arm.

Perhaps it was just as well, she decided. Then he would no longer be asked to endanger his life for some patriotic cause that meant nothing to her and shouldn't to him. Let the ministers in London, let the police and the C.I.D., worry about keeping order in their empire. Private citizens should remain just that, and Hugh had told her often enough that managing both Roxbury and Arran Mhór was sufficiently taxing to keep him well occupied.

One had to consider, too, that if Hugh's arm was indeed irrevocably damaged, he would never again find the same satisfaction in hunting *chinkara* or tigers and boars in the Indian hills, inasmuch as his aim would be sorely affected. Yet even that realization did not cause Eden undue dismay, for to her it meant that Hugh would have to content himself with hunting woodcocks in the forests of Roxbury and never stray far from her side again.

Her eyes opened wide at the thought. What on earth was she thinking? That the two of them would live happily ever after with no more secrets or dissent or resentment between them? That they could put the past completely behind them and settle into the contented life of a loving couple, perhaps with children to bless them?

It didn't seem likely. Not when one considered their volatile temperaments or the fact that Hugh had told her he could never forgive her for her part in the charge on Roxbury's gates.

Eden would have given anything to prevent his being so badly injured, but how could she have known that he would be there? She had thought him safe in the cottage deep in Roxbury's woods with Tom Parker's grandmother watching over him. It was unfair that he should blame her for that, unfair! And yet she could not forget those simple words or the finality with which they had been uttered.

I wonder if he means to send me away, Eden thought, and because it was an intolerable surmise she fled the room and Hugh's presence and went quickly downstairs.

There was little peace to be found there, for the house was filled with strangers, and Eden stopped short on the threshold of the salon, bewildered by the sight of half a dozen unknown men lounging in various chairs about the room. It was obvious that they had been there for some time, for the table before them was stacked with discarded cups of coffee and half-eaten pastries. Belatedly Eden realized that she had not bothered to remove her breeches and boots, and if she needed further evidence of the inappropriate state of her attire, she had it in their startled looks and the sudden silence that settled over the room at the sight of her.

"Gentlemen?" Eden inquired at last, squaring her slim shoulders.

The quietly uttered word had a remarkable effect on them in that they all leaped to their feet in a single, almost laughable motion and made absurd little half bows in her direction. Yet there was nothing the least amusing in the behavior of the burly man who introduced himself as George Trumbull and whose numerous titles, offered in a supercilious tone, made little sense to Eden. She could only assume that he was some high-ranking figure of local authority and that he had come to investigate the events of the night before.

In that she was quite correct, and for the next fifteen minutes she politely answered his questions and those of the others who pressed curiously about her and couldn't help but think that it all sounded positively ludicrous when viewed by the light of day. Yet the gravity of their collective expressions and the fact that her husband lay gravely ill upstairs underscored the seriousness of the matter, and their questions would doubtless have gone on and on had Dr. Blakeney not chanced upon them and seen for himself the white exhaustion on Eden's face.

Incredibly, he managed to get rid of them; once they were gone Eden sank gratefully into a nearby chair and buried her face in her hands.

"I'm sorry you had to endure such unpleasantness, my dear," the doctor said, laying a reassuring hand on her shoulder. "They forget themselves, I think, in their zealous pursuit of the truth."

He went to the sideboard and poured her a brandy. "I don't believe they were particularly satisfied with my answers," she said pensively.

"They'll probably be back," Dr. Blakeney agreed with genuine regret, "and I'm certain there will be others from London arriving before too long. The county is in an understandable uproar over this, and I'm afraid you won't be spared further questions."

"I don't mind," she assured him quietly. "I only hope I can tell them what they wish to know . . . provided I am still here."

"What do you mean?" inquired Dr. Blakeney sharply. "Are you planning to leave Roxbury in the near future?"

Eden, her head resting wearily against the back of her chair, looked at him but said nothing, and a sudden sadness crept to her great, dark eyes.

Nightfall came, and with it a howling north wind that rattled the windows and flung pellets of frozen sleet against the panes. Fires had been lit in nearly every room, and the great house of Roxbury took on a warm and inviting coziness despite its vast size, while a measure of peace crept at last upon its weary, beleaguered occupants.

Thanks to Dr. Blakeney's rigorous objections, the local officials had given their reluctant word not to return until someone of higher authority arrived from London, and the household relaxed at the assurance of a reprieve. The fact that the duke was reportedly resting easier had done much in the way of restoring the spirits of the anxious servants, and most of them went about their tasks with their usual alacrity, though they continued to whisper among themselves and speculate on the fantastic happenings of the night Charles Winton had died at the gates of their home.

Eden, too, had recovered a goodly amount of her composure, and no one could possibly suspect that her outward calm was a mere façade. The troubles and turmoil that weighed heavily upon her mind went unnoticed by all save Hugh, who awoke some time around midnight with a badly raging thirst. A groan escaped him without his being aware of it, and instantly someone moved from the shadows and bent over him. A cup of water was held to his lips, and he drank greedily until its contents were gone.

Falling back against the pillows, he lay still for a time, then turned his head and slowly opened his eyes. Eden was seated in a nearby armchair, her back to him as she stared pensively out into the darkness. The light of a single lamp fell upon her hair, which hung loosely down her back, and illuminated its bright golden highlights so that it gleamed like newly minted gold. Hugh did not speak. He merely looked at her, remembering a long-ago night in a Delhi ballroom when he had likened the color of Eden's hair to ripening wheat and had thought to himself that she was by far the most beautiful woman he had ever seen.

He saw her head turn and the slim, lovely line of her cheek and throat come out of the shadows, and when she looked at him he noticed that the expression in her eyes was faraway and troubled. He held out his hand to her, and she came to him, letting him draw her down beside him. Resting his cheek against her hair, he found he did not have the strength to speak, and so he only held her, feeling the tension in her body and wondering at its cause.

For a long moment there was silence between them, then Eden stirred restlessly, and when she spoke at last her voice was thick, as though she had been crying—or attempting very hard to hold back her tears.

"Dr. Blakeney says you'll be all right now. It was the fever that worried him. How is your arm? Does it hurt very badly?"

Hugh shook his head. He was feeling light-headed and sleepy, and it was undeniably pleasant to feel Eden's slim softness in his arms once again. It may be that he drifted off to sleep for a time, for another lengthy silence fell between them before he became aware of a gentle touch on his cheek. Opening his eyes, he saw Eden leaning over him, her expression grave as she looked at him, and perhaps it was a trick of the light or his own dazed imaginings, but it seemed to him as if she were regarding him with an absorption he had never known before—as though she were attempting to memorize every line and angle of his face and so commit it forever to her heart.

The hand that had been caressing his cheek slid away, and Hugh felt her lips brush his. As she bent forward a stray curl fell across his brow, its touch as gentle as her kiss had been. Then he heard the rustle of crinolines as she straightened, and the door closed softly behind her.

There had been something inarguably final about that sound, but Hugh, drifting in and out of that half-wakeful state that so often follows on the heels of a violent illness, remained unaware of it.

Not until morning, when he awoke with a remarkably clear head, did he recall the events of the night before and attach his own significance to Eden's behavior.

"Where is my wife?" he inquired ill-temperedly of Dr. Blakeney, who had braved the cold and the considerable distance from his home to check on his recovering patient.

"I imagine she's still abed," said the doctor with some surprise. "Why don't you ask the maid to look in on her?"

But the girl who was summarily dispatched to Eden's room returned moments later with the breathless disclosure that Her Grace was not there, and that she had found a sealed envelope on the mantel, which she handed over to Hugh.

"I trust there's nothing amiss?" asked Dr. Blakeney, watching the color leave Hugh's face as he read it.

A thin white line appeared about Hugh's mouth. "I'm afraid there is. She's gone to London. She doesn't say why, only that on no account am I to send someone after her."

"What on earth could she mean to do there?" inquired Dr. Blakeney, shocked.

"Isn't it obvious? Sail for India."

Dr. Blakeney looked on in amazement as Hugh swung himself out of bed, wincing at the pain of his wounded arm and swaying somewhat unsteadily once he was standing on his feet. "May I ask what you intend to do?" he inquired coolly.

"Go after her, of course."

"My dear young fellow, you'll do no such thing! Not unless you care to die on the road, for I assure you that—"

But Hugh was already gone, calling loudly for his valet and turning a deaf ear to the entreaties that someone else be sent to London in his place. A hasty interrogation of the staff revealed the unexpected news that a letter had arrived for Her Grace yesterday afternoon, though the footman who had delivered it into her hand could not be called upon to say where it had come from or what it might have contained. No one else could shed additional light upon the matter, for all were in agreement that Her Grace had appeared quite calm and composed last night, if not a little distracted, which was understandable given the shock of the past few days.

Baffled and angry beyond belief, Hugh strode into Eden's bedroom and rummaged impatiently through her belongings, yet could find no trace of the letter. His head ached abominably, and he was just about to give up the search when his eyes fell on a small box tucked unobtrusively among a collection of hats and gloves on the top shelf of an armoire. Opening it, Hugh was startled to find a military bandolier and other accoutrements that he guessed had belonged to Eden's father. Not wishing to disturb such personal effects, he began to replace them, only to pause as he spotted a bundle of letters in the bottom of the box.

Perusing them quickly, he was disappointed to find that all of them had been written long before the mutiny, and that most of them had been penned by Colonel Hamilton himself. With a growing sense of frustration, Hugh laid them aside and unfolded a sheaf of heavy vellum stamped with an official crimson seal. Though time and the ravages of India's summers had faded the neat lines, he could easily make out the signatures on the bottom of each page. Ram Bundoon Singh was a man not unknown to him. Before the mutiny he had resided near the Red Fort in Delhi and had been considered one of the most highly respected gemcutters on the continent. His painstakingly prepared documents, Hugh saw, contained notorized appraisals of numerous gems and other pieces of hand-worked jewelry belonging to Donan Hamilton, and Hugh was astounded by the value in pounds sterling assigned each one.

He stood frowning down at them for a moment, wondering if Eden had been aware of their existence. Though the documents appeared not to have been touched in a great while, he could not believe that Eden had failed to read them. Was it possible that her abrupt departure for London had something to do with Isabel's jewels? Perhaps the British officer Eden had told him about— But Hugh found he could not accept the possibility that Eden had traveled alone to London to meet Sitka's murderer.

Nevertheless, when he left the house some ten minutes later he rode as though the devil himself were behind him, unmindful of the throbbing of his head and the dull ache of his broken arm. He was accompanied by Pierce, Roxbury's stablemaster, who had refused to the point of rudeness to permit his master to ride alone. Hugh had relented, not so much because he cared for companionship, but because he did not intend to waste further time arguing. He had no idea what sort of trouble Eden was courting, but it seemed highly likely that she had once again behaved in an unthinking manner, which could, as Hugh well knew, prove disastrous for everyone involved.

It was fortunate that the burly stablemaster had insisted on accompanying his master, for they had not ridden above a half dozen miles before Hugh found himself unexpectedly overcome by a damning weakness—to the extent that he would have lost control of his mount had Pierce not seen him sway in the saddle and, reaching quickly across, taken up the reins and brought both horses to a halt. Guiding one by the hand and the other with his knees, he led them to the next posting inn, where he calmly procured a carriage.

Hugh, who was by now sufficiently ill to lack the strength to protest, allowed himself to be helped inside and leaned back against the worn leather seat with his eyes closed. Within minutes the coach had pulled out of the inn yard, and as it turned onto the road it promptly lurched into the first of a nightmare series of potholes, and badly jolted his mending arm. Whereupon Hugh promptly—and perhaps quite thankfully—lost consciousness.

"It was kind of you to come, Your Grace," said the slim young man in civilian attire, running his fingers somewhat nervously through his dark, disheveled hair. "I hadn't expected—that is, when I wrote to you I did not think—"

"That I would come at once to see you?" Eden smiled at him. Though he was not much older than she, she felt a strong maternal need to put him at ease, especially because he seemed so inordinately shy and blushed furiously whenever he looked at her. "Don't you think I would want to hear firsthand about my father? You said you had news of him?"

"Yes," he said with considerable relief, though the truth of the matter was nearer the fact that he had not expected Eden Hamilton to be so disconcertingly lovely—or, for that matter, to be married to a duke.

"You didn't say in your letter how you managed to find me," Eden went on, wasting little time on amenities. They were seated on a bench on the Victoria embankment overlooking the Thames River, a less than ideal location for a private meeting, for the roadway behind them was crowded with the noisy confusion of hansom cabs, carriages, trotting horses, and chattering pedestrians. The sky was overcast and the weather raw, and an unpleasantly damp wind blew upward from the river, bringing with it the strong smell of the tide and the acrid smoke from ships and barges moving slowly through the gray, tossing water.

"It took some doing," the young man confessed. "After all, I wasn't even certain that you were still alive. So many Europeans died in the Meerut Massacre, you realize. But I simply couldn't stop thinking about the promise I'd made to Colonel Hamilton, and wondering if Lieutenant Durlach had kept his word as well.''

''Perhaps you should tell me about him,'' suggested Eden, who was still largely in the dark given that the letter he had sent her had mentioned only that he was a former subordinate of her father's and that he wanted very much to speak to her. Because he had written that his furlough was nearly over and he would be sailing for India in less than a week's time, Eden had departed for London the moment she had been assured of Hugh's recovery. Her haste had clearly proven justified in that Edward Larrimore, adjutant to the commanding officer of the Ninety-second Native Infantry of Lahore, had all but given up hope of receiving an answer and had been planning to sail east the very next day.

Eden knew nothing at all about him or his reasons for seeking her out, but the name Durlach was not unfamiliar to her. Hugh had mentioned a Sidney Durlach several times during the course of his feverish rantings, and Eden wondered if the man was in any way connected with Fred Abercromby, who had been arrested earlier on suspicion of selling arms to Irish rebels.

''I served under your father for nearly three years,'' Edward Larrimore explained. ''You and I never met while in Lucknow, however, for I was just a junior subaltern. Naturally we never mixed socially with our senior officers or their families.''

''I understand,'' said Eden.

''I was with Colonel Hamilton when word of the massacre came to us from Meerut. He requested at once that I ride to the city and see to your welfare. None of us had expected the hostilities to break out there, you see.''

''He must have had a great deal of faith in you.''

Edward Larrimore colored. ''No, I think it was only because I happened to be the most expendable of his men at the time. No sooner had word of the massacre gotten out than the sepoys in our own regiment threw down their arms and refused to take further orders. Two hours later the residency was under siege, and your father couldn't spare another man.''

Yet Edward Larrimore's humble opinion of himself was not entirely justified, in that Eden's father had deliberately chosen him to ride to Meerut largely on the strength of his honesty and unswerving loyalty. Calling the younger man into his office, Colonel Hamilton had charged him with the well-being and safety of his daughter and niece and had, while the sound of mortar fire exploded outside and the screams of the wounded and dying tore through the hot morning air, calmly divulged the whereabouts of his twin brother's jewels and ordered Edward to bring them safely back home.

"And I would have done it," Edward Larrimore continued, "if I hadn't been wounded myself two days later riding through Ferrukhaba. Took a bullet in the shoulder. The sepoys had routed all the local doctors and murdered most of the British, and those left were fighting for their lives. No time to spare for a lowly soldier bleeding to death out in the desert."

Believing himself to be dying, and despairing of carrying out his final orders, Edward Larrimore had been vastly relieved when a detachment of British cavalry had stumbled across him several hours later lying half-conscious in the sand beyond the city gates. Among them had been an officer whom Edward recognized as being from Lucknow and who had listened gravely to the younger man's anxious confessions. He had offered to ride to Meerut in Edward's place and had given his word that both the Hamilton girls and their jewels would be returned to Lucknow in safety.

"I was ill for a very long time after that," Edward Larrimore went on, "and, like everyone else, spent the next eighteen months in hiding. If it hadn't been for the generosity and courage of the villagers of Ferrukhaba, who risked their own lives trying to keep me alive, I wouldn't be here today." He gestured nervously with his hand. "I must confess that I pushed the thought of you and your cousin far from my mind, and it wasn't until recently that I began to wonder, and ask myself whether or not Lieutenant Durlach had been able to keep his promise."

"Anything but that," Eden could not prevent herself saying bitterly.

He gave her a stricken look. "Yes, I've since learned that myself. I received a year's furlough last summer and only then managed to find the time to inquire into the matter. You can imagine my shock when I finally discovered that Lieutenant Durlach was under suspicion for smuggling arms and promoting sedition in native territories!"

A crime for which he had since been arrested, Eden thought, recalling what Hugh had revealed during the course of his delirium. But she found to her amazement that she no longer cared. Not about the jewels or Sir Charles's possession of them, or even the things the young man seated beside her had just revealed to her. She was tired, utterly, indisputably tired, and she found herself longing for Roxbury and for Hugh with something that was very nearly physical pain.

But Hugh had made it clear to her that he could not forgive her for what she had done. She wondered miserably if there was any reason to return to Roxbury at all when it seemed probable that he would spend the rest of his life blaming her for his crippled arm.

"I imagine this has all been something of a shock to you," said Edward Larrimore, looking at her drawn, rigid face.

"Yes," Eden agreed, and got wearily to her feet. She attempted to smile as she offered him her hand. "I cannot thank you enough for getting in touch with me. You've been more than kind. I understand now why my father entrusted you with our family fortune."

Pleased, he returned her smile with one of his own. "I only wish I could have recovered them for you. Perhaps there's still a chance you'll find them?"

"No," said Eden quietly, "I'm afraid they're gone for good." A rueful smile curved her lips. "And perhaps it's just as well. Good-bye, Mr. Larrimore, and thank you."

"Oh, Miss Hamilton—Your Grace!" he called after her, and was nearly run down by a carriage as he crossed the street to her side. "I almost forgot to give you this." He fumbled in his pocket and drew out a much worn envelope of heavy vellum ornately sealed with scarlet wax. "It's from the diwan of Mayar. He asked that I deliver it to you. I've been carrying it with me for months now. That's why it's so crumpled."

A rush of color fled up Eden's cheeks. "From Pratap Rao? What on earth were you doing in Mayar?"

He gave her a sheepish grin. "I must admit that it proved inordinately difficult to find you. I believe I spent the better part of two months on a proverbial goose chase. The authorities in Meerut first sent me to Mayar, where no one seemed to have any idea what had become of you. So I went back to Meerut again and was told to look in Delhi. There they said you'd left for Edinburgh, and since I was on my way to England anyway I decided to write to you as soon as I got there. As luck would have it I discovered when I disembarked in London that you'd arrived here yourself under the escort of the duke of Roxbury. So I addressed my letter to his estate in the hopes it would reach you."

"I suppose I should thank you for your diligence," said Eden gravely. "I don't think anyone else would have spent their furlough in a similar manner."

"It was my duty," he informed her solemnly. "I couldn't have done otherwise."

Eden watched as he walked away from her down the windy embankment, then her attention turned to the letter in her hand. She broke the crimson wafer and unfolded the closely written sheet of paper executed in the flowery hand of Pratap Rao Singh, the diwan of Mayar and Jaji's oldest uncle. Reading it, she forgot the people and the horses and the carriages that surged behind her and around her, forgot the cold gray skies and the tall buildings with their soot-blackened façades that loomed to her back. The beauty of the ancient language of Hind touched within her a long forgotten chord and set it to vibrating, and suddenly the memories were there before her, so real that she had only to lift her head to see the desert shimmering in the heat haze and smell the flowers and the dust and the acrid smoke of dung fires that are the scent and breath and life of India. . . .

"He wants me to come back to Mayar," she told Mrs. Walters a half hour later.

"And will ye?" the older woman inquired curiously.

Eden's expression was troubled. "I'm not sure."

The two women were seated in the parlor of the small but cozy townhouse belonging to Mrs. Walters's sister, Mairi, who had clucked disapprovingly over Eden's wind-chilled hands and cheeks and had hurried into the kitchen to brew her a pot of strong tea.

"I thought the rajah had made trouble for ye before ye left," said Mrs. Walters, who knew something about Eden's past, including her dramatic escape from Mayar.

"Malraj is dead," Eden told her. "Pratap Rao writes that he was found lying in the courtyard below the Tower of the Winds. It's not certain how he fell, but owing to the disappearance of his head syce, or groom, Gar Ram, it's quite probable that he was pushed."

Mrs. Walters opened her eyes wide. "Oh, dear!" she exclaimed on a gasp. "Are you saying he was murdered? That hardly seems possible! No one would dare kill his own king!" Unlike Eden, she was not at all accustomed to the intrigue and violence that underscored the lives of an Indian ruler and his often ambitious subjects and thus could not understand how Eden could make such a shocking assumption. "And you say his *groom* was responsible?"

"Yes. Though he was later discovered dead himself in the garden of the local *kotwal,* the village headman. He had apparently been poisoned, and while some contend it was suicide, I've a feeling it was simply the fact that his past had finally caught up with him."

The British resident, Sir Edgar Lamberton, had taken immediate steps to solve both murders and in doing so had unwittingly uncovered a hotbed of unrest and sedition within the state. Moving quickly, he had taken effective steps to bring the restless natives to heel, and now that a measure of peace had settled over the kingdom and Prince Jaji had been crowned the new rajah of Mayar, Pratap Rao saw no reason why Eden could not return to them—provided she wished to do so.

"And will ye go?" Mrs. Walters repeated.

Eden turned her head and looked about her, seeing not the pleasant furnishings of Mairi's cozy salon but the cool, open rooms of the palace zenana, where she had spent many happy hours of her girlhood. "I really don't know," she said helplessly.

"Have ye thought of His Grace—of your husband?" Mrs. Walters asked, and then blushed furiously at the temerity of her question.

Eden's gaze fell to her hands, which were clutched together in her lap. "I'm not at all certain he wants me back."

An awkward silence settled between them, and both of them were visibly relieved when a small, plump woman bustled into the room with a tea tray in her hands.

"Now, then," Mairi said brightly, setting a plate of scones and a pitcher of clotted cream before Eden, "I want you to drink your tea while it's hot. You're chilled to the bone. I wouldn't be surprised if you've caught yourself a dreadful cold spending all morning down by the river."

She shook her head disapprovingly as she noted the exhaustion on Eden's face. Why, in her day no decent young woman would have dared entertain the notion of driving unchaperoned to the waterfront in order to meet a man she knew only on the strength of a single letter. And while she had no idea what lay behind such odd behavior, Mairi could not forget that her young houseguest was a married woman who by rights ought to practice a bit more discretion. Furthermore, she found it singularly odd that her sister, who clearly felt a measure of responsibility for the girl, had permitted her such scandalous freedom.

Eden shocked Mairi Sinclair a second time by leaving the house again that day to wander alone down the alleys and lanes of the East End, pursued by a restlessness that refused to leave her. Near the steps of a church in Cheapside she bought a gazette from a small boy.

No one paid the least bit of attention to her. The beggars and orphans who plied the streets for handouts were far more interested in the denizens of upper-class London, who could be counted on to toss them a coin or two.

It was in the fashionable West End that they made their daily rounds, leaving the teeming, twisting, narrow streets to the vendors, the seamen, the working girls, and factory hands who made up the polyglot population of the inner city.

It surprised Eden that she should feel so at home there. London, she thought, was at heart no different from such Eastern cities as Delhi, Lucknow, or Pitore. It, too, had its slums and its beggars, its unbelievable poverty and decaying beauty, its lepers and its homeless, and its packs of stray dogs that fought for offal amid the stinking gutters.

It occurred to her as she wandered slowly past the pubs and the taverns and the tiny, cluttered shops that she had never really managed to shake the Eastern sands from her shoes. In fact, the reckless creature Choto Bai had remained more a part of her than the remotely beautiful duchess who, draped in satin and priceless jewels, had moved through the glittering drawing room of Priory Park less than a fortnight ago.

Where exactly was it that she belonged? she asked herself with a pang of confusion and loss. In Mayar, with Jaji and Awal Bannu, or at Tor Alsh with people of her own flesh and blood? Or was it with Hugh, who had given her such unbelievable happiness in the course of such a short, tumultuous marriage?

But even Hugh had left her doubting that he wanted her, and Hugh who had himself once admitted that he did not know to which world he belonged. Eden could not be certain if he preferred the rake-hell life led by the earl of Blair, or playing the landed aristocrat who was the duke of Roxbury, or if he intended to continue in the role of the canny India hand to whom the British government and Indian princes turned in times of crisis.

She realized suddenly that she could not go on living in the shadow of all these men. She was tired of the constant turmoil that had marked the months of her marriage, tired of not knowing what the next day would bring, tired especially of the dragging uncertainty that came with loving Hugh. It was tempting beyond belief to envision herself back in the closely guarded zenana of Mayar, where little more was ever wont to trouble her than trying to decide what she would eat that day, or with whom she would play *shatranj* in the flower-scented courtyard, or which of Malraj's beautiful, unpredictable horses she would ride out onto the plains in the cool of the dawn.

It was beginning to rain again, and the icy water that trickled down her neck brought Eden's thoughts abruptly back to the present. She looked down at the gazette in her hand, unable to remember why she had bought it, and was about to throw it away when she checked slowly and unfolded it. Somewhere on the back pages, she knew, was a listing of the ships of the P&O Line scheduled to weigh anchor that month for the East. Surely there was no harm in seeing if a berth might still be available on one of them?

___ *Chapter Twenty-six* ___

It was remarkable, Dr. Theodore Blakeney pronounced grimly, that the duke of Roxbury had managed to survive the grueling carriage drive back from Bleadney village. A less healthy man would certainly have died, and it was fortunate indeed that John Pierce had possessed the foresight to turn the vehicle around the moment His Grace had lost consciousness. Since he could still not be entirely certain of his patient's recovery, however, the good doctor had charged the anxious Roxbury staff with the dispensation of various medicinal concoctions and above all admonished them to make certain that His Grace did not leave his bed for the next few days at least.

Hugh did not regain consciousness until well into the morning of the third day. He had been given drugs that were intended to stave off infection and reduce the chance of recurring fever, but which also served to leave him feeling light-headed and largely incapable of coherent thought. Furthermore, the broken bones of his arm were mending slowly and causing him considerable pain, and perhaps it was just as well that he had fallen asleep again and slept for hours this time, not awakening until the bleak winter sun, falling through a crack in the drapes, heralded the beginning of the fifth day since Pierce had brought him home.

He opened his eyes to find himself still very much in pain and feeling absurdly weak, yet sufficiently clear-headed to refuse all further medicines and send for Gilchrist, who could be trusted not to treat him like an invalid. He had listened without speaking to his valet's brief description of what had transpired since the storm-

432

ing of Roxbury's gates and had interrupted at last with a single inquiry:

"And my wife? Has she returned?"

Gilchrist cleared his throat, then fell silent.

"Well?"

"No, Your Grace."

Hugh said nothing for a moment, and it was Gilchrist who ventured to add:

"Mr. Pierce went down to London after her, Your Grace. That were on Thursday. The Walters woman said she hadn't seen her for three days or more."

"Good God!" Hugh said furiously, coming up on his good arm, "It takes less than three days to travel from here to the city! She should have returned long before this!"

"If she were comin' back at all."

"What the devil do you mean by that?" Hugh inquired sharply.

Gilchrist said slowly: "The Walters woman seemed to think she'd sailed for India."

" 'Seemed to think'? What in hell does that mean? Doesn't she know for sure? Eden wouldn't simply return to India without telling anyone!"

"Can you be sure of that, Your Grace?"

There was a long moment of silence.

"No, I suppose not," said Hugh at last, and lay back against the pillows. Closing his eyes, he resigned himself to doing nothing, knowing from bitter experience that there was little sense in attempting to leave his bed. After another endless moment he summoned John Pierce and listened without speaking to the stablemaster's description of his trip to London. His lips thinned when he was given an accounting of the details of Pratap Rao's letter inasmuch as Mrs. Walters had known of them. Afterward he issued a series of instructions and then fell asleep again, and did not awaken until the following evening.

By then his fury and frustration had largely faded, and he found himself feeling curiously numb and indifferent— and old. Old because he could not understand what measure of man he was who could not even summon the strength to leave his bed and pursue the vagrant, cunning

child who had played such an unforgettable dance upon
the strings of his heart and then simply vanished from his
life. Eden was gone, of that there could be no doubt, and
if Mrs. Walters was to be believed, she had sailed away
to Alexandria without telling anyone.

Hugh knew, of course, why she had gone. It was what
he had said to her. He remembered clearly accusing Eden
of her unforgivable behavior, yet where he had meant that
she had had no right to risk her life by participating in
the charge herself, she had chosen to place her own interpretation upon what he had said.

Perhaps she felt he blamed her for the fall that had
broken his arm or for becoming involved in the first place
in the theft of Caroline Winton's jewels. Whatever the
reason, it was obvious that she had made the decision to
end once and for all the turbulence of their marriage and
return to the safety of the zenana in Mayar.

Hugh stared up at the ceiling, where the firelight
danced and swayed in golden patterns, and thought that
Eden was not the sort of woman he would ever have pictured as wanting to be safe. ''Safe'' to him had always
meant living a life of boredom, without risks or excitement or the pleasures that come only to those who have
overcome sufficient obstacles and pain to appreciate their
blessings more fully.

And yet it was entirely possible that Eden simply
longed for a measure of peace in her life, and Hugh could
not in all honesty say that she had experienced overly
much of it since her marriage to him. A bitter smile
curved his lips. No, their lives together had been anything but peaceful, and he supposed he couldn't blame her
for returning to Mayar. Or could he?

By morning the entire county seemed to have heard of
Hugh's recovery, for the calling cards that Gilchrist
brought to him with breakfast filled the small silver tray.
Some of them belonged to various figures of local authority, men of considerable influence in the area whose
business with him was pressing; but Hugh refused to see
any of them. He was feeling irritable and in pain, and it
didn't matter to him that there were questions to be an-

swered, or an inquest to be conducted, or that Lord Palmerston himself had dispatched his private secretary to Roxbury and that the man had been waiting for the better part of two days to see him.

Gilchrist had also informed him that Lady Caroline Winton was once again downstairs, and that she was adamant on the score of being shown up to his rooms.

"I suppose I'll have to speak to her eventually," Hugh agreed with a frown, "but not today!"

The last thing he needed—or wanted—was a newly widowed Lady Winton dissolving into dramatic tears at his bedside. Hugh knew her well enough to know that her husband's death did not, in all probability, weigh particularly heavy upon her heart. Doubtless she was more interested in discussing the fact that both of them were now free of the entanglements of marriage, for she had probably already heard that Eden had left him.

"Send them all away," Hugh said tiredly.

"All of them, Your Grace?"

"By God, yes! All of them!"

The door closed quickly on his retreating valet, and Hugh turned his face to the wall. Eventually, of course, he would have to face them, Palmerston's flunkey in particular, and Caroline, to whom he owed at least the courtesy of an apology—and an explanation as to how her jewelry box had come to be locked away in the safe in his study.

In that respect, at least, Hugh reflected, he had not been found wanting, however poorly he might have managed the rest of the recent crises in his life. Thank God he'd retained enough of his wits to remember to send John Pierce out to look for the jewels before some bloody passerby or, worse, one of Winton's rapacious footmen happened upon them. In the company of Ram Dass and several Roxbury grooms, John had made a thorough search of Priory Park's gardens and the countryside surrounding the Wookey Hole. Armed with torches, they had ventured into the cave itself, and it was a measure of the stablemaster's diligence that he had not returned home until he had the oblong velvet box in his possession.

Opened in Hugh's presence, it had revealed a veritable treasure trove of gems. Most of them, quite naturally, would be returned to Lady Caroline, for Hugh could not be certain that her husband had not come by them through honest means, and it was only Isabel's jewels that he could rightfully take for himself. Fortunately he had been able to identify them with the help of Ram Singh's documents.

Regrettably, many of the pieces were missing, while others had been reworked to the extent that they were difficult to identify from written descriptions alone, and Hugh had removed only those he knew unquestionably to be Isabel's. Yet there were enough of them—more than enough, in fact—to pay off Tor Alsh's debts, should Isabel wish to use them for that purpose.

Hugh suspected that she would do so. A recent letter from Tor Alsh had contained both the welcome news of Angus Fraser's unexpected recovery and the cherished hope that Isabel and Davie Anderson would be married come spring. Shy little Isabel, Hugh reflected, had found a good man in Davie, a man she unquestionably deserved.

The thought brought with it an unexpectedly savage pain. Running a hand across his eyes, Hugh was annoyed to find that it was shaking. Ridiculous to feel so bitter at the prospect of someone else finding happiness in marriage! And why in hell should it matter to him that his wife had run off without another thought or care for him? He had entered into their relationship with his eyes wide open, after all, and had known from the first that Eden Hamilton was a willful, unpredictable creature. Even his otherwise unobservant uncle Hamish had warned him of the dangers of attempting to tame her.

I suppose I've gotten what I deserve, thought Hugh, yet he could not remember when he had last felt this wretched and ill—and truly alone.

He would go after her, he decided. As soon as he was well enough to withstand the rigors of the long voyage. And if Eden refused to return with him, he would simply carry her off into the desert as he had once before. And there in the velvet darkness, with no human eyes to witness their passion, he would take her in his arms and kiss her until she melted against him, and he would prove to her with his body, his lips, his hands, and his words that all of his love and longing was hers alone, forever and always. . . .

"Goddammit!" he ground out, and threw aside the covers. It was bad enough that Eden had left him, but did she have to continue tormenting his thoughts as well?

When he appeared downstairs a half hour later, his arm in a sling and his expression wild, he did not need the disapproving looks of his servants to tell him that he had no business being out of bed. He felt sufficiently dizzy and weak to draw the same conclusion himself yet knew that he could not have borne another moment alone in the close confines of his room. He found his desk piled high with paperwork, and for a little while he made the pretense of sorting through it, though most of what he read seemed largely meaningless to him.

Eventually he pushed the work aside and went to stand before the window. A cold winter sun shone down upon the lifeless garden, and a flock of starlings settled with raucous cawing into the barren branches of an elm that grew amid the dead ivy and rhododendron just beyond the frosted panes. Farther out in the park Hugh could see John Pierce exercising one of his horses on the end of a lunge line. It was Vanity, the glossy chestnut gelding Eden had always favored, and Hugh reflected that it was unlikely anyone would be riding him now, for he had always demonstrated an unmistakable dislike for his trainer and grooms. Eden, in fact, had been the only one the animal would tolerate on his back for any length of time.

For some inexplicable reason the thought enraged him. Turning from the window, Hugh summoned his steward and charged him darkly with seeing that his trunks were expediently packed and that the coach was brought round to the front door in an hour's time.

"His Grace wishes to travel?" the elderly retainer inquired.

"It would seem that way, doesn't it?" Hugh countered brusquely.

"Yes, Your Grace. I'm sorry. It's just that Dr. Blakeney—"

A white line appeared about Hugh's mouth. "You forget yourself, I think."

A trace of color crept into the old man's cheeks. "Yes, Your Grace. I apologize."

"I plan to leave the country, Mr. Barrows," said Hugh, relenting, "and I may be gone for some considerable time. I assume you'll look after everything in the interim?"

"As always, Your Grace," the steward answered expressionlessly.

Shuffling out, he closed the door behind him, while Hugh lowered himself wearily into the chair behind his desk and buried his face in the crook of his arm.

Why in hell, he asked himself tiredly, hadn't he simply remained a bachelor? And why hadn't he followed the infinite wisdom of his bearer Baga Lal and sent Eden Hamilton away to Rawalpindi while he'd still had the chance? If he had never kissed her there in the desert, had never held her slender body close, he would never have realized how perfectly she fit into his arms or how much she could excite him. Or how, in so laughably short an expanse of time, she could come to mean so very much to him.

Now it was far too late, of course, as perhaps it had been from the moment he had looked into her unveiled face in the *mardana* gardens and found himself enchanted by its beauty. And while he could not deny that he had had numerous opportunities since then to turn his back on her and walk away, he had not. Simply because he hadn't wanted to. However much she might annoy him with her wild and willful ways, Eden suited him like no other woman, and Hugh knew that he wouldn't change anything about her even if he could. Life would certainly never be dull with her, and he would never be found wanting of anything with Eden at his side.

The study door opened softly at that juncture, interrupting his thoughts with a start.

"Goddammit!" he hissed, enraged at the intrusion. "I thought I'd made it clear that I didn't wish to be disturbed!"

"Still so surly, sahib? *Ohé*, it must mean that thou art not yet recovered."

The softly uttered Hindustani was so unexpected that at first Hugh could make no sense of it. But then his eyes opened wide, and he lifted his head and sat up in his chair, forgetful of the jarring pain of his mending arm and the lingering, throbbing effect of the drugs. There was a rustle of silk, and suddenly a slim, cool hand was on his cheek, caressing him gently, tenderly.

Hugh held himself still. It had to be a dream—it must be! And yet the soft pair of lips that pressed themselves against his mouth were sweetly real, and he could not be imagining the heady scent of sandalwood that enveloped him as Eden leaned closer. He heard her husky voice breathe in his ear:

"I had to come back, Hugh. I thought I'd be happy in Mayar, but the ship hadn't even cleared the estuary before I realized how wrong I was. I asked the pilot to bring me back. . . ." A hint of pain crept into Eden's voice, and her arms tightened unconsciously about his neck. "I made the discovery that it doesn't matter at all where I am: here or in Scotland or India, as long as you are with me. I cannot," she added simply, though her voice wavered, "I cannot live without you and I hope—oh, God! Do you feel the same?"

Slowly Hugh turned his head and looked at her, saw the tears that sparkled in those dark, beautiful eyes and the hope and the pain that brimmed in the depths of the heart she had bared for him. He did not speak, for he found when he tried that his voice broke, so he reached out his hands and brought her slim body against him. Sliding his shaking fingers through the thick, shining waves of her hair, he drew her mouth down to his. And slowly, lovingly, he kissed her.

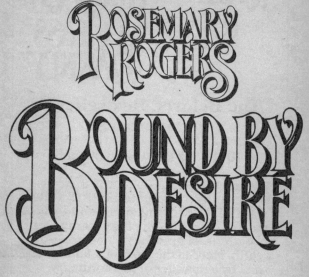